DEAD
UNDEAD

OR SOMEWHERE
IN BETWEEN

Published by Mundania Press
Also by J.A. Saare

The Renfield Syndrome*
The Ripple Effect*

(*Forthcoming)

DEAD UNDEAD

OR SOMEWHERE IN BETWEEN

J.A. SAARE

A Mundania Press Production
Mundania Press LLC
6457 Glenway Avenue, #109
Cincinnati, Ohio 45211-5222

To order additional copies of this book, contact:
books@mundania.com
www.mundania.com

Cover Art © 2011 by Skyla Dawn Cameron
Edited by Skyla Dawn Cameron

Trade Paperback ISBN: 978-1-59426-713-0
eBook ISBN: 978-1-59426-712-3

First Mundania Edition • May 2011

Production by Mundania Press LLC
Printed in the United States of America

10 9 8 7 6 5 4 3 2 1

DEDICATION

To my mother-in-law, who encouraged me to share my stories with the world. I owe everything to you. To my husband, who continues to support our family, care for our children, and doesn't complain when I'm locked away in my writing cave. You are more than my partner, sweets. You are my best friend. To my fantastic critique partners Madelyn Ford and Rosalie Stanton, who read my work, offer advice, and give me so much of their time when they have deadlines to meet. You ladies are the absolute best. To my editor and cover artist, Skyla Dawn Cameron, who holds my utmost respect for doing the job she does while continuing to create stories of her own, stay on top of fellow author and friend Sarah-Jane Lehoux to give us more Sevy and Jarro, and somehow keep her sanity in the process.

Last but not least, an enormous amount of gratitude to the indelible Trent Reznor, who creates the music that inspires many of my stories.

ACKNOWLEDGEMENTS

This book would never have been possible without the assistance of Anthony Fernandez. The time he took to guide me through the streets of New York, the subway system, and the "L" was invaluable. Thank you for spending so many hours taking me through the big city.

CHAPTER ONE

Rhiannon's Law #27: When you're working in a gentlemen's club and one of your dancers takes off those heels, alert the big guns: an ass kicking is on the menu.

Lacey finished her set and started working the room. The flashing lights from the stage mixed with the saturated cigarette and cigar smoke to create a fog effect that surrounded her shoulders in a swirling vortex. Her body was slim and tan inside a white rhinestone bikini, full hips rotating from side to side like a broken linebacker as she prowled toward a table with men in expensive business suits. She bent low, full red lips whispering huskily and plastic breasts straining provocatively. Perfect legs flexed as her spine tilted back, three-inch clear, plastic heels with goldfish floating inside giving added height and muscle tone.

Any good dancer knows how to work the clientele, and Lacey was a pro. She raked in a majority of the house take, and her regulars came from miles around just for a private. She was deceptively young looking, with long blonde hair and big baby-blue eyes, which were a huge part of her attraction. She would never reveal her age, but since I was on the welcoming committee—AKA the Department of Industrial Relations—I was in the know. A twenty-two-year-old that looked illegal as hell.

The men ate that jailbait shit up with a spoon.

"How much for a lap dance, sweetheart?"

I glanced at the owner of the voice, and no surprise, he wasn't anything special. Just another Joe Schmo dressed in his screw-me-best. If I had a nickel for every time I've heard that line, I could quit my blow hole job and retire, enjoying the good life without millions of assholes just like this one who thought they were so quick.

I waited. I knew what was coming next. That's another perk of having asshole customers—predictability.

"I bet you get asked that question all the time."

I gave my sweetest smile. The one that says "aw shucks" on the outside and a big huge "fuck you" on the inside.

Let's see, genius. I'm a female, working inside a bar that just so happens to feature exotic dancers. I have all my teeth, a decent body of my own, and although I hit the big two-five recently, I could pass for years younger. Nope, no one would ever think to ask me that question. Who cares if I'm standing behind a bar peddling liquor? Those bottles could just be another part of my act.

I moved down the drunken assembly line. I had beers to refill, drinks to concoct, and other witty Casanovas with well-researched one-liners to endure.

Erica took the stage. Her tanned skin was like leather, too dark and too fake, matching the breasts she purchased a decade before. I visually stalked her as I refilled a request for Hennessey. Every exotic bar has a queen bitch, and Erica was ours. She lived to start drama, thrived on it. Her damage stemmed from the fact she was the oldest of our dancers and passed her prime a few years ago.

Stripping is not a fair or unbiased career field. Your body and looks are your livelihood. Once those two things go, it's only a matter of time before you punch your last T and A ticket—and Erica's stub was wilting faster than a golden wrapped candy bar that would gain her admittance into the chocolate factory.

"How much for a lap dance, sweetheart?" a familiar voice mocked. I didn't have to look up. I would know that silky baritone anywhere.

"Not now, Disco." My eyes tracked Erica as her number finished and she eased over to Lacey's table. I concentrated on their body language, focusing on Erica's face, paying close attention.

"Bad night?" he asked, peering over his shoulder.

I took a passing glance while he was distracted. He was dressed from head to toe in black, like every other night. It wasn't necessarily a bad thing. The color complimented him.

"Not yet," I answered in my usual wait-and-see voice.

Lacey and Erica came face to face and began talking quietly. So far, so good—shoes on and voices low. Maybe I was wrong, maybe it wouldn't be one of those nights.

Please God, make it so.

"Bartender!"

Another voice I knew by heart, only this one made me grit my teeth and pray for tolerance. I walked to the left of the bar toward Lonnie, the fat bastard of the club. He'd been a regular since I'd joined the BP family, and though he knew my name, he insisted on referring to me as bartender.

I placed my left hand on my hip, bracing myself against the bar on the right. "What do you want, Lonnie?"

"Where's Deena?"

As he spoke, I struggled to keep my eyes on his face and away from his chest. I failed and cringed inwardly. There were random orange stains over his white T-shirt. Ketchup or barbeque sauce, I thought. A rounded Santa Claus belly caused the material to pooch out, creating a little cotton ramp that slid down his chest to the rounded swell of beer gut. I didn't understand how the hell someone could be so clean—his hair, face, and hands were always immaculate—yet he couldn't seem to get food inside that whining hole in his head.

Braced for the worst, I answered, "She's on vacation."

Deena warned me this was coming. She was Lonnie's bartender. The only one to whom he didn't talk down. I had weeks to get used to the idea, but no amount of time in this world could adequately prepare me for dealing with Lonnie.

When he didn't respond, I asked, "Anything else?"

"Crown and Coke." The instant he answered, he whipped his stool around, thereby dismissing me.

Welcome to McDonald's, can I take your order? One super sized, fat assed, pork bellied value meal? Coming right up!

I walked over to the rack and pulled down the Crown. I poured it first, sliding the bottle back, and returned to the main station. A couple of cubes of ice and a dash of Coca-Cola finished it off. I sat the drink in front of Lonnie and he blew me off. Lifting the glass to his lips, he expertly tossed the concoction back.

My gaze darted around the dark, cloudy room. The tables were full, but that was to be expected. The BP wasn't the most exclusive club in town, but we had decent girls, a hospitable crowd, and we kept it clean. Those inclined to visit a topless bar could get their Johnson on in relative safety and enjoyment as long as they kept their hands to themselves.

Old-school David Bowie blasted from the speakers and Destiny took the stage. The dark curtains parted as she sashayed past, the white glow of the stage light bringing attention front and center. One of the few who didn't tan, her pale skin was soft and luminescent in the stage lights, her pink bikini appearing to glow and sparkle. Destiny was one of my favorite dancers. She told it like it was and always kept it real. Like when she used her double-jointed limbs to work the pole.

You can't get more real than that.

"Can we talk later?" Disco appeared in front of me and I attempted to act as if I'd seen the movement, swallowing quietly. The way they moved always creeped me out, so fast it appeared instant. It was unnerving and jolting.

Fucking vampires.

A lush requesting a refill on his Wild Turkey saved me. I reached under the counter to snag the bottle and poured him a little something extra in the glass for the assistance. When finished, I stayed put, feet firmly planted, but I knew I was delaying the inevitable. We would have to speak at some point. I couldn't have Disco showing up like this every night.

"Bartender!" Lonnie yelled.

I rolled my eyes. The most demanding of them all was the shittiest tipper to boot. *What I wouldn't give to shove a bottle of Crown up his ass.*

I unplanted my feet, rubber-soled boots squeaking against the wet plastic floor mats. I always wore my shit kickers, even on nights like tonight. The laced up boots were reminiscent of emo goth punk, but they did far more than help me seem fashionably depressed. The reinforced steel toe was great for crotch shots when I needed to exert a little extra bartender lovin'.

"What do you want, Lonnie?"

"When's Deena coming back?" He didn't bother looking at me. That would take too much effort. Instead, those beady eyes remained locked on the stage—typical.

"When she comes back," I answered flatly. "Can I get anything else for you?"

He shook his head, and I rolled my eyes again.

Poor Deena, her best client was a pot-bellied pig living in the bright lights of New York City. I hoped she was enjoying her time away from this clandestine hellhole while she soaked up the cancer-laced rays in sunny Florida.

A surge of black snagged my attention and I chanced a glance. Disco was there, staring at me. I couldn't read his expression.

Shit.

Why did his un-dead, and I mean "*un-dead*," friend have to show up on the one night I decided to take a breather, shoot a game of pool, and serendipitously rub elbows with Disco and his partner in crime, Cash? I remembered it all like it was yesterday. I was on the nine, slinging the money, when I noticed someone standing over the pocket. When the eyesore in question didn't move after a polite request, I lost my genteel sensibilities and yelled for him to get the fuck out of the way. I realized my mistake, of course, when I took a better look and could see the people directly behind his airy body.

Necromancy—or as it is defined in the dictionary, divination by means of the spirits of the dead—is a bitch, and I hate the hell out of it. I see some pretty insane shit—whether I want to or not. Since the state a person dies in is the state they maintain in spirit, it's a constant box of chocolates, and I don't mean the momma always says kind either.

Death by heart attack—just another day at the office. Death by electrocution— not so bad. Death by car, head sliced neatly open with brain matter galore—beyond all concepts of nasty.

I discovered my nifty talent when I was just a kid. I started seeing deceased neighborhood pets, followed by Mrs. Beaterman mulling over her neatly manicured lawn a week following the heart attack that killed her. I thought it was normal. That all changed the day a drunk driver blew past a stop sign and plowed into my parent's van. When Mom and Dad paid a visit to their own funeral, I knew I had issues.

"Bartender!" Lonnie yelled again, not giving me his attention, gaze remaining on the stage.

I bit my tongue—literally. The sharp edge of my incisor hurt, which was the point. I had to hold it in, or I was going to blow.

"What can I get for you, Lonnie?"

"Will Deena be back next weekend?"

Count to ten. One, two, three, four, five, six, seven, eight, nine, and ten. Got your shit together? Okay, good. Answer the gentleman.

"I don't know, Lonnie." I smiled, speaking through my teeth. "She's on vacation. An *extended* vacation."

"Yo, Rhiannon." Cletus stomped forward from the floor. Muscles that were smooth under the dimmed lights defined his warm, chocolate-colored skin. His bald head gleamed and shined as the overhead lights bounced off the surface and reflected the beams. New York's most intimidating bouncer and I shared a happy working relationship, and the rules that governed that relationship were simple. No lies, no ass kissing, no bullshit. It worked better than most marriages.

"Yo, Cletus," I answered, walking behind the bar in his direction. Everyone made way. No one wants to be in the path of a six-foot-four Mack truck with guns the size of two-by-fours.

"You headed to the gym after this?"

I glanced at Disco who was undoubtedly listening in. "Probably. I missed my set last night. Why do you ask?"

He produced a set of keys. Nothing fancy, just a plain ring surrounded by various scraps of metal that held the power to unlock doors. "Give that to Mike. He's on tonight."

"No problem." I took them and pushed the jangling chain into the pocket on my skirt. I had to pay my dues anyway, and since Mike owned the joint, it was a win-win situation.

As soon as Cletus returned to the floor, the night picked up, and I was thankful. I filled drink after drink, order after order, and I loved it. I didn't want to be in this place any longer then I had to, and Friday and Saturday were the fastest moving nights of the week.

I was filling a shot of Absolut when I heard Erica snarl, "You fucking skank!"

My chin snapped up as my attention turned to the sound of a bitch fight in progress. Erica and Lacey were engaged in a heated discussion at the opposite end of the bar. Fingers were flying and barbs were being exchanged. I topped the shot of vodka off and had just plopped the bottle under the counter when Lacey started pulling off those three-inch, red patent leather, fish high heels.

I ran to the lift and tossed the heavy wood aside just as I shouted, "Cletus!" Someone yelled as his fingers got smashed, but I didn't have time to apologize, and I didn't have time to be courteous. Lacey was barefoot now.

Oh shit.

A few things everyone should know about the women who work in these establishments. They are very savvy. Exotic dancing is a business, and many of them can retire young with sound financial planning. They are excellent actresses. That little show you see up on that stage every night is just that, a show. And they scrap. I don't mean that as in going to the local dump to look for spare aluminum. I mean it as in they will eat your ass for lunch.

Lacey's punch came before Erica could get her shoes off, sending her to the ground. She drew her fist back again, poised to strike, but I grabbed her by the wrist. "Cool down, Lacey," I said evenly. "You don't want to lose your job. Hector is coming over."

That got her attention. The fight left Lacey's body and she stood. I let her go, stepped back, and watched Erica's head slump to the side.

Girlfriend was out cold.

Blood ran in a bizarre line that mixed with her lipstick, as if she were a deranged life size Joker Barbie doll complete with bouffant hair, rhinestones, and fingernails that made it impossible to scratch certain surfaces.

Cletus picked Erica up and tossed her over his shoulder. Her head flopped around limply as he carried her to the curtains, reminding me of a bobble head doll on a car dash.

Hector walked over, addressing Lacey. "Mind telling me what happened?"

"She wouldn't back off. I warned her." Lacey pouted like the diva I knew her to be, appearing her actual age for once.

Hector frowned at her reproachfully for a moment, then his face smoothed and relaxed. The big boss could be an asshole but, for the most part, he was a decent employer. He understood the human condition. As well he should. He profited directly from it.

Hector Fernandez peddled in the most dependable and lucrative of markets—sex. He was all about the good old-fashioned dollar. Those expensive suits he always wore, the Mercedes outside, and the cash in his bank account were a testament to it.

He pushed chin length mahogany hair away from his sublime face, his full lips curving slightly. His Dominican heritage made him a natural ladies' man. He was cut lean, and his body guaranteed you'd wake up happy the next morning.

Women couldn't stay away from him.

"Don't let it happen again," he warned, scolding her as if she were a child who stole a cookie.

"I won't," Lacey promised and leaned over to pick up her heels. She stood tall, spine erect and head held high, and pranced toward the curtains.

"And you, Rhiannon." His dark eyes placed the blame directly on numero uno, and I steeled myself. "You are supposed to be on the lookout for this very type of transgression. Where were you?"

"Doing my job." I crossed my arms defensively. "I'm the bartender, Hector. Not the bouncer."

"Then I suggest you multitask. Or is that too much to ask?"

"Multitask? What do I look like, a fucking secretary?" My temper flared before I could bite it back. Erica wasn't the only one with a big mouth. I was constantly in danger of writing checks my ass couldn't cash, the bearer of a lifelong disease of potty mouth that no amount of soap in this world could properly cleanse.

"If I say so, yeah." Hector nodded and narrowed his eyes in a clear reprimand. "Next time, watch the floor. Butch and Cletus can't cover everything. If you can't handle it, tell me, and I can find someone who will."

He stomped off, his back more than an adequate goodbye. Hector was a man of few words. He said it; you did it. End of discussion.

I released an exaggerated sigh and lowered my head, dropping my guard just long enough for Disco to make his move. His cold hand grasped my arm, and my chin jolted up.

"We need to talk."

"Let go of me, Disco." I would have attempted to yank free but I'd only embarrass myself. Vampires are strong, *unbelievably* strong, and his grip would be as unbreakable as steel.

"Only if you promise we can talk." His blue eyes flashed, striking against his pale skin and golden blond hair. His face was smooth, his jaw strong and squared. With high cheekbones, a straight and lean nose, and full lips, he would forever be a twenty-something looker frozen in time.

"Not here." I glanced around. No one had noticed our little chat yet, and I couldn't afford to lose my job. Personal relations during office hours were a big no-no.

"Where?" His grip loosened as he studied me.

"After close. Meet me outside, around the back."

I waited until he let go before I turned and strode back to the bar. I returned to my spot, apologizing and pouring a free one for the unlucky schmuck with a purple thumb. Tonight was not going to be a good night, and it wasn't even over yet.

I glared at the clock—12:58am. *Wonderful.*

I was on for another hour, and instead of making the gym for some quality muscle burn, I had a meeting with a guy who scared the piss out of me.

"Bartender!" Lonnie's deep bellow ricocheted off the ceiling like a frazzled fart.

I stomped over, feet pounding against the plastic mats, anger coursing through me. I always kept my head with Lonnie, but damn it, this was getting old. Deena would just have to find it in her heart to forgive me.

"What the fuck do you want, Lonnie?" I was aware that my brown eyes were as dark as my temper. The first warning sign you'd pushed my big red button.

His gaze swept over me, starting at my long dark hair, roaming past my chin and nose, and finally resting on my eyes.

He stared at me until I couldn't stand it anymore, and I demanded, "What the fuck do you want?"

"Can I have a Crown and Coke, Rhiannon?" he asked politely.

Although shocked by the swift change in attitude, I managed to keep a straight face as I made his drink. He watched quietly as I poured the Crown, mixed in the ice and cola, and even thanked me when I placed the effervescent drink in front of him.

CHAPTER TWO

Normally, I can't wait for the clock to tick over to 2:00am—that means I've finished working for the man and it's my time—but when those little flashing red LED lights hit 1:56, I started to panic. I didn't have a good feeling about meeting Disco. My internal alarm bell was sounding, a fight or flight instinct we're all born with.

It's called your fucking logic.

No one knows about vampires, although the basic concepts, myths, and rumors are true. They're pasty, stay out of the sun, and have abnormally good looks. They are also cold, extremely fast and agile, and have lethal sex appeal.

The living dead give off what I like to call a vibe. The first time I went clubbing and spotted one, I thought the speakers were blaring and the DJ was shit. In actuality, it was my natural talent weeding them out. They're not dead, but they are dead. It's impossible to describe and equally impossible to ignore.

The first vampire I ever met taught me an invaluable lesson too—don't trust them. He took my best friend home from the club that night, and we never saw her again. She's either dead, un-dead, or somewhere in between. I chose to leave shortly after. Miami was a popular place for the recently non-deceased, and I preferred the company of those who enjoyed the simple things in life.

Like masticating.

It went without saying that the night I slipped up at Shooter's in front of Disco and Cash, I promptly broke down my cues, collected my money and case, and hauled ass out of there. And what do you know? The next night while I did my part inebriating a solid portion of the city population, Cash showed up. He tried to sweet talk me into spilling the beans, saccharine and playful in his antics, until I blew him off good and proper. Since then, Disco had been scouting the lounge, growing more insistent, bordering on frightening.

"Almost set?" Cletus asked, coming around to stand at the edge of the bar.

"Yeah." I snapped out of it, smiled weakly, and reached under the counter for the jimmy club. Deena made it after a drunken asshole came over the counter when she cut him off. She suffered a black eye in the scuffle, but being the cockeyed optimist I loved, took something away from the experience, constructing a deadly weapon using thick electrical wire reinforced with black electrical tape.

I bent over and shoved the black taped length of metal inside my boot. Would the club save my life if I needed it? Probably not. But I sure as hell felt better knowing it was there.

I rummaged inside my pockets. Keys, ChapStick, butterfly knife, cash, and extra set of keys from Cletus—all there. I walked past the floor and pushed aside the velvet curtain. The lights in back were bright and my pupils burned as the retinas readjusted. A little trip down the hall led me past bulbed vanity tables with wigs, rhinestones, and accessories.

Hector was waiting in the back, just as anticipated. His jacket was gone, and his dress shirt was unbuttoned at the neck. No need to pimp for the masses here in the back, and he could care less if I was impressed.

"Got a minute?"

"What's up?" I ambled over, relieved for the distraction. Anything that would keep me from walking outside those back doors sooner than necessary was welcome.

"I fired Erica. She tried to threaten me, and I sent her ass packing. We need a new girl. Do you have the applications from last time?" He reached inside his pocket and produced a cigar. He smelled the tobacco, running the spiff under his nose and breathing in the potent fragrance.

"I put them in your office, in the top cabinet with the older ones. Maybe you could sift through the top choices and I can make some calls."

"Deena won't be back until next week, so I'll need you to come in. Did you ever get a cell? It's too difficult to reach you at home, and I hate answering machines." He put the cigar in his mouth and reached inside his pocket for a lighter.

"What is up with the need for cellular devices?" I complained. This was by no means a new conversation we were having. Hector had been whining about calling my place since I started working for him. "Our parents got by without them. Hell, our ancestors had to get by with a little something called the Pony Express. I don't like cell phones. They are the bane of our society, and I don't want to add to the downward spiral of technology that is ripping Mother Earth a new one."

"Get a cell phone, Rhiannon. It's not a request."

"If you want me to get a cell, you can pay for it. I'm not busting my ass here to foot the bill for something I don't even want." Hector loved his money, hopefully enough to let the cell phone issue slide.

He exhaled a big cloud of smoke, smiling as it released into the air in a billowy cushion of grayish white that flew up to the ceiling like an offering. His curved lips said it all. I was about to become the not so proud owner of a device I couldn't stand. Everyone today had one practically glued to their ears, and here I was, about to join the lemming majority.

"Fine, stop by tomorrow to pick it up." He walked past me, toward the office. I heard a click as the door opened, followed by the crack as it slammed shut.

My shoulders drooped in defeat. *Of all the shitty luck.*

The only way my life could get worse is if I got my throat ripped out. Coincidentally, I was due to leave my place of employment and enter into a darkened alley to meet up with a vampire. So the odds weren't stacked in my favor. Not at all.

My boots squeaked on the linoleum as I strode past the coat rack, walked down the hall, and entered the narrow concrete hallway. The big steel door at the end distorted, appearing too close and then too far, evoking images of *The Shining*. I finally reached it and limply grasped the knob.

I stood there, fingers loose and flaccid. Once I turned the knob, I was sealing my fate. My pride wouldn't stand for beating on the door and screaming like a pansy to be allowed back inside. I exerted my backbone, grasped the knob, and twisted. The door opened with a protest of metal against metal.

I scanned the area quickly and then sagged in relief. The alley was empty. *Thank you God, hallelujah!* The door slammed shut behind me as I rushed down the narrow street. I was dodging a bullet, and I knew it.

The moon wasn't out but the streetlights lit the way decently enough, the circular swells of white shining bright against the darkened concrete. The air was slightly chilly, sending prickles along my skin. I'd have to break out my jeans and sweaters soon.

I hooked a right, keeping my ecstatic pace, until I glanced up.

Disco was propped casually against the wall, his broad back braced against the red bricks. He stood beneath a nearby street light that shone off his hair, the pale honey blond intense. Pulling out a cigarette and lighting up, he waited as I approached. I watched the red tip brighten as he took a long puff, lifted his head, and exhaled slowly into the darkened night.

So much for dodging a bullet.

Some girls get to be prom queen, others get a perfect SAT score, but not me. I was the biggest winner on *The Price Is Right*, and Johnny just told me to come on down.

"You ready to talk?" Surprisingly, his voice was soft and eloquent when he wasn't inside a pool hall or bar.

"Do I have a choice?"

"No." He looked at me, pushed away from the wall, and stepped over.

"What do you want?"

"What do you think I want?"

Let me answer your question by giving you a question. What a cocky bastard.

"This isn't the Psychic Friends Network, and I'm not Miss Cleo." I started to walk past, my patience threshold considerably shortened. "Since you obviously need help I cannot provide, I'll be on my way."

His hand lashed out—cold, hard, and immobile against my arm.

"You can provide *exactly* the help I need." He bent low, whispering the words. His grip on my arm wasn't painful, but it was firm—firm enough that I might or might not have bruises to show for it in a few hours.

"What do you want?" I forced back panic, keeping my voice even.

"I'll be damned." He laughed. "I never thought I'd see you afraid of anything. What's got you spooked, little rabbit?"

"Nothing," I lied, tossing my hair back. The strands cascaded around my shoulders, covering his hand in waves of brown.

"Don't bother lying, Rhiannon." He leaned closer, inhaling softly. His silky blond hair brushed against my nose. "I can smell it."

"What the fuck do you want?" I spat, pulling back my arm. Surprisingly, he let go and stepped away, giving me space. I brought my wrist up and massaged the skin and muscle, keeping my eyes on him.

"I want you to answer some questions." He pulled out his cigarettes and lit up. I didn't see him finish the first one. I guess vampires smoked abnormally fast too.

"About?"

"About what you are." He exhaled as he spoke, and I wanted to ask him how in the hell it was possible. Did his lungs still function? How about the heart? Could you be classified as dead if it still beat? Fucked up questions, I know. That's the point.

"Bartender extraordinaire who moonlights as a pool shark, we're a dime a dozen," I hedged, knowing perfectly well what he meant. From the look in his face, he was expecting it. He inhaled again, taking another long drag before blowing it out slowly.

"Do you really want to do this?" He lowered his chin and studied me intently. "We know, Rhiannon. We spotted you the minute we came into Shooter's. That little radar of yours isn't a one-way frequency."

Well screw my wretched ass sideways! I gave off a frequency too? I contemplated my options. I could continue with the "gee, shucks, gosh I have no clue what you're talking about," or I could pony up, grow a pair, and get this shit out in the open. The truth was I was tired of hiding it. It was burden sitting on the subway watching random John Qs behind white soulless eyes, their spirits trapped in some strange flux between here and there. And I couldn't see how lying would benefit me at the present time.

"Fine." I rolled my eyes and crossed my arms. "You've got me. Cat's out of the bag. What the fuck do you want?"

He grinned, tossed his cigarette onto the pavement, and placed his hands inside the pockets of his coat. "The man you saw that night. Describe him for me."

"What man?" I frowned in confusion. Then it dawned on me. I struggled to remember the night I'd slipped up at Shooter's in front of Disco. I didn't look at the spirit long, only paying attention as I prepared to pocket my ball. "I don't remember much. Long dark hair, maybe in his twenties."

"How did he die?" He watched me from under long dark lashes, moving from foot to foot so quickly the motion seemed constant.

"I couldn't tell you," I answered truthfully. "I didn't pay attention. I just saw a body standing in front of my pocket."

He stared at the ground, eyes unfocused as he internalized my information. I tried not to get antsy, keeping my boots firm on the pavement, but the minutes ticked away and I became uneasy. I bit my cheek, my patience wearing thin.

"Are you off this weekend?" He was still staring at the ground as he asked. I considered snapping my fingers to break the trance, but I wanted to keep them.

"Actually, no, I'm not." I didn't offer any more information. Straight, factual and to the point—this is the no spin zone.

"What about this week?" He stopped staring at the ground and looked at me instead. His eyes were brighter up close, like the clearest span of ocean.

I shook my head. "No again."

It wasn't his lucky night either, but my fortune seemed to be turning a corner. Deena's vacation had booked me solid, which meant I could go around with him all night long. No, no, and did I say no?

"Let me try a different approach. When will you have a free night?" His lips curved mockingly as he waited for my answer.

Rhiannon's Law #37: Don't get so high and mighty. God will only reward that arrogance with a huge bitch slap back to reality.

Don't you absolutely despise questions you can't answer with a simple yes or no?

CHAPTER THREE

I had a date with a vampire. Or was it a date? I was still sketchy on the entire situation, as well as completely mortified. One minute, I was asked about a clear night on my schedule. The next, it was booked. A week and a half had flown by and tomorrow Disco and I were set to meet at the Razor in SoHo.

Deena's absence would have put a severe cramp in my social life—if I had one. I was in and out of the BP all week, and when I wasn't there, I was on the damned scrap of metal that Hector insisted I carry around at all times. He kept my ass on the wire until we managed to hire a new girl. Thank God, we lucked out with Cassie. She was pale and exotic, with raven hair and the never-ending legs of a gazelle.

I leaned across the bar, watching Cassie buff the stage. Lacey had some serious competition for a change. With her striking looks, it wouldn't be long before Cassie had her own stash of regulars.

"Excuse me."

Seeing someone new inside our establishment didn't surprise me. We always had a rotating door of patrons. The man was older, in his mid-thirties at least. His short black hair was neatly combed, his face was smooth from a recent shave, and his brown eyes were warm and inviting.

"What can I get you?"

"Do you have Grey Goose?" He gave a friendly smile when I nodded. "Double shot, then."

I poured his double and turned to hand the drink over. He was waiting, cash in hand.

"Keep the change," he said, exchanging the money for the glass.

"Appreciate it." I bestowed a friendly "thank you for your patronage" smile in return and walked to the backdrop to cash out his drink.

I pushed the button on the register and moved to the right, out of harm's way. The bottom drawer came barreling out of the ancient piece of equipment, and I lifted the metal clip to slide in the twenty. I took the left over cash from the corresponding grooves, slammed it shut, and shoved the remaining eight dollars and change into the tip jar.

"Slow night," he said.

I watched him out of the corner of my eye. He was nursing his drink, eyes downcast, his fingers caressing the rim of the glass.

He appeared harmless.

Rhiannon's Law #16: If it looks like a rabbit, and it hops like a rabbit, run the other way and fast. That shit is liable to tear your arm off *Monty Python and the Holy Grail* style.

"Yep," I answered noncommittally and reached under the counter for a towel.

A new group came in as I was mid-swipe, and I could taste trouble. They were just the type, preppy with egos and attitudes the size of Everest. They were tall, six-foot plus, and built. Muscles formed mounds underneath their designer shirts, and veins bulged from their tanned forearms like juicy spaghetti noodles. They were laughing and talking loudly over the room, apparently juiced up from some other place.

"Three Jack and Cokes," the one in the middle instructed when they made it to the bar, and I immediately dubbed him Abercrombie. The two stooges alongside him would be Fitch and Company. He slid a credit card onto the counter to start a tab, and I nodded and swiveled around to make the drinks. The sooner they picked a table and got away from my station, the better.

I placed the drinks in front of them and reached for the card when Abercrombie's fingers encircled my wrist. "He didn't want ice." He hitched his chin toward Company beside him.

Count to ten. One, two, three, four, five, six, seven, eight, nine, and ten. Breathe in. Breathe out.

"No problem." I pulled my hand away and reached for one of the glasses.

"Just make a new one. It was your mistake."

I shook my head, faking a smirk of regret, and reached for a glass. "Sorry, no can do."

He lashed out and caught my wrist again, squeezing firmly. Once, very bad. Twice, you're treading on thin ice. A third time, please don't find out.

"Why not?" he snapped, demanding an explanation like he was talking to some heinous bitch who'd told him to fuck off when he'd invited her to the senior prom.

The tone did it; I snatched my hand free. "It's our policy. Otherwise, everyone would say they didn't request ice when they did, or vice versa. It's called staying in the green."

His fingers encircled my wrist again, and I saw red. My temper is like a hot haze, licking my veins from the inside. It starts out as a simmer, right below my sternum, and expands. As it grows and builds, I can't think clearly. I discovered my incredibly short hair-trigger after my parents died and I enjoyed a few years inside the fabulosity that is the foster care system. It was something I had little control over.

"If you don't let go of my arm, I'm going to come over that bar," I growled, voice raspy and deep, laced with animosity. "And you see that big ass black guy over there, the one that has the name tag Bad Motherfucker? His name is Cletus, and I'll make sure I yell loud enough so he knows I need some assistance."

Abercrombie let go and didn't stop me when I took the drink. I poured the contents into the sink, reached for a clean glass on the counter, and made a new Jack and Coke—without ice this time. He didn't say a word when I put it down and took the Visa, bestowing an "eat shit and die look" instead. The burning in my chest abated, allowing me to calm down as they walked to the floor to snag a table.

"Well played," the guy from the bar said, and I turned in time to see his lips forming into a grin over his glass of Goose. I'd forgotten he was there.

"We aim to please. Quality entertainment, that's the motto of The Black Panther." I leaned against the backdrop and placed my left leg across the right, attempting to look at ease. Chasing off customers wasn't a part of the job.

"Assholes like that give us all a bad name." He slammed the rest of his glass back and cleared his throat. "I hope you don't assume we're all like that."

"I'm working in a bar where people come for visual stimulation courtesy of naked women on a stage," I said with humor in my voice. "I don't judge anything by what comes through those doors."

He lifted his glass into the air, indicating he wanted another, and I whipped around to make it.

Two more shots of Goose, coming right up.

When I dropped this round off, and he told me to keep the change, I paid out and stuck around. Most of the people at the tables were drinking bottles, which meant the servers were taking care of that end. My night was going to be slow as shit.

"Does that kind of thing happen often?"

I studied Mr. Grey Goose. He wasn't our run of the mill T and A enthusiast. He handled his glass carefully, fingers draped along the top as if he were fondling fine crystal. His fingernails were clean and neatly trimmed. Obviously, he didn't do manual labor for a living.

Meeting his curious gaze, I answered, "It depends. The ones who travel in groups are the worst. Their confidence is bolstered by the combined levels of testosterone."

"You handle yourself well." He made it a statement, nothing positive or negative, just the truth.

"Tons of practice." I shot him a self-depreciating smirk. You bet your ass I handle myself well. I learned the hard way. No one watches out for your interests better than you do. If you wait around for a white knight on his trusty steed, you'll end up eating the television coming at your face.

A commotion erupted from the tables, and I leaned past Mr. Grey Goose to see what the fuss was about. Abercrombie, Fitch, and Company had gotten the attention of Cletus, and he was demanding an audience.

A knowing smile flickered across my face. I loved it when assholes got their due. I plopped my elbows onto the counter and settled my chin on my palms. All I needed was a bucket of popcorn and a lounge chair, and I'd be set.

This was going to be good.

Fitch raised his voice, but Abercrombie's bellows drowned him out. Cletus stood in the middle, trying to diffuse the situation, standing a good three inches over Company, who was the tallest. Company started pointing his finger and jabbed Cletus in the chest. Too bad money couldn't buy intelligence—the drunken asshat was playing with dynamite.

I scanned the room for our other bouncer, Butch, and a nervous pang settled in my gut when I didn't see him. Lifting my chin from my palms, I glanced from side to side. Butch was nowhere on floor. That left one member of security against three impaired men with bad attitudes.

Mr. Grey Goose swiveled in his seat as I walked out of the bar, observing the chaos as well. The voices rose, Cletus's deep baritone in the middle, and all hell broke loose.

Company threw a punch and Cletus pumped back, his left palm deflecting the blow as his gargantuan right arm came back. He rotated at the hip, throwing his weight around, and clocked Company hardcore. The asshole crumbled, taking a snooze in the nastiness of our filth drenched carpets. Abercrombie and Fitch decided to use the chicken shit route of safety in numbers. Cletus took on Abercrombie just as Fitch moved behind them. I reacted without hesitation, running over the floor and coming directly behind him.

Cletus snagged his next meal ticket, locking Abercrombie's arm at the elbow and forcing it behind his back. He fell onto the table in front of them in a loud crash of shattering glass against wood. Fitch started forward, fist clenched, drawing his arm back. I carefully judged the distance and threw my weight into the air, lifting my right foot and pushing off with my left, rotating my leg at the hip and locking my joints in place for optimum impact.

The blow landed at the back of his kneecap, and Fitch staggered, yelling out as he turned. The first pass would just slow him down and leave one hell of a mark, but it served my purpose in buying time.

Butch was back.

Our pacifist bouncer was as tall as Cletus, but leaner. His brown shoulder length hair could be misconstrued as hippy, until you saw him out at night and he allowed it to flow freely.

Butch flipped Fitch's arm under his shoulder, locking his elbow to hold him in place. "Thanks, Rhiannon," he murmured apologetically, applied pressure, and moved the asshole along.

"Anytime."

I returned to my place behind the bar, retrieved my bottle of water from beneath the counter, and took a long swallow. I opened my eyes just in time to observe Mr. Grey Goose gawking at me silently.

"Tons of practice, you say?"

I gave him my first true smile of the evening. "You have no idea."

CHAPTER FOUR

Friday arrived before I was ready. Time always sucked like that, moving too fast when you need a few extra minutes to spare and too slow when you wished it would hurry the hell up. I came off the subway and hustled up the stairs, stopping short. I bit my tongue to hold in my gasp.

The spirit was in bad shape.

His eyeball was missing, the ravaged socket empty. Half the side of his face was gone, leaving behind muscle, shredded tissue and cartilage. His top lip was missing, displaying teeth that dangled from strands of gummy root.

I looked down.

His legs were all kinds of fucked up too. If he wasn't a spirit, there was no way he'd be standing. One knee was bent backward, the foot extended beyond. The other was dangling off his hip, almost detached.

Someone bumped me from behind and shocked me back to the living. I closed my eyes, shook my head, and took a cleansing breath. When I dared to glance back through the maze of people, I spotted him going down the stairs toward the subway. Then I knew what he was—a jumper. I forced myself to look away and walked down the crowded street to meet Disco.

The Razor is an exclusive club, and without the proper hook-ups, you'd never get past the doors. Unlike other places that openly advertised their presence with blaring neon lights and signs above the entrance, this one was very low key. It was located in the southern part of the neighborhood where the older buildings still stood, visible only if you were in the know.

Disco was outside, dressed in his Sunday best—black, black, and black. It was striking and lovely against his pale skin, glossy hair, and bright eyes. I took a deep breath and made my way to the front of the building, past a few people standing in line. He watched me approach with a curious expression on his face.

"What?" I asked defensively. I knew this was coming but it didn't make it any easier. That was one of many reasons I didn't go on dates. It felt like high school all over. That self-conscious girl always resurfaced, no matter how much I tried to squelch her, and teenage angst was bad enough the first time around.

Insecurities are a bitch.

"You look different." He chuckled, appreciative eyes roaming across my face and body.

"Thanks for telling me I look like shit when I don't wear makeup."

Ignoring my remark, he smiled and held out his arm. "Shall we?"

Eyeing him suspiciously, I slipped my hand into the crook of his elbow. The two bouncers—both in black shirts with the word RAZOR etched across the chest—didn't ask for names. One unlinked the rope and the other opened the door. Disco ushered us past, and I tried to savor my one moment of feeling like a British royal attending a banquet or some other such idiocy. Inside, the walls were painted black, and two more doors we had to pass through for actual entrance into the place muffled the music.

Disco slid out of his trench coat, the first time I'd ever seen him without it. His body was tall and lean, rugged muscles evident under the surface of his fitted sweater. His shoulders contorted and flexed as he handed the heavy clothing to the checker.

"Miss," the young blonde girl taking coats said, and I looked from side to side, believing she was speaking to someone else. I finally got hip to the situation and pointed at my chest.

"Me?"

"Do you need to check anything?"

I almost told her if I had something to check, I'd have said so. Everything on my person was something I felt was absolutely necessary to survive a first date.

"Nope."

Disco laughed under his breath. He walked over, turned me around, and pointed at the top of the door. Directly above was a red light—a metal detector. I let out a deep breath, reached inside my pocket for my butterfly knife, and handed it over. The girl smiled and motioned for me to walk under the detector again.

"Fuck," I muttered and leaned down. Lifting my pants leg, I dug the jimmy club out of my shit kicker and glanced at Disco. He was shaking his head and chuckling.

Ms. Coat Checker took the club and handed me a slip of paper, friendly smile gone. I got that a lot. Just because I'm on the lookout for an ass kicking doesn't mean I'm actively seeking one out. It's called covering all your bases.

A man at the double doors opened Hell's Gates, and Disco led the way. The sound was deafening, with speakers all around playing a mashup of Nine Inch Nails and The Beatles. The bass vibrated, tingling my hair and skin.

The walls were a deep blue, with lighting coming from sconces affixed above the booths. Tables were scattered around the central dance floor with metal cages strategically placed along railing. Strobe lights rotated above mirrored windows lined in the corner of the ceiling, pulsating and creating variegated beams inside the smoky area. Unfortunately, my date wasn't the only cold blooded, nocturnal creature. Several littered the dance floor and tables. They all seemed to notice me as I noticed them.

Disco sat down in an empty booth, and I slid in across the table. A waitress appeared out of nowhere, and when I looked up, I knew why. She also sustained herself on a liquid diet.

"You want something?"

"Bottle of water," I said. The place was overflowing with fanged critters, and I didn't trust anyone not to spike my glass. I wanted something delivered to my table neat, sealed, and safe.

Disco shook his head at the server and reached inside his pocket for his cigarettes as she walked away. He clicked his Zippo open, tilted his head to the side, and lit up. After closing the lighter with a flick of his palm, he slapped the square piece of metal onto the table in front of us. Then, he leaned back, watching me.

"So," I said sweetly, leaning forward and flashing an insincere smile, "what the fuck do you want?"

"Have you always been so refined? Your attitude and that mouth." He sucked air through his teeth and grimaced. "Do you kiss your mother with it?"

I answered like the smart ass he knew I was. "I did before she died. Of course, my mouth was clean back then. It took years of trial and error to blossom into the fine outstanding young woman you see before you today."

"I'm sorry." He looked down at the table, idly flicking the lid of his lighter opened and closed.

"It was a long time ago."

Unwilling to take that particular conversation further, I turned to monitor the action on the dance floor. The lights overhead fought the cigarette-induced fog that enveloped the room. It was packed. Both alive and undead intermingled. Their bodies clenched, hips gyrating as they swayed with the music.

A thought came to mind, and I asked, "Do you pick random people for your happy meals, or do you play with your food?"

"It depends. Define play with your food." Disco put out the cig in the nearby tray and relaxed on his elbows. He seemed intrigued by my question, almost eager.

"Play with your food," I repeated. "As in, do you fuck them beforehand, or just take them home and bleed them dry?"

"Jesus!" His face crinkled in disgust, and he reached for another cigarette. The intrigue and eagerness evaporated, replaced with a strange look—as if I'd grown another head. "You have issues, do you know that?"

I shrugged, unfazed by the insult. I was always blunt. It wasn't charming, but it was how I was wired.

The waitress returned and placed my water in front of me. I reached into my pocket for a tip, but Disco shook his head to stop me and tossed a bill on the table. She took the money, thanked him and vanished between the pulsating bodies.

"So do you? Play with your food?" I was morbidly curious. Perhaps I had my own dark tendencies; it would explain a lot.

"For your information," Disco informed me coolly, with a hint of anger, "most of us only take from willing donors. If we're in a sexually compromising position at the time, neither the biter nor the bitee will complain. It's commonly referred to as give and take. So yes, we play with our food, but our food plays with us too. Satisfied?"

Picturing what he described rendered me momentarily speechless. I opened the bottle of water and took a long guzzle. The liquid was cold and burned as it went down. I couldn't force more than three solid swallows before I had to stop, lungs and esophagus ready to explode. A sudden anger formed, fueled by my embarrassment.

I still had no clue what the fuck Disco wanted.

"Can we skip past all the bullshit and get down to business? I know you didn't bring me here to enjoy my suave conversational skills. What do you want, and where do I fit inside that box?" I lifted my fingers and drew an invisible square.

There, it was out in the open, neatly packaged and clearly fucking illustrated.

"We need your help." He toyed with the Zippo again.

Okay, that was step in the right direction. "With what?"

"Several of our people have gone missing, and we don't know where they went or why. It's been weeks, and another two have vanished." He met my eyes and said, "We hired professionals, but they can't see our kind after they pass on to the other side. It all depends on the level of natural talent. You have that talent, and we want to know if you'll help us."

"What makes you think I can see your undead asses the second time around? Isn't the first time enough?" I *so* did not want to get involved with this. I didn't enjoy seeing ghosts, and I didn't go looking for them voluntarily.

"This could benefit you, too." His words were barely hospitable anymore, his annoyance evident. I wasn't surprised. I had that effect on people.

"You know what?" I started to slide out of the booth, ready to make my final farewell and curtain call. I saw dead people because I had to, not for recreational purposes. "I think I'll pass. I'm sorry I can't help you."

His boot came up, crushing the empty space of booth to my side to block my exit. His eyes were glowing, bright blue flickering along the iris. He was angry.

No, strike that. He was pissed.

I couldn't stifle my instinctive reaction, pressing back into the worn plastic cushion, eyes wide and mouth shut.

"Listen to me closely, Rhiannon." His voice was deep and crisp. "You will help us. I'm not giving you the option. I never was. I was simply being polite."

I'd seen some pissed off people in my life. Truth be told, I'd been on the receiving end of some brutal rage myself. But what was burning in his eyes scared the dog shit out of me. My body started to shake and anger licked beneath my skin. I hated being at the mercy of someone else. It was everything I'd struggled to overcome the last fifteen-years of my life, and was my absolute worst nightmare. Control was vital to my existence. Without it, I felt suffocated. But I didn't want to die, even if I had an affinity for the dead, and Disco could kill me before I'd even know he'd cut my throat.

He pulled his boot away, so fast it was there one second and gone the next. His lighter was in his hand and he lit another smoke, seemingly amicable, his moods spinning on a dime. He breathed it in and let it out, watching me, blue eyes normal and sparkling.

"What do you want me to do?" I kept the tremor from my voice. I remembered he could smell my fear, but I'd be damned if I'd show it visibly. I still had my pride.

"I want to take you to a few locations to see what you uncover. I also need to introduce you to someone who's working for us. He's a specialist in the field."

Fabulous. A field trip. Maybe I could see if we could swing by the zoo along the way to pet the zebras, gorillas, and shit. I bit my tongue, telling myself to stop the diarrhea mouth—even if it was only in my head.

Not that I had a choice, but I asked, "Who do you want me to meet?"

Disco lowered his head and lifted his arm, motioning for something.

I narrowed my eyes and scowled. I smelled ambush.

My slitted eyes located him coming over. *Ambush indeed.* I shook my head, ashamed for not seeing it before. I waited until he scooted in next to Disco before I said anything.

He looked the same, short dark hair brushed back, clean button down shirt crisp and tidy.

"Well, hello again, Mr. Grey Goose."

"We didn't formally meet." He reached over the table to shake hands. "I'm Ethan McDaniel."

Oh sweet baby Jesus, bless him. He had no idea who the hell he'd just gotten involved with. I didn't extend my hand, glowering at him from my spot across the cheap ass table. I didn't like to be deceived, and Mr. Goose had done just that. No wonder he was someone I'd never seen at the club. He didn't go to the BP to admire tits and ass, he'd gone to check me out. I hoped he enjoyed the little show between Fitch and me. It was a precursor of what could happen to him.

He looked confused. Pulling his hand away, he tucked it under the table. "Am I missing something?"

"She's abnormally happy this evening and doesn't know how to express it adequately," Disco said. "But she's agreed to help us with our little endeavor. Haven't you, Rhiannon?"

"Fuck you," I snapped.

It didn't have the desired effect. Disco burst out laughing, and Goose looked incredibly uncomfortable. I almost felt sorry for him. Maybe he'd been suckered into this as well. I quickly smothered any sympathy. He had scoped me out, and that made him an accomplice.

"She's totally green." Disco grinned at me, talking to Goose. "She has no idea what to do or what to look for. She doesn't even know anything about our kind."

"Is that true?" Goose observed me with a peaked interest. "Do you even know what level of power you have?"

"Power? Are you joking? Don't tell me you enjoy seeing road kill right before breakfast. One bad corpse can ruin your whole day."

"That goes without saying," Goose agreed enthusiastically, leaning over the table. "But you also have the power to communicate with them. Have you tried that? What about raising the dead? Some of us can do that as well. It's an amazing talent, once fully understood and channeled."

The way he said it...like we were part of a little club—Jesus. He was getting off on this shit. Scratch what I said about vampires being creepy. *Ethan McDaniel* was fucking creepy.

"We are alike, but I'm limited," he continued. "I can't see past the second threshold of death—most of us can't. It takes a natural talent of necromancy. Mine has been developed through years of practice, research, and dedication."

Well, well, well. Tickle my Elmo ass silly. I was sitting across from a person who enjoyed talking to dead people, and if they wouldn't talk, then by God, he'd just wake their corpses up instead. Next to him was a moody, stalking vampire who just might be bipolar and smoked like a corncob pipe.

"Listen." I sighed and reached for my plastic bottle. "I want to get this shit over and done. Can we strive to obtain that goal? I have a meaningless existence, and I can't put that kind of action on hold indefinitely."

"You should quit your job." Goose studied me with his big brown eyes. "It's having a perverse effect on you, being surrounded by all that negativity."

"Thank you, Dr. Phil, for that fine psychological assessment," I snapped and motioned with my chin to Disco. "Why don't you and Oprah here go take a long walk off a short plank and do the world a favor?"

His face flamed and he looked away. Bingo, mission accomplished. Disco couldn't care less. He just stared at me, shaking his head. Cash had probably warned him about my mouth, which begged the next question.

"Where's Cash anyway? Shouldn't you two be locked together at the hip?"

Disco had a cigarette in his hand, moving so fast I didn't see him pull it from the pack. He lit it and took a deep drag. I felt compelled to tell him second hand smoke kills, but he spoke before I could impart my health care advisory.

"Cash vanished the last night he came to see you."

Okay, that wasn't good. Cash, for all his flaws, had grown on me in the week he pestered me. "I liked Cash," I said softly and Disco's head snapped up.

He read the truth in my expression, and his face changed, becoming almost sad. "Everyone liked Cash, which makes this all the more difficult to understand. We run in our own groups, and sometimes we don't get along or see eye to eye, but there wasn't one single person who wasn't taken with him. No vampire would hurt Cash, but only a vampire, or something as powerful as one, could get close enough to him to cause any harm."

"Then what could hurt him? What kind of things can kill a vampire?" I was concerned for Cash and beginning to worry for myself.

Disco's eyes narrowed and his mouth formed a harsh line. "That's what we're going to find out, and once we do, we'll take care of it. Everyone is rattled by these recent occurrences. Vampires are vanishing at a rate of one or two every other week, and it's been ongoing for weeks."

"And you." I looked at Goose. "What have you seen?"

"I've tried to see whatever is available, but I can't see the twice deceased. Perhaps if I visited their place of death, I could. But as it stands, they don't appear to me." His voice conveyed his frustration, and his face mirrored the sentiment.

We were dealing with something powerful enough to overcome vampires. The knowledge freaked my ass out. Anything that could kill a vamp would rip me a new one.

I peered at Disco through my lashes.

He could rip me a new one, too. It was the lesser of two evils. While I didn't trust Disco, I knew I had something he wanted. As long as I delivered, I could return to my blissfully peaceful and mundane life of bartending.

"Where do you want me to go and what do you want me to do?"

"You'll visit the last locations some of our kindred were seen, as well as the places they normally frequented. You saw Jacob at Shooter's, so I know you can see them," Disco said.

"Jacob?"

"The man you so kindly told to get away from the pocket at Shooter's. You described him the night we spoke—twenties, long hair..." Disco watched me, allowing the words to soak in. I could see the undead-dead. Those who bit the permanent gravy train just like the rest of us saps.

"When do I start? I wanted to finish this yesterday," I spoke while I still had my nerve. The steel backbone of mine had turned into a pliable Twizzler stick.

"When are you available?"

"Depends." I thought about it for a moment. "I'm on at the BP four nights a week, sometimes more. Days are better for me, but I know you shrivel and burn in the sun."

His lips turned upward sardonically. "That's why Ethan will be accompanying you. He's a professional. Pay attention, and you could learn a few things."

"Goose is a professional, huh?"

"My name isn't Goose," Ethan corrected me. "And I have free time tomorrow."

"Your name is Goose now, like it or not. And tomorrow is fine. I can meet you after I hit the gym." That would work out nicely. I could get my burn on and then get this shit over and done with as soon as possible.

Goose ignored my ribbing, reached into his pocket, and produced a little metal box. He flipped the lid and revealed a card, which he tossed on the table. "There's my number. Call me when you're ready."

I spun the card on the table with my fingers.

Ethan McDaniel, Paranormal Investigator.

Wow. The man actually made a living from this crap.

The atmosphere in the club charged, becoming palpable, and I frowned, turning my head in the direction of the dance floor.

Good God.

During the course of our conversation, the ratio of alive to undead had changed. For every human in the joint, there were two vampires. Even Miami wasn't this bad.

"What kind of club is this?" I asked suspiciously, the truth revealing itself like an unwelcome surprise.

"A club that caters to my kind. Didn't you know?" The smug smile on Disco's face pissed me off.

"She *is* green," Goose said, sounding both shocked and slightly haughty.

"Sad, isn't it?" Disco spoke to him but looked at me. "If she put half as much effort into honing her craft as she does into expanding her sailor's vocabulary, she could have potential."

I blew them off and stared at the blood guzzlers in the room. Each orifice of the dance floor was crammed as they romanced their dinners. I squinted in concentration as I peered into the dark nooks and crannies. Outlines of people lingered in the shadows, bodies melded together. I had a good idea of what was happening, green or not.

I cringed and averted my eyes. How people ever functioned under the notion vampires were sexy was beyond my comprehension. You were making out with a corpse, formaldehyde not included.

Disco regarded me intently, as if offended by my reaction. Then his face became a blank slate—nothing there but an empty stare that bore me back into the seat.

"Do you hate us so much?"

"It's not personal," I explained. There was no reason to be an absolute bitch. "I just tend to steer clear of things that give me the creeps."

"Don't you mean things that frighten you?"

I didn't bother trying to deny it. He would know if I was lying, and besides, it would explain my reaction. "That too."

CHAPTER FIVE

Canal Street is one hell of a place to discover the real New York. It's not *Bright Lights, Big City*. It's gritty, raw, and crowded. The buildings and streets are dirty. There is garbage scattered along the way, and the rats live lavishly through the waste.

I met up with Goose after my workout. It was early and the street was filling with vendors. The air had just lost the permeating smell of oriental foods, stale smoke and asphalt, but soon the familiar odors would be back in force. As usual there were ghosts galore—having died from both natural and unnatural causes. So far I'd passed four men and two women, only one of which had died violently.

Since Goose was the professional, I decided to grill him with some choice questions, and once I started, I couldn't seem to stop. He appeared to enjoy my interest, answering readily, and I discovered several things.

Not all people will become spirits. Most of them take off to that special place we all go when we die. However, for some, the tie to the mortal world is still strongly connected and they continue to exist. These poor souls usually venture along the same paths they took during their life, only veering off course if they sense a necromancer in the vicinity.

That's where we came in.

Ghosts want to communicate. They want to get a final word out to a loved one, or seek vindication for their untimely death. Afterward, they'll fade to the other side.

We discussed the "yuck" factor, which essentially are the super gooey and bloody ghosts that made me skip all my daily meals. They are perfectly intact, their forms seemingly solid at first glance. The first time I saw one, I scared the shit out of everyone around me by screaming like a pansy and hauling ass in the opposite direction. Thank God, I was only fifteen at the time, and the witnesses to my humiliation reside in Miami.

"The fresher the death, the fresher the spirit," Goose explained, smiling at my harrowing tale. "Most spirits begin to fade over time. The hazier they are, the older."

"I remember a hellacious car accident when I was in high school. Two cars collided head on, and it killed everyone involved. The traffic was backed up for a mile solid. When I finally passed the wreckage, I could see all of them, standing around the police at the scene. If it wasn't for the blood, head traumas and broken bodies, I would have sworn they'd all survived."

Goose nodded. "Very common. Sudden deaths, as you've described, leave the soul in flux. Most will pass over within a few hours, accepting their time here has passed."

"But not all?"

"Not all, no. Some people have strong emotional ties to this world. The ghosts I'm generally retained to contact are those who refuse to cross over and leave behind their husband, wife, or children."

"I haven't seen a child yet," I admitted with relief. "I don't want to either."

"Children are tough." He scooted toward me to avoid a vendor's booth. "I've only dealt with a handful of cases myself, and each of them involved...not so pleasant circumstances."

"Circumstances?" I jumped aside as someone came barreling out of a door with a huge cardboard box.

"Abuse, murder, molestation. I only involve myself if the police are close to apprehending someone. The smallest of things can land a conviction. Children, above all others, deserve vindication."

I absent mindedly touched my stomach, tracing my fingers along the line of my yoga pants, thinking of a time in my past. I knew all too well how children deserved their vengeance.

"Rhiannon?"

Goose's voice snapped me out of it, and I let my hand drift to my side.

"Are you all right?" His face was full of concern, brows drawn together. "You went blank for a minute."

"I'm fine," I answered, relieved my voice was steady. "What are we doing here anyway?"

"We're looking for Baxter Lomen. He vanished after Jacob. Disco said he wanted to buy a few trinkets for his"—he paused, searching for the right term—"female friends. Since this was his favorite place to shop, and we don't know if he visited a jewelry store or an outside vendor, we'll need to comb the area."

"Why do you think he'd linger around China Town?"

"This was his little neck of the woods and his favorite place to be. He had a thing for Asian women, too, if that tells you anything. All ghosts return to their favorite places. It's ingrained in their psyche."

We rounded the corner in front of Beny's Jewelry, and I stopped. Goose kept walking, unaware that I saw something. A few steps ahead, and he whipped around, confusion changing to excitement. But I wasn't paying attention to Goose; my eyes were drawn to someone else.

The ghost stared at me just as I stared at him. His thick hair was dark, his skin barely transparent, and his eyes were the most amazing shade of green I had ever seen. He approached me, and unlike all the times before when I'd walk away, or turn in the other direction, I allowed him to.

"What do you see?" Goose asked anxiously.

"Gorgeous guy, in his thirties maybe, with dark hair and the most vivid green eyes." My words were hoarse, my voice detached.

"Green eyes, that's him!" Goose took my hand. The contact made me jump, but I didn't break it. A strange undercurrent passed between us, a tiny vibration. He was silent a few seconds, and then he squeezed my fingers in a crushing grip. "My God, you can see them."

I tore my gaze away from Baxter to stare at Goose. His eyes were wide in awe and wonderment.

"How do you see him now when you couldn't before?"

"Your necromancy. You're sharing it with me through physical contact."

My attention returned to Baxter. His chest cavity was open wide, and the long white sleeves of his dress shirt were soaked with blood. The fabric dangled in ripped shreds around his torn flesh. His sternum was cracked, several ribs broken or missing, and his heart was gone, leaving nothing behind but empty red casing.

I swallowed back the bile rising in my throat.

"They took his heart." Goose sounded repulsed.

"Look at his wrists." I cringed, fighting nausea. The skin was ragged and raw. I could see white flashes of bone. "He was bound somehow. What kind of object can hold a vampire?"

"Holy ones," he answered, equally horrified. "Anything blessed, especially silver, can keep them restrained. Once it's on, they're powerless."

Baxter's arm extended. The ripped skin splayed out as his hand rose palm up into the air.

"Touch him," Goose instructed, giving me a shove but keeping contact with my right hand.

"Are you fucking insane?" I yelled in disbelief, yanking my hand free, and turned on him.

"My attempts to establish contact through other mediums haven't worked, and I don't have the ability to communicate with him through physical contact. But you do, so touch him!" Goose became impatient when I didn't comply. "Hurry up!"

"Oh man!" I whined. This was not what I wanted to do today. Baxter's face might be gorgeous, but his body was minced. He was waiting, palm raised. I did the spider dance, extending my hand but pulling it back before we made solid contact.

This shit was beyond disgusting.

I held my breath and went for it, fingers sliding past until our palms touched. My hand molded into his as if he were a solid object. The skin was smooth, fingers long. I looked into his face and garbled images flashed in my head.

A dark room, the hard concrete floor stained with blood, silver chains and knives, arms bound, cutting skin, breaking bone, unbearable pain, and then nothing. The images shifted. A bedroom painted lilac, white lace curtains, twin beds. Scratchy music from the record player as it skipped over one section and drowned out the muffled begging coming from the next room that turned to tear-filled cries...

Yanking my hand free, I started to tremble—mind blank, thoughts incoherent—caught in something worse than my temper could ever be. I was suffocating in blind terror, unable to breathe. I bent at the waist, gagging and dry heaving. Someone touched my shoulder, and I reacted defensively, grabbing the hand and twisting at the wrist. I maneuvered the arm around and up, forcing weight into the shoulder joint, pressing down.

"Rhiannon!" Goose screamed in pain. "Calm down! It's okay!"

At first, I didn't understand what he said. My blood was pounding too loudly, chest heaving with adrenaline and fear. Slowly, I came to awareness, and I heard muted whispers. People were watching, appearing cautious, obviously afraid to intervene but too terrified to look away. Goose lay at my feet, his wrist and hand trapped in mine, forcing him to the ground.

I let go and stepped back, folding my arms to mask my trembling. I struggled to pull my shit together, taking measured breaths. Goose rose on unsteady feet, his white polo stained black from the dirty pavement. His usually tidy hair was uneven and messy around his temples.

"What happened?" he asked calmly, hands lifted harmlessly in the air.

A few witnesses stood around while I collected myself, and realizing the show was over, moved along. I glanced at Baxter. He stood waiting. For what, I had no idea.

After a tense minute, I cleared my throat. My voice came out shaken. "He was alive when they took his heart. He was—fuck, you know what I mean!"

Goose's eyes widened in alarm. I've been around enough people to know spooked when I see it, and he was spooked as hell.

"What?" I barked. I didn't go through those memories to be left hanging.

"This has black magic written all over it." He peered at me as he started pacing. "This is not good, not good at all. Harvesting organs while the victim is alive is reminiscent of witchcraft."

"You've got to be shitting me. Granted, what I'm about to say is very naïve, but black magic? You can't be serious."

"How do you think we raise the dead? Do you think that just happens naturally? There's a structured ritual to follow, and that includes magic. Necromancy is just one of the requirements. Black magic works the same. There are catalysts to bring forth the magic, but the ritual and powers are still required to make it work."

"So someone is killing vampires off for their organs? Who would be that stupid?" I was as edgy as hell. The concept of capturing vampires to collect hearts made me sick.

Someone who would willingly go against a force that powerful wouldn't care if they lived or died.

"We need to go to my office. I need to do some digging and research." Goose was deep in thought, fingers on his chin rubbing the skin as he contemplated where to start.

"Oh no." I lifted my hands, stepped back, and shook my head. "I did what I promised. I'm taking my sorry ass home."

I ran off the sidewalk and across the street. I didn't stop when Goose asked me to reconsider, and I didn't look back when he called my name. The constant thuds of my footsteps were the only sounds I cared about as I hauled ass to the L train and went home.

CHAPTER SIX

I arrived to work on the wrong foot. I was jumpy and agitated, constantly watching the doors.

A loud fart would have sent me skyrocketing into orbit.

I tried to focus on the patrons, the music from the stage, and even Lonnie's fat ass, who as luck would have it, reverted to calling me bartender again. It was grueling and tedious, and I just wanted to go home and climb into bed.

Gathering my few belongings, I hit the door after close. I couldn't shake touching Baxter, and it wasn't because of my own personal hang-ups. Embedded in those shared memories was the perception of dread. I could feel his sense of doom, of damnation. He knew his life was ending, but it wasn't death he feared. He was terrified of what came after, because he didn't know if he would go to Heaven or Hell.

I couldn't move past that. His regret at not knowing if he would gain admittance inside the pearly gates because of what he was.

I was curious about the answer myself.

I exited through the back of the building. Pushing open the door with a heavy scrape of metal, I entered the darkened morning dank with mist. I stared at the ground, too confused to pay attention, and nearly busted my ass when I bumped full speed into a hard body. Strong hands held me upright and I threw my weight back, lifting my arms to protect myself.

"Jesus, take it easy." Disco spoke softly, letting go. He was in his normal black ensemble, the collar of his trench coat pulled up and around his turtleneck. He didn't move closer, but regarded me carefully. "Ethan wasn't exaggerating. You did have a bad day."

"Don't sneak up on me like that!" Pulling in a ragged breath, I wrapped my arms around my stomach. I was wrong. I wouldn't skyrocket into orbit. My heart would simply burst inside my chest.

"I wanted to see if you were all right. Ethan said you wouldn't return his calls." Disco turned his blue eyes to my brown ones, and they were full of concern, not demands or expectations.

"Look." I took a jagged breath. "I'm not cut out for this shit. I did what you asked, and now I'm done."

"He told me what you saw. I apologize. I know it wasn't easy, and believe me, I would have done it myself if I could. My friends are dying, Rhiannon. You confirmed our worst suspicions. If you walk away, they will keep dying. Can you turn your back and let others be murdered the same way Baxter was? The way Cash was?" he whispered the last part quietly, bright blue irises shining beautifully behind sooty lashes.

I ran trembling fingers through my hair. Whoever was behind this wouldn't stop. The number of missing vampires made that painfully obvious. Could I walk away and save my own ass, turning my back on them and letting it happen because I was too afraid to do the right thing?

Haunted green eyes flashed in my mind.

"No," I exhaled the word, answering both of us at the same time. "I guess not."

Disco relaxed, standing tall and straightening his shoulders in one agile movement. "I'm relieved to hear you say that." He approached, each step calculated and smooth, stopping just inches away. "Are you all right?"

Was I all right? Not really. My nerves were frazzled. My head was killing me. And my mind kept filtering those images over and over—the chains, the shining blade of the curved hunting knife, the blood—oh my God, the blood. And somehow, tied inside those visions, were ones from my own tormented childhood.

No, I wasn't all right, but I said, "I'll be fine."

He moved, covering the distance, and stopped directly in front of me. "That wasn't my question."

I tried to step back, but he used his speed to place strong hands on my shoulders, keeping me still. His face lowered until just inches separated us. Up close, I could see how pale and smooth his skin was, like polished alabaster.

"Back off," I whispered between clenched teeth. Bringing my hands to my chest, I forced them between our bodies. I couldn't break free, and that knowledge sent my body into unwilling tremors.

"I could be a crass bastard and dig around in that head of yours, just forgoing any manners and say to hell with the impropriety. But I won't, because I want you to come to me, Rhiannon. One day, you will trust me enough to ease your burden on my ears, and when that day arrives, I will gladly listen."

His voice was like plush velvet against my skin. I closed my eyes, biting down on my tongue until I tasted the rusty bitterness of blood. When I lifted my lids, all I could see was bright blue, his irises darker on the edge and lightening near the pupil.

Was he actually capable of reading my damned mind?

I drew in a breath, fighting back panic.

"Answer one question." His hushed request sent a shiver down my spine. "Would you shy away from anyone's touch, or do you just despise mine because of what I am?"

"Okay." I swallowed and cleared my throat. The spark of my temper was small and weak, like flint striking a wet stone, but it felt good nonetheless. "If you were anyone else, your nuts would be taking a long vacation, and the destination would be out of your mouth."

He smiled at that, enhancing his already angelic face. He released my shoulders and I sagged. Righting myself, I shifted my weight to regain my balance.

"Come on, I'll escort you home."

"That's okay, I know the way." I tried to shuffle past, and he placed his body directly in my path. If not for the ripples of his leather coat, I'd have never known he'd moved. I stood stunned as he stepped in beside me. He reached into his pocket for a cigarette, which he promptly lit.

This time, I didn't argue. He would do whatever he wanted. I started walking, breathing deeply until I achieved a small level of calm.

"How do you smoke? Doesn't that require breathing?" I finally decided to ask the questions. If anything, it would break the ice.

"We don't have to breathe, but it's how we form words to speak. It's the reason we can't be killed by drowning. We can hold our breath indefinitely."

"So...your organs function as needed?"

"It depends on the organ."

"Take your heart for example." I avoided looking into his eyes. "Does it still beat?"

He turned swiftly, tossed the cigarette, grabbed my hand, and placed it on his chest. His fingers were cold, the delicate ivory coloring matching my own. I flattened my palm over the softness of his sweater, feeling the solid area over his heart and the steady beating coming from underneath.

"Amazing," I whispered, eyes wide, marveling at the thumping against my fingers. The rhythm was strong and steady. How could you classify someone as dead when they still had a heartbeat and could breathe?

"We are not so different," he said softly, answering my unspoken question.

"How is it possible? Does it ever stop beating?" I was mesmerized by the sensation and felt slightly disappointed when he moved away to walk beside me once more.

"It slows when we haven't fed," he replied evenly, returning to his nicotine fix.

"That's a nasty habit, you know." I wrinkled my nose distastefully and pointed at the cigarette.

"I'll make you a deal. I'll put down the smokes if you stop speaking so crudely."

"Fuck that." I bit my lower lip to disguise my grin.

He sighed, and shook his head, but retained the smile. "You can't say I didn't try."

He followed me like a shadow, quiet but ever present. It was strange making the trip home with someone, because it had never happened before. After we exited the subway, we walked to my street in relative silence, and it wasn't because of my lack of questions. From the moment I'd discovered his heart still beat, my mind went into overdrive.

Then, I remembered a ghost I'd once seen outside my apartment. She'd lingered at the doorway, watching me, but didn't enter the building. The question of their crossing the threshold came to mind. Regardless of the situation, I'd never seen a ghost inside a residence. Although I was certain ghosts could haunt a place, I wasn't sure if they could enter a domain that they weren't tied to. I hesitated, afraid to ask initially, but my inquisitiveness overcame logic.

"Is the myth true? Do you have to be invited into someone's home before you can enter?" I asked the question nervously, fidgeting and staring ahead.

"Are you inviting me inside?"

Shit. I tried to keep my expression blank. That wasn't the smartest question to ask after all. I clammed up, words escaping me, biting the inside of my cheek.

"Yes, we have to be invited," he answered, saving my ass from sheer humiliation.

"Ghosts are the same, or I should say, the few I've encountered near my apartment stop at the door. I wondered if it was connected."

"Ah." He nodded and smiled.

"Thanks for seeing me home." My smile didn't reach my eyes. I felt awkward and uncertain.

He gave a mock salute. "Anytime."

Walking quickly to the door, I yanked it open, stepped inside, and turned to look through the glass. Disco was in the same spot I'd left him, framed by the glow of the street light. I lifted my left hand and swept it up and out in a goodbye wave. He lowered his head in acknowledgement, and I rushed up the stairs.

I refused to breathe until I was safely inside my apartment.

CHAPTER SEVEN

Goose's apartment doubled as his office and consisted of a hodgepodge of all things mystical. With walls painted cream, dark natural wood floors, and a random stuffed critter here and there.

Bookshelves lined the walls with bound pages full of spells and enchantments. The titles were arranged alphabetically, and little objects like assorted stones and rocks were placed carefully in front of the spines. In the ceiling above the wooden banisters were various taxidermies, a squirrel and rabbit among them. They creeped me out something fierce, and I couldn't concentrate knowing their beady little eyes were watching.

I took a seat in the leather chair in front of his desk and settled in. On the edge of his workspace were several thick books, their pages marked with ribbons of multiple colors. Directly in front was a name plate—Ethan McDaniel, P.I.

I snickered. Goose thought he was a private dick.

I closed my eyes and envisioned him chasing a criminal mastermind through the tough streets of New York. Working for the oppressed and down trodden, his feet are swift and his balls are mighty. The visual worked until the pursuit came to a screeching halt and the criminal revealed his Cletus-like physique. What would Mr. Goose P.I. do? Arrest the bad guy and save the day? Get beaten to a pulp and left for dead?

Tune in next week, kiddies, for the exciting conclusion!

"Here we go." His voice echoed from the kitchen, and he appeared holding a steaming mug in hand.

Goose was a consummate gentleman. He opened doors. He offered refreshments. And he didn't interrupt others when they spoke. I was finding it near to damned impossible to hold my previous grudge against him; he was too damned likeable.

"Thanks." I accepted the hot ceramic mug graciously, smiling at him. He was dressed casually while in the comfort of his own domicile. The baby-blue polo and blue jeans made him appear younger and less uptight.

"Where were we? Oh!" He lifted one of the books off his desk, opened it, and flipped the pages. "Muti is a widely used African term to describe medicine, but in recent years, the word has been associated with the excision of body parts from living people. The belief is that pain increases the potency of the organ, as do the screams rendered at its taking. These organs or body parts are then used in medicines or assorted black magic spells, ranging from ones that heal to those that bring wealth and power."

"Pain increases the potency? And they want them to scream?" I shivered, momentarily reliving Baxter's suffering. "That's sadistic."

"Indeed." Goose nodded in agreement and closed the book with a plop. "Which begs the question—why vampires?"

He crossed out of the office, into the living room, and drew the thick curtains around the windows closed. A little click sounded and a warm glow flooded the area, courtesy of the Venetian floor lamp in the corner. He walked to a bookshelf and ran his finger along the wood, locating and then removing a volume from the top. The wood creaked under his feet as he walked back and placed the book on the desk. He opened it, revealing a faux cover that hid various glass vials, and pulled one out. The liquid inside was deep red, nearly black in its thickness.

"Here." He extended the vial and I took it in my fingers, flipping my wrist to study the goopy liquid.

"What is this?" I asked, making odd faces as I imagined the worst.

"Vampire blood," he answered, reclining against the desk.

It didn't seem different from human blood, except the color and consistency was thicker and darker. I held it toward the lamp, twisting the vial. The red was more distinguishable in the light.

"Do I even want to know where you got this?" I peered around the glass and met his steady gaze.

He smiled broadly, nodding his head in approval.

Maybe next time I would get a cookie.

"You want to know exactly how I got that. Vampire blood is huge on the black market. If you drink or inject it, it makes for one hell of a high. It also has the power to heal wounds faster, make you stronger, and does wonders for the sex life. People are willing to pay a high price for what you have in your fingers, and some vampires are always out to make a quick buck."

I was just absorbing the healing faster and better sex life part when the vampires making a quick buck registered. "They sell their own blood?" I asked, completely grossed out. How did that work? Did they keep syringes on hand for a blood draw?

"They do, and they're smart about it. They don't sell directly to seekers. They use reputable underground suppliers where this kind of thing is the norm. They bag it, take it to their contact, swap out goods for the cash, and presto—blood out of body and cash in hand."

"That's nasty. You know that, right?" I stared at him, my opinion validated when he nodded. I wanted to make sure we were on the same page. Then I remembered I was holding a tiny glass container filled with the stuff. My eyes narrowed suspiciously. "And what are you doing with this?" I lifted the vial into the air. "You don't drink this shit do you?"

"I have before, but not for the reasons you assume."

He rose, walked around the desk, and plopped down into his swiveling leather recliner. "The blood in that vial belonged to Jacob. Or as near as we can tell, it did. Disco couldn't get a positive identification from the supplier, so we're going on assumptions. I tried to use his blood in the hope that I could call him with my necromancy.

As you already know, it didn't work."

"I won't tell you how incredibly disgusting I think you are right now. Instead, I'm going to ask you what vampire blood has to do with Muti and vampire organs."

"I think they're connected. I also think that whoever is behind the disappearances got their start in the clubs with blood and decided to move onto something bigger and better. It's that, or a dealer got greedy and started offering new and improved vampire specialties at private gatherings. Either way, our next step is to get invited to a private screening to see what's on the menu."

"Oh man." Images of wannabe vampires came to mind, and an electric tremor shot down my vertebrae. I didn't want to be involved with a crowd like that. I gave Goose my most pitiful look. "Do we have to?"

He laughed, the unexpected sound reverberating inside his apartment. "Why can't you be like this more often? It's refreshing and rather adorable."

"Fuck that shit," I grumbled and felt my face flush as I resumed my normal disposition. *Adorable* was a word with which I never wanted to be associated. No more chocolate. It coerced me into being happy and joyful.

"It was fun while it lasted." He frowned disapprovingly and looked at the ceiling, as if God needed to intervene on my behalf. "And yes, we do have to. Disco got the location of the next blood tasting. It's Friday night—"

"Hold it." I sat up, placing the vial on the desk along with my mug. "I've got work."

"Can't you take the night off?"

He seemed dumbfounded, and I wasn't sure why. Work means you have a schedule, and when it's your day to work, you come in. It seemed like a basic concept to me.

"Sure, I could, but it's a busy night. I can't afford to lose my job over this." I liked my job and the people I worked with. No way was I letting that slip. "That is one condition I'm not budging on."

"Please, take the night off. Getting invited to these social functions is no easy feat, and I'm not sure the opportunity will come again in the foreseeable future. I won't ask again, Scout's Honor." He lifted his fingers and drew a cross over his heart.

"Okay," I agreed reluctantly, and it hurt to do it. I'd never requested off work at the last minute before. I hoped Deena didn't chew me up and spit me out. "But this is it, no more ditching."

"That sounds fair." He sat up and opened a drawer on the desk. The chair squeaked in protest as he reached into the back, searched around, and pulled out a card. He tossed it across the desk, and I caught it with my hands. "That's for your expenses. You'll need to buy something for the occasion. Pamper yourself with a manicure and pedicure. Enjoy yourself."

"What about you?" I tried to picture him in head to toe black, with lipstick and eyeliner.

"What about me?" He frowned, peering down at himself.

"Do you even own a black article of clothing? And who is going to apply your makeup?"

He laughed so hard, I thought his neurological pathways had been fried.

"What?"

He grinned, laughing again, until he noticed my expression. "This isn't that kind of party, Rhiannon. That card is to purchase a dress—a *nice* dress. The people who attend these functions are not young adults with a lingering case of depression. Purchasing vampire blood is an expensive habit, one that requires thousands of dollars each time."

I wanted to gag. I hadn't worn a dress since my prom. "Can't I wear what I did to the Razor?"

"No." He was completely serious now. "These people will notice anything out of the ordinary. You'll need to get a dress, get your hair done—all of it. That's why I insisted you come along and request the night off. These gatherings are exclusive and undisclosed."

My stomach knotted at the gravity of what I was entering into. I stood up, bracing my hands on his desk. "What goes down at these little social functions? I'm not down with guzzling someone else's blood, dead or alive. If that's part of the arrangement, I'm telling you right now, it ain't happening. *No fucking way.*"

"The expectation for you to sample the product will be there, but you can decline. You can say you've recently come down from your last taste and need a breather. It's similar to a wine tasting. People taste before buying, same difference." I could tell he was choosing his words carefully, which told me all I needed to know.

They would expect me to drink vampire blood, no matter what he said to the contrary. I knew what they'd expect, because it is what they went to the tastings for in the first place. My stomach churned, and I could taste the chocolate from earlier. I drew in a huge breath through my nose and released it as I sat back down. I felt icky and nauseous.

"I need to know what to expect, in case I'm forced to taste it." I willed myself not to flinch as I met his gaze.

"I've never been to a tasting myself. I've only heard about them from colleagues. But I have taken blood before." He took an uneven breath, and looked away. "It's instant. The minute you swallow, your eyes, ears, nose, everything, goes into overdrive. It's disorienting at first, then unbelievably empowering. I can easily see why people become addicted to the rush. Once it's gone, you realize just how weak, blind, and deaf you truly are."

The temptation to tell him to forget it and walk out the door reared its head, but I suppressed it. I despised fear, especially my own, and that's exactly what I was experiencing. I was frightened of stepping outside of my comfort zone, of letting go of the little security blanket I'd built so solidly around myself.

And I didn't want to live that way anymore.

"I want something from you in exchange for everything I'm doing," I told him. "When this is finished, I want to know about my necromancy. I want you to teach me how it works."

"Nothing would please me more. You have my word," he promised. Pushing free of the chair, he rose and walked to the bookshelf. He removed a book and placed it into my hands. "As a show of trust, you can take this to read."

The leather bound tome was thicker than any book I'd held, the pages coarse and uneven. I flipped to the first page and studied the freehand script. I scanned through, intrigued by words like summoning, conjuring, channeling and sacrifice, mixed with diagrams and descriptions, lists of ingredients and moon cycles.

"What is this?" I stopped at the page with a full moon and a corpse digging its way out of the ground. My lips came together, forming a thin line as I read the descriptions and necessary items.

"That is the first of my personal journals. I have it all written down, everything I've learned." He cleared his throat and returned to his recliner.

"Please tell me you don't raise zombies on a regular basis."

"No," he said quietly. "It's difficult to do here in the States, and not so easy to explain. It's also very dangerous. Zombies don't feel pain, and they won't return to the grave until you release them."

"Then what exactly do you do." I closed the book and leaned forward to touch the nameplate. "Mr. Ethan McDaniel, P.I.?"

"I help people. People who are mourning. People with missing loved ones. People who need answers they can't have because the person with the information has passed on. When they've explored every possible venue that's considered normal, and all that's left is to wait or give up, they turn to me. I do my best to ensure this is the last stop they have to make." His eyes focused on mine as his tone became solemn. "Placing faith in a medium one doesn't understand is difficult enough, but if people were willing to embrace the truth of what we are capable, could you imagine how beneficial our powers would be?"

I broke eye contact, shifting my focus around the desk. "You didn't add vampires to that list. How did you end up working for them?"

"Eleven years ago, a girl went missing on her way home from Brooklyn College. Her parents filed a missing person report, but it was Disco who retained my services. It didn't take long to find her, just a few days of tracing her normal route. Her ghost was clear, and a simple touch told me all I needed to know. They found her body in a trunk in the Bronx a week or so later. I've been the liaison for his people since then."

"Who was she?"

"Just a girl who was terribly unlucky. She was snatched somewhere between the campus and her house by several not so nice guys on a cocaine binge. She didn't die quickly; they took their time. When it was over, they discarded her like a rag doll, wrapped in cellophane and garbage bags in the trunk of an abandoned vehicle. It didn't take long for Disco's crew to track them, and when they did, there wasn't anyone left for the police to haul into jail."

"Why did Disco and his people get involved?"

"I'm not at liberty to say, Rhiannon," Goose answered after a lengthy hesitation. "Maybe one day you can ask Disco."

"Okay." I didn't pry, aware that I'd trespassed onto some private matter best left alone.

He changed the subject by formulating our plan. He would arrive at nine o'clock sharp at my place, bringing us fashionably late to the shindig in the hope that tardiness would excuse us from the early tasting, as well as keeping us below the radar.

Our plan was simple—mingle, observe, and listen. Anyone who raised a red flag would be marked as a suspect of interest. And we only had one rule that governed the entire stakeout.

If somehow we were caught—get the hell out of there.

CHAPTER EIGHT

Goose said I looked amazing, and I would have accepted his compliment with tact and grace if I didn't feel like a bad Tammy Faye impersonator at a religious rally.

The woman he suggested for my makeover had put a mountain of cosmetics on my face—foundation, powder, concealer, blush, eye shadow, eyeliner, mascara. The only part of me I did like was my hair, which I'd blown out straight. The long pieces fell to my waist like a silk curtain, a few strands of red shimmering in the light thanks to the impeccable dye job I'd received.

My outfit came courtesy of Macy's, and it was something I could live with—a black halter jumpsuit. I never knew such an amazing and smart piece of clothing existed. The back was open to the waist, which was foreign to me, but the legs were long and billowy and hid the new boots I'd purchased to match. Since I lived in shit kickers and Nike's, I hoped I didn't need to haul ass or jump obstacles. If so, I was bound to eat turf.

Goose looked outstanding. His suit was deep navy, almost black, and matched his coloring wonderfully. He wore a light blue shirt with a luxurious navy tie that matched the pants and jacket. His hair was neatly slicked back, and he smelled so good that I pretended to adjust his tie just to take another whiff.

Our driver stopped in front of our destination on Park Avenue, pulling to the empty curb, and my nervousness returned. I was out of my league and completely out of my zone. Whereas I could conform to an emo crowd easily enough, pretending to matriculate from upper crust asshats was too surreal. Goose insisted my stellar attitude and superb language skills had to be put on hold while we were inside the building, which meant I had to keep my big fat cow shut.

It was the equivalent of asking a little girl not to scream the first time she was personally introduced to Hannah Montana.

We walked into the building and signed under pseudo names. Hello, Mr. Receptionist, we're Mr. and Mrs. Hamlin, visiting the Westhouses on the 74th floor, if you please.

Goose kept his arm loosely at my waist, appearing much taller as he focused on his posture. He totally looked the part. As the door to the elevator slid closed, we both relaxed.

"Remember to watch your language, Janet."

I turned toward him, brushing off his lapels and giving him the once over.

"Why ever would you say such a thing, Brad?" I smiled innocently and started to snicker. I loved our names, straight out of *The Rocky Horror Picture Show*. At any moment, I was going to ask Goose to do the "Time Warp."

"Quiet," he shushed me as he fought his own laughter, lips contorting with the effort, and pulled me to his side.

I stood patiently, nervous but somehow excited too. I felt like a spy, assuming different identities and working under cover. The *Mission Impossible* theme echoed through my mind as the lights shifted on the elevator panel. My heart started hammering, and my skin began to tingle. The doors opened, and Goose's arm tightened around my waist, leading us out.

Directly ahead was a man in a black suit. Goose pulled me forward and approached the door confidently. "Brad and Janet Hamlin, we were invited by Marcus Delmar."

He didn't offer any further explanation and he didn't look away.

Jesus.

Goose *was* a bona fide professional.

I started to relax. Mr. Ethan McDaniel P.I. had this shit, no problem. The man in black nodded and moved away from the door to grant us access. Goose reached out and gripped the handle. Opening the door, he motioned me inside. I could hear voices, high-pitched drones with enunciated vowels and leering pronunciation.

I bit my lip, vowing I would not speak unless spoken to. I had two huge strikes against me. I had no formal education—other than the school of bar—and I came from the south. My southern accent wasn't as severe as some, but it was evident, especially in a room full of millionaire northerners.

Goose guided us across the room, toward a huge walk-in closet. He helped me out of my jacket and gently pulled my hair around my shoulders. Sensing my confusion, he led me inside and hung up the garment, showing me where it would be in case we made a speedy departure. I smiled nervously and his eyes tightened. He nudged my chin with his knuckles, and I nodded in understanding.

I would keep my chin up. To hell with the snobby bastards.

He held out his arm and I took it without hesitation. This was a partnership now. I'd have to get used to trusting someone else besides myself.

We exited the closet and walked into a huge room full of people. I suddenly understood the need for snazzy clothes. Everyone was dressed in form-fitted dresses, suits, and designer duds specifically tailored for them. The crowd was older, too. I was one of the youngest in the room, and probably considered eye candy along with the few other males and females with older dates.

There were tables filled with drinks, and hors d'oeuvres were lined up on one side of the room. The wall opposite was open to allow a breathtaking view of Central Park, street-lit walkways as perfect as a watercolor painting.

"So far, nada," I leaned over to whisper in Goose's ear, smiling pleasantly as a server with a tray offered us a glass of wine. I put the glass to my lips and took a small sip. It tasted slightly off, too sweet somehow, and I puckered my lips.

Goose's face tightened, and his eyes narrowed.

As if to say, I told you so.

I would have spit the fluid back up if I could. How stupid could I be? The room changed as the air became crisper, the voices became clearer, and my vision...I saw every minute detail, ranging from the brownish seeds on the strawberries nestled on trays across the room, to the lint on Goose's shirt as he turned to me.

"Oh God," I whispered, wanting to be sick but knowing I had to keep a straight face. I swallowed, aware of my tongue and the sweet taste that lingered on the surface.

Goose moved in against me, a fake smile plastered to his face. He shifted close and leaned down. The feel of his breath against my cheek made me shudder as my legs swayed.

"It will pass in another five minutes or so. You didn't drink much."

"Okay." Even my voice sounded different, like a purr in my ears.

He grasped my hand, and I could feel the heat from his frame as it radiated from his body in warm waves. He slipped my fingers under his arm, wrapping them around, and walked me to the window, giving me something to focus on until the feeling passed. I stared down at the trees and lamps in the distance, and slowly, things dulled. My perfect vision faded until everything was blurry, sounds were distant and slurred, and smells were no longer evident.

"All better?" He didn't turn from the glass, pretending to look outside at the fantastic view.

"Mmm hmm." I vocalized, afraid to speak and hear myself purring.

"Pardon me." A deep voice spoke from behind us, and we both turned to greet the stranger. "I don't believe I've had the pleasure."

He was a big guy who devoted serious time to the gym, with long hair that fell down his shoulders in soft brown waves, and caramel brown eyes that went beautifully with his tanned skin and handsome face. His suit was formal, but he didn't wear a tie, his shirt collar loose and comfortable at his neck.

"I don't believe we have." Goose stepped up to the plate, more seasoned than a award-winning actor from Julliard. He extended his right hand and introduced himself. "Brad Hamlin."

"Jude Mason." He shook Goose's hand forcefully and turned his attention to me.

Goose didn't seem to appreciate the interest generated in my direction when he placed his arm gently around my waist and said, "Allow me to introduce my wife, Janet."

"The good ones are always taken." Jude grinned, full lips pulling away to reveal perfect white teeth.

He reached for my hand and brought it to his mouth. It took all of my control to keep from complaining that I didn't know where those lips had been or what they'd been doing. He brushed them gently across the tender part of skin directly below my knuckle and let go.

"Who told you about our private party this evening?" The question was cordial, but the undertones were blatant. He didn't recognize us, and that pulled a red flag.

"Marcus Delmar," Goose answered, equally unnerved.

Marcus was the supplier for these little gatherings, and when Disco threatened to shut down his operation, he'd gladly given up the goods on tonight's extravaganza.

His was one name the people here wouldn't question.

"I see." The suspicion evaporated from Jude's face. "Then allow me to introduce you to a few of the other guests."

I stuck to Goose like a bad rash, keeping my body in close contact. I could handle a drunken asshole with over one hundred pounds on me, but I was mortified of social interaction with these people.

Jude led us to a large group standing along the far wall, and I knew I was staring at a living billboard epitomizing wealth and sophistication. They reeked of superiority and affluence. Each of the men stood leisurely, accompanied by hard-bodied dates.

"Timothy." Jude breezed into their circle, sweeping around to face us. "We have new faces tonight. Allow me to introduce Brad and Janet Hamlin."

Timothy stepped away from the group. I guessed he was in his forties, but only because of the grey that tinted the black at his temples. His face was still smooth, with only a few wrinkles appearing around the slate grey eyes that matched his suit. He extended his hand, and Goose gave another firm shake before he stepped back.

Everyone quickly made introductions. Timothy's wife, Sarah, appeared years older than her husband, but it wasn't from lack of trying. I could tell when someone worked out, and this woman would give me a run for the money. She was lean and cut; the direct result of personal chefs and trainers. Her black hair, bobbed to her chin, matched her onyx eyes.

Next on the menu were Mark and Sabrina Smith. They were the youngest of the couples, in their late thirties, and extremely well spoken. Mark was handsome with bronzed skin and dark brown eyes, but Sabrina was a real looker. Curly blonde hair surrounded her face in ringlets, deep blue eyes huge inside her heart-shaped face.

Last were Carson and CeCe Parker, both of which gave me a mondo case of the willies. Each had blond hair, blue eyes, and could easily pass for brother and sister. They finished each other's introductions, clung to each other like floatation devices, and made me think we had slipped into a bad episode of *The Twilight Zone*.

The conversation quickly delved into subjects chock-full of words like mutual funds, offshore accounts, and the stock market. The minute they went into that area of expertise, I glanced around the room. Most of the people branched off in pairs—couples I assumed.

"And what is it you do, Janet?"

Sarah's voice echoed inside my ears, and I knew she'd caught me daydreaming. I whipped around and smiled awkwardly. My mind shut down, totally absent of any thoughts or ideas.

Bartender? No. Pool player? No. Ghost hunter? No. Full-time smart ass? No. I was running out of ideas and she was waiting. The room closed in on me as her tiny black eyes came closer and closer...

"You're looking at it," I said for no logical reason whatsoever. *You're looking at it? What the hell was I smoking?* We were busted. I started working out our exit strategy in my head—time to get the hell out.

"What she means is"—Goose pulled me close, squeezing tighter than necessary—"soon, we hope to expand our family. Janet is currently focusing all of her attention on that aspect of our lives."

Ah, smart man. Make me a breeder.

"How wonderful," CeCe exclaimed. She turned to Mark and Sabrina. "Didn't you say you have a little boy?"

"Yes," Sabrina answered softly and Mark nodded.

Sarah shook her head distastefully. "I couldn't have children. I would never get my body back."

"How selfless of you, Sarah." CeCe smirked.

"It's the truth. Some of us are not cut out for Mommyhood." Sarah's eyes slitted and her mouth formed a thin line, making her appear much older.

"Ladies," Jude interrupted, motioning a server over with his index finger, "remember what tonight is about. Just relax."

Everyone took a crystal flute, and when the tray made its way to me, I followed suit, keeping the revolting brew at my side.

"Let's toast." Jude smiled and brought his glass to his chest. "To longevity."

Everyone lifted their glasses and I placed the edge of my glass to my mouth, blocked off my throat, and pretended to take a sip. The wine clung to my lips, and I licked them quickly, tasting that odd sweetness.

"Is something wrong?" Jude asked, and I brought my gaze up. Of course, he'd pay attention. His focus hadn't left us since we arrived. "You don't like the wine?"

Damn it.

I didn't want to drink, and I couldn't look at Goose for guidance. My fingers tightened on the stem of the glass as I brought the rounded swell of fine crystal to my lips. Like before, the sweetness lingered on my tongue, and clarity came on hard and fast.

"Good, isn't it?" Jude's eyes were all over me, and I found vampire blood didn't alleviate one human trait—my temper. I imagined erasing his sneer with a wicked crotch shot that would keep him celibate for weeks, but even anger couldn't overcome the smells that consumed me. My nose took in the scent of perfumes, colognes, starch, and stale air blowing from the overhead air conditioning vents.

I smiled tightly, turned to Goose, and said, "I need to visit the ladies' room."

"Excuse us." Goose lowered his glass and off we went, in search of a throne and a few precious minutes to compose myself.

I'd never dabbled in drugs, so I didn't have anything to compare the rush to. There was no cloudiness or confusion, no stupor induced fog or heaviness. This felt like a perfect high directly following a good workout, when your blood is flowing and your lungs are at full capacity. My body didn't feel detached. Instead, it felt magnified, each part stronger and easily recognizable.

"It's here." Goose nudged me to the left, down a hall. The walls were painted white, with no decorations or adornments covering them. The floor was white ceramic with grey swirls of iridescent pearl mixed within. My eyes saw it all perfectly, absorbing every detail.

"Give me a minute." The purr was there again, thrumming in my ears.

I walked into the bathroom and sat on the toilet. The voices outside were the faintest of whispers, but if I focused, I could hear the conversations clearly. Jude had intercepted Goose again, and his voice carried as he moved back into the room.

This was a bad idea, a very bad idea.

The bathroom door opened, and I leapt to my feet just as CeCe's smiling face peered around the edge. She came inside, closed the door, and twisted the lock. As she moved into the room, her heels created a distinct staccato on the ceramic tile.

She walked to the mirror and placed her small red clutch onto the counter. Checking her hair, then her cheeks and lips, she smiled at me through the glassy reflection. Her bright tomato red lipstick, dress, and clutch all were the same shade.

"You should come to one of our girls' nights. I think you'd like it." She popped open the compact purse, pulled out a card, and handed it over. "Don't worry, it's very hush-hush. Come to that address tomorrow night, around nine o'clock."

The effects of the blood were beginning to wane. I glanced down. The card held an address only, no name or telephone number.

"I'll see if I'm available."

"If you want to know about the real deal, you'll come. This isn't a stuffy get together where everyone has the opportunity to flash his or her money. Take a chance. You won't regret it."

She snapped her clutch closed, smiled, and pivoted in her expensive red heels to walk to the door. When she flipped the lock and stepped back outside, I took a deep breath and slipped the card into my pocket. After checking myself quickly in the mirror, I walked out of the bathroom and went in search of Goose, ready for the night to end.

We stayed for another hour, but didn't learn anything significant. Jude was a supplier, hence his interest in our invitation. Sabrina and Mark quietly mingled around the room, while CeCe and Carson continued to bug me out. The only saving grace of the evening was the wondrous reprieve from drinking anymore tainted wine.

We were waiting outside for our snazzy ride when I noticed Sabrina climbing into a dark limo. The driver was tall, his dark skin closely matching his suit and hat. She slid inside and he walked around, turned, and stared at me. His eyes were an odd shade of green, like deep jade. I stared back until he broke the contact, slid inside the car, and slammed the door. The line moved up and our driver appeared. I sighed in relief, smiling at Goose before climbing inside.

"Enjoy yourself?" Disco asked quietly. He was situated where I couldn't see him, eyes flashing bright blue in the dark.

"Stop doing that!" I snapped quietly. People were still on the sidewalk, and I didn't want them to overhear. Goose came in behind me and the driver closed the door.

"Doing what?" Disco's lips curved into that secret smile he seemed prone to share, and I wanted to climb across the seat to strangle him.

"Sneaking up on people. It's rude."

"Are they out there?" Goose pulled off his jacket and loosened his tie.

Disco nodded. "Is there anyone in particular we should watch?"

"Who is out there?" I glanced out a tinted window.

"Associates of mine," Disco answered, gazing at me from under his lashes. "They're going to take a look at a few of tonight's esteemed guests and see what they can't uncover."

"Good, because we didn't discover much." Goose settled back as the limousine started moving.

"Nothing but a bunch of egos inflated by money," I grumbled. I remembered the card in my pocket and retrieved it. "I did get invited to some super-secret pajama party."

"What's that?" Goose took the card. "Who gave you this?"

"CeCe Parker. She followed me into the restroom, gave me that, and asked me to come to some girls' night thingamajig tomorrow."

"What did you say?" Disco asked.

"I told her I'd have to check my schedule. I didn't want to tell her yes without speaking to you two. To be honest, she gives me the creeps."

"Interesting," Goose said and Disco nodded.

"Uh, hello." I raised my hand. "Anyone care to fill me in here?"

"I say it's interesting because it is, not because there is anything more to it. Can you go to this party? I think it's a good idea. We might get lucky." Goose was studying the card as he spoke.

"About that." I finally had the opportunity to be a money grubbing leech. I hated it, but I'd already lost a shift at the BP. "If I keep going on these little missions, I'm going to expect some sort of compensation. I can't keep missing work and playing Nancy Drew just to keep you boys entertained."

"Certainly." Disco nodded. "We'll start with tomorrow. Can you go?"

Thanks to Deena, I was off all weekend. But did I want to go? Hell no. CeCe was a weird one I didn't want to spend time with socially.

"I can go but I don't particularly want to. That girl isn't dealing with a full deck, and her husband reminds me of Pugsley Addams."

"You won't go alone." Disco's tone brokered no room for argument. "I'll tag along and stay out of sight."

Strangely, that did give me comfort. "I guess I'm going, then."

Goose and Disco managed to share all the essential information by the time we arrived outside my apartment. The driver opened the door and I climbed out, sliding my jacket off the seat and turning to say good night. Goose looked ready to drop, and I told him I'd call him in the morning before nodding by farewell to Disco.

The door closed, and I dug around in my pocket for my keys.

"You look breathtaking," Disco's husky voice whispered in my ear.

I spun around, throwing my weight behind the punch aimed at the sound. My fist made solid contact with his arm, and my wrist locked painfully against his solid frame.

"Stop doing that!" My voice came out pained rather than authoritative, and I brought my hand around to cradle my wrist. It was throbbing in harmony with the wild beating of my heart.

"Let me see." He didn't wait for permission, pulling my wrist toward him. He flipped it over, fingertips skimming across the tender spot where my blue veins stood out prominently under pale skin. "It doesn't appear broken."

"Maybe not, but I jammed the hell out of it." Flexing my fingers, I tested the muscles, and winced as the tendons stretched.

"I'm sorry. It isn't my intention to frighten you so often." He didn't relinquish his hold, brushing his thumb back and forth across my wrist. "I merely wanted to tell you how lovely you look this evening."

"Just call me Tammy Faye," I muttered.

"I assure you, you look nothing like Tammy Faye. Not even remotely similar."

I looked from under my lashes, and his gaze followed the contours of my face, trailing over my mouth, nose and lips. I cleared my throat and stepped back, pulling my wrist into my chest and covering it with my opposite hand.

"Thank you," I said softly, still looking into his vivid blue eyes.

"Most necromancers sense our presence immediately. Why can't you?" Curiosity gave him a boyish appeal. His lips curved as he smiled.

"It's probably because I lack focus and have the attention span of a gnat. I'm always daydreaming, and you're too quiet when you sneak up." I didn't feel it necessary to add my imaginative inner dialogue that was a constant companion in my head.

"And what do you daydream about, Rhiannon?" That husky timbre returned to his voice, giving me goose bumps.

I had lost count of the instances I couldn't seem to formulate words in his presence. Sometimes, he would say things, and I didn't know how to react. Disco was overwhelming, unlike anyone I'd met before, and it wasn't entirely due to fear any longer. I glanced from one end of the street to the other; uncomfortable with the direction the conversation was going.

"I suppose I should get inside. I have a hectic day tomorrow."

"Good night, Rhiannon," he said quietly, voice compelling, and watched as I made a hasty departure into my building.

CHAPTER NINE

Maybe it was the previous night's events or the impending ones to come, but I couldn't relax. My workout had been terrible. I wound up going for cardio and some time on the bag. Mike joined me, inquiring about my change in mood. I told him it was only tension, and he let it go.

I hadn't realized my edginess was that obvious.

I tossed my keys down on the cherry wood with a loud clank of metal when I walked through the door and pushed the button on my answering machine. Only Goose had called. He was unfailingly polite, even when speaking to mechanical devices.

My growling stomach led me into the kitchen. I groaned when I cased the fridge. The shelves were nearly bare. I slammed the door closed and opened the drawer under the coffee pot, sorting through the various menus from local take out. I decided on Chinese, calling in beef and broccoli from Mr. Magoo's.

After walking into the tiny living room, I plopped on the couch and tried to decide whether I should read or give my decrepit television a shot. I chose my faded and tattered copy of *Jane Eyre*, flipping to my bookmark, which was a simple piece of ripped paper. The cover was bent, white creases marred the outside, and the spine was loose. I had fallen in love with Jane in high school, and no matter where I went, I always carried a copy along with me.

A knock at the door sounded right as Jane was preparing to deny St. John for a second time. I frowned as I stood, placed the book face down on the coffee table, and walked to the door. I looked through the peephole and grinned. Unlatching the chain, I turned the lock, and opened the door.

"Can't stay away, can you?"

Goose smiled. "Can I come in?"

"Sure." I let him inside and showed him over to the couch.

"I'm sorry to intrude. I tried to call first."

"I was at the gym. I just got home actually." I sat in the chair opposite him and wrapped my arms around my knees. "Not that I'm complaining, but what brings you here?"

"Some information a colleague faxed over. Sharon lives in Los Angeles, where there's a steady undercurrent of supernatural activity. I called to see if any strange happenings had taken place recently, and this is what she shared." He tossed a notebook onto the table and sorted through the papers until he found the one he wanted me to read.

I quickly skimmed over the story.

Three victims, all unidentifiable, were found in the rubble of a fire that ravaged a condominium. There were no witnesses, no suspects, and no leads.

"I know I'm slow on the uptake, but I'm not seeing a connection." I read the short clipping again. Nothing rang a bell.

"Sharon told me everyone who deals in the underground blood market in L.A. got pretty worked up over that fire. The girl that died was Reese Worthington, and the two young men were her cousins, Tyson and Matthew Crescens. They were big suppliers to the upper crust in L.A., and had been for a long time. They fell into an accidental friendship with a group of vampires in the area and became intermediaries. When that fire happened, everyone took notice."

"Couldn't it just have been a freak accident? Fires do happen from time to time." I tossed the paper onto the table.

"At first, everyone thought it was. Then this happened."

He handed me another slip of paper. My brow furrowed as I read the article.

Six dead bodies found with organs missing, the bodies amazingly preserved.

"Vampires," I whispered. "They're dying there too."

"They *were*," Goose said. "And I'm stressing *were* here. The fire with Reese, Tyson, and Matthew happened first. The vampire bodies were discovered a couple of weeks later. That's when the connection was made. Sharon works for a group of vampires in L.A. On a hunch, they sent her to the location the bodies were discovered. She didn't get anything. She doesn't see the twice dead. But she did ask questions. The vampires that the cousins worked for went missing too, all six of them, within days of the fire. After that, everything went quiet."

"How long ago did this happen?"

"About a two months before Jacob went missing." Goose met my eyes, making sure I understood what he was indicating.

"They're here now," I breathed, doing quick math inside my head. "How many vampires have gone missing since this started here?"

"Seven." Goose stacked the papers back into the folder. "If we don't find out who's doing this, they are likely to move again. Time is working against us."

A loud bang at the door caused me to jump, and I laughed nervously when I realized my food had arrived. Swiping the money off the table, I scurried for the door. The deliveryman wasn't Chinese. In fact, his bronzed skin and dark hair screamed Hispanic. I pushed aside my momentary humor and traded my money and a generous tip for the enticing smell of fried rice.

After I placed the food on the counter in the kitchen, I returned to the living room. I was too restless to sit, and paced back and forth in front of Goose.

"This just keeps getting worse."

Goose nodded and said, "Disco has called together the vampires in the area to share what he knows. Right now, their only defense is to use extreme caution. If they sever ties and stop the market, whoever is responsible might move along."

"How does that work?" I stopped pacing and faced him. "Are there little vampire clubs or something?"

"It's similar to normal families. There is the head of the house—the one responsible for creating one or several of them. Vampires show fealty to the original creator of their line, as do any fledglings they create. Some branch off, going their own way, but most choose this lifestyle."

"But in this case, other families were targeted. Not only Disco's, right?"

"I don't think Disco's family is being targeted specifically. I think it's random."

"What about the blood dealers? Who's spoken with them?"

"There are only four suppliers in the city—Marcus Delmar, Chris Devey, Lorence Smith, and Dexter Martin. Their clients are the upper crust—like we met at Jude's tasting. At this point, they are in just as much danger, if you take what happened in L.A into account."

I perched on the edge of the recliner, bracing my elbows on my knees. "So where do we go from here?"

"I'm going to check out a few of the people from the party, namely Jude Mason. We need to find out if anyone at that tasting made a move from L.A. recently. That's where we'll find our answers."

"Do you think it's an inside job? As in the buyers are responsible?"

"I don't know. Right now, my instincts are telling me to stay near those who use the market steadily and know where they can get the goods." Goose paused then cleared this throat. "Do you have a gun, Rhiannon?"

"Yes."

I purchased my Ruger LCP a month after waiting for my license to be approved. Hector insisted I get one, especially for the rare occasion when I needed to make a trip to the bank with his money. I practiced on the range once a week at West Side.

Goose seemed impressed. "Keep it handy."

"Should I take it with me tonight?"

"Disco's tagging along, so I wouldn't think so. Besides, this is a party, right? I think you'll be safe." His chocolate brown eyes flickered in the direction of the kitchen. His nostrils flared and his stomach rumbled audibly. "Shouldn't you be eating?"

"Don't change the subject." I grinned at him playfully as I stood to walk into the kitchen. "I hope you like beef and broccoli."

CHAPTER TEN

Goose left a few hours later, and I had to force myself to get ready. I didn't want to go to CeCe's party, but delaying my foray into the weird and freaky wouldn't accomplish anything aside from making me look like a messy grunge chick.

I styled my hair straight, left it loose, and dressed functionally in slacks and a black turtleneck. If anything, I would suffer the nut jobs in comfort. I put on my makeup, pulled it all together with red tinted ChapStick, and stepped down the carpeted hallway to retrieve my shit kickers. When the jimmy club was tucked safely inside, I grabbed my keys, butterfly knife, and money. I'd forgotten to charge my cell, so I decided to leave it behind.

By the time I left my apartment, it was already dark. Streetlights illuminated the street in big fat halos of light.

"Hi, Disco." I was relieved he'd chosen to stand in my line of sight instead of jump-starting my heart as he seemed so prone. He was still difficult to see in the shadows, dressed in black.

"Rhiannon." He moved away from the car he was leaning against. "You look beautiful this evening."

"Flattery won't get you anywhere with me," I joked. We walked down the street, steps in harmony.

"What will it take?" he asked, staring into the darkness.

"Do you really want to know the answer to that question?" I laughed under my breath. For all he knew, I'd require a lifetime of servitude.

His voice smooth and enticing when he answered simply, "I do." He grinned at me, eyes sparkling.

"How about some answers? Nothing excites a girl more than knowledge." I didn't mention the fact it would ease a shit load of my concerns.

"What would you like to know?"

I started out with a good one. "Can you really read minds?"

"Yes." He was facing forward, not meeting my eyes.

"But you don't read mine?"

"No." He shook his head, blue eyes focusing on me briefly before turning away.

"That will get you somewhere with me. I value my privacy." I hoped being honest would keep him honest too. Respect garnered respect. "What about crosses, holy water, and sleeping in coffins? Is any of that true?"

"We don't particularly care for crosses, holy water can melt off our skin, and no, we don't sleep in coffins." He smiled at the last part.

"That's good to know." I glanced over and his face was blank again, offended by something I said. I spoke in rush to clarify my previous statement. "I don't mean it like that. I meant it would suck to sleep inside a hard little box every night."

He grinned wryly. "I suppose it would."

I inspected him closely. He appeared to be in his late twenties, and that was pushing it. With his unblemished skin, he could easily pass as younger, but there was no way to know for certain.

"How old are you anyway?"

"If I answer, will you answer a question for me?" His eyes flickered over, but this time, they stayed put.

"Maybe." Some answers were easy, others no so much. It all depended on the subject, and Disco loved personal questions.

"I was born in 1837." He barely drew a breath before he asked his question, not allowing me time to absorb just how hocking old he was. "Where is your family, Rhiannon?"

"Dead," I answered curtly. "A drunk swiped our van one afternoon on the way home from the beach. My parents died instantly."

"How old were you?"

"Technically, you've had your one question," I said, but answered, "I was ten."

"So young..." His voice trailed off, and he looked at me with a mixture of pity and sadness, which pissed me off.

"Don't," I snapped, furious at being pitied. "Don't you dare feel sorry for me. Bad shit happens to everyone, and my number was up. It's called life."

"Who cared for you?" He asked the question innocently enough, unaware of the ramifications and depth that one answer entailed.

The truth was, no one cared for me. Psychotic people put me up in their house of depravity while horrific things took place. Sure, things got better. After I was given to a real family who gave a shit.

"The state of Florida," I responded after a moment.

We walked the remaining distance to the Long Island Rail Road in silence. He didn't pry, and I didn't ask any more questions, each of us content to share space without the complication of conversation.

We sat next to each other in an attempt to be inconspicuous, which wasn't easy. Disco didn't look like your average guy, and when he nailed you with those eyes of his, you could sense something absolutely lethal lingering beneath the surface. People didn't know if they should mug him or stay the fuck away.

A sane person would choose the latter.

Halfway to our destination, the train stopped, and a few people stepped on. I was too busy focusing on my clothing to notice the new passengers. Wearing head to toe black meant Disco and I matched perfectly. We couldn't have planned it better.

His body shifted closer, and I peered into his face, instinctively braced to push him away. He shifted closer, wrapped an arm around my shoulders, and I found it impossible to tear my gaze away from his bright blue eyes.

"Relax, Rhiannon. I'd prefer to do this than rip apart the three sloughs that just boarded the train, if you don't mind."

"What are you talking about?" I didn't glance around, not wanting to be obvious. He leaned even closer, and I held my breath.

"The three men that boarded the train at the last stop are thinking rather unpleasant things. I'd like to show them that acting on those impulses would prove detrimental to their throats."

His hand came up, touching my hair at the temple, following the strands down to my shoulder. He was so close, I could smell him—sweet and earthy, with a hint of cloves and cinnamon. He looked into my eyes, and heat overtook my body, drifting along my skin as I started to tremble.

Breathless, I forced the word from my mouth. "Stop."

He lowered his eyes, and suddenly, it was easier to think. The trembling lessened, and I was back in the seat on the train. When the doors opened at the next stop, I watched the three young men in jeans and leather jackets exit. They turned and gave me the kind of attention that tells you they've imagined your naked body contorted and used in all sorts of disgusting ways.

Disco removed his arm from my shoulders, and I scooted toward the window. The rest of the trip was awkward. I was aware of him next to me, and the lingering hint of cloves continued to tease my senses.

We exited the train and walked in silence, arriving at Stony Brook with fifteen minutes to spare. I wasn't at all surprised that CeCe would live here. It was a privileged area.

"I would like to monitor your thoughts after you cross the threshold," Disco said unexpectedly.

"Uh." I shook my head. "I don't know."

"I won't listen the entire time," he reassured me. "Only at intervals, in the event something goes wrong."

"I really don't like the idea of you in my head," I said. "It gives me the willies. Besides, you could hear more than I want you to."

"I won't take advantage. I give you my word."

My mind had too much baggage trapped inside that I didn't want him or anyone else to see, but he could have listened in without asking. That had to count for something.

"Okay. But no digging around in there."

We stopped at the brick mailbox marked with the white plastic numbers 243. The property was isolated, the houses nearby hidden behind trees. The numerous windows were spaced far enough to allow the light to cascade onto the manicured lawn. The large two-car garage door was shut, three cars already parked in front.

I was late.

Maybe that had been CeCe's intention all along.

I turned toward Disco. "Where will you be?"

"Right here." He gave me an encouraging smile. "If you need me, I'll hear you."

"Then here goes nothing." I gave my head and shoulders a good shake to loosen up, took a deep breath, and started walking toward the house.

CHAPTER ELEVEN

There is such a thing as hell, and I had walked willingly inside.

CeCe herded me into the living room the moment I walked through the door, offering various wines and cheeses, and introduced me to her other guests.

Marcia wasn't much older than me, a lithe brunette with cocoa skin and shining black eyes. She said she worked in commercial television, and with her lovely complexion, I could see why. Treenie was in her thirties, with big blue eyes and blonde hair trimmed into a stylish pixie. Amanda was a high school boy's wet dream with mahogany hair, tanned skin, and huge breasts.

I chose to sit as far away from them as was possible—as in all the way across the fucking room. They kept touching each other intimately, staring at me all the while, their hungry gazes lingering for far too long.

I cautiously sipped on my glass of wine and was happy to discover that the contents didn't contain so much as a trace of vampire blood.

At least one part of the evening was looking up.

"We're so glad you joined us, Janet." Marcia gave me a bizarre grin.

"Thanks." I cleared my throat and tried to remain distant but friendly.

CeCe announced that a big surprise was due to arrive. Otherwise, I would have made my apology and gotten the hell out an hour before. I kept expecting the women to strip off their clothes and go at it at any moment. Their lingering kisses told me that before the night was over, all four of them would probably end up in the same bed together.

"Have you ever met a vampire?"

"Nope," I lied smoothly.

She batted her eyelashes, voice becoming raspy. "They are liquid sex."

Women with a hard-on for the dark side. How appealing.

I remembered Disco was listening and tried to keep my thoughts under control. Changing my train of thought, I picked at a loose thread on my bell sleeve while silently recanting random nursery rhymes. I was into the third line of "Mary Had a Little Lamb" when a loud knock ricocheted off the high ceilings. I turned to watch as Marcia, Treenie and Amanda rushed out of the room, their high heels clicking on the floor.

I heard CeCe's high-pitched voice as she invited someone inside. The girls chimed together, their excited chatter changing to husky murmurs. As their footsteps approached, and I stood anxiously, an inner warning chimed inside my head.

"And this," CeCe's said, her voice a seductive purr, "is who I told you about."

My heart stopped beating as a massive spike of adrenaline surged through my veins and the world seemed to stand still.

Oh Christ almighty, oh my dear God.

CeCe had invited a vampire into her house.

He was huge, well over six-feet tall. His long black hair flowed straight down his thick, broad shoulders. He was dressed almost entirely in black, the blue silk shirt beneath his jacket being the only non-leather item of clothing. He moved like all vampires, with grace and precision.

This was not what I expected.

I needed to get the hell out.

"A surprise indeed." The floorboards creaked as he came forward. His eyes remained on me, but his head turned in CeCe's direction. "You did even better than I expected. Thank you."

My thoughts somersaulted when he crowded my senses, seeping into my subconscious. The women clung to him, wrapping hands around his shoulders and waist, moving in synch with his steps as he drew near. I glanced at Treenie, then Marcia, and finally, Amanda. Their eyes were glazed, oblivious to everything in the room—except him.

My eyes grew wide in alarm and comprehension.

"What's your name?" he whispered, and each syllable seemed to caress my skin.

I closed my eyes and fought the compulsion to tell him whatever he wanted to know. When that didn't work, I bit my tongue. The pain gave a temporary reprieve, allowing me to think rationally.

"Someone who's leaving."

I tried to take a step, but stopped, my feet refusing to work. I tried again, and but my legs felt like dead weight. Each instruction I sent my brain stopped short at the stem, my body detached from the command center.

"But you just got here." He stepped closer, voice dropping an octave, deep and inviting. Liquid heat swept through me. My body sagged and my eyes closed. He was invading my mind, and I could feel him all over me. His tongue swept along my skin, teeth nipping at the sensitive flesh at my neck. His fingers traced the line of my jaw and collarbone, past the hollow on my throat, toward my breasts.

"Stop." My growl was husky, like a seductive rasp.

I bit down on my tongue again, hard enough to taste blood. I closed my eyes and attempted to clear my thoughts. Tears sprang into my eyes with the effort, but it wasn't enough, not nearly enough.

"Wesley!" Carson's voice broke the spell, echoing through the house as the front door slammed closed.

The vampire turned his head and I reached inside my pocket for my butterfly knife. I yanked it out and fluttered the blade in my hand, changing it from benign to dangerous in a singular movement. My heart throbbed painfully as I strategized. Carson was between the door and me. I had to get past him.

"I'm calling dibs on..." Carson stopped mid-sentence, eyes narrowing as he walked into the room and saw the knife.

What a fucking sleaze bucket. He was in on this shit too.

"I was just leaving." My voice came out shaky. I looked up and locked gazes with Wesley.

His eyes were amber.

Radiant, beautiful amber.

He rolled me under, promising exactly what he would do, showing me just how much I'd enjoy it. His hands were cool, brushing across my body in sensual, teasing movements. His tongue delved into my ear, his breath brisk against my skin, fingers tracing the counters of my bra as his thumbs thrummed my nipples. His mouth found mine as he ripped at my clothing...and I wanted him to. I wanted to feel every inch of him against me, along me, inside me.

I loosened the grip on the knife and it slid past my fingers until I held the blade. The sharp bite of metal into my skin cleared my head, and I squeezed, absorbing the steel deeper into my flesh. Warm blood coated the spaces between my fingers, dripping in big fat drops to the floor.

I wanted to run, but I couldn't. My head was clear of him, but my traitorous body wouldn't listen. I struggled to tell my feet to obey, to take one step, then another.

"This one will require a special session." Wesley smiled, elongated canines prominent. "Do we have any chloroform left?"

"I'm one step ahead of you."

A cloth covered my mouth, and though I wanted to struggle, I remained passive. The room shifted, becoming fuzzy as my breathing slowed.

Wesley pulled Amanda into his arms. His hands traveled along her body while the other three caressed him, their hands grasping and squeezing, moving lower...

Then everything vanished into nothing.

CHAPTER TWELVE

I woke with a pounding head and a dry mouth. I slowly opened my eyes and attempted to focus in the dim lighting. The haze distorting my vision changed to an orange hue that covered the room, flickering and moving across the ceiling. The familiar smell of fire permeated my nose, and I stifled the groan that threatened to escape my lips. I turned my head to the left and could see the outline of bottles along the kitchen counter in the darkness.

Everything came rushing back, and I realized I was still on the floor where I'd fallen.

Grunts, groans, and feminine cries combined with the sound of skin slapping against skin. I forced my aching head around. Wesley was on the carpet and Treenie was underneath him, braced on hands and knees. They were naked, bodies coming together in forceful, animalistic thrusts.

CeCe and Amanda watched from the couch, naked as well. Their hands moved back and forth between their thighs as they groaned and panted. The smell had come from the fireplace, which was the only light source, glowing rusty orange against their skin.

I felt bile rising from my stomach and I swallowed, holding my breath.

I was in the middle of a goddamned vampire orgy.

"Rhiannon?"

I opened my eyes, blinking to adjust my sight. "Disco?" Relief coursed through me at the sound of his voice, but I couldn't locate him in the darkness.

"Shh!" Disco's voice whispered inside my head. *"Don't talk out loud. You have to get outside. Can you do that?"*

I chanced a glance toward the living room. Treenie was ass up in the air, her full breasts flush against the rug, mouth wide and eyes closed. Wesley pounded into her with enough force to push her forward, his lush hair covering both their bodies.

"Where are you?"

"Don't talk. Think of what you want to say, and I will hear it. I'm outside, Rhiannon." A trace of urgency entered his voice. *"Can you make it to me? I cannot enter the house."*

"Yes," I thought back. I would make it to him because I had to.

My body protested as I turned to my side, and I decided to stay on the floor, dragging myself as not to draw attention. My right hand was slick against the wood, and I lifted it into the air. A long deep gash oozed inside my palm, several of my fingertips cut deep into the fatty tissue. I pushed aside the pain and nausea and continued to pull myself along the wood, sliding in slow motion across the floor.

"Carson," Wesley yelled, and the slapping sounds ceased. I froze, terror seeping into my chest. "Someone's awake."

"Fuck!" Carson's voice came from the kitchen. He murmured something I couldn't make out, and Marcia's lust-filled voice whispered in response. He came around the counter, naked and totally aroused.

Standing on unsteady legs, I bounded for the door, and made it past the counter before Carson's arms snaked around my midsection. He shoved a soft piece of cloth over my mouth again, and I brought my right leg up and thrust the heel of my shit kicker into his shin.

"Son of a bitch!" he grunted, arms going lax.

When my feet hit the ground, I ran for the door. His hand wound through my hair, yanking my head back. He shoved the cloth over my mouth and I swung my arm around, planting an elbow into his ribs.

"Fucking bitch!" He released my hair and turned me. This time, he didn't bother with the cloth. He drew back his arm and punched me dead-on in the mouth. The world spun and blood poured from my lips. I twisted with the blow, landing flat-faced on the floor.

I stayed down, waiting for him to make another move. Blood seeped past my lips and poured onto the polished wood like deep red paint. I closed my mouth, swallowing and gagging. My gaze drifted down the hallway to my left, and I saw a back door.

It was made entirely of glass; I could see outside.

"Let's try this again." He flipped me over and shoved the cloth over my face. His fingers slipped on my bloody mouth, and he used his clean hand to apply pressure. I shifted my weight and held my breath, waiting for the right moment.

When he moved between my legs, I drove my knee up with all the force I could muster. I felt the spongy tissue give way under the bony strength of my knee as I made solid contact with his balls. He groaned and fell on his side, hands coming up to cup himself.

I shoved his body away, stumbled to my feet, and his hand lashed out, latching onto my boot. My feet flew out from under me, and I went down hard, chin cracking the floor. Blackness threatened, and I worried I might pass out.

"Wesley said to wait, but fuck it. He can go second for a change." Rough hands pulled my turtleneck free from my pants and tugged at the slacks. A deep-seated fury erupted. I would not let this happen without a fight.

No fucking way.

I reached out with my left hand and grabbed a handful of his blond hair. I twisted it as hard as I could, balled my fist, and when his chin came up, punched him in the nose. There was a nasty snap as his head whipped to the side and blood gushed from both nostrils.

When his corresponding blow connected with my jaw, I saw stars.

His hands cupped my breasts and moved down to my slacks. I brought my leg up, and he shoved my arms above my head, locking them in place with his free hand. I didn't protest, pretending to be as limp as a rag doll. I waited as his tongue ran along my face and down my throat, shaking violently as his other hand let go of my trapped arms and started groping my body, squeezing my breasts painfully.

I stretched my fingers, my leg still clenched around his hip. The jimmy club had come loose during our struggle and was visible over the rim of my boot. I got my fingers around the taped metal and tugged. The tape slid against my slick hand, and I gripped it tightly.

"That's it," Carson groaned and rubbed his crotch between my legs, a considerable erection grinding against me.

"You got that right!" I snarled, raring back with all the strength left in my body.

The club struck him in the temple, the sound a mixture of a dull thud and a splitting crack. His eyes widened, then closed, and he collapsed on my body. I shoved at his shoulders, pushing him down as I tried to free myself. His body was dead weight, and it took several long thrashing stretches to get loose.

I crept to my knees, standing on wobbly feet. The room spun, and I threw out my arms in an effort to keep balanced. With the jimmy club squeezed tightly in my hand, I staggered down the hall. I focused on one thing—the beckoning glass door only a few feet away.

"You don't want to run." Wesley's voice came from the kitchen, and that same erotic enticement coursed through my veins. "It's our time now. Wouldn't you like that?"

Our time together, his voice promised in my head, *just the two of us. No one to interfere, and no one to interrupt.* He would bring me to climax repeatedly, giving me pleasure I'd never experienced in my life.

Forcing one foot in front of the other, I pressed my lips together so that my split lip burned and pulsed. I pushed forward even as a part of me demanded I stop, knowing if I didn't I would be lost.

"I know what you are, little necromancer. Don't be afraid." Wesley's voice came directly from behind me, and his words were compelling, speaking to my mind, telling me I needed to wait for him. I wanted to wait for him. I would beg and plead for what he could give me.

"You'll love everything I plan to do to you."

"Fuck you," I whispered, adrenaline and fear overcoming lethargy.

I forced my feet to obey, screaming one word repeatedly in my rebellious mind. *Run.* Don't stop. Run! I would not go to him, not if I had a choice. Each springing step brought the glass closer, and I knew without hesitation I'd rather eat every single shard than to let him touch me.

I didn't slow down, turning my body in the air at the last possible moment before crashing through. It hurt. A blunt pain scorched the left side of my body as I braced my arms around my head to protect my face. I pulled my knees into my waist and waited for the painful crash into the cement. I was aware of solid arms surrounding me and pulling me close. I started to flail, attempting to break free. I didn't make it to my freedom only to condemn myself now.

"Easy, Rhiannon," Disco murmured. "I'm here."

I stilled instantly. It was Disco. I had made it outside, and he was waiting for me—just as he promised. My body erupted into uncontrollable shivering, my teeth chattering in my ears. The harder I tried to fight it off, the harder I shook.

"Gabriel?" Wesley's voice had lost the seductive edge. He sounded confused and worried.

I burrowed into Disco's chest, turning my face into his body. His arms tightened protectively. I didn't want to see Wesley's amber eyes, or hear his alluring voice in my head.

"What are you doing here, Wesley?" Disco growled. "You're supposed to be in Nevada."

"I no longer wish to feed off sluts and tramps who should pay me for the pleasure I bring out of them. I can go where I want, when I want. Who the fuck are you to interfere?"

"No one, until you force yourself on the unwilling. That's beneath us, even for an incubus." Disco's chest rumbled as he spoke, and I could sense the anger rolling through his body.

"She would have come to no harm by my hand. The human male lost his temper, even though I informed him specifically that she was to be mine. Return her to me, and I'll prove this truth to you." His voice shifted and it sounded as if he were moving closer.

"Don't!" Disco thundered. "I should kill you myself."

"Why are you angry? She bears no mark. She is unspoken for and unbeholden. I am within my rights to feed from any human who is free of another's claim. As a necromancer, she would give me triple the energy I need. Return her to my care, and I will tend her injuries and erase this night from her memory."

"Listen to me closely." Disco bit out each word, pulling me into the shelter of his arms and chest. "She is beholden to me, and is here tonight on my orders to investigate the deaths of our brothers and sisters in the city. My word serves as her mark, and I don't want to see you near her again. Do you understand?"

"How the hell was I supposed to know that? I would never knowingly feed off of someone who is marked."

"Perhaps in the future you should stay away from her kind. They don't fall so easily into our mind trappings, and you may not be certain the exchange is consensual."

"I will take it under advisement."

"You'd better do more than that," Disco snapped. "I want you to clear the memories of everyone inside. None of them are to have any memory of tonight." Disco's voice deepened, angry and unforgiving. "I don't want the male who attacked her to see the light of day. Take him somewhere his body will never be found. Correct the wrong he has committed this night."

"I'll see to it."

I heard the crunch of glass as Wesley returned to the house, and my body sagged. I hurt all over, and when I tried to open my mouth, I gasped. The ripped skin along the crease of my lip had sealed, and the movement reopened the cut. The world shifted as blackness threatened to pull me under.

"I'm taking you home, Rhiannon. Is that all right?" Disco asked softly against my hair.

"Yes." I felt reality slipping away, and I welcomed the darkness that surrounded me and took away all the pain, until there was nothing but blessed black.

CHAPTER THIRTEEN

I could hear voices, soft and distant, becoming distinct. I assumed I was dreaming, perhaps another vivid nightmare resurfacing. I stilled my breathing and didn't move, expanding my hearing to listen. A door opened and the conversation was no longer muffled.

Individual cadences and dialects rang inside my ears.

"She got the shit pounded out of her, that's for sure. And she's bruised from head to toe. Gabriel said she ate a plate glass door to get outside."

"No shit? She went through a glass door?"

"Yeah, man, she's tough as nails. Wait until you see her. Just keep it down. Gabriel will have my ass for coming in here again. He's already on the warpath."

"I heard. Peter said he sent Paine to track down Wesley. I guess he wasn't as forgiving once he got home and Nala cleaned her up."

"That's her? She's so little."

A hand touched my shoulder, and I opened my eyes. Two young men—one light, the other dark—were standing next to the bed, eyes growing large in their beautiful faces. Since vampire movement was the only way a voice from across the room could be standing beside me in the next instant, it was an obvious giveaway as to what they were.

I lurched up and cried out as pain shot through my body. "Shit!" I moaned in agony, collapsing against the pillows.

Everything hurt.

"Oh man, she's awake! Get Gabriel. I'm getting the hell out of here."

I stared at my aching arm, bandaged from wrist to elbow. The hand on the opposite side was wrapped up as well; little strips of taped gauze surrounded individual fingers. I shifted and groaned. My entire left side throbbed, and I knew that each place my body struck against the glass would be purple.

Disco appeared at my side, and I didn't try to move, content to stay still so long as it left me pain free. "Where am I?" I asked, wincing as I licked my lips and touched the tear on the side. It was ragged, twisting around the crease.

"I asked if I could bring you home. You indicated that was acceptable." He spoke in a pacifying tone, careful not to move and jostle the mattress as he sat beside me.

"We're at your house?" I wasn't in the mood to argue. I was too tired and too sore.

"Yes."

"How badly am I hurt?" I hoped the prognosis was better than I felt.

"Nothing is broken, but you could use stitches in several areas on your body," he informed me evenly, "and you're bruised all over."

"I've had worse." I attempted to sit up again, and the pain along my ribs stole my breath as I pushed with my arms. I gave up, breathing in short pants.

"I wanted to wait until you were awake to ask. There is no reason for your pain or injuries to linger. We can take care of that right now, if you'll allow it."

My brain computed this information quickly. Of course he could help me heal—vampire blood. I hurt like hell, but the idea of ingesting blood didn't appeal to me, no matter how remarkable the results.

"I'm not sure that's such a good idea."

"Please, Rhiannon. You're suffering needlessly."

I peered into his face. His brow was furrowed, blue eyes conflicted, and his wheat blond hair was tousled and unkempt. It wouldn't be that difficult, a couple of quick swallows of the stuff, and I'd be good as new. From the look I was receiving, Disco would take matters into his own hands whether I liked it or not.

"Okay," I agreed numbly.

His face smoothed, tension evaporating. He stood and walked to the nightstand. Pulling open the drawer, he lifted something out. A sliver of bright metal flashed in the light as he returned to my side. He lifted his sleeve to expose his wrist.

"Oh no." I closed my eyes, shaking my head, understanding where he intended to get the blood. "I thought you poured the stuff into wine or some shit. I can't drink that from your body."

"Why not?" He held the sharp edge of the knife over his skin. The iridescent handle flared red and pink as he paused, staring at me in confusion.

"Because it's disgusting, that's why."

"For someone who prides herself on being such a hard ass, I would think this would be easy." He shot me a look that mirrored his disappointment.

I tried to sit up again, forcing myself upright. The room spun and a wave of nausea hit as my head began to throb. I lifted my hand to my face, exploring the swelling along my jaw with cautious fingers. I didn't want to know how bad I looked. Two good jabs to the face and a plummet to the floor ensured I was black and blue. This situation was all kinds of messed up, but it could have been much worse.

I could have woken at CeCe's with Wesley and his nut job sidekick Carson ready for round two.

"How did you know Wesley anyway?" It hurt just to speak.

"We can discuss this after." Disco lifted his hand, made a decisive cut, and placed his wrist near my mouth. The blood flowed thickly to the shallow wound, welling out in a dark ruddy pool. "You must hurry, Rhiannon, or I will have to pierce myself again. We heal quickly, even with blessed silver."

He thrust his arm closer.

My hands trembled as I touched his cool skin, fingers gently wrapping underneath. I closed my eyes at the last moment, opening my mouth and praying I wouldn't gag when I swallowed. I took the blood from the surface. It was cool and incredibly sweet, with just a hint of spice. I lifted my head, prepared to release his arm.

"No." Disco moved closer, his voice slightly shaken. "You have to take more."

I hesitated before my mouth descended. The blood on the surface was nearly gone, and I had to suck gently. Disco groaned and I felt his right hand running along my back, fingers twining through my hair. I swallowed, and it hit. Differences in my perception shifted instantaneously. My vision cleared, my hearing opened...and my body started to heal. The gashes on my hands and arms started to tingle painfully, as well as the nasty tear on my lip. I tried to pull away, but Disco's hand cupped the back of my head.

"More." His voice was hoarse and thick, his hand pressing gently on my neck.

I drew on his arm, taking the sweet, spicy liquid into my mouth. My body stopped throbbing, the soreness ebbing away to nothing. I sucked again, and then again, drinking more of him. He relaxed, gently rubbing my back.

When the flow ebbed, I forced myself to stop. He lifted his wrist to his mouth and ran his tongue along the wound. When he lowered his hand, nothing was there, the skin unblemished.

Everything magnified, the room seemed to come alive and breathe. My gaze rested on Disco, moving along his arm, up his shoulder, and stopping at his face. My breath caught. I was completely wrong. Disco had never been a twenty-something looker. He was far more than that. With my perfect vision, I could see his beautifully flawless skin, so smooth, like lustrous ivory.

I reached out with my bandaged hand, touched his temple, and traced my fingers along the contours of his cheek. His skin was incredibly soft, cool and silken. My focus shifted from his skin to his eyes. The irises were a mixture of blue and aqua with black along the edge. The inner brilliance emitted from golden flecks embedded deep within. His lashes were exceptionally long and dark, framing his eyes beautifully.

Something warmed inside me, an unfamiliar heat I had never experienced surfacing. The compulsion to move closer was overwhelming. Eager fingers longed to touch his full bottom lip.

Would it be as soft as it appeared?

A female voice spoke through the door. "Gabriel, may I have a word?"

I shook my head clear of the emotional spider web and saw Disco frown in frustration before I averted my eyes. He rose, returned the knife to the drawer, and walked to the door.

My eyes quickly darted around the room.

Red curtains interlaid with golden threads covered the walls and windows, each one held aloft by bronze colored poles situated along the intricately crown molded ceiling. Directly across from the bed was a desk. The dark wood stretched for several feet, matching chair legs that were visible underneath. To the right was a fireplace with wood stacked neatly inside an iron grate.

Lifting my injured hand, I flexed my fingers. When I experienced no pain, I ripped apart the bandage, twisting the gauze around and around until I could see my skin.

The gash was sealed.

I quickly pulled each strip from my fingers and the bandage from my forearm. The cuts were nothing more than thin lines. A long pale furrow of sealed skin ran from the outside of my elbow to my wrist, appearing the same as the gash on my hand.

When I lifted shaky fingers to my mouth, the torn skin was gone, the edges sealed.

I leapt out of the softness of the mattress, landing on socked feet and steady legs. I stretched down, bringing my hands to my feet, finding my shit kickers on the floor next to the bed.

No pain, no discomfort. If not for my heightened senses, I would have felt totally normal.

I straightened, amazed and slightly terrified.

"Paine has returned." The voice from the hallway was lovely, soft and melodic. "You asked to be informed when he arrived."

I swiveled to see who had spoken, but Disco's body blocked her from view.

"Thank you. Tell him I'll be down shortly."

Disco closed the door and walked back into the room. He observed me guardedly, sliding his hands into the pockets of his expensive black slacks.

"When will this pass?"

"A few days," he answered quietly. He stepped around the edge of the bed, stopping a couple of feet away.

"Days?" I winced. "Why so long?"

"Taking blood directly from our bodies is different. You're feeding not only on the sustenance, but also on our essence, the very thing that gives us life. You couldn't achieve this level of healing from blood poured into a glass. You'll adjust. The disorientation is only temporary and will subside."

I flopped down into the mattress, hips sinking into the softness of the feathers. I eyed Disco warily, following his movements as he lifted his left leg and perched on the edge of the bed.

"Did you know what was going to happen in there tonight?" He and Wesley had known each other, and that made me nervous. I didn't believe Disco was the kind of person to set me up, but I'd had serious lapses in judgment before.

"I didn't until I saw Wesley entering the house, and by then, it was too late. I tried to tell you to get out, but you already suspected something was wrong. When your mind went blank..." He took an uneasy breath. "I was very relieved to hear you again."

"What is he?" I shivered as I recalled Wesley's voice inside my head.

"Do you know what an incubus is?" I nodded and he continued, "Wesley is one of the few who exist. Using sex, he can control the mind of any female he chooses."

"Not me," I stated angrily, remembering the women who'd surrounded him as though he was a Greek God.

"No." Disco tilted his head admiringly. "Not you."

"Does that sort of thing happen often?" I kept repeating four words in my head—please God say no.

"No." He sounded annoyed, and when I looked at his face, his lips were drawn tight. "Wesley moved to Nevada where his talent could be put to good use. I don't know why he came back. Perhaps he was bored, or maybe he wanted to reconnect with his family. He lived here originally."

"What's this business about marking?" I waited until he met my eyes and continued, "What was that all about?"

He didn't look away, irises becoming teal. "When humans become close to a vampire family, or they wish to enter into it at some point, they are marked. This serves as a warning that they are spoken for, so no harm comes to them."

"Have you marked me?" I tried to contain the tremor in my voice.

"No," he answered quietly and my shoulders sagged in relief. "That is a personal choice only you can make. Although, I think you should consider it, especially now."

"No." I shook my head. "I'd rather not. After this is all over, I want to return to my normal life."

"You'll never return to your normal life, Rhiannon. I know that isn't what you want to hear, but it's the true nonetheless. The longer you remain unmarked, the greater the danger you place yourself into." Disco's voice was laced with regret, but also a willful determination.

"That's not true," I argued, grasping at straws. "Take Goose. He leads a normal life." It was a bad comparison, and I knew it. Goose wasn't normal. He dabbled in all things kooky and surreal.

"Ethan was marked by us years ago."

I panicked, standing up and striding across the room. I stopped, facing the wall, staring at the swirling golden threads stitched intricately inside the velvet curtains. Goose was marked; that explained a lot. No wonder he was so gung-ho about helping.

He was a part of the fucking family.

"Rhiannon, talk to me." Disco's voice was inches from my ear, and I realized he'd silently crossed the room to stand behind me.

"I want to go home." Wrapping my arms around myself, my chaotic mind grasped for a solution. I would move. That would solve everything. It had worked before, and it would work again.

"Moving won't change anything. It will only delay the inevitable." His hands came up, gently enveloping my arms.

"You said you would stay out of my head," I snapped through clenched teeth, agitated with myself for feeling the way I did. I wanted to be furious and resentful. Instead, I found my body aching for the feel of his delicate fingers across the surface of my skin.

"I have respected your wishes. You spoke aloud." He moved closer. I could feel and sense his nearness.

"What do you want, Disco? Or should I call you Gabriel?" I closed my eyes, forcing my sensitive peepers to take ten.

"I want you to stop being so afraid. I want you to feel safe and protected. I want you to show me the real you, no more false pretenses or facades. And I want you to trust me. You can call me whatever you wish; by the name chosen on the day of my birth, or the one intended as a joke. Both will lead you to the same man."

I resisted the temptation to let it all go, to leave all the burdening shit I'd carried behind in the past, but forgetting your mistakes made you prone to repeat them, and I would never allow myself to be placed in a helpless position again.

I felt split down the middle, absolutely torn.

"Some people are beyond repair, and I'm one of them. I can't be fixed, not by you, or anyone else." I opened my eyes and stepped away from the wall. Walking to the bed, I reached for my boots.

Disco rounded on me, eyes flashing in anger. "Why won't you tell me what happened to you? What has bound you so tightly you cannot let it go? Let it out, Rhiannon. Expel the taint from your life so you can move on."

"I won't ever tell anyone about it," I responded flatly and shook my head, zipping the boots up one at a time. I hated ending the night on a sour note, but it was safest thing—for both of us. "And I think it's time I went on my way."

"You can't just leave," Disco grumbled, raking a hand through his hair. It was the first time I'd seen him lose his composure, and the knowledge that I was responsible made me feel like shit. "Are you certain you want to go? You don't want to discuss this?"

He moved across the room in a burst of speed, standing across from me in one moment and in front of me the next. He made sure not to touch me, but it wouldn't take much to bridge the gap.

I sighed, changing my mind and offering an explanation I hoped he would accept. God help me, I cared about what he thought.

How the mighty have fallen.

"The girl you want to know died a long time ago. She's gone, Disco."

"She's still there." The gold shifted in his irises, becoming bright. "You choose to keep her locked away in a place that festers and rots. It's a shame; she deserves better."

"Have you finished analyzing me yet?" I snapped. He was doing the one thing I couldn't stand for, asking for something beyond my capacity to give.

"For now." His eyes reflected the light. The gold was truly stunning, as if the iris was a three dimensional display of color—black edges, shifting blue as the base, and liquid gold on the top.

"I want to go home." My voice lost any anger, becoming deflated.

"As you wish." He cupped my face in his hands, thumbs brushing my jaw tenderly. Those gold tinged eyes rolled me under, erasing the room, sending me into darkness.

CHAPTER FOURTEEN

Birds were chirping outside, serenading worms, hatchlings, and nests. I smiled and stretched, breathing in a deep lungful of fresh morning air. I had the worst nightmare, but now, it was over. I was home, in my bed.

No more horny vampires who fed from slutty women.

No more blood...

My eyelids flew open.

I wasn't at home, and I wasn't in my room.

A ceiling fan rotated in a slow motion above me, causing the thin cream-colored curtains at the window to flutter. I sat up, eyes wide. The striped comforter keeping me warm matched the robin egg blue interior of the room, and contrasted with the antique cream-colored dresser and nightstand.

Someone was outside the door. I could hear the floor creaking with each footstep.

My socked feet slipped on the polished wood as I slid from the bed. Padding across the room, I paused to glance in the full-length mirror on the back of the closed door. Other than a case of bed head, my face was completely normal. There were no bruises, and the cut on the edge of my mouth was gone. I inspected my hand. The white lines were barely visible on my skin. I flexed my body and it responded with no aches or pains; muscles strong and ready to go.

Grasping the tarnished golden handle, I turned until the latch gave, held my breath, and said a prayer that the door wouldn't creak as I peeked out. Beady-eyed stares greeted me from the top of bookshelves, and a growl rumbled inside my chest. I knew exactly where Goose was. I could hear him shuffling about as he prepared breakfast.

I glided into the strawberry kitchen, thus dubbed by me because of all the kooky strawberry decorations inside. Goose had it all—strawberry salt and pepper shakers, a strawberry paper towel holder, a strawberry sugar jar, and a strawberry cookie container. He even had a strawberry teapot, complete with matching cups and saucers.

I snuck up from behind and said, "You and I are going to have to work on our communication issues."

An egg slipped from his hand as he whipped around. I rushed forward, catching it in my palm before it hit the ground, and shoved aside my temporary shock. This was about Goose and his failure to communicate, not my ability to save falling objects with superhero-like reflexes. I put the egg back into the Styrofoam carton, anchoring my hands on my hips, and stared him down.

"Why didn't you tell me you were marked by Disco's people?"

"Hello and good day to you, too, Rhiannon. It's wonderful to discover you're so pleasant in the morning." He narrowed his eyes and hitched his chin in the direction of the bedroom. "How did you sleep, by the way? I hope better than I did. The couch isn't very forgiving on my back."

"Oh no, you don't." I snorted. "You will not play the victim. Did you have any idea of the shit I went through last night?"

His expression softened. "I'm sorry. I should have insisted on going with you."

"Why? So the big bad vampire could mind fuck you too?" He paled and I said, "Oh, for Christ's sake, I'm joking!"

"That's not very funny." He cracked an egg on the edge of the bowl and tossed the shell haphazardly into the trash.

"Without humor, I couldn't survive insane shit like this. I would lose my mind." I smelled fresh coffee and followed the aroma. A freshly made pot sat waiting. I pointed to the machine. "May I?"

"I had planned on surprising you with breakfast, including coffee. So yes, you may." He started whisking the eggs, wrist and arm moving effortlessly.

"All right, Martha, tell me about this business between you and Disco. I want to know why the hell you didn't let me in on the fact you were part of the family." I grabbed a mug and pulled it down. The damned thing had Christmas trees and eight tiny reindeer on the shiny surface. Oh well, at least it wasn't strawberries.

"It's complicated." He poured the eggs into the pan, moving a plastic spatula along the bottom.

"Lucky me." I smiled sardonically and took a seat at the table. "I have all day."

"Necromancers don't have it easy. We can see the dead, communicate with the dead, and in some cases, we can control the dead. That's a very dangerous ability when you live in a world where dead things co-exist among the living."

"I'm waiting," I prodded when he didn't continue.

"For our own safety, it's generally advised that we find a group of people who can offer protection. Necromancers are sought after because some of us have the capability to overcome vampires if we so desire. It's uncommon. Only three such people exist that I am aware of, and all of them are marked." He pulled the pan from the stove and emptied the eggs onto a waiting plate.

"And you?" I asked. "Why did you decide to allow Disco to mark you?"

"It was the smart decision, and the right decision. All of us have to find security, and if it's offered by someone you trust, you can't ask for more. I could have found myself bound to a group that loaned me out for profit, or demanded I only work directly for them. And that does happen, more often than I care to admit."

He filled a plate with eggs and two slices of toast, slid it across the table, and sat down, folding his arms across his chest.

"What does it mean anyway? Do you actually have a mark?"

He removed his thick Tag Heuer watch to display an intricate splash of lines and dots along the width of his wrist.

"It's just a tattoo?" I exhaled a sigh of relief. A tattoo was easy. Where did I sign up?

"No." He shook his head as he refastened his watch. "You have to swear fealty to the family, and it's a lifelong commitment. You also have to give a blood exchange, which allows them to find you no matter where you go. It links you together."

"Hell no," I breathed.

"It's not without benefits. How would you like to look any vampire in the eye and maintain control? Their mind-twists don't work so well once you've entered the fold. It's a double-edged sword. And the best part is your necromancy. Once the gate is opened between you and them, you'll discover just how far your abilities go."

He rose from the table and went for coffee.

"I was interested in understanding my abilities," I said, "but if joining the home team is the means to that end, I'll have to pass."

"Goddamn it!" Goose roared, no longer happy go lucky Ethan McDaniel P.I. He faced me, his tone harsh. "Pay attention to what I'm going to tell you, and don't interrupt with your sassy smart ass comments. This isn't funny anymore. You don't have many options left, Rhiannon. Once word gets out that a necromancer is floating around unmarked, it's only a matter of time before undesirables start sniffing around. That badass attitude of yours won't hold an ounce of water with the kind of people you're about to meet. And they're coming. Hell, they may already be here. So you think about what Disco offered, and you think about it real hard."

He took a deep breath, turned around, and filled his mug.

I didn't know if it was the information shared, his anger, or the look he gave as he forced me to listen, but I kept my mouth shut when he walked back over, sat down, and rested his elbows on the table, clasping the mug with both hands.

"I understand there are things in your past that keep you distant, but this is something that even you can't tackle alone. I don't want to see you broken, and that is exactly what would happen if you're marked by the wrong people." His concerned brown eyes locked on mine, and his voice softened. "They won't ask for permission. They'll force you to give fealty. And once they have it, they'll own you. I don't think you'd survive something like that. Not for long."

"I don't understand. Why us? Why are we so important? How would they even know if someone is marked or not? Can't I just say that I am?"

"Because that connection between the living and dead flows through us and they can absorb it. If they are hurt or weakened, they can draw strength from our life force for themselves. The mark is a living thing. They can sense it, just as we can sense the spirits around us."

"It sounds dangerous," I said, unable to conceal my fear.

"It is." He looked at me, stressing the importance of his words. "That's why you have to trust those you align yourself with. A selfish person won't care if you live or die because of their needs. They'll just suck you dry, and if you don't survive, wait until another comes along to repeat the cycle. Are you starting to get the picture now?"

I cradled my head in my hands. I got the picture. I was being forced to choose between the lesser of two evils again. It sucked and pissed me off something fierce, but it also scared me shitless.

"Do you trust Disco?" I lifted my head, gazing across the uneaten plate of food to catch Goose studying me.

"Implicitly," he answered, never breaking eye contact.

"Damn it." I reclined in the chair and stared at the ceiling. I could see the tiny little bubbles where the paint had dried too quickly, my vision still shaper than normal.

"What other reason besides your affinity for isolation do you have to say no?"

"He wants more of me then I'm willing to give."

"Like what?" Goose kicked my chair.

I sat up, frowning at him. "What did you do that for?"

"You have the worst manners. It's rude not to pay attention to the person you're speaking with. Now, stop avoiding the question. What does he want that you can't give?"

I hesitated and answered, "He wants my trust."

"Your trust?" Goose echoed. "Why is that too much to ask for?"

"I don't trust anyone." I stared at him unapologetically, anger simmering within. I allowed the emotion to wrap around me like a familiar blanket.

"Then come to some kind of understanding. Your life is worth swallowing a bit of pride, isn't it?"

"It's not that simple." I squirmed in my seat, uncomfortable about treading into unknown territory. "I don't want to relive my past. Not for anyone or anything. I just want that part of my life to stay dead and buried. Is it so wrong to want to forget?"

"No, that sounds like a positive thing. And if you mean it, you can start today by letting your past baggage go. You can't claim you want to forget when you keep memories around as a defense mechanism."

"You skinny ass version of Dr. Phil." I scowled. "I swear to God, you should get into talk show television."

"Call me whatever you want, but you know I'm right. You keep watching out for what you expect to happen, and you're going to be blindsided by something you don't."

"I'll tell you what." I compromised grudgingly. "I'll think about it."

"Baby steps are fine with me." He grinned over his mug and took a huge gulp.

"How did I get here anyway?" I looked around the kitchen. Even the wallpaper had strawberries. Willy Wonka popped inside my head, his wicked little voice repeating, "The snozzberries taste like snozzberries," and I snickered.

"Disco doesn't have a standing invitation into your home, so he brought you to mine. What's so funny?"

"Your strawberry hard-on." I motioned at the strawberry basket in the center of the table. "Did you just wake up one day and decide, 'I want to collect strawberry kitchen gadgets and shit, time to visit Pier 1'? It's kind of weird, like you're a closet Suzie homemaker."

"The wallpaper was here when I got the place, and I accessorized. So sue me," he grumbled defensively, giving me the evil eye.

"Hey, whatever floats your boat, shortcake." I laughed. "But if you ask me to go to rummage sales to find that all elusive strawberry toothpick holder, I'm having you committed."

I pushed the chair back, grabbed my untouched plate, and walked over to the trash. I was usually starving in the morning, but I had zero desire to eat. Another side effect of new spidey senses, I guessed. I tossed the food into the garbage, rinsed the plate, and placed it inside the dishwasher.

"Thanks for breakfast. I suppose I should get a move on. I still have to go to the store, and I probably should swing by Mike's for a quick workout. Where are my shit kickers?"

I walked out of the kitchen and spotted my black leather boots near the door. I snagged them in my hand, sat down in the chair across from his desk, and slid them on.

"Wait!" Goose hurried out of the kitchen. "I checked up on Jude Mason. So far, he's clean. He works down on Wall Street in foreign exchange. I'm looking into Mark and Sabrina Smith next. It's no surprise they used an alias, so I have to track them down."

"How do you plan on doing that, Sherlock?"

"Mark said he worked real estate, so I'll start by looking for an agent."

"And how do you know he wasn't making that part up too?" I waited expectantly, smiling and leaning back in the chair, crossing my arms.

"I don't." He shrugged. "But it's a starting point."

"Be careful. They might be into some kinky shit. Do *you* have a gun, Goose?"

"Very funny." He pretended to laugh as he moved around the chair. "Rhiannon..." He waited until he had my undivided attention and said, "When I took that first case for Disco, I wasn't green. I knew about the dangers and the pitfalls of flying solo, but I did it anyway. I was too damned cocky for my own good. I almost regretted it too, when Deidre and her crew came calling."

"Deidre?"

"The head of a local vampire family in the area."

"She tried to force you to join them?"

He nodded. "I got lucky. Paine and Adrian were trailing me the night she showed up. I don't want to think about the flipside of that coin."

"Paine and Adrian?"

"Two of Disco's people. You would have met them if you'd stuck around last night."

"Maybe next time." I hefted my ass away from the shiny leather and strode toward the door. I wanted to crack a joke or to be a smart ass, but he was so serious I didn't bother. Besides, I did have to think it over. I didn't want to get stuck working for some schmuck like Wesley who would use me for a little something extra.

Pausing with my hand on the doorknob, I looked over my shoulder and told him, "I promise, I'll think about it."

CHAPTER FIFTEEN

The vacation was fun while it lasted. Deena had a message waiting on my machine when I arrived home, telling me to come in to work ASAP. Two girls who covered the floor were out, and she couldn't handle the bar alone on a Sunday. I was actually looking forward to the normalcy of bartending, which was incredibly pitiful, sad, and depressing.

When I arrived, things were just starting to swing. There were only two tables unaccounted for, and Cassie was on the stage. I walked through the mass of bodies and came around to Deena, hoping like hell that she didn't ask about the missing jimmy club.

She looked exceptional dressed in a slinky backless top and black pants that rode her tanned hips like a second skin. Her long chestnut hair was straight, and long, and flowed over her shoulders.

"Rhiannon, I need an Amaretto Sour, Cape Cod, and a Grateful Dead, pronto!" She didn't even look at me, slinging drinks left and right.

With that, I got to work, pouring, mixing, shaking and stirring. I didn't have the opportunity to stop and look around. As time wore on, and particular guests became inebriated, I was bombarded with orders. The varying tones and cadences of the patrons lit up my ears. The minutes passed, the pain increased, and my head started to pound, tiny pinpricks inside my ear canals burning white hot.

"Deena," I yelled across the bar and tried not to wince. "I'm going out the back. I need a minute."

"Oh shit!" She glanced in my direction. "Please tell me you're not getting sick. We're not even close to peak."

I didn't answer, cashing out a Rum and Coke, and hauled ass out of the bar. The strobe lights burned my retinas, so intense they were almost blinding, so I stared at the floor. I fought back an impulsive gag when I saw all the dark marks from dirty shoes that probably stepped in dog shit at some point.

When I made it to the dark curtain, I tossed the obtrusive material aside. The smell of stale smoke assailed me, and I covered my mouth with my hand, barreling past Lacey as I raced for the bathroom.

When I reached my destination I slammed the door closed with a deafening boom, lunged for the toilet, and landed painfully on my knees, dry heaving. Nothing was inside my gut but vitamin water from a couple of hours before. I gasped for air, swallowing repeatedly as tears streamed down my face from the violent spasms.

"Rhiannon?" Lacey's voice was blessedly muffled on the other side of the door. "Is everything all right?"

"S'okay," I mumbled and cleared my throat. "I guess I'm still sick."

Her footsteps retreated and I allowed my legs to collapse, the right side of my body hitting the wall and sliding down. The linoleum was cold, but I didn't dare look down. I was certain it was equally filthy, and I didn't want to be sick again. I closed my eyes, breathing deeply, and waited for my head to clear. The tingling burn inside my ears subsided, and the ringing dissipated.

I stood on shaky feet, using the wall for support, and staggered to the sink. After washing my hands and erasing any of the grime from the floor, I swished my mouth out. The bitter taste of metal lingered, and I closed my eyes.

The new vampire associates of mine were seriously cramping my style. I couldn't work tonight. Returning to the bar with all the noises, lights, and overwhelming smells would only bring another wave of sickness. I composed myself, averting my eyes from the mirror, too afraid of what I might see staring back at me.

Hector was waiting when I opened the door, his handsome face a combination of concern and annoyance.

"What's the deal, Rhiannon?"

I tried to look as pitiful as possible, and it wasn't difficult. "I'm sick."

"Then take your ass home. Don't spread that shit around my club." He hurried away, staying clear of whatever funk I'd become the unwilling host of, and intercepted Cassie along the way.

I didn't need to be told twice.

I tried to block out the sounds from the club—the catcalls, blaring speakers, and Lonnie's lard ass barking at Deena. My feet seemed to be lighter with each step that led me down the pasty hallway and closer to the prospect of blissful silence. I didn't know how in the hell Disco dealt with the intensity. It wasn't a high I endorsed.

The metal against metal sound of the door scraping made my ears ring, and I sagged in relief when it closed with a reverberating slam. I absorbed the sounds of the night, reveling in the relative quiet, knowing I would never take silence for granted again.

Suddenly, my nose and eyes kicked in, super senses working triple time.

Someone was coming around the corner, and fast.

My necromancy flared on its own, an odd humming that rippled inside my body. I knew who was on the way, and it wasn't Disco. Goose's warning echoed inside my head. They would come, he'd said. Well, screw my wretched ass. He was right.

Three vampires came around the corner, dressed similarly in dark gothic clothing and shaggy hair. They stopped several feet away, allowing me room, which was downright noble of them. The tallest stepped away from the group.

"Rhiannon Murphy?" He kept his tone even and welcoming, like a Jehovah's Witness who just wanted to share the gospel. "I'd like to have a word."

I stood perfectly still. How in the hell did they get my last name? Maybe they'd asked at the bar. No, I thought immediately. Deena and Hector would tell them to go play hide and go fuck themselves before they gave away any employee information.

"This isn't a great time for me."

"That's too bad." He motioned to his companions. "Because it's the only time we have."

The door to the BP scraped open with a shrill screech of metal, and my stomach bottomed out. I didn't turn around to see who it was. My nose easily distinguished the floral smell of Paul Sebastian Design—Deena's favorite perfume.

"Rhiannon?" Deena's soft lilt carried to my ears. "Hector said you're still sick. Do you need anything?"

I turned my head slightly and called over my shoulder, "I'm fine, Deena. Go back inside. I'll call you later."

The door slammed shut, and I heard her heels clicking across the pavement. *Double damn!* She had come outside. Mr. Suckface seemed delighted by the shift in events; a smile spread across his face.

"I feel bad asking you to come in," Deena said, smiling at the tall, dark, handsome leech boy when she stopped at my side. She looked up and down his body and purred, "Is this a friend of yours?"

Jesus. It figured. Deena would never think of dating someone inside the shit pit, but once she dipped outside, her freak was on.

"I'm Evan," Evan greeted her casually, his voice going husky as his eyes appeared to shimmer.

Deena quit moving as soon as the words slipped past his lips, as still and quiet as a stone monument.

"I wouldn't recommend that," I snapped. "Our bouncers will come looking for her. She's the only bartender in the place tonight, and it won't be long until she's missed."

"Then we should get going." Evan turned and offered his arm. I glowered at the appendage, wishing super human strength was one of my newfound abilities so I could rip it off at the shoulder joint and knock him over the head. His smile widened and he lowered his arm, moving closer to Deena.

He extended his hand to touch the cheetah paw print tattoo that encircled her bicep, and I snarled, "Don't you even think about it, asshole." Reaching into my pocket, I wrapped my fingers around the carved beaded chain within.

He stepped away from her and approached me instead. His dark eyes flashed as he growled, "The first thing I'm going to work on is your attitude."

"Take a number." I dug out the rosary, griping the cross in my fingers. "There's a long line."

I extended my hand, beads cascading along my palm, and shoved it into his face.

I learned three important things in that instant. Father Rooney blessed my rosary perfectly, vampire flesh stinks like scorched plastic when it burns, and they are perfectly capable of screaming when it all goes down. His shout bounced off the brick walls in a blaring roar that seemed to carry from the pavement to the sky. He covered his face with his hands, bending over as shaking fingers accessed the damage.

I grabbed Deena's arm to get the fuck away. "We have to go inside. Now Deena!" She staggered with each tug, unmoving and unresponsive.

The other vampires rushed us. One snatched Deena, wrapping his arm around her neck. The other shoved me into the wall, cracking the base of my skull against the bricks. Evan reappeared, and he was pissed. The taste of rosary I'd bestowed left little connect-the-dot holes spaced along his face.

"That wasn't an intelligent decision." His long, white, canines gleamed. My attention stayed riveted on them. God they were huge, pointy, and sharp.

The metal door to the club opened again.

"What the fuck? *Butch*!" Cletus barreled out, moving faster than a man that big should. I knew he wouldn't be strong enough to stop what was happening. No amount of protein shakes and fitness in this world would change the fact that he was a mortal man.

Then, I heard the sound of a shotgun being pumped.

Buckshot, on the other hand, just might save my ass.

"I suggest you pieces of shit get the fuck out of here," Hector spat, his hands holding the sawed-off steady. I knew he kept Big Betty in his office, but he'd never pulled her out for some quality time—until now.

Butch came at a run. He stopped next to Hector. His gaze flickered over every person in the alley as he assessed the situation. Mr. Kung Fu was probably thinking of inventive Bruce Lee ways to take them all down.

"Enjoy the reprieve while it lasts," Evan whispered. "See you around."

He turned and walked away, footsteps unhurried on the concrete. Solid hands released me and I staggered, watching as the other two followed him.

Of course they wouldn't want to bring attention to what they were. If they'd taken out all of the employees in the back alley, it wouldn't be easy to hide.

"Jesus fucking Christ!" Hector's voice boomed inside my ears, and I turned to look at him. His normally tan skin was a sickly shade of white. "What was that about?"

"They wanted money." My voice was shaky, making the lie credible. Things could have gone south in a hurry, and not just for me. I panicked, searching for Deena. She was out cold, head arched back and hair dangling in soft waves down Butch's arm.

"Let's get you inside." Cletus's deep and reassuring voice was a welcome sound in my ears.

I followed Butch as he led the way. Destiny was just inside the hallway, observing with fear and excitement. She moved out of the way and frowned in disappointment when Hector directed us to his office. I slumped down on the bench along the wall and Butch gently laid Deena on the couch, placing her head against the cushions for comfort.

"You two, get back out there. The bar's closed for the time being. If anyone bitches, tell them they can fuck off." Hector pointed to the door and demanded, "Close that behind you."

Butch exited first, with Cletus close behind. The door smacked shut, making the blinds clack against the window. Hector removed his jacket and tossed it over the back of his chair. He loosened his tie, pacing back and forth.

"I want to know what the fuck is going on with you, Rhiannon." He spun around and leaned across the desk, caramel eyes angry. His normally attractive face was harsh, lines creasing his forehead.

"Nothing is going on with me," I replied evenly, meeting his anger head on.

"Don't lie to me." He spoke through tightly clenched teeth, jaw muscles ticking.

"I'm not lying!" I hated lying to Hector, and if he kept pushing, I wasn't going to be able to. "Why are you blaming me for some coked up assholes looking to score?"

"Let me play this out for you, *jodona*." He pushed away from the desk and reached for his jacket. "You better get your shit together tonight. When you come back to my club, I don't want any more strange people lurking around. I might not work the floor, but I'm always aware of what goes down here. This is my business, and I won't let you fuck with it. No matter how good you are at your job."

He stormed out, slammed the door behind him, and my body sagged.

Of course Hector would have noticed everything—the visits from Cash and then Disco, taking a week off unexpectedly, and now the altercation on the back of the property. This was his baby, his livelihood, and I was threatening it. No wonder he was livid. I'd be pissed too.

Deena moaned and I knelt beside her. She opened her crystal blue eyes. They were confused but clear. I breathed a sigh of relief, smiling at her.

"What happened?" She groaned, palming her forehead.

"I almost got robbed, but you saved my ass." I wanted to laugh and cry at the same time.

"I did?" She thrust her hands under her body and pushed herself upright.

"Yep." I moved away and stood, smiling down at her.

"I remember coming out to make sure you were okay...but that's all."

"It's all over now."

"Are you still sick? Shouldn't you go home?" She rose from the cushions, apparently feeling all right.

"I'm still going home, but I need to make a phone call first."

She seemed torn, trying to decide if she should comfort me or return to the floor. Deena was always on top of her job, so I wasn't surprised her first inclination after being mind-fucked would be to get back to work.

"Okay, if you're sure." She frowned at me skeptically.

"I'm sure. Call me later."

I waited until the door closed behind her before I allowed myself to crumble to the floor. Goose was wrong. I wasn't being offered a choice. This was Survivalism 101. Pick something you can live with, or suffer the consequences. But he was right about one thing—I would never survive in an environment where I was controlled. I'd rather join my parents and pass over to whatever the hell was on the other side. I just hoped my own private purgatory didn't entail walking this Godforsaken earth like the rest of the lost souls.

My hypocrisy only went so far.

I dug the phone from my pocket, my trembling fingers skimming across the Motorola Razr. I yanked it free and my heart started to pound, palms going clammy. Rising on wobbly legs, I started to pace in a tiny circle.

This shit was permanent. Goose said lifelong commitment—as in forever.

I felt eyes on me and stopped, glancing out the window. The dusty blinds were opened just enough for me to see Hector. He was still pissed, watching me with a troubled expression, his hair cascading carelessly around his face. He stared long and hard before he adjusted his tie and walked out of my line of vision.

I held out the phone, staring at the tiny digital screen before opening it. I scrolled through the few numbers in the memory, locating one in particular.

With my stomach churning and my heart pounding, I took my leap of faith. I pressed *send* and placed the phone to my ear. When he answered, I was proud that my voice sounded rock solid and steady.

"Goose, I need to talk to Disco."

CHAPTER SIXTEEN

To say I felt awkward would be an understatement. I was sitting in a room surrounded by Disco's family, and they wouldn't stop staring.

Goose had taken the spot beside me on the vintage love seat, but it didn't ease my tension. I squirmed under their scrutiny, wiggling from time to time against the hard tapestry cushions. I felt totally out of place, like a cockatoo on display at an exotic bird show.

After I'd called Goose, things fell into place—for the most part. I'd been forced to submit to another mind-twist to keep the location of their home a secret. One minute I was outside the BP with Disco, the next, I was sitting in an elaborately decorated room surrounded by strange faces. The mind-warp was a shock to the senses and a bitch on perception. I couldn't account for the lost gaps in time, and my memory kept trying to connect the blank frames.

I studied the vampires I'd been introduced to the moment I'd snapped out of my mind funk. There were eight of them total—six men and two women. Each one was lovely, skin luminescent and flawless, eyes twinkling in the red cast of from the fireplace.

Jonny and Sirah sat directly across from me on the couch, Adrian and Nala situated beside them. I didn't have to be told they were in relationships. The men made it clear with hands draped possessively over crossed legs or around shoulders. Standing behind them were Landon and Corey, the two pranksters who had come to see me the last time I'd paid a visit. To the side, lounged casually in chairs, were Peter and Paine.

Of all of them, Paine freaked me out the most. His thick brown hair fell to his chin, complementing his lovely ivory complexion and masculine features. But all of that beauty disappeared when you looked into his eyes. They were dead, totally hollow and empty. Looking into those deep pools of liquid obsidian made me cringe, and when he met my stare and saw my reaction, he smiled.

I quickly averted my gaze and glanced at Nala. She was staring, just like all the others, but in a different way. Each time I caught her bluish green eyes, she produced a friendly smile.

Disco came into the room and my heart started thrumming, adrenaline making me queasy. Goose explained the details over the phone, preparing me for what would occur. The family would convene to discuss the potential candidate. Then, each has a vote. If you're invited to the fold, you give fealty to the family, accept their promise of protection, and get a big old chunk taken out of you to seal the deal.

"You know why we're here, so let's get the ball rolling. I'll start with you, Jonny." Disco walked to the fireplace, standing in front of it. Since my arrival, I'd avoided making eye contact with him, still uneasy about our prior encounter. He didn't seem upset or angry when he came to escort me to his home, but he kept to himself, unusually quiet and somewhat melancholy.

"You're sure she can see the twice dead?" Jonny studied at me speculatively, his dark hair short against his head, brown eyes cautious. He was dressed to impress in an expensive navy business suit with a lavender tie.

"I am." Disco nodded.

"Then it's simple. I vote yes." He looked to Sirah. His fingers ran along the matching lavender dress she wore before returning to her bare knee.

"Sirah?" Disco asked.

"She's a novice at her craft, you admitted it yourself. Why do we need another necromancer? Ethan has always gotten the job done." She spoke with a hint of arrogance, which allowed me to place her. Sirah was the ice princess of the household, complete with bouncy blonde hair and big blue eyes.

"Her capacity and talent will extend far past my own," Goose said. "All she needs is time and instruction, which I plan to give her personally. I assure you, she is an asset."

"I'm sorry, Ethan." She narrowed her icy eyes in my direction. "I'm voting no."

Goose shrugged. Judging by his reaction, he already knew how she planned to respond.

"Adrian?" Disco put his hands behind his back. He wasn't happy with Sirah and didn't attempt to hide it.

"It's a no brainer. If Ethan has that much faith in her, who am I to argue? I vote yes." He gave me a boyish smile, as friendly as Nala's.

"Nala?" Disco relaxed, smiling.

"I've already told you my answer, but I'll repeat it for the sake of propriety." She smiled at me again, and my lips curved at the corners in response. "I vote yes."

"Landon?" Disco lifted his gaze to the blond standing behind the couch. As far as outward appearances were concerned, he seemed to be the youngest, twenty-years old or so at the time of his conversion.

"Hell yeah!" he exclaimed and muffled laughter erupted inside the room. Corey slapped him on the back and his playful demeanor vanished. He coughed and cleared his throat. "I vote yes, too."

"Corey?" Disco fought a grin by coughing and covering it with his fist.

Corey's soft brown eyes twinkled. He winked at me and smiled. "She's got my vote."

"Peter?" Disco shifted his feet in that bizarre motion that gave the illusion he was moving but standing still.

"Majority decides, and the majority has chosen yes. Therefore, I vote yes as well." He glanced at Sirah and a small smile tugged at the corners of his mouth. I wasn't sure if he voted yes because of the reason he stated, or if spiting her was motive enough.

"Paine?"

The atmosphere in the room seemed to thicken, and I felt the tension radiating from the people around me. All the attention I held dissipated; the focus on exactly one person.

"Peter said it best." Paine's onyx eyes turned to me, and my breath caught in my throat, making it impossible to breathe. Time seemed to stop as we studied each other and he said, "Yes."

"It's settled." Disco sounded relieved. "Paine and I will take it from here."

The space went from occupied by eleven bodies to a paltry four in a matter of seconds. They emptied the room, vanishing with unnatural speed. Paine watched me from his chair, reclined, legs splayed out. I shifted anxiously, and Goose patted my knee with his fingers.

"It's your turn, Rhiannon." Disco's teal eyes were intense when he spoke. "Once you devote yourself to us you can't walk away. The commitment is binding and lasts as long as you live."

As long as you live—those words made me feel as if I were selling my soul. An inner part of me, the one that insisted I remain a free spirit, demanded I get up and walk out. I grappled with the words, trying to remember them as Goose had instructed. I frowned, brain sputtering.

This was not the time to have stage fright.

"I swear fealty to you and yours, placing myself into your keeping and devoting myself to you as you devote yourself to me." The words came out in a rush, and I whispered to Goose from the corner of my mouth, "Is that right?"

"That's right," Disco answered for him. I shifted uncomfortably in the couch, looking away. "Ethan explained that Paine is in line to take my place in the event something unexpected happens, and for that reason, he must taste your blood. Did he not?"

"He did." I nodded, staring at the floor. I could feel the weight of his stare.

"Did he also warn you of his particular ability?"

"He did," I repeated.

When Paine touched me, he would know all my secrets, including ones that hadn't occurred yet. He was both blessed and cursed with flashes of the past and the future. He would know what it was like when I was born, just as he would know how it would be when I died.

Paine rose from the chair in a fluid movement and said, "Wait outside, Ethan."

Goose smiled in encouragement as he walked around the chairs and past Paine. I bit my tongue and pressed my lips together, preventing the words "don't go" from escaping. He walked out of the doors and closed them behind him, the click of the latches cementing the reality of what I was allowing to transpire. I swore I wouldn't show fear, but it was impossible to hide.

They could smell it.

"You play the hellion pretty well." Paine smirked, striding over. "But I'll know if it's all for show. Is that what frightens you?"

"No. But it has to bother you knowing how all your brothers and sisters are going to bite the big one." I didn't mention the personal guilt related to seeing what happened to Jacob and Cash. After all, soon he would know all of my dirty laundry too.

"It does," he admitted, voice deep and contemplative. "And I'm about to see how you die as well."

He knelt beside me, ebony eyes probing as he opened his hand, palm up. I nervously extended my own and he pulled me to him, turning my arm to expose my wrist. I took a deep breath to steady myself. Disco remained in front of the fireplace, but his gaze was riveted on us. I avoided looking at him, returning my attention to Paine. He grasped my forearm and hand tightly as his hair fell forward, obscuring him from view.

"I give you my protection as a member of this house," he whispered against my skin, mouth widening, and his elongated canines sank deep.

Whoever went around spreading the juicy rumor that vampire bites are erotic and sexy are full of shit. His teeth didn't pierce or poke, they tore through the muscle and tendon in my arm. I hissed, jerking and trying to pull away on reflex. He kept my arm firmly in place, fingers digging painfully into my skin, and I sniffed back the tears that threatened to spill from my eyes.

His teeth pulled free of my agonized flesh as he sucked gently with his mouth and tongue. The intense burning faded to a sting, and then a dull pulse. He stopped abruptly, mouth tight over the wound. The moment passed and he drank again, pulling on the skin, his steady swallowing soft in my ears. When finished, he ran his tongue along the surface of the wound, sealing the skin together. Only then did he release my arm.

He stood, towering over the loveseat, pushing heavy brown hair clear of his face. He studied me with an odd expression, almost tender and curious. Quickly it vanished, replaced by dark and dangerous eyes.

"Welcome to the family," he said softly. With a nod to Disco, he left the room, pulling the doors closed without turning around.

I studied my wrist. Little white indentions ran along the surface, tiny little dots and slashes—teeth marks. I recognized them as being the same as those hidden beneath Goose's watch.

"I thought it was supposed to turn black." I spoke aloud to break the strained silence of the room.

"Not from his bite."

"Why didn't I have to take from him? I thought the connection was established by exchanging blood?"

The loveseat sank beneath the weight of Disco's body. "If something happens to me, you'll be expected to exchange blood with the new head of the family, which is Paine. For now, you're connected with him, and that's enough."

I ran my fingertips along the raised welts of skin, each smooth but also firm, almost iridescent. "Does he tell you? How we die, I mean?" Although it meant I was extremely morbid, the knowledge that Paine knew how I would die didn't bother me.

"No." Disco's voice was strained. "He refuses to share what he knows with anyone."

"Why?" I glanced up, into Disco's eyes. I could make out the gold flecks inside the irises with my faultless vision.

"People who know how they will die change their behaviors in an attempt to avoid the circumstances. Paine doesn't want to interfere with the time someone could spend productively, in happiness. So he swore he would never share what he knows, and to my knowledge, he never has."

"It seems to have taken a toll."

"Everyone knows the ones they love will die. Even immortals are aware death doesn't play favorites and our time could be cut short, as we are not infallible. But I don't think anyone ever truly thinks about the limited span of time given to each of us. It is a different awareness for Paine. He knows with absolutely certainty everyone will die. Whether it occurs tomorrow, or five hundred-years from now."

"I guess it nixes potential friendships," I said, pity creeping into my voice.

"I braced myself for anger, not your understanding, in regard to Paine. I thought you'd be livid that he knew the things you've sworn to keep hidden."

I sighed, a mere whisper of air against the crackle from the fireplace. "I don't have a choice. I'm angry about that. But he didn't intentionally seek out the information. If he goes around sharing what he knows, that'll be a different story."

"Paine won't say a word, I can assure you. He keeps to himself, but when he does interact with us, it's very superficial. Your secret is safe with him." Disco spoke the last part begrudgingly, and when I dared a look in his direction. He was frowning.

"Do you want to know that badly?"

I stared into the shimmering depths of his eyes. Coming into the fold was not the only monumental change I would have to accept, there was still the matter of trust.

"I do," he acknowledged.

I reached for his hands, the warmth of my fingers encompassing his cool skin. He watched me, his intense gaze ravaging my face as I placed his palms against my cheeks.

"Once you know, don't mention it or bring it up again. Not now, not ever. That's all I am able to give you." I closed my eyes and waited, trembling when his right hand laced through my hair, the left caressing my jaw.

"No," he murmured softly. "One day you will tell me, and it won't be because you feel obligated or pressured. Until then, I can wait."

I lifted my lids and his face was there, his breath soft and sweet in my nose. My throat constricted as our eyes clashed. He pulled my hair teasingly, angling my head to the side so he could place his mouth against my left ear.

"Where do you want your mark, Rhiannon?" His words were sensual, husky, and filled with underlying promises.

"On my wrist, maybe?" My voice cracked. "Like Goose?"

His breath teased the skin on my throat. "I don't think that suits you."

"Then where?" I groaned, anxiety changing to something else, skin tingling and sensitive.

"Here." He pressed his mouth against my throat, and my entire body erupted in heat, flames licking beneath the surface of my skin.

"Okay," I agreed rashly, bringing my left hand up to grasp his back.

He twisted his body ever so slightly, teasing the skin along my nape with his fingers, lightly skimming the surface. Soft lips replaced them, rubbing in a delicious friction on my throat. I felt teeth follow the same path, gently scraping the top of the skin, stopping above the pulse on my neck.

He moved his left hand down to grasp my arm firmly. The right remained entwined in my hair, pulling me closer. I felt his body surge forward and I tensed, unable to resist the urge to avoid the inevitable pain from this bite. My breath stuck in my throat as he sank his teeth deep, scoring the pulsing vein cleanly.

My free hand connected with his arm, fingers digging into unyielding muscle. The pressure vanished as teeth eased out of my neck and his mouth surrounded the bite. He sucked gently, tongue lapping against the ravaged skin. The sharp, stabbing pain vanished, a dull ache left in its place.

He drank in deep greedy pulls, crowding my neck until I felt lightheaded. My grip loosened as he shifted his body, reaching for something I couldn't see. Blood trickled freely down my neck in a thin red line when he lifted his head, flowing past the hollow of my throat and into my sweater.

"This will only take a moment," Disco promised and pressed something soft against the deep punctures in my skin. I watched from sleepy eyes as he removed a black piece of cloth from my neck. His mouth descended, and his tongue moved over the ragged holes gently. He worried at the skin longer than necessary, and I gasped for the second time, but not in pain.

"It's done." His voice sounded deep and far away. "It's your turn."

He pulled his sweater over his head and threw it carelessly to the ground. The tiny blessed silver knife he'd used before appeared in his hand. He made the incision at the hollow of his throat and pulled me into his arms so that my face was level with his chest.

There was no protest, no argument. I remembered the taste of his blood, and some sinful inner part of me wanted more. Disco sighed at the first draw of my mouth against his skin. He pulled me closer, his hands wrapped into the hair tangled down my back. My sleepiness disappeared. His blood filled me with a newfound energy. I lost track of how many times I swallowed. All I could fathom was the incredibly succulent taste of his blood; cool and sticky sweet, with a hidden touch of cinnamon and cloves.

When the blood began to trickle, I reluctantly pulled away. My eyesight, hearing, and sense of smell were already heightened, so I didn't experience any of those disorienting symptoms. Instead, I felt amazing, as if I could jump off a building and fly. Disco held me close and I looked into his eyes. Something I couldn't explain overcame me in that instant, and I reacted.

My lips brushed Disco's as I ran my hands along his solid stomach, fingers skimming the contours of his chest and shoulders. His initial shock was short lived. He rolled with me on his chest, rotating our bodies so I rested against the tapestry cushions, and pressed his hips between my legs.

I tasted the metallic bitterness of my blood on his lips and shared his lingering essence by pulling the tip of his tongue into my mouth and sucking softly. He growled, hands rough against my hips, dragging me downward. Uncontrollable warmth spread through my body, in places I wanted him to touch, and I ground my hips deliberately against his pelvis, moving my hands lower, latching onto that perfect mound of flesh on his ass to pull him against me.

He ripped his lips away. "You can't know how badly I want this," he groaned next to my ear, kissing the tender spot just behind. I didn't speak, using actions to convey my agreement, bringing my hands up to cradle his face and draw his lips to mine.

But it wasn't enough, not nearly enough...

I raked my nails up and down his back and brought them around to his chest. His skin was cool and firm. I arched my back, pressing my aching nipples against him, desperate to ease the burn.

"Rhiannon." He pulled away, hands holding either side of my face to prevent me from interrupting him. "I want to take you to my bedroom and love you until the sun comes up. But if I do, you'll hate me in the morning. I would despise myself for allowing that."

"I don't understand." I attempted to wiggle free, eager to taste him again. "Is it STDs? I know you can't get me pregnant."

"No, our kind doesn't transmit or get infected with diseases. But damn it, I want you to come to me because you want me, not because your libido has been altered by my blood. I can't be certain this is something you'll be proud of tomorrow."

It felt like lightning bottled inside my skin, the tendrils of electricity burning and quickening in my veins. I struggled to find my inner strength, but it was difficult. I'd never been so sexually charged in my life. His fingers were gentle against the sensitive flesh on my neck, and each tickling brush threatened to break my resolve. When I finally managed to speak, my words were raspy.

"You're right. I'm sorry."

"It's not your fault," he murmured.

I was keenly aware of each solid inch of him pressed against my body. His muscular stomach was firm, his pelvis snug and heavy between my thighs. His frame melded perfectly to my own, his coolness muting the flush emitting from my skin. I stifled a groan of frustration.

"Maybe it would be best if you sat on the other side of the room," I whispered hoarsely.

He chuckled and lowered his head, smelling a lock of my hair. Slowly, he pulled away. I sat upright, staring at his bare chest and shoulders, which were cut, defined, and smooth. His abs were equally mesmerizing, visible hip bones disappearing beneath his slacks. I peered up and saw him studying me, eyes equally intense.

"It will take longer for the sexual drive to dissipate." He broke eye contact, reaching for his discarded sweater.

I wanted to be sarcastic, but damn it, I couldn't. I was still battling the desire to leap from the cushions and tackle him to the floor. He tossed the sweater over his head and yanked the material over his body. His head popped out, blond hair ruffled and unkempt around his face. The effect was devastating, especially with my raging hormones.

I managed to find my voice. "Are we done?"

"For now." He lowered his chin, grinned wickedly, and his dropped his voice an octave, oozing with sexual innuendo. "Unless there is something more I can do for you. Is there anything else you would like me to do for you, Rhiannon?"

"Bite me," I snapped and winced at my choice of words.

His grin intensified, eyes glinting. "I already have."

CHAPTER SEVENTEEN

"What can I get you?" a dinky little girl with blonde hair and pigtails asked cheerily. She looked rather adorable in her little brown apron and black dress, but I wasn't in the mood to be peppy.

"A tall double mocha latte, please." I needed the caffeine and fast. It had been a long night, and I hadn't slept at all.

She rang the order up, wrote my name on the little Styrofoam cup, and placed it on the counter behind others awaiting concoctions of their own. I paid with cash, stuffed the remainder into the tip jar, and stood back until my jolt of caffeine was ready.

As I waited, I fiddled with the collar of my turtleneck. The mark was there, inked in black. It looked odd against my pale skin, but served as a reminder of the previous night's events.

All of them.

My name was called and I collected my java before some other person attempted to whore themselves off as me. I'd seen it happen before. Some people don't care if they steal directly in front of you. I exited the building and made my way down 59th Street, toward Central Park.

Sabrina and Mark Smith, otherwise known as Carolyn and Max Starkey, lived in Uptown Manhattan. It turns out Goose is lottery-winner lucky. The first upscale real estate firm resulted in pay dirt. Max even had his very own picture in the phonebook, nestled next to an ad that insisted, 'Don't delay, Call today!'

Since Max's office was in a building right next to the park, we could track him easily and he'd never be the wiser. This meant I could enjoy the urban wilderness and fulfill my nature cravings.

It was a win-win situation.

As I entered the gate, the hair on my nape stood on end and my skin started to crawl—the early warning sign that a ghost was in the nearby vicinity. Usually, I would see maybe a half a dozen spirits during a routine day. I'd already surpassed that number since I'd left my building, and it was only 11:30 in the morning.

I found an empty bench in the mall walkway and took a seat, sipping my coffee. The air was brisk and fresh, children's voices drifted to me from different distances, and the shades of green were brushed beautifully in my sight. I smiled, content to have a moment alone, taking another swallow of chocolaty goodness.

I knew Goose was there before he spoke, aware of his unique power, able to sense and distinguish it.

"Should I ask?"

"Nope, there's nothing to tell," I quipped, cup affixed to my lips.

"Oh, Rhiannon." He shook his head and chuckled as he sat beside me. "You're a terrible liar."

He'd taken my advice about wearing casual clothing. His shirt was still uptight—white cotton with matching buttons down the middle, starched and pressed to perfection—but he wore jeans and a pair of brown leather timberland shoes.

It was a step in the right direction.

"So where is it?" He looked up and down my arms for my mark.

"Wrong." I struggled to squelch a moment of embarrassment.

"He didn't..." He pointed at my neck.

"Yeah, so?"

"Most familiars are marked on the wrist. It's a sign of servitude as the hand is extended outward in offering. The neck, on the other hand, is an intimate part of the body. A mark there indicates you're far more than just an asset to the family. It's meant as a warning."

He leaned over. "Can I see it?"

"Good God. What is this? Show me yours and I'll show you mine?" I shook my head in exasperation but did as he asked, pulling down the neck of my sweater to display the mark.

"Yep, that's what he did. He bit you right where everyone would see. I knew something was going on, but I didn't know it went that deep. Do you want to tell me what happened last night?"

"No, not really." I smirked unapologetically. "But I would like to ask you about this change in my perception. Since I left my apartment, I've been bombarded. If I don't see ghosts, I can feel them all around. What's that all about?"

"Your ability is coming to the forefront," he answered. "Our powers are generally weak on their own. They have to be manipulated, molded, and then harnessed. However, even the most practiced necromancer cannot achieve the level of awareness one does by becoming a familiar to a vampire. We see dead people, and vampires are considered dead."

"So it's normal?" I breathed a sigh of relief. "I was worried."

"I think so. Your abilities are greater than my own. Soon we'll know more. If you're agreeable, that is."

I arched a brow. "Agreeable?"

"The best way to learn is by experience, and I can give you that. The work is dependable and pays well. Most of my clients come by word of mouth."

"I don't know." I hedged. "I like the job I have. It's something I know, something I'm good at."

"You can't bartend forever," he argued. "You need something you can fall back on. Being a member of Disco's family will always ensure you have a place to go, but I know you, and you like your independence too much."

"Tell me something." I quickly changed the subject. "Why does Disco's family call him Gabriel instead of Disco?"

He tensed. "You finally noticed that, did you?"

I nodded. "Aside from you and Cash, no one else calls him that."

"I usually refer to him as Gabriel, but since you weren't aware of his given name, I wanted to make you feel comfortable."

"So where did Disco come from?" I knew I was blushing, I could feel my cheeks burning.

"Oh no." His eyes widened and he shook his head back and forth slowly. "No wonder you won't tell me what happened last night."

"Stop analyzing me and answer the damned question," I snapped, glaring at him.

"The nickname came about as a running joke that got of hand. Cash was the only one who kept it going. Gabriel hates being called Disco, and Cash loved to get under his skin."

I shifted uneasily; he still stared at me like I'd grown another head. "Stop looking at me like that. I was just asking."

"I can't help it; this isn't like you at all. I know the blood exchange changes things—including mood and body chemistry—but this is beyond any kind of scientific explanation."

"You know." My voice was laced with sarcasm. "I love being reminded of just how fucked up people find my company. One minute, I'm asked to be more loving and sweet. In fact, someone once told me it was downright adorable. But when I actually give the public what they want, they think I'm suffering from a chemical imbalance. Thanks, Goose."

I felt it again; that inner humming that signaled something otherworldly was close by. This time I couldn't ignore the feeling, it was too intense, too compelling.

"Do you feel that?" I glanced around.

"No." Goose looked at me, mildly concerned. "Feel what?"

I stood and took off in the direction of the undeniable pull. I knew Goose was behind me; I heard him asking to be excused as he bumped into someone in an effort to keep pace. My feet flew across the path, rubber soles scraping against the concrete, hair flowing behind me as I quickened pace and shoved past a group that blocked my way to the front of the Bandshell. My skin prickled with an unfamiliar energy, the surface rippling pleasantly.

"Rhiannon." Goose snagged my arm, jerking me to a halt.

"You can't feel that?" I couldn't believe he wouldn't at least feel *something*. The humming grew stronger with each step. I stared down the path, gaze affixed in the direction of the vibration.

"No, and you're starting to scare me." He placed his hands on my shoulders and spun me around. "Look at me."

I couldn't look at him, eyes riveted toward the pull. So close, if only I could get there.

"Look at me!" he snapped, shaking my shoulders forcefully.

It took effort, but I did as he asked. His lips were tight, lines forming around his mouth, and his forehead creased in worry. His chocolate brown eyes met mine, ensuring I was with him and not somewhere else.

"What does it feel like?"

"Like a humming on my skin, but from the inside out." I gazed down the path, to the fountain at the end. "I'm going down there. I have to."

"All right, but slow down. You control what you're feeling, not the other way around."

He released me and we started walking—together this time. A breeze shifted through the trees and my nose filtered the multiple scents—a hotdog, meatball sub, Chanel N°5, Hypnose cologne, grass, leaves, dirt, freshly poured cement and exhaust fumes.

It took all of my restraint not to jog as the need to see what existed beyond intensified. I drew a deep breath through my mouth and allowed it to escape slowly through my nose. I could see the drop from the stairs ahead, The Bethesda Fountain beckoning in the distance. The sounds of splashing water and voices assailed my ears, multiple conversations taking place at once, combined in a mash of incoherent whispers.

I cleared my throat, using the rumbling sound inside my head to clear my mind. We descended the stairs and stopped at the base of the fountain. Two ghosts were perched together, holding hands, interacting with each other. I'd never seen anything like it before. The spirits I'd encountered were always detached, seeming out of place in the world around them, but not these two.

Their clothing was from the seventies, her long brown hair parted down the middle and his styled in a mop top. My mouth dropped in realization. I could see them, *really see them*. The colors weren't faded and their features were clear.

"What do you see?" Goose sounded calm, but I could tell he was attempting to mask his excitement.

I didn't speak, reaching out to him.

Goose's fingers wrapped around mine and our palms connected. I didn't know why he didn't perceive the same things I did, but at least I could share them with him. A few seconds passed and then his hand squeezed in mine in a rapid succession.

"It's a residual." He laughed softly. "You're witnessing something that occurs when a moment imprints in time. Normally, it happens in the location of a tragedy, like at Ground Zero. But this...this is formed from sheer happiness. You can feel the bliss."

I nodded and pulled him along with me. The pull didn't stop there. We walked down East Drive, weaving through people with strollers and on bicycles. This time, Goose didn't discourage me when I scurried along. I started jogging, bobbing through the people who stopped to look around and enjoy the scenery. As we neared the green expanse of the Great Lawn, my heart started fluttering in my chest.

I released Goose's hand and ran my fingers through my hair in an attempt to ease the crawling sensation, goose bumps forming all over my body. I could see them from the distance, and I put on speed, flying over the grass.

I stopped just beyond the edge of the trees. "Oh..." I said the word in an exhaled breath, awestruck. I took Goose's hand and gave him a moment to process everything.

"My God," he finished. I didn't chance a look, but I knew his eyes were as wide as mine.

They were everywhere, spirits from the past frozen perfectly in time. The lush green grass was occupied at every nook and cranny, every detail crisp and clear—from the plaid polyester blanket underneath the couple in the shade, to the old-fashioned football held firmly under the arm of a man in shorts and high socks with red stripes at the top.

"How is this happening?" I asked in wonderment, completely unafraid.

"You're receptive to it." Goose turned his head as the ghostly image of a dog ran into the trees, its shaggy brown hair bouncing with each lunging stretch.

"Can we touch them?"

"I don't think so," he said. "They aren't ghosts, per se."

I pivoted, locating the dog in the trees. His snout pushed something I couldn't see. The object became visible only after the animal chomped it between his teeth. He started running with the yellow tennis ball, and I stepped directly in his path, tugging Goose's arm in the process. The dog passed through me and I whipped around, watching as the mutt ran back to the open grass.

"I guess that answers that question." I laughed.

"This is extraordinary. Imagine the possibilities, the opportunities. We could visit historic locations across the world and witness everything with our own eyes. The Coliseum, Stonehenge, the Seven Wonders of the World." He spoke in an excited rush.

"Slow down." I glanced at him. "I still have a lot to learn, remember? I'd prefer to take this one step at a time."

"I know, you're right," he demurred. "I'm excited by this information, naturally. The necromancers I'm aware of don't meet often, and our time together is often restricted and constrained. With you, there are no boundaries."

"Don't tell me." I snickered. "You're in a club that gathers together like raving Trekkies to share secrets of the afterlife. I bet you even have an Enigma CD you crank up to get in the mood."

"Don't be silly." His face lit up with an enormous grin. "We listen to Enya, not Enigma."

The humming dissipated, my body reverting to normal as that unnatural part of me received satisfaction. We stood together, staring for a few moments longer.

"I suppose we should get back to work." I sighed, casting a gaze over the shapes in the grass one final time.

"Come on." Goose yanked gently on my hand and pulled me back into the expanse of trees that formed a canopy overhead.

"Distract me." I exhaled a lungful of air, tossing my cup into a nearby trashcan. "Tell me what you know about Max and Carolyn."

"Not much." He cleared his throat, back to business as usual. "On paper they check clean. They've lived here for four years, and they've never owned residences anywhere near California. Max got into the real estate business for pleasure. He's financially set as his family owns a chain of Slumberwood Hotels across the world. Carolyn comes from money as well. Her parents struck it rich selling a patent that preserves fruit for extended periods of time."

I chuckled. "Do you mean those little bags you buy for bananas?"

"I'm sorry. I didn't delve into the specifics of her parent's fruit protection invention. Next time, I'll be more thorough."

"Do that. Otherwise, I'll have to tell everyone what a slacker you are." We exited onto East Drive and I asked, "So why are we meeting here, anyway? Couldn't you handle this alone?"

He hesitated. "I wanted to make sure you were all right."

"Oh my God." I snorted in disgust, walking faster. "You're like a worried mother digging around for dirt."

"It's not like that. But like it or not, we are a team now. And I know what you're going through."

I refrained from addressing what I was going through. Instead, I let my attention wander over the people lined up on Cat Rock. The dip in temperature had brought windbreakers and sweaters out in force, T-shirts and shorts were virtually non-existent. Soon, Christmas would arrive, and a blanket of snow would cover the trees, stone and metal statues, and fairytale castles.

"Stop." Goose gripped my arm. "There he is."

Diverting my attention to the Tisch Children's Zoo, I located Max Starkey. Carolyn was with him, her hands on the handles of a three-wheeled black stroller.

"I guess he's taking lunch with the family," I said quietly. "We should wait until they leave and follow him."

"Definitely." Goose nodded his agreement.

We stayed put, pretending to chat and shoot the breeze. It wasn't difficult, the area was usually chock-full of people doing the same. Max eventually reappeared with his family, Carolyn pushing the stroller, their child held securely in his arms. My heart sank and a lemony bitterness crept into my mouth.

The little boy was perhaps four or five, and obviously ill. A New York Yankees ball cap covered most of his tiny head, and two red hearing aids were tucked inside his ears. He clung to his father with a huge smile splayed across his face, and a surge of protectiveness overcame me, intermingled with disbelief.

I shook my head. "It can't be them. They were probably at the tasting to get blood to give to their son. You said everything else checked out, and it would make sense. Vampire blood heals."

Goose frowned. "You know what they say about appearances and deceit?"

"Come on, Ethan." I used his actual name to make my point. "Do they look like they could attack and kill a vampire? Seriously, they'd be mincemeat. There is no possible way."

"I'll agree that it appears highly unlikely."

"More like improbable. We don't have an unlimited timeframe here. We need to move on to suspect number dos." I lifted two fingers into the air, flicking them back and forth.

"I'll make you a deal." He acted as if he was pacifying an unruly child, and I had to avert my face so he wouldn't see my smile forming. "We follow Mr. Starkey the rest of the day, and if he checks out clean, then fine. We have to meet Gabriel tonight anyway. Marcus, Chris, Lawrence, and Dexter have agreed to meet and share information. At this point, client confidentiality isn't a high priority."

"The suppliers?" I asked and he nodded. "Why wouldn't they share all the information they had from the start? Don't they realize how serious this is?"

"They do now. That tip from Sharon proved invaluable. None of them are willing to go gently into that good night, and with all of them together in one place, we can start to connect the dots." He stared at Max and his family. They had moved out of the zoo and were walking along the path ahead of us.

"Come on." He indicated we should follow.

I fell in at his side and for once, I really hoped I was right. I didn't want Max and Carolyn to be the monsters we were searching for.

CHAPTER EIGHTEEN

Max Starkey didn't make an appearance until later in the evening. He hailed a cab and we quickly followed suit. I never believed I would have the opportunity to utter the words, "Follow that cab," but I did. It was strangely liberating and exciting to work covertly.

I felt like a Bond girl.

We trailed him home and nothing spectacular occurred. Max was just another man returning to his domicile after a hard day at the office. Fortunately, Goose agreed to insert our nosey asses elsewhere, and I took him up on the offer of a cab ride home.

We hit my street after the sun had dipped below the horizon. The sky was painted with the last lingering hues of orange and yellow, which cast dusty shadows against the buildings and enveloped the trees in a warm glow. Dusk was a lovely time of the day, right before the creepy crawlies came out to play.

"Thanks for the ride." I braced myself against the faux leather seat inside the cab and gripped the door handle, ready to escape to my apartment for a few moments alone for the first time since the morning.

"Not a problem." His eyes narrowed and he gazed past me, out of the window. Surprise and humor replaced his worried expression. "I was going to ask you to call me so we could go together tonight, but I don't think that's necessary. I'll see you there."

"What?" I frowned, turning to look at my building.

Disco reclined casually against the wall. He was watching our cab, lips curved in a private smile. He wore a tight grey turtleneck with black slacks and the customary trench coat.

So he *did* own a different colored piece of clothing.

He looked as irresistible as he did the night before, even more so if that were possible. My insides clenched and I felt that all too familiar heat return to my lower extremities.

Goose laughed and I whipped around, narrowing my eyes at him.

"What?" He mocked me, shoulders shaking as he chuckled.

"I'll see you later." I climbed from the cab and slammed the door behind me. It wasn't as if Goose knew anything, but I still felt completely naked, as if everyone had been in that foyer to see me act like a brazen hussy.

I took my time approaching Disco as the cab resumed its trip down my street in a cloud of smoke. I wasn't sure what he wanted, but I was sure of what my body wanted, and I wasn't going there again.

"Good evening, Rhiannon." The mocking tone from the evening before was still there, and he looked happier than a pig in slop.

He was enjoying himself—damn him.

"Isn't it too bright for you?"

"The sun is no longer in the sky. The rays that continue to shed light are not harmful."

"Uh-huh." I cursed my inability to look away from his enticing bright blue eyes. I ground my teethed together and forced myself to stare at the blades of grass growing between the concrete at our feet.

"How was the stakeout?" There was laughter in his voice. He really was enjoying this. "Did you learn anything useful?"

"No... I mean, yes, we did. We don't think Max and Carolyn have anything to do with this. They're probably interested in the healing properties of vampire blood for their son. He's ill." I risked a look into his face.

"I see." He shoved away from the building, moving his tall frame within inches of me.

"Why are you here?"

"There are things we need to discuss before we go to the Razor. I was hoping you'd agree to speak with me. Am I mistaken?"

"I didn't realize there were more things to talk about, but I'm okay with it. What's up?"

He looked away, but not before I saw a smile resurface on his face. "Do you think we can do this in a more private place?"

Oh...yeah. Of course, he would want to go inside my apartment. Fair is only fair, right? I walked to the door and pulled it open. "Come in."

"Thank you." He nodded graciously and stepped inside my building. There was no going back now.

We stomped up the stairs and walked to the last door on the left. The little metal numbers had fallen off months ago, leaving behind a residue stain in their likeness. I'd learned shortly after I'd moved in that my landlord couldn't be bothered to fix cosmetic issues. He had drains and toilets to unclog.

I unlocked the door, pushed it open, and reached for the lamp on the nearby table. Disco waited patiently at the door—unable to cross the threshold—and I felt like a dumb ass.

"Come in," I said again, and he stepped inside and closed the door quietly.

I emptied my pockets, plugged in my phone, and checked the machine. Deena had called and sounded worried. I contemplated calling her back but decided against it. I'd call her later when I had the chance to speak freely.

"Nice place," Disco said, walking into the living room. He looked out of his element, filling the small space completely. I considered telling him, "Welcome to the real world, Mr. Wayne. Alfred is on a permanent vacay but make yourself at home," but decided to keep things mellow.

"No, it's not. But it's mine, and I'm not picky." I grabbed myself a bottle of water from the kitchen and followed him into the living room. I turned on the lamp next the couch, flooding the room in a soft glow. He took my recliner, so I walked to the couch and nestled at the opposite end.

Disco picked up my tattered copy of *Jane Eyre* and flicked through the worn pages. "Jane Eyre?"

"Is there a particular reason you find my choice of literature so strange?" Maybe he assumed I was illiterate.

"No, not at all." He put the book back where he found it. "It was immensely popular when I was a child."

I couldn't think of anything witty to say. He'd probably been alive to see the book the first time it was printed. Hell, he could have possibly met Ms. Bronte herself. I slipped my feet along the edge of the couch, placed the water on the vintage coffee table, and unzipped my shit kickers. After I yanked them off, I scrunched my toes and exhaled in bliss.

"The first reason I'm here..." He pulled an envelope out of his coat and tossed it to me. "Since you're a part of the family now, you'll receive a monthly compensation. This means you'll need to be on hand whenever and wherever we need you. Which brings me to the second reason." He shot me a look that indicated he knew I wasn't going to be happy. "I want you to quit your job. Finances won't be an issue, and you should focus on learning from Ethan. The next few months will be intense, and the less stress you experience, the better."

"And if I refuse?"

"Then you refuse. I don't expect you to do everything I ask." He sat back in the chair, his elbows braced on the arms, his long pale fingers interlaced over his stomach.

"I'm sure it's not a coincidence that I had a similar discussion with Goose while we were out today, so I'll tell you the same thing I told him. I'll think about it. There has been a massive overhaul in my life, and I need something that remains solely mine." As I spoke, I flipped open the envelope. My eyes grew wide at the amount of cash inside. I closed it and held the yellow paper aloft. "How much is in here?"

"Enough. But if you need more, don't hesitate to ask. You don't strike me as a frivolous spender, so if you need something, I would assume it is a necessity." He glanced around as he spoke, and I wasn't sure if I should take what he said as a compliment or an insult.

"How do you get this kind of money?" I shook the envelope. "You live in a mansion and don't appear to have gainful employment. How does that work?"

"I purchased a claim in an oil company years ago, expanding my interests as money came in from the venture. It proved to be lucrative"—he motioned toward my upright hand—"as you can see."

"What's that like?" I asked curiously. "Having vast amounts of wealth and power combined with one hell of a long lifespan?"

"A mixture of things." He studied me as he answered. "To have immortality is to be free. You can explore the world, see all of the things you've dreamed of, and time is not an obstacle. You can be just as youthful when you visit Rome as you are one-hundred years later to visit Ireland. However, as with anything, there are consequences. While we have no limitations, the mortals we care for do. It's the one heartache we all share."

"I never thought about it to be honest. I assumed you all remained in your tight-knit circle."

"Some do." His voice softened as he became reflective. "But sometimes people intersect our path, and although we know better, it's impossible to do the right thing and leave them alone. That's when complications arise."

"And your family? Are they random complications?" I leaned halfway off the couch to snag my bottle of water.

He nodded. "With the exception of Paine, we've known one another since childhood. Our grandfathers established a friendship during the Revolutionary War. We were raised on corresponding plantations that were passed down through the family. All of that changed, of course, during the Civil War."

"You fought in the Civil War?"

"We did. Would you like to hear the story?" I nodded enthusiastically and he continued, seeming pleased with my interest. "We were born in West Virginia during the same summer. Our parents were good friends, and because of that, we all grew up together. Our siblings intermingled constantly at both plantations. In fact, Paine was betrothed to my younger sister, Isabella." His smile vanished and his tone became somber. "The burden of loyalty and where to fight wasn't an easy one. Paine's family owned a few slaves to work in the home and around the farm, but not my family. My father cropped for profit, and when the time came to choose sides, there was a division. Paine chose to fight for the Union. I fought for the Confederacy."

He stopped, blue eyes growing dark as they glazed over.

"What's wrong?"

"Nothing." The serious look vanished, and he returned to his story. "Paine and I had a huge falling out over that. Many families did. The war turned fathers against sons, brothers against brothers. For years, we managed to avoid one another, until we met on the battlefield in Cold Harbor."

"Cold Harbor?" I couldn't believe my ears. I was actually conversing with someone who had experienced what I had read about in history books. "Really?"

He laughed, but there was no warmth or joy in the gesture. "What a waste that was; a complete massacre. A gap formed in our lines, and a group of blue coats pushed through, completely unaware their comrades alongside them were off course. They were sitting ducks, and the first volley of shots killed most of them. When reinforcements arrived, it erupted into chaos. It was dark and impossible to see, and we all fired at random. I don't remember how I was hit. One minute, I was standing. The next, I was in the dirt, struggling to breathe.

"When I came around, it was pitch black, and someone was next to me in the shallow cover of fallen trees. It was Paine. He'd seen me when his unit approached, and when I was hit, threw me over his shoulder and got the hell out. Unfortunately, as he took cover, a stray ball caught him in the back. I don't know how Marius found us. He changed me first, then Paine. Afterward he carried us to a deep grave carved into the earth. We stayed there until the sun descended the next day. When we woke, our human lives were over."

He stared down at his hands. His story was unfathomable, and completely extraordinary.

"Who is Marius?"

His smile didn't reach his eyes. "An old family friend of my grandparents'. An aristocrat who'd ventured over to explore the new world changed him. He severed the family friendship after several years when he didn't age and reappeared decades later, claiming to be a distant grandson. After the war began, he tracked my progress. It wasn't difficult for him to stay out of sight. If we move at our natural speed we're not easy to detect."

"But..." I frowned in confusion. "Why would he follow you?"

"He knew I was the only male child in our family, and he didn't want to see the family line vanish permanently following my death. Although we've argued over the fundamentals from time to time, as our kind cannot have children. I'm not exactly carrying on anything."

"And Paine? Why did he change him?"

Disco smiled, and this time the gesture was real. "He said coming across one who wore blue and one who wore grey, side by side, content to die as long as it be together, said more for the potential of the human race than anything else he'd seen."

"What happened after? Did you go home?" I tried to picture how it would be back then. No transportation, no telephones. His smile disappeared, and I worried that my question was too personal.

"We couldn't return to our divisions or to the war. The sun would have killed us. We had to make the trek home at night. Marius insisted we leave for the west immediately, but Paine wouldn't deviate from his course. He wanted to see Isabella and take her with us. When we made it to my family's plantation, we couldn't enter the house, so we had to wait until she ventured outside. That's when Paine got the first taste of his ability. When he touched her, he knew a future with him would result in a painful and excruciating death. Marius cleared her memories and we left, making the trip to California where we lived for several decades. Afterward, we returned here, and settled down permanently."

"Where is Marius now?" I took a sip of my water. After what he shared, I couldn't help but look at Disco differently. He wasn't just a vampire. He was someone who had once been very much human. If he continued to soften me up, I'd be Silly Putty in his hands in no time.

"He decided to take a sabbatical to see the world a long time ago. He drops postcards in the mail here and there, to let us know he's still out there. The last one came from Spain." He grinned, shook his head, and checked his watch. "We'll need to leave soon."

I rose from the couch. "I just need a few minutes."

"Rhiannon, will you do something for me?" Disco's smile was sheer enticement, and I chose to nod instead of speak. "Wear what you did that night we met at the Razor."

"What's wrong with what I have on?" I peered down at myself, pulling at the hem of my turtleneck.

"I can't see your mark," he answered quietly, the golden sparks in his eyes flaring.

"Oh, right." My cheeks flushed as I recalled exactly how the mark he wanted everyone to see came into being. "I can do that, sure."

I released the breath I'd been holding when I made it to the safety of my room and told myself to get a grip as I retrieved my clothing. I silently left the room, peering to the right. Disco was flipping through my copy of *Jane Eyre*, seemingly lost in the pages.

After pulling my hair into a clip, I quickly jumped inside the shower. When I was finished, I flung back the curtain and reached for the towel only to discover that I'd forgotten it in my rush to evade Disco's attention. I eyeballed the insignificant hand towel over the sink, grimacing as I made peace with the fact it was my only hope.

My clothes protested and clung to my sopping wet curves, sticking versus sliding on as I dressed. I ran my hands down my body to make sure everything was in place, picked up my dirty clothing and placed it into the hamper, and pulled on the door to escape the sweltering room.

Disco was exactly as I'd left him, sitting in my recliner, engrossed in the woes of Ms. Eyre. I snagged my shit kickers, pulled them on, and reached up to remove my hair clip when Disco stopped me.

"Leave it up."

I paused and glanced at him. "Excuse me?"

He peered up from the book. "Leave it up. It looks nice off your shoulders." His eyes locked onto my throat.

"Sorry, I've filled my quota of requests for the day." I released the clip, let my hair fall around my shoulders in soft brown waves, and smoothed any stray strands into place.

My mark was visible enough without drawing more attention to it.

I met Disco's eyes and the golden embers were burning from within. He placed the book on the table and rose in one fluid motion. My insides melted as he neared, until we were mere inches apart, and delicious warmth flowed through me. Shaking my head clear, I took a step back and braced myself for what was to come.

It was going to be one hell of a night.

CHAPTER NINETEEN

Marcus Delmar was moderately attractive. His black hair was short, the color striking with his dark blue eyes. He was only about four inches taller than I was but had shoulders as broad as barn. He wore clothes that emphasized his build, his dark navy sweater and slacks snug, as if specifically tailored for him.

Chris Devey was a blond version of Marcus with hair cut in the same manner—short and neat. His honey brown eyes were wary as he monitored us cautiously. He went all out casual in jeans and a black T-shirt, biceps expanding as he flexed his muscles.

Lorence Smith looked totally out of place. He was the only one of the group to wear a business suit, creamy white and pinstriped, perfectly ironed and pressed. His coffee skin was smooth and creamy, and his hair was neatly trimmed. He smelled amazing, even from across the room. If he was nervous, it didn't show. He remained utterly still and impassive, speaking only when addressed.

Dexter Martin reminded me of someone from Baywatch. He was tanned, athletic, and possessed All-American boy good looks. His honey blond hair was long on the top, coming around his forehead in a purposely-sloppy display. He was dressed in a nice polo shirt and khakis, cementing the illusion in my head. His curious, ice blue stare darted over to me repeatedly.

In fact, he had been staring at me since I'd entered the room with Disco's entourage.

When we had arrived, we entered the Razor through the back, climbing a flight of stairs into an area situated above the club. The private room was decadent and lavish. Expensive red velvet cushioned chairs and couches filled the space, the Venetian glass floor lamps emitting a serene glow. A large hand-knotted rug was the central feature on the dark hardwood floor, lending a hint of coziness to the room. Lights from the club shone through the one-way glass, giving everyone a glimpse of the happenings below.

Even though the area was large, it was crowded. There were liquid dieters all around, including ones who had lost family members to whoever was behind this insanity. Oddly enough, other than Cash and Jacob, none of the missing vampires shared a connection. I was painfully aware of the power in the room, and it emitted from two sources—Disco and Joseph.

Joseph had one hell of an intimidating posse, far larger than Disco's. There were twelve of them in all, minus Baxter of course. Joseph also had an ace in the hole—the necromancer I had sensed the minute they approached the building.

Sonja was my age, if not slightly younger, and my polar opposite. She had collected her hair at the top of her head, allowing multicolored strands of blonde, pink, purple, and blue to fall around her face. I was certain she wore contact lenses; her violet colored irises were too bright to be natural. She was dressed in skintight leather, the painted-on pants clinging to her hips, her matching vest lifting her breasts up and out. I noted she was marked, as I was, directly where everyone could see.

I'd wanted to sit on the sofa when we arrived, but Disco kept me at his side. Goose was on my left, and Paine stood to Disco's right. Behind us was the family, all at the ready for whatever might come. The tension inside the room grew with each passing minute.

Everyone wanted someone to blame.

"Time is running out," Joseph snarled heatedly. "You promised you would handle this, Gabriel. Since Jacob was the first to go missing, I agreed, but now I want to take control of the situation."

Disco's anger simmered just below the surface. It was evident he didn't take kindly to someone insinuating he was incapable of finishing what he started. "You won't find any new information. Ethan has been diligent in his efforts, and so far, we have nothing. We have to flush out the person responsible, and the only way to do that is to cut off all the blood supplies and leave one channel open."

"And how will you choose the dealer that puts his head on the plate?" Dexter asked in a voice as boyishly appealing as his looks.

"Flip a coin?" Joseph narrowed his eyes at Dexter. "All of you peddlers deserve to burn. After this fiasco, no one from my house, or any other I'm tied to, will ever share their blood. Soon, you will have to seek other avenues to keep yourselves thriving. We are the ones who actually need blood to survive. Not parasites seeking a high, like you."

"You are not the only resource, Joseph, but I'll take it under advisement." Dexter's smile didn't waver. "I propose that Lorence be the one to facilitate our plan. So far, he's been the one with the least to lose, since he's been keeping all of his information to himself."

"It's called client confidentiality." Lorence's voice was as smooth as butter. He was obviously an educated man; you could hear years of study in every syllable. "I have shared all of my knowledge with you, have I not?"

"Sure you did." Dexter continued goading him. "After we threatened you with the consequences."

"Boys," Paine interrupted them, stepping into the middle of the room. "We'll decide who gets the red ribbon after the important people in the room have the opportunity to talk. Don't make me throw you out of my club."

The words registered, and I gawked at Paine. The Razor was his. No wonder Disco brought me here for our little date. I bet all of the family had sat at the window and observed our entire conversation.

What bastards!

"Of course." Dexter's smile returned, but it was forced. He took a step back, and as his jaw clenched, I realized he was biting his tongue.

"Ethan can lead Sonja to the location where he intercepted Baxter, and she can establish a connection to speak directly with him. Flushing people out using these"—Joseph motioned toward Dexter—"leeches might work. But when time is of importance, a name or face would benefit us more."

"She won't gain anything more useful," Disco said.

"Of course she will. You want to give her that opportunity, don't you?"

A strange sensation breezed across my skin, and I drew a shaky breath to calm myself. My nerves were rattled from the close proximity to Disco, as well as being surrounded by so many of his kind. They gave off their own strange hum of power, which had the capability to become overwhelming.

As the silence stretched, I peered up at Disco. He was frowning, full lips drawn into a tight line. I glanced at Joseph, who wore a knowing smile. Sonja had closed the distance between them, her hand on Joseph's arm.

"What is going on?" I whispered when Goose grasped my hand. He didn't respond immediately, but when he did, my blood iced over.

"Sneaky bastards," he murmured. "They're using some sort of power to glamour Joseph's words."

"How does that work?" I had to read Goose's journals soon. Being ignorant wasn't what I was being paid for.

"I'm not sure. Joseph is the energy source, and he's using his bond with Sonja to do it." Goose kept his voice quiet and hushed. "We have to break the contact. I need you to get to Sonja."

"No problem." I hoped it would work one of two ways. Either I got a piece of the bitch, or the ensuing chick fight would break everyone out of the funk she'd started.

Goose released my hand and stepped forward, his body effectively blocking mine from view. I stayed on his ass until his body jerked and I was able to see the hand clamped around his throat that prevented him from advancing any further. Whipping to the right, I came face to face with Rainbow Brite and grabbed a fist full of her brightly colored hair. One good yank was all I needed. The contact between her and Joseph was broken, and I thrust her to the ground, causing her leather pants to chafe against the wood.

Voices chimed in the room in the same instant, furious and disbelieving.

Shrieking, Sonja jumped to her feet and rushed me. Her hands grasped my shoulders and I balled my fist, rotated at the hip, and delivered a devastating uppercut to her chin. Her jaw snapped back and her feet lifted off the ground before she crashed to the floor. I stood stock still, mouth gaping in shock and disbelief. The vampire blood I'd ingested had increased my strength. She would pay a hefty price when she came around.

Joseph lifted her lifeless body in his arms, his green eyes shimmering in fury. The mamma jamma next to him stepped forward, intent on crushing me in arms the size of jumbo jets. I thrust my right foot back, getting into a position to defend myself.

Suddenly, Paine appeared. He grasped the bigger vampire's forearm and forced him around. "Do you want to know how you go, you fat ass piece of shit? Because I know, I know everything"—Paine's face contorted, as if in agony—"Paul."

Paul shook his head, mouth hanging open. I didn't know vampires were so uptight about death, or so terrified. Paine let go of Paul, reached for me, and pulled me against him. I was caught off guard by the contact. Disco indicated Paine didn't touch anyone unless it was necessary. Paine checked me over before he guided me back to Disco's side. Goose was rubbing the dark indentions on his throat, and I patted his arm consolingly.

"You should know better Joseph." Disco bristled in anger. "Is this what we've come to?"

"I could say the same to you," Joseph snarled, cradling Sonja to his chest. "We are tired of waiting, and I gave you the opportunity to do this your way. Now it's our turn."

"You can't taint the blood supply. It would kill too many people and raise too many questions. Can't you see that? If people die with our blood inside their bodies, the human laboratories will pick it up. It's a risk we cannot take."

"Who cares if it kills off a few humans?" Joseph scoffed. "They are nothing to us. Human science won't be able to decipher anything; they'll cast the anomaly aside. It wouldn't be the first time our blood has unwittingly found its way into human hospitals."

"I refuse to take part in this," Dexter interrupted loudly, stepping forward. "I will not knowingly endanger the lives of anyone I deal to. If that's your plan, forget it."

"That is not our plan." Disco nailed Dexter with a dangerous glare. "We have information from all of you, and more importantly, we have Rhiannon."

Joseph's eyes narrowed. "Am I supposed to be impressed that you obtained a new familiar?"

"I didn't tell any of you because she was not yet marked, but now that she is beholden to our family, there is no need for secrecy." Disco's extended his hand and I laced my fingers through his. The connection was immediate. A comforting energy surged between us, filling a void that I wasn't aware existed. "Rhiannon can confer with the twice dead. It was she, not Ethan, who communicated with Baxter."

Joseph's face changed as his green eyes homed in on me. It was then that I really took him in, comprehending why those glorious set of peepers seemed so familiar.

Green eyes—just like Baxter's.

"Brothers," I whispered.

"I want to see." Joseph handed Sonja to Paul and closed the distance between us with vampire speed.

"No, you don't." I stepped back. I knew what it was like to see a sibling suffer. Nothing good would come from sharing what I had seen.

"Don't tell me what I do and do not want." He extended his hand, palm up, and I shivered as I recalled it was the exact same thing Baxter had done when I'd faced his ghost in front of Beny's.

I closed my eyes and drew an unsteady breath, attempting something I'd achieved only once before. I thought aloud in my mind, hoping Disco would hear. Nothing happened so I glanced at him, squeezing his hand. I silently shouted the words I wanted him to hear in my mind and replayed that sense of fear and despair Baxter exuded when we'd touched. I wouldn't share that knowledge with his brother. Not if I had a choice.

Disco spoke for me. "She wishes to spare you pain in your loss."

"I have the right to know!" Joseph yelled. He didn't wait for permission. He grasped my hand and green eyes filled my vision as his brother's face flashed through my mind.

I felt the cold concrete, the slice of the blade inside my flesh as it rubbed against bone, the terror I would forever be punished in hell for what I was—a demon, a blood drinker, a monster. Just as swiftly, the images changed to twin beds, music on the record player, pain-filled cries in the next room.

I attempted to break free, terror overcoming everything else. I was aware of Goose, Paine, and Disco, all yelling in anger.

"I apologize, *piccola*." Joseph's hoarsely spoken words had no meaning in my broken mind. "Allow me to undo the harm I have wrought."

Cool hands pressed against my cheekbones and my skin warmed as the sun shone upon my face and shoulders. I smelled the salt from the ocean, heard the waves as they crashed into the surf, and felt the gritty sand between my toes. A breeze ruffled my hair, and I turned toward the sound of someone speaking my name as I breathed in the hot salty air.

My mother's voice was full of laughter as she ran across the beach with my father chasing after her. She was lovely, ebony hair hanging down her back and around her shoulders as she spun around, opening her arms. My father lifted her into the air, spinning in a circle, the water and sky met behind them, forming a snapshot in my mind.

The image melded into another sunny day. A young boy with a baseball glove, raven hair hanging loosely around his face, old clothes covered in dirt and grass stains. He was laughing, running across a field, his green eyes shining. He reached into a glove, pulled out a ball, and held it aloft, grinning proudly.

"Rhiannon." Disco's voice penetrated the vision, and it dissipated. I was once again inside the dark, dimly-lit room above the club.

I cleared my throat and struggled to orient myself. Joseph had returned to his group, and I was standing once again between Goose and Disco.

"Don't you ever fucking do that again," I wheezed at Joseph.

"I'm sorry." He sounded genuinely regretful, the two words laced with pain. "One of my abilities is to meld the memories of two individuals together, just as my brother did."

"Adrian," Disco said. "No longer do we shield our talents. If you see anything coming, say so."

"It's about damned time." Adrian exhaled as he responded, sounding relived.

"Joseph, we agreed to meet without benefit of talents or persuasions, and you broke both of those terms. As the oldest families in the city, there is no reason for us to fight amongst ourselves." Disco sounded tired, his usual silky baritone heavy and solemn. "I propose Dexter provide the blood while we monitor his progress. But we will not taint the supply. We will not murder innocents."

"And if that doesn't work? How long are we expected to wait?"

"I don't see why we can't work together," Paine interjected. "That would be the logical thing."

"I offered." Disco looked at Joseph as he talked. "But only if we work together."

"I'd like a moment with you, Gabriel." Joseph sounded equally exhausted. "Would everyone excuse us?"

You could cut the tension with a knife. Everyone waited apprehensively for Disco to speak.

"You heard the man."

Paine motioned toward the exit. "Downstairs everyone. Let's go."

Joseph's people went first. Rainbow Brite was finally coming around. Her head shifted on Paul's arm, and she groaned. I was sure she was going to have one hell of a headache. Marcus, Chris, Lorence, and Dexter went next, carefully avoiding each other as they made their way down the stairs. I waited until Goose started down before I followed.

Everyone pressed against the walls as Paine strode past. He unlocked the door beneath the stairs and stepped through, allowing the music from the club to fill the hallway. Sonja was on her feet, and she walked through the door with Paul holding her steady. Jonny and Sirah went next, followed by Peter, Landon, and Corey. Nala and Adrian hung back, lounging against the wall.

Paine waited until everyone went through then allowed the door to close. We were in the far corner of the club. The music was deafening.

"Stay with her," Paine told Adrian and motioned at me.

"You got it." Adrian nodded, taking Nala's hand. "Come on, Rhiannon. We'll wait at the bar."

Paine moved and Adrian led the way, shouldering past the people in our path. The walls were painted blue, like the rest of the club, the only light source coming from the open area at the end. Adrian walked around the left of the dance floor. Vampires packed the place, with a few people spread out among them. We walked under the cast iron stairs that led to the DJ booth and underneath the booth itself. There were several empty seats at the edge of the bar, and Adrian sat at the far end with his back facing the dance floor, Nala close by his side. Goose slid into a swiveling chair next to them, and I did the same.

"What would you like, Rhiannon?" Nala yelled over the music.

"That's okay." I shook my head. "I'm fine."

She gave me a full-on smile and returned her attention to the dance floor. She was wiggling in her seat, and I knew without asking she wanted to pull Adrian out there with her. It was a shame to let her outfit go to waste. She looked ethereal in a black skirt and billowing aqua shirt that matched her eyes.

"Why don't you two go dance?" I hollered over the noise.

She didn't yell, but her voice lifted an octave. "We're supposed to wait with you."

"What's going to happen? Go on!"

She turned to Adrian, yelled something, and his face went blank, as if he were concentrating on something important. He nodded at Nala and she smiled, bounding from her seat. He instructed Ethan to stay put and followed the path she made to the floor. He pulled her close and caressed her back as they started to dance.

"They are quite the pair." Goose words echoed my own thoughts.

"If we can't enjoy the same thing for ourselves, at least we can live vicariously through them," I yelled back, grinning.

Within minutes, the crowd thickened. Every square inch of the room was covered. I glanced at the mirrors above the dance floor.

"Do you see Adrian and Nala?" I leaned closer to Ethan so we could hear each other.

"They were on the floor, but I don't see them now," he yelled. "No wait, here they come!"

I scanned the crowd and located an angry Adrian pushing his way to the bar with Nala close behind him. I laughed and turned to Goose, but my smile evaporated when I found a scowling Evan in his place.

Evan grabbed my arm and pulled me off the stool. "Your reprieve is over."

Goose stood, coming to my defense. "I wouldn't recommend that."

"Piss off." Evan pushed him into the wall and yanked on my arm again. A warm haze of outrage spread through me, and I lost my shit.

I'd had enough of this asshole.

I lurched back with all my strength, pulling him up short. Lifting my right foot, I brought my weight down on my heel and planted it into his toes below. Grasping his arm tightly, I drove my left knee into his groin. If he'd been a human male it would have left him cockeyed for days. I guessed the family jewels were either non-existent or just plain vampire durable.

He snarled and wrapped his fingers around my throat. I gasped as he applied enough pressure to cut off my airway. I rifled in my pocket for the backup butterfly knife I'd collected before I left my apartment, pulled it free and fluttered it open effortlessly, and flipped the heavy handle in my grip. I knew vampires healed quickly, so I chose a decent location. I plunged the blade into his neck between his shoulder and collarbone.

He cursed and let go of my throat. Grasping the handle, he pulled the blade free. Blood poured down his skin and into his shirt in a dark red current, and then trickled to a halt as the wound closed.

I straightened, gasping and heaving. I was fucked. I was out of weapons, and num-nuts was back for round three.

"You're going to regret that in about three seconds," Adrian said as Nala's hands gently enveloped my arms.

Paine appeared out of the bodies, obsidian eyes furious. His hand shot out in a movement too fast for my eyes to see and Evan dropped to the ground. Nala pulled me out of the way as Evan's face connected with the floor with a resounding thud.

"I told you to stay with her," Paine snapped at Adrian and Nala. He walked over and pushed my hands away from my neck. Peering down at my throat, his fingers gently explored my sore skin.

Adrian stared at Paine with a baffled expression. "I checked ahead. She was in the clear until the floor overflowed and I saw him coming. It's not my fault you have so many people in this shit hole."

I slapped Paine's hands away, and he narrowed his dark eyes at me. Unperturbed, I informed them, "I don't know if any of you noticed but I had his ass."

Retrieving my knife, I wiped the blade on Evan's shirt before flicking it closed and sliding it into my pocket. I didn't like an uneven playing field. Being small and female was bad enough. Adding another physical handicap, like inferior strength, sucked.

"You three can get rid of him." Paine pointed at Evan and then held out his hand. "Come with me, Rhiannon."

Goose, Adrian, and Nala appeared shell-shocked but recovered quickly. Adrian grasped Evan by the arm and dragged him across the floor. I eyed Paine warily, but did as he asked, sliding my hand into his.

He took me back to the hallway, past the restrooms, and released my hand to unlock the door to the back area. After pulling open the door open he motioned me inside and locked the door behind us.

He leaned against the wall across from me. His dark hair fell around his face but didn't obscure his ebony eyes from view. His black dress shirt was loose around his pants with the top buttons undone, exposing a portion of his chest and throat.

He looked as alluring as he did lethal; a dangerous combination.

"What's the matter?" I asked after a lengthy silence.

He answered by stepping forward, his large hands grasping my face, onyx eyes focused.

"What the fuck are you doing?" I yelped and struggled to get free.

"I can't see your future." His black stare locked with mine, filling me with trepidation. "I can see your past, and I can see your future through the eyes of others, but I can't see it from you."

I stopped thrashing as the meaning of his words sank in. "You can't?"

He shook his head. "I haven't touched anyone in over one-hundred and forty years without seeing how they die or what tragedies will touch their lives. But you... you're totally blank."

"You've seen me through the eyes of others? What's that supposed to mean?"

He dropped his hands and stepped away. "I can't answer that."

"Why not?"

"It's not beneficial to know anything about the future, especially events that you would be tempted to change." He leaned against the wall once more, watching me.

"But you can save the lives of the people you care about. Isn't that worth something?"

"Every action, every choice we make, has an impact on the future. There is such a thing as free will, but there is also fate, and the two do intersect." His tone changed, sending a chill up my spine. "If someone cheats death, then everyone in their life will be affected by the ripple that follows it. Every decision by a dead man becomes a new form of the future, with different outcomes and tragedies. Most of the time, those you care for will suffer because they are in the path that was never intended to exist. So no, it's not worth something. All I can do is shoulder the truth alone. I can't intervene, no matter who the person is or how much I want to."

Now I knew why he was so detached. Hell, I would be too.

I murmured lamely, "I'm sorry."

"I'm only telling you this because"—he paused—"I want you to understand that I'm not a Magic Eight Ball. I can't deviate from the given course."

"Well shit." I rolled my eyes dramatically. "Does this mean I can't shake you to find out if I can expect to make it home before the sun comes up?"

He smiled, chuckled softly, and his cold eyes warmed. The change was baffling and took me by surprise when he answered, "Ask again later."

CHAPTER TWENTY

Disco and Joseph came to the agreement that from this point forward it was a combined effort. That meant Rainbow Brite, Goose, and I had to get together for a play date. Since I'd broken rule number one of happy fun-time etiquette—thou shall not hit—I didn't think it was going to be a fun day, but we'd see.

I was willing to forgive her dumb ass for attempting to pull one over on us so long as she didn't hold a grudge for my power drive to her chin.

I hopped off the 7 at Bryant Park and walked over to 5th Avenue. Most people ventured to the New York Public Library to get their reading fix, but there was always at least one group of tourists who had to see where *Ghostbusters* was filmed. Screw history. They wanted movie magic, damn it! I once saw an overzealous fan straddle the lion statue only to fall off into the barrier along the side. I almost felt sorry for her, but let's face it—no one forced her to be a moron.

The library was beautiful, quiet, and unlike the movie depicted, the ghosts in residence left you alone. Most of them walked along the rows of desks, completely content in their own little universe. One in particular always roamed around the McGraw Rotunda, fixated on the Moses mural. I dubbed her Zippo after Moses's wife, Zipporah. I hoped I didn't burn in hell for the blasphemy.

I arrived early, too anxious from the previous night to sleep or sit still. Paine was surprisingly easy to talk to and seemed excited at the prospect of having someone nearby who wasn't susceptible to his ability, but I didn't have the opportunity to heckle him with more questions. Disco and Joseph called everyone back upstairs within minutes to lay out the master plan.

The blood supply was to be diverted through Dexter, and he wasn't happy about it.

In the meantime, Lorence, Chris, and Marcus couldn't deal anymore until they got the go ahead, unless they wanted to become chew toys. They also couldn't leave town, forced to wait and offer any help we felt was necessary.

Sonja, Goose, and I were to pool our resources, and hopefully, stir up some ghost juju. The goal was to make contact or unearth new information before the heart snatchers chose to move on.

The people seated at the library tables were scattered about—most with books and pencils—scribbling notes and ideas for new inventions that would make them millions. I placed my elbows on the desk and braced my chin on my palms, daydreaming of what life might have been.

A camouflage satchel barreled in front of me, stopping just inches from my arms. I pulled back and looked up in surprise.

Sonja looked completely normal. Sure, her hair was in a vast assortment of the rainbow, but it didn't look too bad cascading with the long blonde strands over her shoulders. Her beautiful light blue eyes shone through her thick, dark-rimmed glasses. No wonder the contacts from the night before were so vivid, there was barely any pigmentation behind them.

She was dressed down in faded blue jeans with a navy blue sweatshirt tied neatly around her waist. Her simple grey fitted T-shirt had NYU across the chest in a coordinating navy color.

The only thing that gave away her nightly activities was the mark on her throat.

"You'll catch bugs with your mouth hanging open like that," she informed me haughtily, hands on her hips. Her fingernails were painted perfectly, in bubblegum pink no less.

"Touché." I nodded in admiration and closed my mouth. A girl after my own smartass heart. Maybe this wouldn't be so bad after all. I looked her up and down one more time, motioning at her pep rally best. "I take it Mommy and Daddy don't know their little girl moonlights in leather with vampires after dark?"

"My parents are dead, if you must know." She pulled out a chair, eased onto it, and tossed multicolored strands of hair over her shoulders. I was tempted to ask how in the hell you achieved a dye job like that. Was it even real hair? "Do yours know about your nasty penchant for violence?"

"I'd imagine they do, if that business about looking down from Heaven holds any water." I returned her smile, rubbing my knuckles under my jaw. "How's the chin?"

She glared at me through the dark frames of her glasses. "Fine, no thanks to you."

"I'm just trying to be polite," I said, unable to suppress a grin. I *was* trying to be polite but also maintain my dark sense of humor.

"No, you're not," she snapped, drawing a quiet reprimand from a person two rows over. She crossed her arms over her chest and fumed in silence.

Damn. Our play date wasn't going well, and I did promise Disco I would be on my best behavior. I leaned over to whisper, "Of course I am." I pointed at the NYU shirt and tried to start a lukewarm conversation. "What are you going to school for?"

"Archaeological Anthropology." Her eyes flittered up and down my torso, accessing me. "What about you? Do you attend college?"

I had taken classes when I arrived in New York four years ago, but it didn't last. Not after I fell into the pitfalls of rent, utilities, and food. Somehow I didn't think imparting the knowledge I'd maintained a 3.9 grade point average during that time would impress her all that much.

"I graduated from Dilligan's in the Bronx with a degree in bartending. I work over at The Black Panther now."

Her nose crinkled and her lips pursed together. Barbie didn't know whether to run for the nearest shower, stick around and hope for the best, or haul ass out the door and tell Joseph fuck it. I could sympathize. If she pulled out rollers and fingernail polish, I was liable to upchuck all over the polished wood floors. Sometimes you just have to see the bright side of the situation. In this case, we both knew the sooner we got the job done, the sooner we could bid each other a not so fond farewell. I definitely wouldn't be braiding her a friendship bracelet anytime soon.

"How...ambitious."

I shrugged, refusing to take the bait, and sat back in my chair, waiting for the Goose to arrive. He and Ms. NYU would go together like peas and carrots.

We didn't wait long. Goose came into the room calm and relaxed, a navy satchel slung across his shoulder. I felt out of place. All the cool kids had nifty bags, and all I brought were my pockets.

He slid into the seat next to me. "I hope I'm not late."

"Nope," I said and offered a smile.

Sonja didn't comment; she reached across the table, and pulled her bag into her lap like a sullen teenager. Goose had plenty of experience dealing with this sort of behavior recently, so if he noticed, it didn't bother him.

He sorted through his bag for a heavy tome and placed it on the table. "I've been thinking. Why is it we haven't been able to communicate or locate the spirits of any of the twice dead through our own natural outlets or by ritual? Why has it only been by chance?"

I frowned and answered, "I assumed it was because the spirits had passed over."

"That's what I thought too. It would account for the reason we haven't seen any other souls besides Baxter and Jacob. But what if it's because their souls were exorcised, forced over to the next plane so that no one would have the opportunity to seek them after?" He flipped through the pages until he found the underlined passage he sought. "It isn't uncommon after we raise the dead to order them permanently to rest. Of course, that is invoking necromancy to the fullest extent of the word, not the sciomancy we are more prone to use."

"I don't see a spell," I whispered, glancing over what appeared to be one of his personal journals. His handwriting was more difficult to read this time.

"That's just it," he said. "There isn't one. When we reanimate a body, it requires oils, blood or a sacrifice, incantation, and a circle to return a form of life. Ordering the spirit on to the next plane would require someone aligned with the church. Someone ordained to exorcise spirits."

"It would make sense." Sonja joined in the conversation, sounding excited. "That would keep whoever is doing this hidden."

"You think a priest is killing vampires?" My voice rose in alarm, and I got the dreaded 'shh.' I cringed in apology and lifted my fingers to my mouth in embarrassment.

"It would also explain access to unlimited holy relics. Someone could bless enough rope or silver to contain several victims at once," Goose explained in a rush.

Sonja cast a glance around the room. "With that kind of power, there is no limit to what someone could do."

"Explain this one to me," I said softly. "Who can trap a vampire? Holy relics, demonic priests, and logic aside. How would someone lure one in? Think about it. After the first few vanished, vampires got wise. There wouldn't be easy targets anymore."

"So far, they only share one connection, and that's donating to the blood market," Goose said.

"No. They also share the"—I crooked my index fingers into bunny ears for emphasis—"*big* connection. As in, they suck blood full time for a living."

"I don't see your point." Goose stared at me dumbly, and I rolled my eyes.

"And you're supposed to be smarter than I am?" I sighed. "You told me that some necromancers have the power to control the dead, right? Why haven't we considered the possibility that vampires are easy to target because they are, you know—*dead*. Why haven't we accounted for the fact that maybe one of *us* is lending a hand here?"

"If that's true, the ramifications could be devastating." Alarm crossed Sonja's delicate features. "The only vampires who would conceivably be immune would be masters with familiars, and that's not a guarantee."

I looked from one to the other. "Why would they be immune?"

"You really should read a book sometime," Sonja snapped.

"I'm sorry," I quipped back, keeping my voice muffled. "The local Barnes and Noble is all out of *Necromancy for Dummies*, but I'll be sure to stop by this afternoon and see if they're back in stock."

Sonja leveled a stare at me. "It's because they are tied to the living through us, just as we are connected to the dead through them. They can't be lured or controlled by something with power over the dead if there is a spark of the living inside them. Still, a necromancer that powerful is a danger to all of us, especially if they are unmarked and unmonitored."

"I need to call Sharon," Goose said. "If we can pin down the name of someone who left L.A. around the same those murders went down, then we might get lucky."

"What are you going to do?" I asked half-jokingly. "Call up for a list of the necro-Trekkies in the area?"

"Actually, yes, I am." He glared at me and I writhed in my seat. I hated that look. It sent me back twenty years, to Mrs. Adams's first grade class. It was the first evil look of my existence, and the most indelible.

I glanced around the library and asked, "And what do we do in the meantime?"

We could always ingest a bundle of knowledge while we waited. Actually, the walking encyclopedias didn't need to beef up their ghoulish knowledge. That hardship would fall directly upon me.

"We make emplacement charms. With all that's happened, we can't be too safe." Sonja sorted through her bag. "I brought all the necessary items. We just need to find a place to invoke them."

Goose pushed his chair away from the table and rose. "We can go to the park."

He led us out of the library, past the ropes, and out the door. He hooked a left at the base of the stairs, walking to Bryant Park from 42nd Street. The streets weren't crowded, and when we entered the cover of trees, we easily found an empty table. The weather was amazing, a nice brisk seventy-degrees and sunny.

I loved New York in the fall.

Sonja took two plastic baggies from her satchel. The first had little white plastic things that reminded me of the prongs you use in the board game, *Life*. The big fat circle on the end looked like an enormous head, while the thin rectangular shape was the body. The other baggie held three tiny pieces of wood attached to a thin red string.

She handed out the white pieces of plastic, and then emptied the tiny wooden circles into her hand. "Once we activate these, we'll be able to find each other in a given radius should the need arise. Any safeguards are better than none."

She handed out the pieces of wood by the red string. I took mine and studied it. It was made out of some kind of porous wood with a tiny clear stone embedded into one side.

I glanced up, watched her pull the circle off her little piece of plastic, and jab her index finger. A red dot swelled, and she ran it along the charm on the opposite side of the stone. I looked at Goose, who was doing the same.

"What exactly am I poking myself for?" I asked like the bumbling ignoramus I was.

"Your blood activates the charm. See the stone? It will glow when you approach the person the charm belongs to—watch." Sonja held hers out and I cupped it in my palm. The little gem shone a vivid bright blue. I let go and reached for my little piece of plastic. Poking my ring finger, I mimicked what I'd seen. Within seconds, my stone was glowing bright blue as well.

"Groovy." I nodded and smiled. "Are you making these for everyone else?"

"It's a form of earth magic." Sonja barely contained her irritation at my questions, but I gave her Brownie points for the effort. "Since the earth is a living, breathing thing, the charm only works with living people."

She shifted her attention to Goose. "Now we need to exchange them."

We went counterclockwise. Her to Goose. Goose to me. Me to her.

I stuffed my charm into my pocket. I wasn't sure if it would come in handy, but if I got into a tight spot, at least they'd know where to send the cavalry.

"Don't let anything made with salt touch that," Sonja warned. "It will nullify the spell."

"No sodium, got it." I nodded, and she looked ready to explode.

Goose placed the Sonja's charm in a zippered pocket on his bag and said, "I think we should try to channel Jacob. I want to meet at my apartment tonight for a séance. My living room already has a circle marked, and I have all the necessary items."

"I can do that." Sonja took a seat, crossing her blue jean clad legs. "The three of us should have more than enough energy to bring him around. Do you want to try to contact any of the others while we're at it?"

"It can't hurt." Goose pulled a business card from his bag and passed it to Sonja.

She inspected it thoroughly, as if she were trying to ensure he didn't use Kinko's for all his printing needs. "There's my address. Let's all meet at say... seven?"

"Sure," I answered. "That will give me time to hit the gym."

Goose pulled the bag over his head and settled it across his body. "I'm going home. I need to call Sharon to see if she can offer any help." He gave me a reproach-ful look. "Try to stay out of trouble."

"You know me."

He hustled off, carefully avoiding people in his path. I chuckled when he tripped on a non-existent something on the ground, struggling over his own feet. It was a universal law. To maintain that delicate balance someone had to excel at one thing and do piss poor in another. Since Goose had an Einstein brain, it was only fair that he have Steve Urkel-like reflexes.

Sonja was staring at me. I couldn't get a read on her expression. On one hand, it seemed she was genuinely interested and wanted to make nice. On the other, she seemed to hate everything I represented because I was something she didn't understand. Maybe it was both. Or maybe it was the result of eating something that didn't agree with her that morning.

"Joseph said you saw Baxter. Is that true?"

"I did." I was uncertain of where she was going with the question and that made me a little uncomfortable.

"Was it—" Her voice faltered and her eyes brimmed with tears. "Was it fast?"

Comprehension struck swiftly. Baxter didn't just leave a brother behind. I was hardened, but tears usually worked me over, especially when they were tears of loss. I averted my eyes, knowing that I couldn't lie to her and realizing the truth wasn't what she would want to hear.

"He didn't focus on the pain," I confessed. "If anything, it was fast because his mind was elsewhere."

"Where was it?" Her voice caught, and I knew I was screwed.

"He wanted to know where the next stop was going to be, and if he was getting a ticket to the pearly gates." I blew out a shaky breath and dared a cautious glance in her direction.

"We spoke about that a lot." She smiled sadly, her ice blue eyes brimming with unshed tears. "He wanted to believe there was a Heaven, even for them. But he couldn't shake the fear of what came after if he was wrong."

"Then we can only hope wherever he is, he's in a good place."

"No," she corrected me angrily. "We will make sure he goes to that place. When this is over, I plan on using your help to ease his soul to the other side."

I didn't know what to say, so I decided to call it a day. I pushed back my chair and stood, ready to leave the park and get something to eat before I went to the gym.

"Are you so spiteful you can't even help a lost soul find rest?" She spat out the words, heavy tears spilling down her cheekbones in salty trails.

I heard myself speaking before I could weigh the consequences. "No. If I can help ease him to the other side, I will."

Damn tears, they always melted me.

I didn't open another window of opportunity for her to speak as I walked past the table and out of the park.

CHAPTER TWENTY-ONE

Mike's Gym is not extravagant or exclusive, the machinery isn't state of the art, and you won't find a specially trained nutritionist in the building to help you count those dreaded calories. What you will find is a good place to work up a sweat, get your ass in gear, and make sure your heart and muscles pound and throb until you're ready to drop.

I decided to take it easy for my workout, taping up my wrists and donning gloves to work the bag. It was a great cardio exercise and helped me focus on my form. I learned a long time ago that the bag wasn't some simple piece of equipment that people could use to look good. If utilized properly, you could hone your strength, balance, and coordination.

I stopped when the light outside dimmed. After I retrieved my duffel from the locker room, I hit the shower. Once my body was freshly scrubbed, I pulled my hair into a ponytail, creating a faux bob with wisps of hair falling loose. I tossed on my clean clothes, dressing for comfort and not ass kicking, and studied myself in the mirror.

My mark managed to peek out from the sweater, especially with my hair off my shoulders, but was only notable if you were staring. My comfortable best was probably Sonja's definition of slouch fest. I returned to my duffel, pulled out my makeup and slapped some on. It wasn't a total loss. I managed to pull off the look that gives the impression you're not trying too hard but you really don't need to.

"Hey, Rhiannon." Mike motioned to me as I rounded the corner and approached the lobby.

He was standing behind the counter, all veins, tan, and muscle. I cringed when I looked at his arms. The pronounced blue veins were super juicy and thick. He kept his hair buzzed short, and his shiny scalp showed clearly through the blackish stubble.

"You have a hot date or something?"

I broke into a smile and laughed. "No, it's nothing like that. I have some work to take care of and I figured I should at least look halfway decent."

"Did you leave The Black Panther?" He and Cletus were tight. He probably thought he was being kept outside of the loop.

"Nah, I'm still over there. I'm just helping out a friend."

"He must be some friend. You've been coming here what, over a year? And I've never seen you dressed like that."

"Trust me." I snickered. Even picturing Goose and me together as a couple was too much. "If you saw this guy, you'd apologize for even thinking that."

I hiked the duffel over my shoulder and walked outside. The sky was pink now, turning purple fast. If I hit the subway in time, I just might make it.

"Pardon me." A lithe, blonde woman approached me, her words eloquent and clear. "Rhiannon Murphy?"

I turned as I responded, "Yeah."

She was in gym clothes, but her voice gave her away. She wasn't here for the workout. She held herself too rigid, too uptight, and too damned uppity.

"Hi, my name is Rachel Greene." Her eyes were a lovely liquid brown with green centers. She seemed nervous. "Is there somewhere we might speak?"

"That depends." I nailed her with my no-nonsense stare. "What do you want?"

"Can we please go somewhere private?" She sounded desperate, big two-toned eyes practically pleading.

"Listen." I gave a fake half smile. "This is as good as it gets. If you need to talk to me, talk. I have somewhere to be, and you're making me late."

"I apologize for the intrusion." She drew her shoulders up and back, straightening her spine. "I'm a private investigator hired by Carrie Shaw."

My blood turned to ice, and my heart began to race. "Fuck off," I snarled. *Carrie Shaw.* That was one name I didn't want to hear today. No fucking way this shit was happening to me now. I turned to walk away.

"Please, Ms. Murphy." She kept pace beside me, talking quickly. "Mrs. Shaw is devastated by what happened, and she wants to make amends. She asked me to locate you. She wants to meet with you and express how truly sorry she is."

"Tell her to go see Jennifer Cunningham if she wants someone to apologize to."

"Ms. Cunningham is unavailable—" She stopped talking when I skidded to a halt and came face to face with her.

Something unhinged inside me. Something I'd kept locked way for years. "I want you to listen to me, *real fucking good.* You and I both know Jennifer isn't unavailable. I can tell you *exactly* where to find her. She's been living in the Florida State Mental Hospital the last eleven years." I was breathing heavy, my body shaking. I balled my hands into fists, telling myself repeatedly to keep it down, to keep it cool.

"I'm aware of Ms. Cunningham's circumstances, as is your foster mother." Her voice softened, perhaps in an attempt to come across as apologetic. She addressed me carefully. "But this is about her speaking with you. She has changed and wants to set things right. She's been trying to contact you the last few years. All she wants is the opportunity to ask for your forgiveness."

"Don't be so goddamned stupid." I bit out each word through clenched teeth. I couldn't even smile at her shocked face, I was too hot. It took all of my restraint to keep from screaming at the top of my lungs. Stepping closer, I bumped against her retreating body. I wanted to shake the piss out of her, but I chose another route.

This moronic woman was nothing more than a stranger I'd never see again, someone who wouldn't make my stomach sink or my skin crawl when I passed her in the streets because I knew she was aware of the demons from my past. In light of my circumstances, she was the perfect outlet for everything I'd kept locked away for too long.

Rachel Greene was in the wrong place at the wrong fucking time.

"Did Mommy Dearest tell you about the sick things she let go down in that little Christian household of hers, Rachel?"

Her face blanked and she gave a pitiful nod. I wanted to laugh. She didn't know. She didn't know anything at all.

I could remedy that.

"No?" I shook my head and gave her a hard look. "Fuck it. I'll tell you myself. I moved into that cesspool when I was ten years old. Jennifer was only two years older, but you wouldn't know it to meet her. The first time I met the poor kid she had the eyes of an old woman, and after those first few weeks, I knew why. You see, Ray Shaw, Carrie's husband, liked his girls young. He used to say when it sprouted hair, it was too old. That's the kind of sick bastard I'm talking about. And he'd been enjoying time with Jennifer for a couple of years before I came into family."

"There is no reason for you to be crude, Ms. Murphy." She folded her arms and looked at me with clear distain.

"That's not crude." I laughed spitefully, my voice laced with menace and years of pent up resentment. "*This* is crude. Every fucking night I listened to Jennifer crying and begging in the guest bedroom. Only I wasn't the only one who heard Ray telling her to shut the fuck up and take it all. So did Carrie Shaw. She knew about everything, and she didn't do shit. She sat back while her husband raped a child under her own roof. Night after goddamned night. Hell, the heartless bitch washed the sex stained sheets every morning."

"I don't have to listen to this." Mortified, she turned to walk away.

I grasped her forearm, fingers biting into her skin. "Oh, you'll listen," I snarled, snaking my fingers around her wrist. I reminded myself to keep it down. "You came to me, remember?" I continued without her permission. "He was in the middle of raping Jennifer the first time he let her know I was next on the menu. She was sixteen by then, and I'd just turned fourteen. I was a brand new freshman in high school, and he didn't want someone else getting to that virgin pussy of mine before he could. Those were his words *exactly*."

"Let go of my arm," she snapped. Her eyes were huge saucers, and her face had turned a sickly shade of white. Maybe she wasn't aware of what had happened inside the little house on Bridge Street, but so help me God, I was going to tell her.

"One Thursday night, he tells Jennifer, 'tomorrow its Rhia's turn.' He taunts her with the different ways he's going to tear me apart, and then he pounds her so hard she can't walk the next morning. But there was a little something Ray didn't count on, a miniscule problem decent fathers don't worry about contributing to directly—teenage pregnancy. Jennifer found out a week before that she was in the family way, and that's when her mind started to slip. She went batty, hearing voices and seeing things that weren't there, losing her shit and saying delusional things."

Rachel Greene had stopped struggling. She was listening now, probably too disgusted to turn away. It was like the train wrecks you always hear about—too much blood and carnage to stomach but too distracting to ignore. That's the way it worked with sick shit. You couldn't help but watch.

"The night he came after me was the straw that broke the camel's back. He took me into the bedroom, stripped me bare while I fought his ass tooth and nail, and told me he was about to get a piece of tightest snatch in the world. Jennifer waited until he was distracted before she came into the room, yanked his head back by a handful of his balding hair, and slit his throat with the serrated kitchen knife we used to carve the Thanksgiving turkey. She sawed so deep she scored the bone and nearly cut his depraved head clear off. But I didn't care. I was glad the sick bastard was dead."

She stood silent and unmoving, mouth slight agape.

"Do you want to know what happened after?"

She nodded and I smirked. Of course she did. Every good story has to have a twisted ending. "Jennifer lost it. The combination of abuse, fear, and desperation drove her to a place that no normal person could ever understand. But God help her, she loved me. In those years, we formed an unbreakable bond, and she swore she would never let anything or anyone hurt me. Too bad that mind of hers was shattered. She was so far gone she could only imagine me being placed in a home with pervert just like Ray. So she shoved the sick fucker's carcass out of the way, climbed onto the bed, and told me after she killed me she would kill herself. She sank the same blade she used to kill Ray into me five times before the police arrived. It took murder to get Carrie off her worthless ass, but by then, it was too late. Jennifer got shipped off to the loony bin, and the last time I saw her, she was so lost she couldn't even tell you what day of the week it was."

I let go of Rachel's arm and stepped back, oddly deflated and empty. "Don't come here asking me to meet with Carrie Shaw. I sure as shit will not make that bitch feel better because she decided to get a conscience after all this time and can't sleep at night. I haven't slept well in fifteen-years."

"She said it was bad, but she didn't divulge those details." Rachel's eyes were huge, her oval face full of revulsion, and, I was pretty sure, a dash of pity.

"Why would she?" I shrugged, my destructive frustration ebbing. "She was always the kind of woman who only cared about herself. Sure, Ray beat the shit out of her, and she had to walk a fine line just like we did. But I'll tell you this. When she discovered abuse could be dealt out elsewhere, she didn't think twice about keeping her ass out of the line of fire. She was the adult. It was her job to protect us. She couldn't even do that because she was too concerned about her own ass. People like that don't change."

Rachel cleared her throat in an attempt to regain her professionalism. I bet she didn't handle many cases like mine. If she did, I hoped she was royally fucking compensated.

"What would you like me to tell her?"

"Tell her that if she sends anyone else to find me, I won't just come for a visit. I'll come knocking on her front door for payback. And when I do swing by, I'll stop by the hospital and make sure to bring Jennifer along with me." I nodded at her and started back down the sidewalk. The sun was almost gone now, and the streetlights were coming on.

I was going to be late. *Damn it to hell.*

"Wait," Rachel called out and I stopped.

"You said she was pregnant. What happened to the baby?"

I chewed on my bottom lip as I strolled back to where she stood. People appeared on the sidewalk, and I didn't want to offend the general public, so I kept my voice down.

"When the police arrived, there was so much blood they didn't see the knife. They could tell by the compromising position we were in that Ray was a demented piece of shit, and they automatically assumed it was a case of self-defense. They pulled Jennifer off me, went to work on my injuries, and that gave her just enough time to bury the blade from tip to hilt inside her belly button." I smiled at her stunned expression. "I'm pretty sure that took care of it."

CHAPTER TWENTY-TWO

I was more than fashionably late to Goose's soiree, and I dreaded knocking on his door. I wasn't in the mood to be around people, my mind stuck somewhere in the sands of time.

The last time I saw my foster sister was the day I left Miami. She didn't know I was there. She looked so lost, her once gorgeous hazel eyes empty, her flaxen hair greasy and stringy. Her psychiatrist kept her well medicated. It was the only way to keep her from killing herself or someone else.

Jennifer was classified psychotic for good reason.

I took my time walking down Goose's street. Brooklyn Heights was a nice area and relatively safe to wander alone. It was quiet now, with only a few people walking along the sidewalks. I unwittingly drifted into Never Never Land, sorting through my past, present, and future. Things didn't turn out the way I thought, and I wasn't sure how I'd reached this point. Now that I was here, I didn't know what to do or expect.

I thought of Disco, and that wrenching sensation of being torn in two overwhelmed me—something that happened each time I pictured his face or those heavenly golden blue eyes. I had never been so conflicted in my life. Normally, I knew exactly where I stood in situations, but not so much anymore. The black and white areas that governed my decisions just took on a huge middle ground of grey.

My daftness proved to be my undoing yet again. I thwacked into an older woman with her mixed breed ankle biter, our shoulders knocking each other off course. I took the "watch where the fuck you're going" in stride, nodding and muttering a half-assed apology, eager to get downwind of the Icy Hot wafting from her body and into my nose.

I closed my eyes and groaned when I heard chuckling. Disco was gentleman enough to laugh out loud and announce his presence instead of startling the piss out of me, but it didn't erase the fact he was laughing.

Being humiliated always made me cranky.

"You *do* have a short attention span," he teased.

I glanced up. He was waiting on the stairs, eyes sparkling in amusement. Dear God, would I always find ways to look like an asshole in his presence?

I was grateful I'd decided to make the extra effort with my appearance, because he had too. He was dressed in black, as usual, but in a different style, without the trench coat. The shirt was a nice long sleeve button down, the collar open around his throat. He'd also left his honey blond hair unkempt, and I worried he might have read my mind that night I'd thought about just how amazing it made him look.

"Laugh it up," I grumbled.

He was busy taking me in, starting at my feet and working his way up. He approved of my change of attire and wanted me to know it, taking his time and allowing his eyes to linger. I looked away, annoyed by my awkwardness.

"You look delectable." He used his uncanny speed to close the distance between us. I gazed up into his eyes, utterly transfixed by the shifting colors. "I'm going to buy an entire wardrobe consisting of things just like this for you."

How do you respond to a remark like that? I had no clue and, at the present moment, I didn't care. His close proximity made me remember the heat I experienced on the couch in his foyer, and this time, I couldn't completely fault the blood. I was attracted to Disco whether I wanted to be or not, and he knew it. The smart thing to do would have been to back away, but I didn't want to. That grey area expanded, melding black and white together until there was no concept of right or wrong.

His right hand came up, fingers nestling against the back of my neck. He brushed his thumb down my throat, pushing aside the material obscuring my mark from view. The first graze of cool skin against his bite made my knees crumble. I dropped the duffel and sagged. He anticipated just that or he used his speed, pulling me close, keeping me upright. I braced myself with my hands, grasping his muscled bicep and waist, gazing into his face.

Disco's eyes were mesmeric. The multilayered colors sparkled like vibrant jewels. The ocean blue base was darker, the vortex on top a beautiful array of violet, green, and teal. The black circle along the edge dipped inward, creating a pattern reminiscent of flower petals. Glowing on top were the dazzling flecks of gold, brilliant in the dark.

His face descended, lips coming toward my own. He wanted me to know what he intended, giving me the opportunity to push away. His eyes engulfed me, growing larger as he closed the distance. His lips lightly grazed mine, and I closed my eyes, the whisper of air leaving my mouth captured in his.

Butterflies erupted in my stomach and chest, a delicious heat spreading through my limbs. I opened my mouth and his tongue delved inside, gentle but insistent. The moment I reacted, caressing his tongue, he groaned and crushed me tightly to his chest.

He tasted addicting, and when he deepened the kiss, I mirrored his lapping, swirling my tongue in harmony with his. My heart pounded as my awareness heightened. Tracing the line of his jaw with my fingers, I skimmed over his throat, forging a path to his heart. The solid, steady beating helped bring me back to reality.

I opened my eyes and he lifted his head, my gaze caught once again in those enormous pools of blue. Suddenly I knew what I'd missed, the most minor of details.

"No smoke," I murmured.

"What's that?" He enclosed my hand in his and held it against his chest.

"Did you quit smoking?"

"You finally noticed?" A broad grin spread across face. "I was beginning to wonder if it even mattered. I can forgive the oversight now, seeing as you have a tendency to over look things with your impressive attention span."

"Why did you quit?"

"Don't you know?" When I shook my head, a breathtaking grin lit his face, making his eyes shimmer. "I felt drawn to you the first time I saw you, Rhiannon. I've tried to deny the complexities of my feelings, but every time I'm in your presence, they always return. Our kind experiences all things intensely, and emotions are equally difficult to suppress. As selfish as it makes me, I won't hide the way I feel for you any longer. I couldn't if I wanted to. The least I could do is put down the cigarettes you so obviously detest."

I was flattered, taken aback, shocked, and totally scared out of my goddamned mind. A gambit of emotions assembled in one huge helping, served on a tiny did-you-see-that-coming plate. Words escaped me. So many thoughts scattered through my mind that was unable to formulate a coherent response. Kissing someone because you felt an attraction, I could handle. But when you gave up a habit to impress that special person, well, that meant something else all together.

"It doesn't change what I am, does it?" His eyebrows drew together as he misinterpreted my silence.

"It's not that," I managed to say. I wasn't good at emotional shit. Extending that fragile part of me was something I never allowed. It was my cardinal rule for staying safe. The deepest wounds are inflicted by those you care for. Anyone can kill you physically, but being brutalized emotionally was an entirely different matter.

"What is it, then?"

"As clichéd as it sounds, it's me. I'm not...I don't...damn!" I growled at myself in annoyance. I not only looked like a douche; I sounded like one too. "I haven't had many boyfriends, Disco. I'm not saying that's what you meant when you said..." I groaned in mortification.

Fucking hell, I couldn't even do this right!

He waited while I tried again.

"I'm not good at relationships or depending on other people. I've been on my own since I was fourteen. It's how I've lived the last nine years of my life."

"Do you want to spend the next nine like this?"

The question hurt on several levels. Especially as it implied something was wrong or disturbing about how I lived. I knew I wasn't normal. Most people thrived on some level of companionship. Me? I didn't even own a Chia Pet.

"I don't know."

His lips pressed against mine, hard and demanding. The hand at my nape pulled my face closer, allowing him to devour my lips. I responded automatically, sexual instinct taking over. No matter what rules I had regarding my life, they couldn't govern my reactions to him. I met each thrust of his tongue with my own, fingers clutching at his neck and shirt.

He placed his hands on each side of my face, pulling away, and forced me to look at him. "You can't deny how you feel about me any more than I can about you." He breathed the words against my face, a silky timbre seeping into his voice.

"This is completely insane," I argued feebly. "And it would never work."

"Why don't we withhold our judgment until we know that for certain? I'm not asking for your soul, Rhiannon. I'm only asking you to take a chance. How long has it been since you've done that? Allow yourself to fall. I'll catch you."

His lips skimmed across my cheek and I closed my eyes, attempting to think rationally. "You could have any woman you possibly wanted. Why can't you pester them?"

It was a serious question that came out laughable. I realized subconsciously I wanted to do what he asked. I was in serious danger of pressing my luck.

"Sirah asked the same question." He chuckled against my hair.

"Maybe you should listen to her."

"When she said that, I knew I was making the right decision. None of us put stock into anything that woman says. Actually, we all agree if Sirah advises something, do the exact opposite. She inadvertently gave you her seal of approval." He ran his hands down my arms, causing the skin to tingle.

"I'll think about it." I attempted to move away.

"No." He shook his head, peering down. "If you think about it, you'll find a million different reasons to say no." He tugged me gently, closing the distance between us. "Have dinner with me."

I squirmed anxiously. "You don't eat food, and I don't like eating alone."

"If you don't want to have dinner, tell me what you'd like to do, and we'll do it." His fingers squeezed my arms and then began gently massaging the sore muscles.

I smiled uncomfortably, words husky. "Listen, I appreciate what you're trying to do. This kind of thing doesn't happen to women like me. But don't you think it's best if we assess the situation and cut our losses beforehand? I'm not worth the headache you're sure to have if we take this any further. And no offense, but I don't see you as the going to the movies and taking a walk in the park kind of guy, which is what I assume normal people do when they date...if that's what you're asking for in the first place."

"Women like you?" He chuckled in amusement, shaking his head. "A date is exactly what I'm asking for, and a movie and walk in the park is fine. What about tomorrow night?"

"With everything that's going on, I don't think now is the appropriate time." I didn't want to say no, but I had to try and wiggle out of this. I was holding a can of kerosene while standing next to a blazing pit of fire.

"We could both use a distraction and there is no better time than the present. What time should I pick you up?"

I had heard this tone before. It was the same one used when I declined his offer to escort me home. He wouldn't take no for an answer, even if I argued.

"I don't think it's a good idea—"

"What time?" Again, he forced me to meet his incredibly beautiful blue eyes, which was cheating.

I tried to glare at him, but my eyes betrayed me. "You really want to do this? The first time wasn't incredibly successful, if you recall."

"First time?" he looked and sounded confused, two things I never encountered from Disco simultaneously. His face lifted into a mischievous smile. "That wasn't a date. Not in the slightest."

"No? Just an opportunity to let your family watch me squirm." This time, my glare was genuine. Envisioning all of them observing us that night pissed me off. With everything going on, I'd almost forgotten about my anger regarding it.

"I can't deny Paine was there. It is his bar after all. Now, stop avoiding the question. If you don't give me an answer, I'll simply wager a guess. Either way, I'll be knocking on your door tomorrow night."

"Fine." I scowled but I was equal parts annoyed, flattered, and excited. Damn my hormones to hell and me right along with them. I was sealing my own fate. I could only blame myself. "How does seven o'clock sound?"

"It sounds perfect." He smiled, eyes vivid and bright, the blue impossibly clear. "I'll be there."

He kissed me again, and I figured to hell with it. I already had one foot in the door. I slid my hands under his arms, gripping his back through his shirt. This time, Disco was different. His full lips were gentle, bestowing a multitude of soft kisses that were both endearing and sweet. Something I hadn't experienced in years came to life, the tiniest fluttering inside my chest, and I pulled away before the emotion could intensify.

"I should go inside, I'm already late." I looked past him to the door. I was going to be interrogated by Goose, reamed and teased mercilessly. I returned my focus to Disco, suspicion creeping over me. "What are *you* doing here anyway?"

"Joseph and I accepted Ethan's invitation to observe tonight. I wanted to wait out here for you, away from prying eyes."

"Great," I muttered, palming my forehead and groaning at Disco's soft laughter. Everyone would get to witness my utter lack of knowledge when it came to my ability firsthand.

I sighed and braced myself.

What was one more humiliation?

CHAPTER TWENTY-THREE

When Disco and I arrived, everything was set. Goose moved the rug from the center of the living room to reveal a large intricate pattern painted into the wood. It wasn't like those depicted in the movies. This circle consisted of three interlocking patterns. The first design was a normal red circle, which formed the base. The second pattern, above the red, was painted white. The final design was painted black.

I was to sit outside the circle, as were Goose and Sonja. Disco and Joseph were told to stay completely out of the room and watched from the entranceway.

Goose informed us we would attempt to contact Jacob first. If we got lucky, Sonja would work as a medium, offering to channel his voice to answer crucial questions. If everything went according to plan, this would be easy.

Naturally, I knew it was too good to be true.

Goose pulled a tiny vial from his pocket, unscrewed the lid, and put a finger on top. He flipped it over in a fast motion, down and back up, and placed the anointed finger on his forehead, drawing a cross with the shiny liquid on his finger. He said something in a foreign language and walked to Sonja, who did the same thing. She returned the tiny bottle to Goose, and he walked to me.

"Take some of the oil on your finger and make the sign of the cross on your forehead."

Goose extended the vial to me. Inside, there were sprigs of what I distinguished immediately as mint. I took a sniff and wrinkled my nose at the potent aroma. The liquid was thick and clear with a gold tint. I made the sign of a cross on my forehead as instructed.

"The words you speak need to carry conviction so you'll need to say this in English. Repeat after me—protect me and keep me, thus no harm shall befall me."

"Protect me and keep me, thus no harm shall befall me," I repeated dutifully.

Nodding, he took the vial and screwed on the tiny black lid. "No matter what happens, stay outside of the circle. Understand?"

I frowned at him. "If it's Jacob, what's the worry? Isn't he a good guy?"

"Not all spirits can resist the pull that comes from body snatching. If he communicates through Sonja, his soul will remember what it was like to live. He'll see through her eyes, smell what she smells, and feel everything she touches. That's why we light the candle in the center of the circle. It acts as a tether. If he refuses to withdraw after our questions, we will force him out and back to the flame. But if you cross the circle, you become the tether, and his spirit will remain until we can exorcise it." He narrowed his eyes at me in a clear reprimand. "Just stay out of the circle."

"No problem." He didn't need to worry. I wouldn't enter that circle if Ed Mc-Mahon was holding my million dollar Publisher's Clearinghouse check inside.

Goose walked past the circle and lit the candle in the center. It was a large, black pillar with a dark, well-used wick. He watched until the flame was strong, and then took his seat at the edge of the circle. I thought he would hit the lights and do this wacky shit in the dark, but he left both floor lamps as they were, and I could see everything clearly.

Goose and Sonja closed their eyes, and I mimicked them. I had read the pages from Goose's journal that shared information about this, so I wasn't totally unprepared. An incantation was sometimes necessary but not always. You started out by singling out the spirit, forming a mental picture of the person, and calling to them with your mind and necromancy. I drew on my past memory of Jacob, which was crap. All I could remember was dark hair and shooting off at the mouth.

Nothing happened, and the minutes slowly ticked by.

As with anything, being in a position that required silence and concentration made me doubly aware. A trickle of cool air breezed across my skin, carrying a mild electrical current. I opened my eyes and gasped. Jacob's face was inches from my own. His eyes were blue but looked opaque. His face was blank, as all spirits' faces were, and being up close and personal helped me appreciate just how scary that was.

"Jacob Newman," Goose said the name evenly, without emotion. "We summoned you here in an effort to bring your killer to justice. Aid us in this, so that you might rest peacefully."

Jacob stood, and the motion brought his empty chest cavity directly into my line of sight. Even without the truest clarity, the visual was revolting. His black shirt was cut down the middle and parted like a vest, the skin along his chest peeled back and ripped away. Some of his ribs were cracked in half and few were missing. His sternum was shattered, the lower portion completely gone. I could see his spine; the pink meat of muscle and cartilage infused together. His heart was missing, leaving behind a clumpy mess of veins and arteries mashed into a goopy blob of thick and thin strings dangling from the mass. His wound extended to the gut below, revealing the sausage-like strands of his intestines mixed with shards of white bone that flashed starkly against the pink tissue.

I gagged, covering my mouth, holding my breath to fight back nausea.

"I invite you to use my voice to speak," Sonja said calmly.

I watched as she closed her eyes and took a deep breath.

Jacob vanished—there one second and gone the next—and Sonja started to twitch violently. I peered at Goose in a panic, but he was calm. Sonja stopped moving, and when her lids lifted, her eyes were as white and as opaque as Jacob's.

"What happened to you, Jacob?" Goose asked.

A detached, male voice came from Sonja's mouth. "The dark man appeared, and I followed. I don't remember how I got on the ground. The chains holding my hands and feet burned. I couldn't move."

"What is the dark man, Jacob?"

"Evil."

"Who is he?"

"He is death."

"Where did he take you?"

"I don't know."

"What do you remember?"

"Pain."

Joseph called out from the other room. "Why can't he answer these questions?"

"Because he doesn't know." Goose kept his tone level and quiet, as if addressing someone next to him.

"We need more information than this." Joseph's tone was clipped and he started to pace.

"Jacob," Goose addressed the spirit again. "We have someone who can communicate directly with you by touch. But she is not a gateway, and you must leave her when she obtains the information necessary to solve your murder. If you fail to do this, we'll be forced to exorcise you, and your spirit will remain locked between dimensions. Do you understand?"

Time passed, the seconds painfully slow, before Jacob answered. "Yes."

Everyone, with the exception of Sonja, stared at me. I shook my head, laughing uneasily. More one-on-one spirit time? No fucking thanks.

"Nu-uh. No way am I doing that shit again."

"He won't have access to your memories this time," Goose said. "That only occurred because of Baxter's unique ability. All you will share are his memories and thoughts, and more importantly, you will see the face of this person he calls the dark man. We have to know what he looks like, Rhiannon."

I groaned, closing my eyes. I didn't want to wimp out with everyone watching. "What do you want me to do?"

"Enter the circle," he instructed.

"What?" I snapped in disbelief, opened my eyes, and glared at him. "You just told me not to enter that thing."

"The plan has changed." Goose's eyes were slitted in annoyance, but his voice stayed steady. "Stop being a baby and enter the circle."

"Why can't he just step out and come to me?"

"For the same reason Disco and Joseph were instructed not to enter. This entire room is blessed." He lifted his index finger and rotated it around his head. "Jacob cannot leave the circle. That is the only area in the room in which he is allowed. He's borrowing Sonja, but only so long as she agrees to it. She can break the contact at any time."

"This is some fucked up shit," I muttered, rising to my feet.

I wished Ed was inside the circle with my check now. I deserved that kind of compensation for walking into a magic circle with a "possess me" bulls-eye centered on my chest. I didn't look at Disco as I prepared myself. If I saw anything less than total confidence from him, I wouldn't have the balls to do this.

I held my breath, closed my eyes, and stepped into the circle. The room changed, a heavy and oppressing atmosphere shrouding me. My breathing increased and the tempo of my heart accelerated. I removed the elastic from my ponytail, let my hair fall free, and combed my fingers through the tangles to soothe my nerves.

Sonja slumped forward and back. Her eyes opened; the normal icy crystal blue greeted us instead of the milky white. The pressure inside the circle intensified and I had to fight the compulsion to step out. Jacob's form reappeared inside the circle. His dead eyes focused on me, and he started over. I knew why I didn't notice his injuries before at Shooter's. His shirt was black and blended with the hole in his chest. His short sleeves displayed the wounds on his wrists clearly, the flayed flesh spread outward to reveal solid bone.

"Oh God."

He didn't lift his hand as Baxter had, stopping mere inches away. I stared straight ahead. I didn't want an up close view of his innards again.

"You will have to touch him, Rhiannon." Goose's voice sounded miles away. "Baxter reached out because his ability dictated touch. Jacob didn't have an ability that required physical contact."

"Oh man." I squirmed, extending my fingers. My shoulders crowded my neck and my spine curved in revulsion. I decided to touch his face. It was as good a place as any. At least the skin there remained unmarred by injury.

At the first tentative contact, I saw a face I couldn't place, but it was one I'd seen before. The man was dressed in a simple black suit and tie, his body tall and thin. His black skin was dark and smooth, and his narrow, distinguished face contained a pair of large oval eyes in a lovely shade of jade.

A frame of blackness, then another image quickly replaced it. I was face up on the floor of darkened room, no windows, no doors. Just concrete and the strong fragrance of Clorox and blood. My ankles and wrists protested in agony. Thin metal pressed against my flesh, melting away my skin. There was an empty spot in my brain—a big blank space where my memories should have been. How did I get here? Who had brought me to this place? I struggled against the bindings and stopped; each movement sent the chain into my bones.

The dark man came, wearing nothing but solid black pants. He began to chant in a strange dialect, and fear seeped into my chest. He produced a silver blade from behind his back. The knife shimmered in the blackness, glinting with each rotation of his wrist. The tip was sharp, a clean edge meant to slash. The thick silver spine was etched in a circular design that ran to the silver bolster, the handle a deep black material that looked like stone.

I looked into the face of the man with the milky green eyes. He was smiling as he brought down his hand with the knife. The razor edge slid into my welcoming skin like butter. I screamed; the dark man closed his eyes, and his head rolled back as he looked to the ceiling.

He lowered his face with the movement of the knife. I felt myself splitting—a painful slicing that ached and tortured. Pressure radiated from my chest in a dull agony when he contacted bone. I screamed again, thrashing against the bindings. The blade was placed on top of the fresh skin on my chest, and I opened my eyes in horror.

He brought himself to his knees, plunging the metal into my chest, tearing through the skin and bone in a horrible crunch that reverberated through the room. I wailed, screeching in anguish, each new broken bone as painful as the last.

A deeper slice took my breath away, somehow more devastating. A slurping sound followed and my life began to ebb. The blackness surrounded me, but not before my dying eyes saw the heart cupped in his hand—my heart—and it was still beating.

"It looks terrible, doesn't it?" Jacob's voice was much deeper then Sonja could project.

I snapped to attention and I saw him standing across from me. He was perfect, no hole in his chest, his black shirt intact. His dark hair was actually deep brown and his eyes were light, sparkling champagne-hazel. I glanced around. We were not where he died. Instead, we stood next to a table at Shooter's. There were no sounds of wood meeting cues, or balls colliding. We were the only two people in the building.

"What is this?" I spun around, confused. "Where are we?"

"I'm afraid I've taken liberties with you," he confessed, smiling just the same. "I've done what Ethan asked me not to and merged into your body. Don't worry. It's only so we can speak. Right now, we're locked together in your mind. See"—he motioned at the area around us—"I let you choose a familiar location."

"So we're having an actual conversation?" I felt like I was in *The Twilight Zone*. Everything felt so real; I could even smell the talcum powder.

He nodded and smiled. "It was the only way I could speak directly to you. It's difficult to formulate words through a host body. The brain functions differently. Sort of like two hard drives working with different software. Not to mention, this is a private conversation, two separate entities sharing information independently at the same time."

"Wow." I walked to a table and lifted a cue. It was solid, as was the table. I could shoot a game if I were so inclined.

"Don't get too comfortable," he warned. "That is how you're tricked and the spirit takes over. You'll begin to believe all of this is real, and eventually, you'll forget all about how you got here."

"Sorry." I placed the cue back on the table and faced him.

"I've imposed on you for one reason." He feigned a wince. "I have unresolved business here, and even if you attempted to release my soul, I would remain because of it. I'm asking you to give your word that you'll do as I ask so I can finally get some rest."

The request wasn't unreasonable. "What would you like me to do?"

"Go to the closet in my bedroom. You'll need to walk all the way inside, to the back. On the top shelf, you'll see a plain, brown shoebox. I need you to give that box to Gabriel, along with a message. Tell him I found it at a random pawn shop a few years ago and wanted to find the right time to return it to him, but"—he shrugged—"something got in the way."

"I thought you were going to tell me to kill someone," I said, nervous laughter escaping. "Delivering a shoe box is a piece of cake."

He shook his head sadly, hazel eyes heavy with regret. "No, it's not cake, but it's something I have to do before I can leave this plane and move on to whatever it is that awaits me."

"I give you my word. I'll get it to him."

"Thank you." He bowed his head, and hair tumbled around his face. "I'm in your debt. If are such things as guardian angels, I'll return the favor."

"Wait." I lifted my hand to stop him. There was something I had to ask. "What's it like being a spirit?"

"It's not so strange. You know what you need to do and what you need to accomplish."

"So you're aware...of everything after you die?"

"Are you aware of everything after you're born?" he responded cryptically.

The pool hall vanished and I heard Disco's voice, drowning out all the others. I was back inside the circle, slightly dazed but standing on steady legs. I blinked rapidly as I acclimated to the change in scenery. Goose and Sonja were pulling things out of several cardboard boxes, sorting through the contents frantically.

"You told her to go in there!" Disco thundered. "What were you thinking?"

"I found the thistle!" Sonja's voice was thick with panic. "Where's the sandalwood and yarrow?"

"We'll get him out of her! I didn't think Jacob would do that!" Goose yelled back, sifting through a box before angrily tossing it to the side. "Where the hell is it? The yarrow should be in there!"

I held back a grin but allowed myself a huge, inward smile. Now they cared. Step in the circle, Rhiannon. Go get possessed, Rhiannon. I took a peripheral peek at Disco and Joseph. Joseph was watching but it was obvious that he didn't give a shit. I didn't mean squat at the end of the day.

Disco's expression, on the other hand, made my heart ache.

Concern, worry, and anger marred his beautiful face. He would eat Goose's goat when this was said and done. I was surprised the revered necromancers in the building didn't notice Jacob had gone. The room felt entirely void of energy.

I took a deep breath and turned to Disco. His brows lifted in trepidation and doubt, his lovely eyes darkening. I rolled my eyes and shook my head, and the look disappeared. He started forward and then glared at the entranceway, unable to cross the threshold of the blessed room. Since he couldn't come to me, I went to him instead.

Goose and Sonja were still squabbling with each other when Joseph saw me, green eyes narrowing dangerously. "She's been taken over," he snarled.

"What?" Goose and Sonja asked concurrently. They whipped around and gasped.

"Don't let her leave the apartment!" Goose shouted.

The minute I was clear of the barrier, Disco yanked me into his arms. His body stiffened and he held me at a safe distance, staring down guardedly. I tried not to notice the emotion etched across his face, but some of it seeped past anyway.

His voice mirrored his confusion.

"Rhiannon? Is it you?"

"Yes, it's me. If Ethan and Sonja would mellow the fuck out, they'd know it too. Jacob left. He passed over to that bright shiny place in the sky."

Disco glanced over my shoulder, his body remaining tense. He didn't totally trust me, but that was cool. I wouldn't trust me either.

"He's gone," Sonja confirmed, sounding pissed. I'm sure she didn't like being caught with her panties down—poor girl.

Disco pulled me to his chest, and I went into his welcoming arms without argument. It felt good to lean on someone else for a change. After tonight, I deserved the break.

Tomorrow I could return to being the hard ass bitch everyone expected.

CHAPTER TWENTY-FOUR

The night wasn't a total bust, but with my luck, that was bound to change. After everyone recovered from my Linda Blair stunt and I explained what I had seen—sans the private discussion with Jacob—we called it a night. Everyone was anxious about the dark man, especially me.

I couldn't shake that nagging feeling I knew him from somewhere.

Disco had a car at the ready to take him home, and he offered me a lift. I knew it was a ruse. Disco could run faster than the car would move down the street. He just wanted to get me alone again. Even knowing that, I accepted. There was no time like the present to get my promise fulfilled. Jacob deserved to rest peacefully, and I wanted to see what was so important.

When I told Disco I needed to go to Jacob's room, he was suspicious. He asked questions that I refused to answer and stopped speaking to me when he realized it wouldn't do him any good. The drive to his home was agonizing.

We pulled into the gated drive and I could see the mansion in the distance. I wasn't aware places like this existed in New York. The house was enormous, with a red brick exterior and windows that gave the visage of watchful eyes.

The driver pulled up along the circle that formed the driveway, and I didn't wait for him to open the door. I climbed out the moment the vehicle stopped and raced up the stairs. One bonus with Disco—he was so fast I never had to be concerned about waiting for him to catch me.

The door opened before I reached it, and Nala appeared.

"It's wonderful to see you, Rhiannon." She greeted me and stood aside, smiling past my shoulder. "Welcome home, Gabriel."

"Escort Rhiannon to Jacob's room, please." Disco strode past us, gliding down the hall to the left.

"What is that about?" Nala's asked, frowning.

"We contacted Jacob. He had a request before he crossed over. I need to go to his room."

She motioned to the stairs. "Follow me."

Nala led me up the winding staircase and to the right, the wood barely creaking under our feet. Paintings, antique furniture, and tapestries adorned the painted walls. Heavy drapes along the hallway obscured the windows.

We passed two doors before Nala came to a stop.

"This is Jacob's room," she said softly, reaching for the handle. After stepping inside, she flicked the light switch and waited for me before closing the door behind us. "If you don't mind me asking, what are you looking for?"

"It's back here." I walked to one of two doors in the room, hoping I didn't accidentally pick the wrong one. When I pulled open the door, I looked for a switch. My vision was finally beginning to fade, and I couldn't see as well in the dark anymore.

"Here." Nala brushed past me and turned on a light, flooding the room in a yellow glow. I hurried to the shelf along the back wall. The brown shoebox was right where Jacob said it would be.

"I need that shoe box." I pointed at the shelf. "Can you reach it?"

"Sure."

Nala motioned for me to step aside. She leapt on the pads of her feet like a large cat, grabbed the box, and landed quietly on the cream Berber carpeting.

She handed the box to me and I ran my hand along the cardboard surface. It was a plain old shoebox, nothing special. Yet something inside was so important Jacob risked being stuck between dimensions to tell me about it. That made the contents invaluable.

I carried the box into the bedroom and sat on the bed. Nala stood close by, watching. "I don't know if I can open it," I said, inhaling a breath of courage. I placed the box in my lap and lifted the lid. Various colored rags were scattered inside. I pulled them out one by one, until I uncovered a rectangular blue velvet box at the center.

I lifted it carefully and popped open the lid. A bracelet was nestled inside, the platinum metal radiant and untarnished. The squares that made up each link held square blue sapphires with two tiny round diamonds flanking each one.

"Oh no," Nala said and sank down beside me on the mattress.

"I don't get it." *All of this to return a pretty piece of metal and gemstones?*

Nala looked from me to the box and back again. She drew in a deep breath before exhaling softly. "Years ago, Gabriel met a young woman named Sienna. They were an item for several years before she got into trouble." Nala smiled sadly, reaching to touch the bracelet, and I handed her the box. "Sienna became involved in very dark magic, conjuring and summoning demons. Before long, she was indebted to one."

"Demons," I whispered in disbelief.

"The world isn't the place you imagined, Rhiannon. I'm about to tell you something that will get me into a spot of trouble with Gabriel. But you have the right to know, and I refuse to keep you in the dark any longer." She lifted her head and met my eyes. I nodded, encouraging her to speak.

"The first vampire was created from a demon named Ahriman. He raped the human witch who summoned him using the guise of glamour. He appeared before her as a handsome, lost traveler, only revealing his true form after his evil seed found life in her womb. The witch died during the birth of her son, and Ahriman took the boy with him to Hell. He shared his story with other demons whose names had been spoken, and therefore, were bound to cross dimensions to the people who summoned them."

I waited while she paused, patient until she continued.

"Demons cannot cross into our dimension without just cause or conjuring, but the half-breed children possessed free rein to travel at will. Soon, demons realized they could litter the world with their kind and started twisting conjuring contracts, using glamour and creating offspring to take over the world. It wasn't long until half-breeds discovered that by draining someone dry and exchanging some of their tainted blood, they could create a less powerful but equally dangerous hybrid. This new race still retained a soul, so they couldn't bask in God's sunlight to smite him, or visit the abyss of Hell, but they still required blood to survive."

"Vampires?" I guessed and she nodded.

"After several decades, priests started to battle the most unclean on earth, hunting them down. The smart ones returned to their dimension. The ones like us were left behind."

She cleared her throat and shifted uncomfortably on the bed. "Sienna practiced black magic in secret, and her curiosity proved to be her undoing. Demons don't normally bother with mortals. They find them too weak and too predictable. However, when someone gains the name of a demon and summons them to do their bidding, they bring attention to themselves. The one Sienna got involved with was particularly nasty. Morax demanded her servitude in Hell for his services after the fact. Demons love to spin deals, and you have to be careful with what you agree to. They will trick you if they can. You can count on it."

"And she was tricked?"

Nala nodded. "She had no choice but to come clean with Gabriel. If he were any less of a man, he would have turned her away. But he didn't. He loved her, even with her faults. It took time and assistance from Marius, but we worked out a bargain with another demon named Zagan. Morax owed him a debt from years before, and Zagan agreed to use that debt to wipe Sienna's slate clean if one of us offered a favor of his choosing in the future. Gabriel accepted the offer and agreed to a debt owed for a debt paid, sealing the deal."

My stomach churned. "So where is she?"

Nala lowered her head, staring at her hands. "Paine never touched Sienna. Had he done so, I don't believe he would have allowed Gabriel to make that bargain. Sienna wanted to wait to become one of us, believing she had plenty of time. But she wasn't like you, Rhiannon. She didn't know how to protect herself or fight back. The men who abducted her made sure she suffered horribly before she died. When we found her body, all of her belongings were gone." She returned the box to me, smiling broken-heartedly. "Including the bracelet Gabriel had given her."

"The last few weeks have been the most fucked up of my life, and *that* is saying something," I told Nala. I closed the blue box and returned it to the cardboard one. I left the pieces of cloth out, closed the lid, and ran a trembling hand over the top.

"I felt the same way when Adrian told me the truth. It's a huge pill to swallow, and we all have been there. Even Gabriel." Nala touched my arm. "Just remember anything is possible. Look who you're talking to. Did you ever imagine you'd be having a conversation with a vampire?"

"No," I laughed. Even after I'd learned vampires existed, it still took years to accept it. "You said Gabriel owes a favor to the demon that cleaned the slate. What did he have to give up?" I pictured Disco making the selfless sacrifice and felt terrible for judging him so harshly in the past.

Nala stood and paced, her feet barely skimming the surface of the carpet.

"The debt hasn't been honored yet. We won't know what price Gabriel will pay until Zagan comes to collect. Netherworld creatures don't have a concept of material wealth or belongings. They derive pleasure from misery and chaos. That's the only reason Zagan agreed to the bargain in the first place. The opportunity to spite Morax was too good to pass up. Whatever is in store for Gabriel will consist of those things, you can be certain of it."

"Shit."

She stopped pacing and faced me. "You needn't worry about things you cannot change or prevent. Fearing the future won't make anything different. It will merely ruin time that should be better spent. Gabriel deserves to be happy. After Cash disappeared, we feared he might leave us as Marius did. But he didn't because of you. Somehow I don't think you're the type to allow fear to keep you away from the things you want most."

I cracked a smile. "I don't let anything run me off once my mind is set. Thanks for telling me this, Nala."

"If you ever need to speak to someone, my door is always open. I will never relay anything that we talk about to anyone without your permission. Gabriel isn't the only person who is happy you joined us; so am I. Adrian is a wonderful companion, but sometimes I long to speak to someone else about things he wouldn't understand." She pointed at the box. "Will you give that to Gabriel tonight?"

"A promise is a promise."

"Then let's go find him."

We left the bedroom and walked back down the hall. Nala stopped at the top of the stairs, looking left and right, and her nose flared briefly. Before long, she relaxed, and we descended the staircase to the right, past the entranceway and down another hall. The tiled floor matched throughout, a stark white with tiny black squares in the center. Nala walked silently, but my sneakers squeaked each time my foot lifted into the air.

We stopped in front of a set of huge wooden double doors at the end, and I recognized them immediately.

"I'll leave you two," Nala said. This time her smile wasn't real, and she rushed past me in a blur too fast to perceive.

After grasping the long golden handle in my fingers, I opened the door and stepped inside. Disco was waiting on the loveseat, in the same place he had marked me just days before. One look in my direction told me he was still angry, but he didn't say a word, giving me the silent treatment. The chairs Paine and Peter had used the night I'd been accepted into the family were gone, leaving an open path.

I crossed the room, sat beside him, and cradled the box in my lap.

"I'm sorry," I said quietly and got the response I was hoping for, gaining his attention. I extended the box to him. "I would have told you everything in the car, but since this was about you in particular, I was afraid to say anything until I actually had what Jacob wanted me to give you."

He frowned as he accepted the box, blue eyes cautious.

"Jacob wanted me to tell you he found it a few years ago in a pawn shop and was waiting for the right time to give it to you."

I could see Disco's chest still as his breath caught. He flipped the lid off the box and let it fall to the floor. He stared at the velvety blue box inside, and my heart ached. His mouth tightened, drawn eyebrows so close together they almost touched. He pulled the box free, lifted the lid, and closed his eyes after one glimpse of what rested inside.

I didn't say anything, unwilling to interrupt his grief. The only thing that remained of the girl he once loved could fit inside a tiny blue box. I was sure the pain was incredible, especially after thinking the bracelet would never be found.

He closed the lid and placed it back inside the shoebox with trembling hands. "Did Nala tell you?" he asked hoarsely.

I nodded. "I hope you don't mind. When I asked her, she couldn't exactly say no."

"No." He cleared his throat, staring straight ahead. "I don't mind."

"Would you like me to go?" I shifted on the cushions, prepared to leave and give him time alone.

"Don't go." His right hand came out and touched my thigh. "I want you to stay."

"All right." I settled back, glancing around the room.

"How did Jacob tell you where to find this?" Disco placed the lid back on the shoebox. "I thought you only saw how he died."

"He decided to venture inside my body so we could have a little chat." At his curious look, I explained, "As weird as it sounds, it wasn't that bad. Jacob said he couldn't cross over until this was given to you and asked me to take care of it." I paused and tried to find the right words to convey how badly I felt. "I'm really sorry about not telling you...and about having to be the one to give you this."

"Don't be sorry. I'm glad you were the one to give it to me." He leaned over, plopped the box onto the floor, and turned to face me. "Living an eternity means you never get used to death, but you learn to accept it."

"You must miss her." I offered a weak smile as my gaze drifted uncomfortably away from his.

"I did," he admitted. "And I regret the harm that befell her that I feel responsible for. But Sienna is gone. Nothing I do will reverse the past. And I'm fortunate, because someone else has come into my life." He leaned across the sofa, moving closer. Then he whispered into my ear, "If her death taught me anything, it's this. Cherish the time you have. Don't worry about tomorrow. Right now is all we are promised."

Those words were my undoing.

I closed the distance, turning my body, and clasped my hands behind his neck. Our lips came together, his tongue darted inside my mouth, and I met each thrust, moaning against his lips, pulling his face closer, twining my fingers in his hair.

I dimly perceived him standing with me in his arms, striding out of the room, and carrying me up the stairs. I was aware on some level that once this boundary was breached things would change forever between us, but I shoved it into the back of my mind. I was tired of thinking, and Disco was right; we might not have this moment again.

Now all I cared about was being with him.

A door clicked open and then shut. I opened my eyes.

We were inside the same room I occupied after the Wesley incident. Disco eased me onto the bed as he shifted his large frame beside me on the mattress. He lifted his head. Thick blond hair fell in every direction, framing his impossibly golden blue eyes.

"If you want to leave, say so now. I'm not sure I'll be able to stop if this goes any further." He was panting softly, eyes fevered and eager. I could feel the tension radiating from his body.

I brought my hand up and watched my fingers brush across the black buttons of his shirt, feeling his cool, solid muscles beneath. A wave of shyness and apprehension swept through me. I had attempted to have sex one time in my life and couldn't go through with it.

My voice trembled, betraying my emotions. "I'm afraid."

"I would never hurt you." He spoke thickly, his fingers skimming lightly across my jaw. "If you're not ready, I'll stop now."

"I want this," I whispered, meeting his heated gaze. "I want you."

He lowered his head and kissed me gently, without any expectation. His tongue brushed against my lips, prodding them open. I felt his fingers stroking my hair before they traveled to my neck to hold me tenderly. It was staggering that someone so powerful, so dangerous, could be so gentle.

His mouth breezed across my face, light and tender. I felt cool air blowing into my ear, followed by the tip of his tongue as he traced the sensitive shell. I gasped when he sucked in, the sound and sensation causing my body to clench. My right hand grasped his forearm, fingers digging into the shirt. His mouth moved down and he pushed aside the neck of my sweater, nipping at my mark. Like before, desire shot through me in a lick of heat.

"What is that?" I groaned, writhing on the bed.

"Scar tissue from our bites become erotic zones on the body." He bit down and I cried out as unfamiliar warmth erupted between my legs.

"Oh my God." I was barely able to contain the tendrils of heat and prickles inside my skin.

"Just wait," he promised. "You are so beautiful. I can't wait to see all of you."

His fingers brushed against the skin on my waist, lifting my sweater. I didn't feel shy. I was too absorbed in the unbelievable sensations he was wringing from my body. The sweater came off easily, and he tossed it to the floor.

He didn't take such precautions with his own clothing. He ripped his shirt off, sending buttons scattering into the air. His skin met mine in a wave of silky coolness, like touching solid marble, and I shivered involuntarily.

"I'm sorry, I forgot," he murmured against my mouth, starting to rise from the bed.

I grasped his arms. "Where are you going?"

"To start a fire. You'll get colder before we're finished. We don't produce body heat, and I'll steal away your warmth faster than you can produce it." He grinned at me wickedly. "I take that back. You'll produce more than enough, but not at the start."

"Then light the kindling here, the fireplace can wait."

He slid over me and I ran my fingers along his chest. His muscles were perfectly defined, smooth and solid. His coolness was a bit strange at first, but erotic as well. He was like a living, breathing, seductive statue, with eyes as blue as the ocean after a storm.

I slipped my hand under his arm and outlined the dip of his spine, tracing the hollow edge with my fingers. He kissed me again, lifting his hips up and over. His knee gently nudged my legs apart, and he settled between them, placing his weight at the apex of my thighs.

I felt his fingers tugging on my jeans. The button slid out easily and the zipper came apart. He broke the kiss, sat upright and leaned backward, intent on taking them off, gently pulling at the cotton on my hips. He stopped mid-tug, eyes unbelieving and focused on my abdomen.

My stomach sank. *Damn it.* I'd forgotten about my scars.

"Oh, Rhiannon." He traced one of the thick white crescents with the pad of his finger. When he glanced up at me, his gaze held a mixture of pity, a newfound understanding, and anger. "Who did this to you?"

"If I asked you to do something important for me, would you?" I refused to look away.

"You know I would."

I motioned for him to come back to me, and he eased his body over mine, bracing himself on steady arms.

"I want you to see." He tried to argue, but I pressed a finger to his lips. "Sometimes the person you trust the most is the hardest one to explain something to. Don't force me to relive everything all over again, not with you. If you really want to know the girl I used to be, you have to see why she stays so safely hidden. Do you understand?"

"I don't want to force myself on you."

"You won't be." I stroked his back, urging him closer. "You'll be easing a tremendous burden. Once you know, we'll never have to mention it again. You can make this so much easier for me." I added in a whisper, "Please."

I knew he made the decision when his eyes shifted from teal to steely blue. He leaned forward to plant a kiss on me, lips soft against mine as he placed his hands either side of my face, and closed his eyes.

I felt him inside my head then, like the fluttering of butterfly wings. He was calm initially, but it wasn't long until his body went still. I could feel the rage emitting from him as his arms started to tremble.

He reopened his eyes and the golden specks inside shone like liquid metal.

"If he weren't dead already, I would kill him myself."

He rose to his knees and lifted me, tossing back the comforter with his free hand. He placed me on top of the pillows and covered me with the blanket before he slid in and pulled me into his arms. Reclining against the headboard, he strummed his fingers through my hair.

I was too astounded to speak. This was not what I expected when he finally looked inside my warped mind. I rested my cheek against the cool skin of his chest and enjoyed the motion of his fingers as they threaded through my hair before gently caressing the skin on my back.

"I just want to hold you," he told me, his voice a smooth, soothing caress once again. "I'm going to hold you all night and keep your nightmares at bay. Close your eyes and think of somewhere you've always wanted to go. I'll make sure you get there."

I don't know if I closed my eyes because he asked me to, or because the temptation to have one night's sleep without nightmares was too tempting to resist. Either way I lowered my lids and nestled against his chest. His fingers flittered across my hair and skin, and I relaxed, sighing contentedly.

It didn't take long to reach the pinnacle between dreaming and wakefulness. I found myself at the beach with my parents, that last day we were together as a family. I heard the joyful laughter of a child—my laughter. Mom and Dad danced together in the sand, and my heart brimmed with the love I felt. The salty air blew my hair into my eyes, and I thrust it away, turning my attention from my parents and the ocean crashing into the surf.

A lone figure watched us from further down the beach, his blond hair shining in the midday sun.

CHAPTER TWENTY-FIVE

I woke and sighed blissfully, shifting my body against something hard, solid, and surprisingly warm. My lids lifted and a white expanse of smooth luminescent skin greeted me.

"Did you sleep well?" Disco whispered against my head, brushing his fingers along my arm.

"I slept amazing. Thank you," I murmured, placing my hand on his chest.

Something was different, and it took me a couple of seconds to place the change. His skin was markedly cooler on the opposite side, but only by degrees. He was as warm as I was beneath the comforter.

"Am I keeping you warm?"

He squeezed me gently and said, "You are, and it feels unbelievable."

I tickled the skin on his stomach with my fingertips, pushing aside the blanket to outline the muscles along his abdomen. He drew in a ragged breath and tensed, the fingers in my hair ceasing to move. He had a trail of blond hair that led from his belly button down. I followed it with the pads of my fingers. The hair was as soft and flaxen as the hair on his head.

"What time is it?" I asked, toying with his stomach.

"I'm not sure." His breath hitched as my fingernails scraped along his skin. "The dawn came an hour ago."

"How are you still awake?" I brought my fingers back up his chest. The white skin was perfect and smooth. I shifted my body to look at him and rested my palm across his heart, directly over the steady beating.

"We don't require sleep like you do," he answered roughly. "It is only the sun we cannot venture into."

"What's wrong?" I asked innocently, knowing good and damned well what the answer was. I could see it in his striking multicolored irises.

He flipped me over and buried me beneath him. His eager mouth found mine as his cool tongue moved past my lips and vanished deeply inside. I grasped his back, fingernails raking into his skin. He felt good pressed against me, and I remembered how close we came to crossing that elusive bridge between us.

"I won't stop this time," he warned. Breaking the kiss, he stared into my eyes. His expression was harsh as he fought to maintain control.

"I don't want you to."

He leapt from the bed in an agile movement, removed our shoes in a matter of seconds, and gently tugged at the legs of my jeans. Once he pulled the clothing free, he tossed the jeans to the floor, until all that remained were my black cotton panties and bra, and removed the last of his clothing. I felt shy, but he didn't give me the opportunity to become self-conscious. He returned to the bed faster than I could see.

"I won't do anything you don't want me to do," he promised, lowering his head to kiss my ear.

He blew into the canal, teasing the lobe with his teeth and tongue. His kisses drifted past the tender flesh behind my ear, down to my mark. He bit down. Sharp teeth and pure erotic bliss overcame me. My body thrashed, and I pressed my face into his chest, breathing him in, clutching his hair in my fists. He bit down again, using greater force, and my breath came out in spurts.

His lips descended, barely touching the skin, stopping at the hollow of my throat. He placed a kiss into the soft, sensitive flesh, raining affection along my collarbones. His mouth skimmed across my chest, his hands coming up to cup my breasts. His thumbs brushed across the nipples through the lace and the hot spasm in my stomach extended, soaking my panties in liquid heat.

"I'm taking this off," he told me, reaching behind to unclasp my bra. I arched my back and he pulled the flimsy material away.

The cool air hit my bare skin just before his mouth covered an aching nipple. His fingers worked at the other breast, teasing the responsive area with his thumb and finger, rolling and pinching the taut flesh. I had never experienced anything so erotic in my life. Sounds caught in my throat as I pushed my head into the pillows.

A desire flourished inside me, an emptiness that needed release. I moaned aloud, lifting my hips and digging my fingers into his shoulders. His tongue flicked and sucked in a repetitive movement, mirrored by the deliberate motions of fingers on the other side.

I couldn't remain still. I felt hot and needy. I writhed under him, rubbing against his cock along the inside of my thigh. He released the nipple from his mouth and moved to the other breast; his fingers worked at the now wet, pebbled skin while his mouth teased and tormented.

He released my breasts, kissing each softly, and made a trail of kisses along my stomach. His tongue dipped into my belly button and I groaned. Reaching for his plush blond hair, I threaded my fingers through it. He moved lower, pausing to graze his lips across each scar along my pelvis.

Fingers crept up to pull the panties from my body, and he eased them down each leg. His face continued past my hips and the first wave of awkwardness overtook me.

"Wait," I gasped.

"What's wrong?" He paused with his fingers around the delicate bones of my pelvis.

"I've never..." I flushed. "No one has ever done that before."

"You've never been with anyone like me before. Why should this experience be anything but new? Trust me, Rhiannon. I've been dying to taste you."

He continued his chosen path, blond head going lower as I stared at the ceiling, trembling uncontrollably. His hands parted my thighs, his cool breath brushed the folds of sensitive skin, and his face descended.

I had heard stories about oral sex from women at the club. Most of them swore they preferred it to the actual thing. I never understood what the fuss was about until I experienced the first touch of his tongue, parting me, exploring where no one had ever dared kiss before. Disco's mouth settled over me and I sucked in air, making mewing sounds in my throat, arching my back and grasping the sheets in my fists. The pleasure was unbelievable, so good I wanted to scream.

"Disco." I moaned his name, unable to remain motionless as he continued, writhing as if on fire.

A pressure started to build in my stomach, a summit so close that all I needed to do was reach out to take it. Each flick of his tongue brought it closer, then closer. I clenched my fists, closed my eyes, and embraced the climax that was surfacing, wanting to know what waited for me at the other side.

I was almost there.

His tongue flicked my swollen clit—once, then repeatedly—and sent me over the edge. My body felt as if it exploded, becoming pure light. I thrashed with each new wave of pleasure that assaulted me, soft whimpers escaping my throat. I rode the high for as long as I could, until it left my body limp and sated. A wave of euphoria swept through me and I stilled, lax and breathless.

"Delicious, like warm vanilla sugar," Disco growled against my stomach, kissing the scars again, lavishing attention on each one.

He followed the same trail back up, returning to my breasts. His mouth latched onto a nipple and his fingers returned to the opposite side, leaving me gasping. His lips brushed against my sternum, kissed the hollow of my throat, and traced the curve of my neck. I moaned and placed my hands on the contours of his back and shoulders. I pressed my face into his throat, breathing in his own tantalizing scent, pushing against him so that his skin would cool the hot flush spreading over me.

He pulled away and stared down with adoring eyes, the blue depths shifting with each layer, the gold still visible but not as much as before as my sight no longer as strong or as viable.

"This is it, Rhiannon." He kissed my lips reverently. "If you want to say no, the time is now. I will love you the rest of the day without taking that extra step if that is what you want. I would love nothing more than to spend the morning tasting you."

"No." I shook my head, leaning up to kiss his neck, brushing my lips along his smooth skin. "I want you. I want this."

"Then look at me," he whispered hoarsely.

I looked into his eyes and felt him prodding at the core of my body. I trembled all over, hands and shoulders shaking as he eased into the welcoming liquid warmth created by his mouth and my arousal. His body was still cooler and therefore easy to distinguish from my own.

He moved, carefully pushing forward. He was large and foreign inside my body, the more of him I took in, the greater the discomfort that intensified. I tried to relax, eager to experience this new brand of intimacy.

Suddenly, he stopped, and his glorious blue eyes expanded in surprise.

"You've never done this before." He made it a statement, not a question.

"Is that a problem?" I felt my face burning again. I thought a girl was supposed to be embarrassed by having too many sexual partners, not too few.

"No, it's not a problem. It's an honor. One I've never been given before." He kissed my forehead tenderly, and brought his hands forward to cup my face. "I swore I wouldn't hurt you, and I'll do my best to keep my word. Stay with me."

He continued staring into my eyes as he moved forward again. I tensed at the odd inner burning and dug my fingers into his shoulders, gasping softly. He stopped and retreated, giving me a moment before starting again. The burning returned and I breathed through my nose, tensing beneath him even as I ordered my muscles to relax.

He cursed, pulled away, and pressed his lips to my neck.

His mouth settled over my mark, teasing the area with little nips. Heat surged beneath my skin as he bit down, bringing on that swamping erotic euphoria, and he joined us together in one hard thrust.

The pain was as intense as the orgasm that came with it. I screamed without sound, my voice box failing to work. He was deep within my body and I convulsed, burrowing my fingers into his skin, lifting my shoulders off the mattress. I turned my face into his shoulder, holding him tightly until the shudders subsided.

"Are you all right?" he whispered against my ear, remaining completely still.

"Yes." I was barely able to speak, my body reeling from aftershock tingles.

He gave me a moment to become accustomed to the intrusion. Then, pausing to touch his forehead to mine, he withdrew. When he slid back into the heat of my body the sharp burning was replaced by a feeling of fullness. He buried himself completely within me and released the breath he had been holding.

"Christ," he groaned, throwing back his head. The light above surrounded him, framing his perfection for my eyes. "You're so warm and tight. You feel wonderful, Rhiannon. Perfect."

He started moving in a slow, steady rhythm, lowering his mouth to kiss me, caressing my face with his hand while moving in gentle exquisite movements. His practiced fingers grasped my hips, encouraging me to match his rolling thrusts. The delicious heat started to spread, rushing through my limbs until I mirrored each motion without his guidance.

"There you go," he whispered huskily and brought his hand between us, rubbing my clit. "Come for me, Rhiannon."

Trembling started anew. My body heated as my skin prickled. I squeezed his hips, acclimating to his rhythm, and matched it. I reached for that explosive feeling once more, tumbling over as my body lifted and detonated yet again.

My moans were lost inside his mouth as he kissed me, moving harder and faster. His tempo increased, his hands pressing roughly into my hips, holding them in place. Our bodies moved together in unison and I gasped into his mouth, my body complacent under him as he reached for his own version of heaven.

He thrust into my body in one sharp stroke, bringing himself into me until all I could feel was him, both inside and out. His entire body shuddered, I felt him pulsing within me, and a cool wetness overcame the heat where we were joined. He groaned into my hair and blanketed my body like a brisk breeze.

Hoisting onto his elbows, he peered down with concern and worry. "Did I hurt you?"

"No, you didn't hurt me. I'm wonderful." I laughed through shallow intakes of air, pressed a fast kiss to his mouth, and fell back on the pillow. He relaxed, returning my smile. He lowered his head and kissed my throat, nuzzling my ear.

"Thank you for trusting me," he murmured, pressing a kiss to my mark. "You won't regret it, I promise you."

"Thank you for making it worth the wait," I teased, biting my lip as a smile formed. I could definitely see why people enjoyed the experience. I was already thinking about round two.

He slowly pulled himself from the heat of my body, lifted away, and rose from the bed. My protests were silenced as he pulled me into his chest and took us across the room. Pushing open the door across from the bed, he carried me into the bathroom. Lights flickered and surrounded us, glowing brightly against the white tiled floors and wallpaper.

"What are you doing?" I asked anxiously, aware of our nakedness in the bright fluorescent lighting.

He opened the glass door to the shower and stepped inside. "I'm going to take a shower with you."

A steady spray of water shot from two different spouts on the adjoining walls as he fiddled with the levers with his free hand. He waited until the water heated before lowering me to the ground. My bare feet touched the cold tile, and I crossed my arms over myself. Without my shoes, I only came to his chest. As if sensing my shyness, he pulled me into his arms and turned so the water streamed down his back and over our skin.

I glanced down at the trickle against my leg and gasped. I knew people often bled the first time, but not like this.

"What's wrong?" He moved away and peered down.

"The blood," I said weakly.

"I'm sorry, I should have warned you." He pulled me back into his arms. "That's me, Rhiannon. Our body excretes blood. It's the source of our life, and it inhibits all our bodily functions."

He pivoted so I was under the warm stream. Tilting my head, I allowed the water to cascade through my scalp, causing wet hair to cling to my back. The duel showerheads steamed up the space, fogging over the glass, giving the illusion of cover.

Disco reached past my head and pulled a clean cloth from the shelf inside the stall. He held it under the soft rain from the shower and ran it along my back in soothing, circular motions. He cleansed each surface thoroughly, taking extra care as he ran the cloth along the soreness between my legs. He was gentle, removing the traces of himself and my virginity. Being with him like this felt more intimate then our time in the bedroom.

When he finished with my body, he started on my hair, massaging floral scented shampoo into the thick strands before helping me rinse it clean. Then he embraced me in the shelter of his arms, his chin resting atop my head in the steaming shower. His hands teased the skin at my back, and I gripped his waist as we swayed back and forth in the stall.

I didn't know what tomorrow held for either of us, but for the first time, I really didn't care.

I was ready to start living again.

To hell with the consequences.

CHAPTER TWENTY-SIX

This was what it was like to be young and completely enamored. I felt as if a part of me remained behind when I climbed into the car and started my trek home. I didn't want to leave and would have remained with Disco all day if I didn't need things like a toothbrush, deodorant, fresh underwear, and clean clothes.

I made it to my apartment before eleven. Once I unlocked the door, I tossed my things onto the table. The answering machine was blinking and I pressed the button, listening to messages from Goose and Hector. Goose wanted me to call him when I got the message, and Hector informed me that if I didn't make it in on time the next day I could find other gainful employment.

I cringed when I replayed the second message for clarity. If I wanted to keep my job, I had to put in some serious ass kissing effort.

I was starving, a ravenous appetite returning at a bad time. I still hadn't been shopping, and the kitchen was empty. Digging through the cabinets didn't help. I didn't even have an emergency can of soup in the cupboard. I walked down the hall and into my bedroom, yanking off my sweater along the way. I would get some shopping done, call Goose while I was at the market, and after I brought everything back home, I'd go back to Disco's.

I intentionally chose clothing Disco would approve of, deciding to wear the soft grey cotton sweater that fell to my hips and the tattered blue jeans I wore in high school. I slid on new underwear and quickly dressed before rushing to the bathroom to brush my teeth.

I was looking at myself in the mirror, affixing a clip to keep my French twist in place, when I recognized the face from Jacob's vision. My reflection mirrored the horror I experienced with the epiphany. My mouth gaped and my eyes grew wide. How could I have forgotten those jade green eyes and that dark skinned face? Jacob had shown me that his killer was in a plain black suit, just as I'd seen him dressed after Jude Mason's party.

I had looked the bastard dead in the eye.

Rushing into to the living room, I paced the circle formed by my recliner, sofa, and coffee table. I thought about the little boy held aloft in Max Starkey's arms and tried not to imagine what a vampire like Joseph would do if his parents were somehow involved.

Should I tell Disco of my discovery? That would be the intelligent thing to do. Besides, he would have to know eventually. Still, I couldn't shake the image of the sick child from my mind, or the way his parents looked at him. He was just a kid. I couldn't knowingly lead vengeful vampires to his doorstep.

I decided to call Goose. His home machine picked up, and I disconnected before prompted to leave a message. I tried his cell with the same result and grew annoyed when it clicked over to voice mail. I left him a brief message, explaining he should call as soon as he could. Slamming the phone back into the cradle, I crammed my pockets with my keys, knife, money, and cell, and started for the door.

I froze, hand on the knob.

There was something else I might need.

I returned to my bedroom and pulled down the little black box on the top shelf of my closet. My Ruger was already loaded and the extra magazine was full. I attached the holster to my jeans, slid the gun inside, and placed the extra clip in my pocket. I had to dig out the manufacturer's warranty papers to find my license. I shoved it into my back pocket and hoped like hell I wouldn't need to explain why I was carrying a firearm.

I left my apartment and headed for the subway. I was anxious the entire trip and made a conscious effort to keep my arms crossed and my sweater down so no one would notice the gun on my hip. When I came to my stop, I tried to picture the conversation I was about to have with Max Starkey. He had to know how dangerous this shit was, and I had to know what the hell was going on.

I didn't hesitate when I reached the glass doors that announced I'd found my realtor's haven, pushing on the lever and striding confidently inside. It was a nice clean space, not too frou-frou or uptight.

The portly receptionist looked up from her computer, her friendliness evaporating like water on hot summer asphalt when she got one good look at me.

"Can I help you?"

I lifted my chin and smirked at her. "I'm here to see Max Starkey."

"May I have your name?" Her arrogance wavered ever so slightly. She couldn't tell if I was legitimate or not.

"Janet Hamlin. Tell him Jude Mason introduced us. He'll know who I am."

I kept a face straight face. If this didn't work, I was sure I could take Bertha Sue. Too bad I didn't bring a box of Twinkies to distract her.

She lifted the phone to her ear and pressed a button, watching me the entire time. I considered picking my nose to see how she'd respond.

"Mr. Starkey? There's a Janet Hamlin here to see you. She says a Jude Mason introduced you. Yes sir, I'll send her in." She informed me with a clipped voice, "He'll see you."

I didn't ask where he was, strolling past her desk, toward the doors situated along the back. Each of them had little nameplates screwed into the wood and I glided past until I found his name emblazoned in gold plating.

Bingo.

Max was seated behind his desk and had his hand on the telephone when I walked in. "Ms. Hamlin," he said politely and gestured to an empty chair. "Would you please close the door behind you and take a seat?"

He looked completely professional, as relaxed and courteous as he did at the tasting. His suit was understated but expensive, the light blue tie matching the tiny stitching on the pinstripes on his jacket perfectly. His dark skin and deep brown eyes gave me the same impression I had the first time around. He was boyishly handsome and appeared as trustworthy as an eighty-year-old school teacher. Goose was right. Appearances certainly were deceiving.

"Sure." I put my best smile forward as I closed the door and slid into the chair across from him. I nested into the comfortable leather seat.

"What can I do for you?" He remained polite and smiling. Not what I had expected. He returned to his seat and leaned back, the chair creaking as the springs shifted under his weight.

"I'm here to ask you some questions," I responded, equally cordial.

"Regarding?"

Well hell. I had this all planned out and then he went and screwed it up. He wasn't playing into the asshole mold I'd prepared for, and I couldn't do the good cop bad cop routine. I decided to go with blunt force honestly. You can't beat it.

"What can you tell me about the market for vampire hearts?"

"Pardon?" His friendly smile faltered and he looked at me as if I'd lost my gourd. He was good, real good.

I repeated myself. "Vampire hearts. You know what I'm talking about, so don't try to deny it." I narrowed my eyes.

"Ms. Hamlin, I assure you I have absolutely no clue what you're talking about." He sounded offended and confused. His voice lost the friendliness that was present just a second before. "I'd appreciate it if you didn't bring black market business into my office. Please leave."

"Oh no, you don't." I shook my head and launched toward his desk. We were finally getting somewhere. "You know what I'm talking about. I saw your driver, Max. I saw him through the eyes of a dead man."

"Are you on drugs?" he asked, mortified.

"No, I am not on drugs," I snapped. How did I become the weirdo here? He was the one living a macabre version of *Driving Miss Daisy*. "But I do see dead people. One of the vampires you killed paid me a visit."

"I think you need professional help." Max pushed his chair back slowly and rose to his feet.

"Wait." I took a deep, calming breath. *Count to ten. Breathe in. Breathe out.* "If you don't know what I'm talking about, then tell me this. Why did you get into the car with the man I'm talking about?"

"What man?"

"The man from the party. I saw you and Carolyn get into the car with him."

"The car—" His expression changed as the light bulb went off in his head. He stared at me distastefully. "My son has been gravely ill, Ms. Hamlin. That's why my wife and I attended the party in the first place. As you can probably imagine, we were eager to get home that evening. When Mrs. Gilstead offered us the use of her car and driver, we graciously accepted." His lips thinned. "If you have questions about the driver, I'd take them up with her. I would suggest you try a different approach, however. This one won't win you any contests."

"I don't remember a Mrs. Gilstead," I said like a moron. At least my instincts were correct. I'd rather look like a lunatic than find out the Starkeys were responsible.

"You were introduced to her." He eyed me like a nasty piece of toilet paper that stuck to his shoe on the way out the john. I really had to work on my presentation and delivery.

"I was introduced to several people, but Mrs. Gilstead was not one of them." I sorted through my mental vault and couldn't recall anyone with that name. If she was there, I was positive our paths had never crossed.

"She and her husband Timothy were standing with us when Jude introduced you, Ms. Hamlin. I remember clearly." He paused, then added, "You don't seem to be functioning on a rational level, if you don't mind my saying so."

"Timothy," I said. My own light bulb went off, accompanied by a brain screeching alarm. I remembered. Ms. Hardbody and her husband with slate grey eyes and hair reminiscent of George Hamilton. "Timothy and Sarah Gilstead."

"That's right." He nodded but frowned at my expression. "Are you all right?"

"Yeah, yeah." I rolled my eyes, stood, and stumbled around the chair. I had to get out of here. Disco needed to know what I had learned, and I had to speak to Goose.

"Are you sure?" He came around the desk and reached for me. I threw my hands up and he stepped back, eyes flaring enormously.

"Listen to me, Max." I spoke quietly and looked him dead in the eye. "You might think I'm crazy, and that's fine. You don't have to believe a word of what I'm about to tell you. But if you love your family, you'll take what I say to heart." I pressed into his personal space, speaking clearly. "Stay away from the Gilsteads. They are into some heavy shit, and you don't want to be in the middle of it. I promise you."

"You're not talking about the tasting, are you?" A well-founded fear crept into his voice. Good man. He was starting to believe I wasn't some crazy loon paying a social call.

I shook my head and never broke eye contact. "I'm not talking about blood or anything else that's consensual. Your friends are murdering people—*my* people. And you don't want to be involved with my people, Max. They're the type to bleed you dry and leave your corpse to rot. When the reckoning comes"—I lifted my hand and made an arch, pointing across the room—"you'll want to be way the fuck over there. Do you feel me?"

"Yes," he answered in a hoarse croak.

I nodded in approval, turned around and opened the door, and stepped into the hall. I walked past the receptionist, smiling at her shocked face when she told me in a superficial voice to have a nice day, and I gave her a parting gift—my middle finger.

Retrieving my cell, I dialed Goose. His voicemail clicked over and I was forced to do the most annoying, rude, and discourteous thing anyone can with a phone.

I spammed him.

I kept calling his number, over and over. On the fifth try, I heard the click that indicated he'd pushed talk.

"Rhiannon?" He sounded annoyed and as if he'd intentionally muffled his voice so someone else couldn't hear. "I planned on calling you after I finished here, but when you kept calling, I was afraid something was wrong."

"Where are you?" I was out of breath from jogging along. I stopped on the sidewalk and waited, not hearing him well through the speaker.

He didn't answer right away. "I'm following a lead."

"Tell me you are not going after Timothy Gilstead."

When he didn't respond, I had my answer. My chest constricted with panic and I tasted bitterness rising from my stomach.

"Listen to me. The man who killed Jacob works for them. You have to get out of there, right now. Do you understand? Get the fuck out of there!"

"Are you serious?" he hissed into the phone, voice muffled.

"Would I fucking lie?" I snapped. "That night we left the tasting I saw Max and Carolyn Starkey getting into a limo. Their driver was the same person who killed Jacob. I don't know why I didn't place him immediately, but it's him. He was even wearing the same fucking suit."

"Then we need to pay a visit to Max and Carolyn—"

I cut him off. "I already did. It wasn't their car or driver. Sarah Gilstead said they could use the limo to get home to their son." I dodged people on the sidewalk, cursing in annoyance. "Leave whatever you're doing and meet me at Disco's. This shit can't wait."

"I'm leaving now." Wind crept into the phone and I could barely hear his last two words. "Be careful."

"You be careful." I could take care of myself, but Goose was a walking target. "I'll see you at Disco's."

I hung up the phone and hurried to hail a cab. The sooner I got to Disco's, the better. I walked to the street to flag down a yellow submarine when something lodged into my lower back. A hand grasped my arm from behind. I opened my mouth, prepared to give a good tongue chewing to whoever was moronic enough to push me.

"I wouldn't recommend that," a deep male voice said into my ear. "The Taser I'm holding against your spine will incapacitate you. We can do this without resorting to that, but if you push your luck, I'll be forced to use that option."

"Who are you?" I tried to get a look at the face behind the voice, but failed. "What the fuck do you want?"

"We'll get to that shortly."

He nudged me toward a black Lincoln waiting on the street. I took the smallest steps possible. If I got inside the car, it was game over.

Rule number one that all girls must learn. If you're told to lie down on the floor during a robbery or to step inside a waiting car during a kidnapping, you're not doing yourself any favors by cooperating. You are essentially handing the bastards responsible a loaded gun and giving them express permission to shoot you in the head.

He opened the door, and I tried to bolt. Twisting around, I lunged to the side.

"I warned you."

A pained gasp caught in my throat as an explosive burning shot through my spine and radiated through my entire body. Hands directed my tumbling form forward, into the waiting seat. My arms drew to my sides in involuntary jerks, going on and on, and I passed out.

CHAPTER TWENTY-SEVEN

I came to with an aching head and weak body. My neck protested when I forced my chin off my chest. Fresh oxygen rushed to my numb muscles and they roared to life, stinging and tingling. I tried to bring my hand around to rub the ache, but my arms were trapped behind me. I opened my eyes and waited for them grow accustomed to the darkened space.

I was at the far end of a rectangular room with one door and no windows. The walls were painted dark to match the floor and ceiling and, aside from a table behind me, the room was empty.

My heart lodged in my throat. I knew this place. I had been inside Jacob's and Baxter's bodies on that hard concrete floor. A large white circle was painted on the pockmarked concrete with a six-pointed star drawn in the middle. The hexagon center had little metal hooks buried deep into the ground, connected to thin silver chains. The surface was stained, and the brownish black coloring flared out from one area in particular.

A surge of despair welled into panic. I threw my weight forward, trying to propel myself, but the chair was hard and immobile. My struggling only caused the rope around my wrists to cut into skin. I pushed up with my feet in an attempt to stand. When that failed, I tried to rock from side to side.

Pressing my head against my shoulder, I glanced down. The damned chair was bolted securely to the floor. I tensed my shoulders, fighting the ropes around my hands, ignoring the pain as coarse material bit into my skin.

The door opened and I froze, listening as the hinges creaked. I had said working for Disco was accepting the lesser of two evils and I would probably get killed. I was about to find out if my premonition was bound to meet fruition.

Timothy Gilstead didn't have the same flair now that I knew he was a sociopathic asshole. His grey eyes flickered over to me and he smiled, shaking his head. The son of a bitch looked at me as if I was an honored guest. He closed the door and ambled over.

"Mrs. Hamlin? Or should I use your real name?" He smiled as he stopped directly in front of me and folded his arms. His baby blue dress shirt pouched out where the starch was extra thick.

"That depends," I answered in an agreeable tone, smiling deceptively. "Can I call you a despicable murdering asshole?"

I didn't take Timothy for the kind of man to hit a woman, but he gave me a nice ear-ringing slap across the face. The burn was intense, and I knew the blow would leave one hell of a mark. I opened my mouth, rotating my jaw in the socket.

"I thought attending NYU would have made you smarter somehow." He was breathing heavy, still angry. "I suppose no amount of quality education can buy common sense. Perhaps you need a little incentive to keep that lovely mouth shut."

His sudden movement regained my attention. He strode to the door, opened it, and whispered to someone outside. I pressed the smarting side of my face along my sweater, attempting to soothe the sting. If I made it out of here, I knew the first thing I was going to do. I was going to track Timothy down and kick his pearly white teeth down his goddamned throat.

Footsteps approached, and I watched Timothy return. Someone else followed and I nearly gave myself away, attempting to hide the automatic response that comes with recognition. Big boy vampire, Paul, stepped into the room. He seemed as docile as a puppy—frighteningly different from the vampire who was ready to take my head off at the Razor.

The soft squeak of rubber soles against concrete came from the door and a little boy appeared, dressed in a thin, white cotton shirt and black pants. His dark skin was flawless, black hair shortly trimmed. He glanced in my direction and smiled. Big milky-green eyes stared back at me.

Pure fear produced a debilitating adrenaline spike. I could feel what he was, even if my mind refused to accept the fact.

"Lie down," the boy instructed and Paul obediently sat on the floor and stretched his body out in the center of the circle. He didn't make a sound when the silver chains were drawn through the hooks, wrapped so tightly about his wrists that they started sinking into his creamy flesh. His hands were secured first, then his ankles. Timothy stepped away and the little boy surveyed the work, finding it satisfactory.

"Wake."

Paul started to hiss and thrash, each movement causing him more pain than before. He whipped his head from side to side, eyes wild and confused. A pitiful sound of agony escaped his lips.

"Shh." The boy lifted a finger to his lips, and Paul went silent. I watched in disbelief as he thrashed in suffering but didn't make a peep, muted like a television station.

Timothy peered over at me and said, "Amazing, isn't he?"

I couldn't speak; too humbled, mortified, and just plain scared. The boy didn't look to be any more than seven or eight years old, but I could sense the evil in him. He might have died when he was a child, but his true age was something I'd never encountered. The power emanating from him was massive, and I was awestruck.

"Good," Timothy said smugly. "It seems you realize the dire straits in which you find yourself. Now that we have your attitude under control, I can offer my most sincere apology. We hoped it wouldn't be necessary to involve anyone other than those essential this time around, but unfortunately, your master is one of the most powerful in the area. Kibwe couldn't pass that up."

"Your master has a most unbelievable talent." Kibwe had the voice of a child, speaking in clear but accented English. He smiled enthusiastically at me, exuding happiness. "The ability to manipulate perception is rare and something I must have for myself."

The ability to manipulate perception? I grappled with what Timothy said earlier about NYU and easily slid the puzzle pieces together. I didn't know if it would be to my benefit or detriment to inform them I wasn't Sonja and that my master sure as shit wasn't Joseph.

"What the fuck are you?" Disturbed, I looked him up and down. He appeared to be a little boy. He even sounded like one. However, he wasn't a child and hadn't been one in quite some time.

Timothy started forward, arm poised to strike, but Kibwe moved with vampire speed to stand before me. He held his small hand aloft with a sadistic grin spreading across his face that made me wish I could shrivel up and disappear.

"I was once as you are—a kindred conveyor of the dead. A plague assaulted my village, bodies torn apart and drained of blood. I was summoned by the elders to speak to with the spirits about the lingering death that continued to consume us. My maker witnessed this exchange, and was intrigued by my power. He made me into what you see before you."

I shifted quietly in the chair, my back pressed against the wood. His angelic face studied me with rapt attention and inquisitiveness.

"You could see spirits?" I eventually asked.

"Oh, yes." He grinned, revealing tiny white teeth.

Eyes averted, I spoke softly, wanting answers and trying to be as non-confrontational as possible. "I don't understand. Why would you kill your own kind? They haven't done anything to you. Why would you want to hurt them?"

"I must eat of their body and take their power directly into myself. Therefore, death is required." He shrugged his thin shoulders nonchalantly at my revulsion. "It is necessary. The heart is the organ that sustains life. It generates all of the power we hold. To devour power is to take it into one's self."

"You killed them...so you could take their power?"

Goose and I were way off the scent. He wasn't using the organs for magic. He was using them to empower himself. God knows how many hidden talents he possessed. He was older than any vampire I'd ever known. I was sure of it. And the way he handled Paul told me his necromancy had crossed the all-powerful threshold; he could control all of the dead, vampires included.

"No." He shook his head and smiled. "Those who keep me protected also must be given their due. Eating of our flesh can slow the aging process indefinitely, did you know that?"

I shook my head in return and looked away, swallowing down nausea.

"Drinking from our life's blood will hinder father time, but only so long as you partake. My people have been loyal to me for centuries. Those vampires taken without talents I deem worthy are a given to my coven as a courtesy."

I whipped my head around and stared at Timothy. He had willingly participated in the murder of innocent people and devoured them like a fucking Happy Meal.

"You disgust me, you rotten piece of shit."

At first, he blanched. Then his face turned an angry shade of red as I kept going.

"Get as mad as you want cannibal Lecter. You can pretend you're all high and mighty in front of the masses, but I know the truth, you nasty bastard. I hope you choke on the shit."

"Let me silence her, Kibwe." Timothy stepped forward, and I met his hate filled glare head on. "They will come for her dead or alive."

"Don't let her sharp tongue slice you so deeply." Kibwe sighed, giving me a chastising look. "The danger of a strong wit is the capacity it carries to unravel. You must control yourself. Her petty words cannot harm you unless you allow them to."

"Are you the one responsible for the deaths in Los Angeles?" I asked bluntly, fear turning to wonderfully delicious anger.

"Such a tragedy that was." Kibwe shrugged his fragile looking shoulders. "The girl was too curious for her own good. She should have left well enough alone."

"And what do I have to do with all of this?" I wriggled my hands, keeping my shoulders still.

"I have taken your master's right and left hands." He lifted his tiny fists into the air, pointing at Paul and then me. "He will come for you. They always come for those most important to them. He also wants revenge for the death of his brother. That was how I tasted his talent. The memories his sibling shared gave me everything I needed."

"What if you're wrong?" He might look like a child but he was nothing more than a sick, sadistic, murdering little bastard.

"I am never wrong." His broad smile made me want to vomit. "I'll show you. Ask me a question. Any question."

"Are you going to kill me?"

He frowned, his annoyed expression truly making him resemble an unhappy child. He glared at me, gauging the possibilities of the answer.

Eventually, he answered, "No."

A knock sounded on the door, and Timothy strode across the room. Kibwe continued to stare at me with uncertainty. That had to be a good sign. If he didn't have a clue what my future held in store, there had to be hope. The whispered voices were too quiet to distinguish, but I attempted to hear, homing my ears. I continued to work my hands back and forth. The burning was worse. Tiny fiber splinters embedded deeply in my skin, splicing the flesh.

Timothy came back inside and walked over to Kibwe, stopping just short of physically touching him. "They are here. Our people can sense them all around."

"That is good." Kibwe turned away from me, and faced Timothy. "I must complete the sacrifice of this new one, and as he has no talents worthy of my notice, I will honor you with the strength of his life."

"I am most grateful."

Timothy knelt down and I stifled the gag in my throat.

The child vampire ran his dark hand through Timothy's hair, whispering something inaudible, treating him as if he were the child. When he stepped back, Timothy stood and turned in my direction.

"Fucking cannibal," I snarled, but he didn't react this time. No doubt happy he'd be chowing down on vampire for dinner.

"What do we do with her?" Timothy asked.

"Let her witness. When I have finished, I will feast on her blood and break her master's bond. Afterward, we will leave this place. I must hurry. There is little time to spare." He waved at the door, his delicate fingers moving in a way no child's would. "Leave us."

Timothy gave a quick bow and hurried off, speaking to the people waiting outside. The sounds of footsteps faded along what I assumed was a hallway. Panic consumed me as I tried to think of a way to get free. Although the struggle against the ropes hurt like a bitch, I pushed aside the pain. I didn't want Disco and his family walking into an ambush. It was bad enough if Joseph was already here.

Kibwe removed his shirt and yanked the thin white cotton over his head. His dark skin was flawless and pristine, his chest concave and stomach distended. His tiny fingers grasped the pendant at his neck and he spoke an incantation. He rested his chin on his chest as words carried from his lips, his voice changing from that of a child to a man.

Kibwe didn't shift so much as he changed. His body grew taller, and his muscles shimmered underneath his ebony skin. The boy transformed, aging until the man responsible for killing Jacob stood before me.

What the fuck.

"This charm was spun by the most ancient of demon magic. A gift from a witch who served in the hell dimension under Lucifer's very own familiar." He allowed the charm to drift from his fingers and down the dark expanse of his chest. He raised his face, closed his eyes, and breathed in deeply. "Your blood smells exquisite." He reopened his eyes and met my terrified stare, his irises glowing amber. "When I have finished my work, I will drink you dry. If you survive the thirst, I will consider bringing you into my fold. Would you like that?"

"You might look like a man, but we both know your dick is nothing more than a Vienna sausage." I kept working at my hands as I spoke. "I don't dig pedophilia."

"You are an amazing creature." He smiled admiringly, the silky tenor of his voice deep and smooth. "We'll see if you retain that self-assured nature when I rip apart your throat and drain the life from you."

I could see the blade shoved into the back of his pants as he passed my chair, its oddly slanted hilt unwelcomingly familiar. The muscles corded in his shoulders with each step as he stepped over Paul's squirming form and faced me.

"Speak," he whispered.

Paul's pained cries filled the room. His wrists were tortuously raw and open, but he continued in his attempt to wrench free. I followed his example, struggling with my own bindings.

Kibwe hoisted the knife by the slowest of degrees. He built the tension as he lowered the weapon, bringing the blade down slow and steady. Paul thrashed pitifully, eyes glued to the sharp metal coming toward his chest. Kibwe lifted Paul's shirt, ripped the material, and splayed it wide. Paul's chest moved up and down as he drew terrified breaths, his rib cage rising and falling in rapid succession. Tiny red dots formed on his skin in a sparse, uneven pattern.

Dear God. He was sweating blood.

The blade slid into his stomach, and Paul cried out. I winced, knowing all too well how deep that pain went. As he had with Jacob, Kibwe tilted his head back, as if pulling the horrible cry into his ears. He started to chant in a language I didn't recognize as he slid the knife up from Paul's stomach, toward his chest.

"Yo, fucknut!" I yelled.

If Kibwe heard, he showed no indication. I thrashed like a mad woman, yanking my arms against the restraints and kicking my legs. I felt the warmth of my blood, sticky and thick where the rope had frayed my skin. Paul's screams incensed me, and I started making my own sounds of exertion, embracing the pain as though it could set me free. When my efforts didn't work, I relied on sheer desperation.

I felt my right hand ease past the rope, the skin stinging like a thousand needles.

I continued staring at the carnage before me. Kibwe was engrossed in his task, dragging the blade through pliant muscle and skin. I bit down hard on my lip to keep any sound from escaping when I pulled my left hand free, leaving fresh skin behind.

I only had one option, and it didn't bode well. I had to rush Kibwe. I didn't know where my gun was, and the butterfly knife in my pocket would take too long to dig free. Since he was the oldest vampire I'd ever encountered, I was playing Russian roulette.

Breaking free, I charged across the room like a deranged battering ram but didn't make it far. Kibwe's hand enclosed my throat, lifting me easily from the ground. Squeezing his wrists with both hands, I thrashed like an injured animal.

Carrying me across the room, he rammed my back into the wall with a dull thud. The heels of my shoes banged against the plaster as I struggled for air, gripping at his wrists with my hands, fighting to breathe as air and saliva gurgled in my throat. He tilted his head from side to side, studying me from multiple angles, yellowing eyes glowing. Suddenly, his clenched fist came into my vision; his thumb was so close I couldn't bring it into focus.

"*Ndoto,*" he whispered as he released my windpipe.

I drew in a huge, ragged chunk of air just as he opened his hand and blew something dark and foul into my face. It smothered me, constricting the newfound flow of oxygen. He let go and my body dropped, legs barreling to the ground as dead weight landed on fragile knees. The burst of agony that should have followed the distinctive snap of breaking bone didn't follow. I clutched my throat and rubbed my eyes.

The room shifted, the walls taking on new patterns and colors, a virtual paint by numbers with irregular squares and circles that moved and kept me off balance. I swayed but didn't fall. I closed my eyes but could see everything. Nothing worked as it should, and the harder I tried to bring it all together, the faster my grip on reality slipped.

The ground rushed up to meet me, but the impact didn't hurt. Worn, green carpet padded my fall, absorbing the impact, and brushed against my face. I lifted my head, heart racing as I comprehended where I was.

Fear, panic, and desperation choked me, and I watched in terror as Ray's black loafered feet stopped inches from my face.

CHAPTER TWENTY-EIGHT

"Get off your lazy ass!" Ray's rough hands grasped my arms, his fat fingers digging into my skin. "Where's your sister? I'm not buying the bullshit about a study group after school."

I shook all over, unable to speak. The pads of his fingers slapped my face, stinging sharply. I remained stunned and silent, too petrified to make a sound.

"Did you hear me, Rhia?" He slapped me again, using his full hand, harder this time. "Look at me when I'm talking to you."

I lifted my head and focused on his nose. I knew not to make eye contact. If he saw my fear, it would excite him. I swallowed, nervous trembling trickling down my back and along my extremities as my fingers became numb. I balled my hands into tight fists.

"Where is Jennifer?" His hands caressed my arms in a gesture that was anything but fatherly.

"I...don't...know."

"You...don't...know," he mocked. His tone changed to a husky whisper. "What should we do to pass the time until she gets home?"

His fingers maneuvered down my arms, gliding behind and gripping the flesh of my back, going lower until he grasped the thick portion of my hip and thigh. He closed the distance, his rancid breath hot against the skin on my neck.

I pushed him away and ran through the living room as he roared, "You frigid little bitch!"

After yanking open the bedroom door, I stumbled through and slammed it closed behind me. I squeezed my eyes shut, leaning against the solid wood. My breathing was loud in my ears, resounding in my head.

"Sweetheart," a gentle voice said, and I felt something tug my shirt. "Sweetheart, I need you to open your eyes. I need to shine this light into them."

My body swayed from side to side then shifted roughly as I bounced around. I lifted my lids and gazed up at the bright light shining into my eyes. My lashes fluttered against my cheeks, and I lifted my hands to ease the burn that came from momentary blindness.

"You're going to be fine."

I squinted to block out the light. The woman speaking had on a vest with various pockets and a stethoscope around her neck. Her pale skin was lovely, the red stain on her cheeks, and the pink tint to her lips, natural and breathtaking.

"We're going to the hospital right now."

Hospital. My stomach barreled into my throat. Not the hospital. That meant it was over. That meant they were gone. I started to wiggle and discovered that I was unable to move my neck. I was strapped down to a hard surface of some kind.

A blur of white confused me until I recognized the ceiling above, speeding by in square flashes. Multiple voices assailed my ears, overriding each other. The brightness changed to darkness. I found I could sit up, and so I did. After carefully rising from the bed, I walked to the door. It was quiet now. I couldn't detect anyone or anything. I reached out for the tall hospital door, pulled on the silver handle, and stepped through.

It was a dreary day. The sun was hidden behind heavy grey clouds that threatened to empty at any minute. The air was thin as I dragged it into my ravaged lungs, exhausted by hours of crying. The pastor read the final rights as the caskets lowered into the ground.

Side by side they went—ashes to ashes, dust to dust—my life, my family, slowly descending into their final resting place, entering the cold, dark earth. I stood beside the now-occupied graves and listened as dirt was tossed onto the wood, cracking and sliding along, cascading to the ground below.

I lifted my head, fixated upon the battered form of my parents. Dad was beyond recognition. Half of his once-handsome face gone, and his cheekbone was missing along with the eye socket. Mom's beautiful long hair was hacked off on one side, revealing a wide gash that ran from the front of her skull to the back. They watched me behind empty eyes, and I called to them, but their expressions remained blank and emotionless.

I covered my face with my hands as tears tumbled down. My chest racked with silent sobs and wails of grief. I heard an odd noise, like a headboard banging against a wall, and lifted my head from my knees.

It was dark.

Jennifer's quiet begging came through the thin plaster. Ray told her to say she wanted it harder, to please give it to her harder. She said it back, voice cracking. A loud slap reverberated in my ears followed by a harsh reprimand. She went silent, and the repetitive thumping and squeaking of well-used mattress springs followed.

I buried my head into my knees again, praying for God to change me into something else, into some other creature who could escape from the hell that was my life. I huddled as deep into the closet as possible, hiding amidst clothes, shoes, and forgotten toys. Jennifer's cries mingled with the sound of Ray's moans. I covered my ears, rocking back and forth, humming as loudly as I dared.

When the door flew open, I freaked out, screaming and shoving back into the clothes. It was my turn now, and no one would be able to stop him this time.

Ray always got to me in my dreams.

Strong hands reached for me, circling my arms, drawing me toward the light. I resisted, fighting with all I had. If I lost here, I would lose everything. I resorted to begging and mindless pleading, content to stay hidden in this dark place. My pride be damned.

The hands forcing me out were firm and insistent, pulling me ever forward from the comforting dungeon. The darkness dimmed as an orange glow neared. I pushed back, slamming my eyes closed, unwilling to leave safety behind me. A forceful tug forced me away from the comforting cover of darkness. The warm rays of the sun surrounded my body, wrapping me in a sheltering cocoon.

"Rhiannon." Disco's voice was so very welcome that I crumbled, afraid to open my eyes and see what new nightmare waited. "Look at me."

I shook my head, breathing heavily as tears streamed unbidden down my cheeks. It was a trick. I would open my eyes and Ray would be grinning back at me.

Chilled hands cupped my face, and I felt Disco's equally cool lips brush my own. I could smell the scent of cloves emitting from his skin, taste his cinnamon-laced breath against my mouth. I tentatively reached out to touch his familiar body.

"You're safe now." His fingers wrapped inside my hair and pulled me closer. "Open your eyes and look at me."

I held my breath and did as he asked.

Molten pools of golden blue stared back and me; the most beautiful eyes I had ever seen. My bottom lip quivered, and I gasped for air as fresh tears fell from my eyes. His thumbs brushed across my cheeks and he gave me one of his beautiful smiles.

"*Disco.*" Sagging into his arms, I released all of the pent up terror and fear. His name had never been so welcome on my lips.

"Do something for me," he whispered against my hair.

"Anything."

"Call me by my real name."

I nestled my cheek against his solid chest and whispered, "Gabriel."

He held me securely in his arms, swaying back and forth. The crash of the waves breaching the sand got my attention, and I looked past him. I breathed in the muggy air, tasted the bitter salt on my tongue. We were at the beach I had visited with my parents. He had brought me to the one place I felt most secure—my happy place.

"Is this real?"

"You're dreaming, but this is different. Not at all like the time before. Something is feeding off your fear and using it against you." He moved away, holding me at an arm's length to look me in the eye. "None of this is real, but if you allow it to continue, it will consume you. You're going to have to wake up."

"How do I wake up?" A flash of terror seared my chest. What if I couldn't wake up?

"I'll help you, but first we need to talk. Everyone outside is trying to get into the warehouse, but something is controlling our people and making them turn against their own. Two of Joseph's kindred have already been killed. Do you know why?"

"It's the vampire responsible. He can control the dead, even vampires, and he's been eating the hearts of others to take their powers. He wants Joseph now. That's why he took me. He thought I was Sonja."

"We can't enter until he's dead." Disco's eyes focused as he tried to formulate a plan. He studied me carefully and asked, "How badly are you hurt?"

"I think I've broken my knee," I answered calmly. There was no reason to worry him.

"It has to be you, Rhiannon. I don't like it, but if we delay..." He shook his head, clearly angry at the lack of options. He looked up. His steely determination showed through his frustration. "Our kind can regenerate from almost any wound inflicted, but mortal ones are the hardest to heal."

"I don't know if I'm strong enough."

"You are." His grip on my arms increased and he kissed me. I took comfort in his succulent sweetness, placing it to memory. He pulled away, bent down, and brought our foreheads together. "I'll be there with you. Trust me. Now wake up, Rhiannon." He shook my arms forcefully and yelled, "Wake up!"

My eyes flittered open, and I stared across the cold, dark concrete. The light overhead reflected clearly, creating a shining path across the room, and I rotated my head.

Paul's spirit was standing over his body, and Kibwe was holding his now severed heart aloft. The large, silky-red organ was still beating. The necromancer's back was facing me, but I could see his uneven breathing as he chanted.

I raised my pounding head inches from the ground, shaking the cobwebs loose. My right knee was throbbing, and my wrists stung, but I didn't have time to think about it. I managed to sit up, finding myself weak and unsteady.

"*I am here, Rhiannon.*" Disco's voice washed over me, through me. "*And my strength is now yours.*"

The lethargy, weakness, and headache vanished—replaced by strength, power, confidence, and purpose. The change was unbelievable.

I felt indestructible.

Suffused with Disco's strength and fortitude, I made it to steady feet without a sound. He had finally opened that special connection we shared, unlocking my mark. I searched for a weapon, spying my Ruger on the table and clip beside it. I retrieved both, slipping the pistol into my hand.

Kibwe was lost in a chant, and I watched Paul's spirit dissipate before my eyes. Kibwe was banishing his soul. I didn't know how I knew that for certain. I simply did. That's why we couldn't communicate with victims. They were trapped in limbo. It wasn't enough to take their lives. Kibwe was stealing their rest as well.

I called on my anger and it answered readily. The flame called fury licked under my sternum, spreading outward. I stepped toward the circle, my right leg pain free but lagging behind. Disco was there. I felt him like a shadow in my mind. Present but silent.

Paul's form was nothing more than a haze. The time to act was now. I steadied the gun, angling the pistol to left side of Kibwe's back, aiming for his heart. The clip slid quietly into place and I braced my left hand, my trigger finger twitchy as I cocked the gun.

Kibwe tried to move with his impressive vampire speed, but I started unloading the rounds the instant one slid into the chamber. The clip only held six shots, and the small caliber bullets would ricochet along his insides like a pinball machine, but it still wouldn't do the job.

I watched him sag forward when the sixth shell entered his torso, and Paul's heart flopped from his hand into the empty chest cavity it had once inhibited. I dropped the pistol and snatched the shining weapon at Kibwe's side. The blade was blessed silver, which meant the wound wouldn't close immediately. I grabbed his hair and yanked his head back. His wide green eyes stared up at me in bewilderment.

"This is for Cash, you son of a bitch." I flipped the knife to a backward angle, gripped the hilt, and slid the sharp blade into his throat.

The edge was true and sank deep, gliding through the path of my choosing. Blood spurted and poured down his chest in a thick, steady flow of exquisite red and pooled on the floor below. Flailing hands attempted up to staunch his river of life, but it was too late. I continued to push the knife deeper, until I met the resistance of solid bone and scored through it.

Kibwe lurched forward and I instinctively reached out to stop him. My hand wrapped around the leather string tied to the amulet around his neck. It tore free, dangling from my fingers.

The man before me shrank, reverting to the form of a child. The wound was much worse like this, the head nearly severed but for a splice of bone and flesh. The delicate body flopped on the floor, bubbles of air mixing with blood around the wound, spreading over the floor in a crimson stain.

"*We are coming.*" Disco spoke in my mind and the energy abruptly drained from my body.

I sank to the ground, ears ringing as the knife bounced off the concrete in several decisive chinks before coming to a rest beside me. My right knee burned and pulsated. The injury was so severe that my jeans stretched as far as the material would allow. I opened my fingers and stared at the amulet nestled inside my palm. It glowed like amber, with a tiny black teardrop glistening inside.

Timothy thrust aside the door and raced into the room. His eyes widened when he located his master's fallen body. His scream was one of hate and rage.

His body slammed into mine, causing the back of my skull to smash against the concrete floor with a crack. I was defenseless and too exhausted to put up much of a fight. I lifted my hands in a feeble attempt to ward off the blow from the blessed knife he now gripped. He slammed the blade into my chest, and I sucked in a painful wail of air. He tried to pull the weapon free, but I grasped his hand, holding the knife in place.

If he pulled it free, I was as good as dead.

We struggled for a minute, until my grip ebbed. My bloody hands slipped against his, covering us in sprays of crimson. We thrashed back and forth, his strength unwavering, mine faltering. I had nothing left to give. I could taste the metallic bitterness of blood as it seeped from my mouth. I was suffocating, unable to draw in vital air.

I closed my eyes and let go, imagining my parents waiting for me, envisioning us walking to our beach and staring into the setting sun together. Timothy tried to tug at the blade, but it was slick and hard to grip. Each attempt brought gurgles from my lips as warm wetness poured from my mouth and nose, and trickled past my ear into my hair.

Timothy disappeared and I stared up at the dark, grey ceiling. The florescent light bulb in the center of the fixture flickered.

The pain was less now. It wouldn't be long.

When Timothy returned, he stood with one leg on either side of my body. He stared down at me, holding my Ruger in hand. Aiming the gun at my face, he roared, "I'll have your heart, you fucking bitch."

The mechanism clicked as he squeezed the trigger, but nothing happened.

I laughed weakly, the sound more of a cackling mew than anything else. Leave it to Timothy not to check the clip or the chamber, ignorant bastard. It didn't matter. I didn't have long left anyway. It was getting dark fast.

He scowled, lifting his arm, ready to get some use from the weapon even if he had to throw it.

My words came out bubbly, barely understandable as I spoke through bloody lips. "Fake it until you make it, you sorry sack of shit."

I struggled for air, my lungs screaming for essential oxygen. My body fought itself, demanding what it needed but I was unable to provide. I choked on my blood, gagging instead of breathing. The pain inside my chest was dull and immense. I seized on the concrete, limbs contorting in a death rattle. I felt my body relax as I slipped free of the pain. A peace settled over me, and my dimming eyes saw the finality of my death through Timothy's elated face.

My soul detached from my body, leaving the empty casing behind. I didn't have to look around the room. I could see and hear everything. I knew that Timothy was rushing for the door, but he was out of luck. People were down the corridor. I also knew three bodies were on the floor, bunched together, drenched in blood.

And one of them used to belong to me.

"Thank you," Paul said quietly.

"You're welcome." My voice wasn't a voice. There was no sound, yet Paul heard me clearly. I looked at him. He was whole once more. I glanced down at myself. So was I.

"Are you going to go?"

"Go where?"

He smiled and pointed behind me. "We can go together."

I turned my head first, then circled around. The entire wall was gone, replaced by a glorious white light, brighter than the first blanket of fresh winter snow. It thrived, alive with welcoming tendrils, casting swirling rainbows that lengthened and stretched toward us.

It was difficult to turn away, but somehow I did. My gaze rested on the lifeless body I was leaving behind. The knife was still embedded in my left breast, the hilt smeared, the silver tinted red. Blood stained the grey sweater in a large circle. More of it had dribbled free of my bluish lips and welled on the floor.

Paul drifted past, stepping closer to the light. The rays seemed to reach for him, making contact with his body until he shone in its brilliance. The shimmering molten white surrounded him, and he stepped past, becoming one with the glorious radiance.

I followed Paul, intent on basking in those mysterious beams that sang of all the wonderful things I'd always wished for—serenity, peace, safety.

Disco, Goose, Sonja, Joseph, and Paine burst into the room. I heard Goose's horrified cry, Paine's confused babbling, and Disco's heartbroken roar. But I couldn't rip my eyes away from the light. It was so beautiful, so breathtaking, and it *sang*. The most glorious, divine, and pure music chimed inside my unworthy ears.

A jolt pierced through me, a painful tug on my soul. I stopped my trek, confusion overcoming my desire to cross the room.

"You will remain here, Rhiannon." Goose's voice accompanied the next jolt that seared through me. I was being pulled back, forced to remain as the light in front of me started to move into the distance.

"Look at us!" Goose demanded, and I turned to that undeniable voice, unable to disobey the order. Goose and Sonja were holding hands, their eyes focused directly on me.

"Get her back here now or she's crossing over!" Goose yelled, voice urgent and uncompromising, although his attention remained riveted on me. "You don't want to leave this world. You still have so much to do, Rhiannon."

Unable to do anything else, I took in the scene before me.

Disco's bleeding wrist hovered over the mouth of my former body. His lips were moving quickly as he screamed at me, angry that I would leave without a fight. Paine pulled the blade free from my chest and blood rushed out, absorbing into the sweater. He cut his wrist with the blade and held it over the gaping wound. Our blood mixed as his seeped down into the jagged hole.

An unsteady thud shifted my perception, rocking the room. The glorious music from the light started to fade and I spun around, bereft and saddened as the melody and radiance drifted away, turning into a fog.

Something inside me shifted, and I no longer stood pain free above the fray. I was on the cold ground, brutal shards of agony radiating from my chest and lungs.

"She's back!" Disco's voice was heavy with unshed tears, and I shifted my barely functioning gaze overhead, desperate to see his face. He kept his wrist at my mouth, rubbing his skin across my lips.

"You have to stop feeding her." Paine's voice was soft—so unlike him. "If you don't, she'll start to change. Stop, Gabriel."

Disco pulled his wrist away, eased his hands under my body, and lifted me cautiously as Paine moved back. Strong arms surrounded me, trapping me securely against his chest, and I went limp within them. He didn't say another word as he squeezed past Goose and Sonja and strode from the room.

Tucking my hands under my chin, I wrapped my fingers around the necklace clutched safely in my fist, the surface of the once warm amulet going strangely cool against my palm.

EPILOGUE

Four Weeks Later

I crossed the sunny street, exiting the lot of the local Super Store Family Grocery. Both of my hands sagged under the weight of black reusable bags as my muscles flexed. The vampire blood had faded over a week ago, no longer enhancing me with abnormal strength, vision, and hearing. I was just a regular girl grocery shopping on a Saturday morning.

Okay, maybe not *totally* normal. But the grocery shopping part was true enough.

I smiled at Jerry—Disco's personal driver on loan to me while my knee continued to mend—and he returned the gesture. He stepped out of the car in his crisp white shirt and dress slacks, opened my door, and confiscated my bags. I thanked him, climbed inside, and took a load off.

Paine's blood bound the flesh and bone in my chest while Disco's had done the rest from the inside out. But there was extensive damage, and by the time my lungs and chest were working properly, the remaining injuries were left to sort themselves out.

Since any more blood could trigger a change, I had to suck it up and see a doctor. He informed me that my kneecap was cracked, but was miraculously healing, so I could continue to live life like the rest of my fellow *Homo sapiens*.

It had taken a week to find out where our mole was. Someone had been feeding information to Timothy Gilstead, inaccurate though it may have been—how in the hell he confused Sonja's platinum rainbow dye job with my Plain Jane style and dark mane was beyond me. As it happened, Lorence Smith didn't want to help us because he was knee deep in the shit. Timothy had approached him about a new drug of choice and made him an offer. If he gave up the identities and whereabouts of certain individuals, he would be lucratively compensated. And the best part was they worked on a schedule, so they'd be leaving the area afterwards.

No fuss, no muss.

It's a shame with all that money Timothy didn't hire better help. All of us—Disco's family and Joseph's—were tracked for days. When Paul was taken, Timmy boy gave the okay to bring Sonja in. The asshole with the Taser might have gained an advantage over me, but I got the last laugh. Thank God, he seized the wrong girl. Sonja might have the smarts, but I had the cojones.

We are all special in our own way, I suppose.

As for Lorence, he wouldn't be peddling anything anymore. He was on an extended vacation somewhere under the ground with Sarah Gilstead. He went running to her when the ship started to sink and took her down with him. You have to love that kind of commitment.

My pocket started buzzing and I dug out my phone, smiling when the incoming number flashed. I chewed on my bottom lip as I placed it against my ear.

"Hello?"

"I'm picturing how you looked beneath me this morning—flushed, excited, and out of breath," Disco purred into my ear. "When will you be home?"

"I just finished here. I need to unload everything at the apartment and change," I rasped, picturing him above me, his powerful body moving in and out of my own, and a wisp of heat ran from my head to my toes.

The car shifted as Jerry climbed inside and buckled up.

I shifted uncomfortably in my seat but it didn't alleviate the burn.

"Wear the present I got you," Disco whispered in a husky timbre. "Give me something to look forward to."

"The last time I did that, you shredded them." I giggled, trying to keep my voice down. The creamy lace bustier with the intricate black threading didn't last long. He'd ripped it from me within seconds, too eager to access the body underneath.

"I'll buy more." He chuckled, then lowered his voice seductively. "Wear the red one for me."

"I'll surprise you."

"Then I'll be waiting...hurry."

The phone clicked and I lowered my hands to my lap, smiling at the screen. The sneaky bastard had crept into my heart when I wasn't looking, and now he had a key to it. Letting go was terrifying, but Disco had done as he promised. I just had to believe he would be waiting to catch me before I hit the ground each time I fell.

Jerry helped me with the bags and walked me to my apartment before returning to the car to wait. I checked the machine. Deena had called again. She'd managed to talk Hector into giving me a much deserved vacation—one that ended in exactly one more week.

She wanted to make sure I was coming back, but I was still undecided.

It took longer than usual to put away the food. I'd bought mostly non-perishable things. Fruit and vegetables didn't last. I stayed at Disco's—*Gabriel's*—too much for that.

I snickered and shook my head. Gabriel didn't particularly care for his nickname. He'd gotten it one Christmas after Nala adorned his room with a spinning mirror ball, and as a joke, he'd kept the damned thing up for a year. The name pretty much stuck after that, an ongoing joke that spanned a decade.

After hanging the black bags in my laundry closet, I walked into the living room. The amber pendant was where Goose had left it. He refused to take it with him, and seemed spooked as hell when he touched it. Since he refused my pleas to research the damned thing, I was going to take it with me when I returned to Disco.

I twisted the amulet between my fingers, studying the stone. I could feel the faint hum it gave off. The slightest surge of power tickled my fingertips. Spun from

Lucifer's very own familiar—whatever that meant.

I shoved the amber chunk into my pocket and went into the bedroom. Pushing the door across the carpet, I looked down to monitor the movement of my right leg. My limp was less pronounced now, more of an achy reminder.

Reaching out blindly, I prepared to push aside the door to my mirrored closet, when I got glimpse at the reflection.

My mouth opened and I gasped, eyes going wide. Glowing orange irises with golden-yellow iridescent centers flashed back at me. It had human features—feminine yet boyish—with high delicate cheekbones, a thick sloping nose, and full lips. Ivory colored skin was marred at the temples and neck with protruding stains of black. Bronze colored hair flared out in every direction. The clothing was unisex. A button down shirt rolled up at the cuffs, russet-brown slacks and matching loafers completing the outfit.

I stepped away from the mirror and the reflection of the fire-eyed creature. The sky behind it was red. Strange animals crawled over what appeared to be desert sand. The wind whipped around them, manipulating the dust into miniature tornados.

The creature stepped forward, its leg wobbling, distorting the parameter of the mirror. The glass swayed and rippled, giving way as a foot slid from the glossy surface. The overwhelming smell of burnt sulfur permeated the room and stung my nose, causing my eyes to water. The thing stepped free of the mirror, standing just inside my bedroom.

"I am Zagan. Do you know why I have come?" Its irises glistened like oil on water, a sheen radiating and glowing at the same time.

"Oh shit."

"You do know. Excellent." It smiled at me, displaying perfect rows of white teeth. "I have come to collect my due."

My heart hammered miserably in my chest. Running wouldn't help; my leg wasn't up to par, and the demon came through a thin piece of glass, which meant it could travel in ways I couldn't conceive of.

I gulped, waiting quietly. I thought nothing could scare me anymore.

Bull-fucking-shit.

"What are you going to do to him?" The thought of something happening to Disco made my heart contract.

"We do not give answers freely, but as you did not summon me, I will oblige your curiosity. I seek reimbursement of his debt through you, Rhiannon Murphy." It extended a finger, twisting its head to an unnatural angle, displaying more teeth. "The mark you bear and the blood within your veins solidifies Gabriel Trevellian's dominion. That which he owns is subject to the bargain."

I swallowed thickly and asked, "What do you want?"

"You are in possession of Marigold Vesta's amulet. I require that, as well as one other payment to consider the debt settled."

It took a step forward, smiling maliciously. Unexpectedly, it stilled, pupils becoming snakelike. Thrusting back its lips, it bared fangs. "You reek of Heaven's light." The demon stepped away from me, snarled, and dropped the human façade.

"You mean this?" I pulled the pendant out of my pocket and the flaming eyes sparked, burning liquid gold. I took an unbalanced step backward, covering the charm with my fingers.

Zagan snorted, keeping a distance between us. "Yes."

"And the other payment?" I asked warily.

The demon paused, stared at me angrily, and inhaled again. Shaking its head and coughing, it cleared its nose in repeated snorts. "The delivery of a message."

"A message?" I asked suspiciously. It sounded too easy.

"I require the amulet and a message delivered, nothing more." Rusty citrine eyes stared me down, the pupils in the center shifting to a vivid lime green. "I wished to have you serve as my pet in perdition, but God's hand still lingers on you."

I said a prayer to God, thanking Him for allowing me to bask in the light the pearly gates, if only briefly.

"What kind of message?"

Zagan smiled impishly, dipping its long narrow chin, staring at me through heavy bronze-lashed lids. "I want you to tell Gabriel Trevillian our debt has been settled."

"That's it?"

It couldn't be that easy. *No fucking way.*

"That's it." The demon nodded and smiled again, white teeth sparkling.

I didn't see how this could be a bad deal. The debt would be paid. The amulet would return to Hell where I was sure it belonged. And I was on my way back to see Disco. I could settle everything in less than an hour.

"If I give you the amulet and give Gabriel the message, then it's done and over?"

"Yes."

"Nothing more than that?"

"Nothing more than that."

Wary but hopeful, I extended my hand with the amulet. "Okay."

"You accept the deal?" it asked, teeth gleaming, eyes ignited.

I hesitated before answering, "Yes."

"Excellent!" Zagan clapped spidery hands together, the nails at the tips long and rounded. It reached for the amulet, took it, and held its breath until it was at a breathable distance from me.

"Pick a number." It danced back and forth on long limbs, grinning gleefully at the pendant in its hand.

"What?" I frowned, caught off guard by the request.

"Pick a number," it said again, smiling playfully.

I wanted to leave and get to Disco. I had just made a bargain with a demon for him. If that didn't show him the magnitude of my feelings, nothing would.

"Pick a number," Zagan repeated, becoming moody, staring at me through slitted eyes. "And you will be able to deliver my message."

Spotted Dalmatian puppies came to mind, and I blurted, "One hundred and one."

"One hundred and one." Zagan cackled, lifting its head. After a pause, a grin spread across its face, becoming a terrifying smile. "Now, for the second part of our bargain."

The demon's androgynous face contorted as it came toward me. The eyes slit, opal pupils crackling like snake eyes, teeth sharpening into miniature triangles of white. The black patches near its temples spread out, marring the skin in big uneven splotches.

I stumbled back as the putrid stench of sulfur stole my breath, falling at the side of my bed, staring up in horror.

"Deliver my message and all debts are paid."

Long, lean fingers touched my forehead, burning my skin. My room disappeared. Flashes of color, images of unknown faces, and the hurried sounds of traffic, death, and sulfur combined. I screamed, equilibrium off kilter, and fell back, crashing through windows of color, some in shades I'd never seen, faster and faster.

The world came to a deafening halt and I wretched, vomit overflowing from my stomach in painful heaves. I turned onto my knees, spewing out my lunch while holding my stomach. My muscles protested and heaved until there was nothing left to expel and the world stopped spinning. I wiped the back of my hand across my mouth and stilled.

Instead of carpet, I'd vomited onto asphalt. I sniffed through my nose, eyes watering with unshed tears, and lifted my head.

The sun was setting, maybe another forty-five minutes until it sank behind the horizon, and I was in a filthy dead end alley. I lifted myself on wobbly legs, swiping my mouth with my fingers to make sure they were clear of any leftover up-chuck.

I didn't know what the hell Zagan had done but it couldn't be good. My hair on the nape bristled, warning me that something was very wrong. I was in SoHo, not far from the BP, but the street was deserted. There were no animals, no people crowding the sidewalks, no cabs on the street. And most frighteningly, there was no sound.

I plodded along, looking around for any signs of life. Was I in another dimension? Did Zagan lie and send me to Hell anyway? Movement caught my attention, and I whirled around anxiously. A man was scuffling down the street with a black garbage sack, moving as fast as his thin legs could carry him. His hair was buzzed short, jeans and T-shirt worse for the wear.

"Excuse me!" I yelled.

I tried to intercept him, but he ignored me, walking faster. My knee protested as I struggled to keep pace. Catching up with him, I touched his arm. He lost his balance and his bag fell to the ground, along with several books and pieces of paper.

"Look at what you did!" he screamed, bent down to collect his things, and shoved them hurriedly into the plastic bag.

"What's the problem?" I asked, picking up some of the books and collecting them in my arms.

"The sun is setting, that's the problem. I never should have come out this late, and from the looks of it, neither should you!"

He snatched the remaining books from my hands and stood, leaving some of the papers scattered on the sidewalk at our feet. He took off in a frantic jog, the black plastic bag rustling in front of him.

I fell back on my ass, the busted knee throbbing miserably. A newspaper was next to my hand, and I when I saw the headline, I lifted it with trembling fingers, certain it was a joke.

The header, printed in Old English text, identified the newspaper as *The Blood Times*. The feature article was entitled, "The Future Of Blood Supply As Human Numbers Dwindle." I scanned over it, reading about something called The Renfield Syndrome; a virus that had wiped out a majority of the population during the third world war between humans and vampires.

I flipped the paper over with shaking hands, staring at the classifieds.

People were presenting themselves on the market, offering blood and servitude in exchange for eternal life. There were details, as if they were nothing more than varieties of livestock on the open market—male, female, fat, skinny, tall, short, young, and old.

They even mentioned blood type.

I pulled the shaking paper toward my face, reading the bold date at the top right hand corner.

October 28th, 2112.

I didn't have to do the math. It was simple. Add one hundred years to 2011 and carry over the one. Zagan had sent me into the future, using the number I'd picked from the top of my head as his marker.

I lifted my gaze toward the darkening sky as reality sank in.

I was in the same dimension, but now humans were the endangered species, vampires were out of the closet, and here I was—sitting on my ass while the sun dipped below the horizon, bringing on the night.

Rhiannon's Law #101: Never make a deal with a demon. They are evil bastards that will screw your ass over and send you back to the future.

Where the hell did Doc park the DeLorean?

AUTHOR'S NOTE

Three years ago, I went to my husband and told him I wanted to write a book about a woman who worked in a strip club as a bartender and saw dead people. He said, "That sounds nice," and I immediately sat at my PC (I didn't have a laptop at the time) and started writing the book you are currently holding in your hands. *Dead, Undead, or Somewhere in Between* introduced me to so much in the publishing world, including things I wasn't prepared for. I won't go into that, aside to say that I was very excited to be able to reclaim the book, work on it, and return it to readers as it should have been in the first place. I hope you enjoyed the revised edition, as well as the bonus material included as a way to express my thanks for purchasing my work.

For those who want to kill me for the ending, allow me to say that Rhiannon's journey will continue in August when *The Renfield Syndrome* releases at my wonderful publisher, Mundania Press. I'm currently working on the third novel in the series, *The Ripple Effect,* and have a feeling there will be several more installments before Rhiannon is finished with me.

Thank you for taking a chance on my work and for giving me time in your reading chair. Without your support, none of this would be possible.

All My Best,

Jaime AKA J.A. Saare

BONUS MATERIAL:
EYES ON ME

Not too long ago, my friend and enormous Disco fan, Bells, told me she would love to read about the first encounter between Rhiannon and Disco. Eyes on Me *takes place prior to* Dead, Undead, or Somewhere in Between, *and introduces you to Rhiannon, Disco, and their ill-fated friend, Cash.*

Rhiannon's Law #51: It's a crime *not* to take a fool's money. If they are stupid enough to put it on the table, be smart enough to take it off their hands. Stupid is a stupid does—so don't be stupid.

Lining up the short shot, I decided not to baby the ball but to send it rocketing into the tight corner pocket using a bit of draw to make the cue roll back nice and fancy. The moment the money shot arrived to its destination, I slowly eased from my crouch, slid my stick onto the table, and faced my opponent. I could have asked for the dinero he owed me, but it wasn't necessary. He was already reaching into his back pocket for his wallet. The poor bastard didn't seem too happy about his first hand introduction to Law #51, but I relieved him of his crisp and shiny Andrew Jackson just the same. His expensive Meucci with the ivory and jade inlay told me he had plenty to spare, and besides, it was a slow night to hustle.

"Funny, you didn't play this well twenty minutes ago," he informed me as he passed the money over.

"That's because I wasn't warm yet." Accepting the bill with a smile, I hiked my chin in the direction of the table. "You up for another round?"

He allowed his stick to slide through his fingers, until the plastic bumper rested on the floor, and wrapped both hands around the shaft. "Are you going to let me break?"

Smirking, I lifted my index finger to my forehead, swiped it across, and asked, "Do I have stupid written across here?"

"Excuse me," a smooth, husky southern baritone drawled.

The hair on my nape rose on end, tingling as my heart hammered a fast staccato. The gift of necromancy told me what was standing behind me; a familiar and unwelcome hum accompanied the vibration under my skin. I would have welcomed anything else at the moment—a battered wife, the victim of a gunshot wound to the head, a machine operator who lost their grip and fell into a meat grinder. Anything but what I knew stood at my back.

As I turned toward the voice, I steeled myself to remain expressionless and titled my chin to look into the face of the newest challenger to step up to the table. He was dressed in his fuck-me-best—a snug black T-shirt that displayed his defined, muscular torso, blue jeans that molded to his thighs like a worn, second skin, and battered combat boots. Strands of dark red hair fell across his forehead, his ocean blue eyes vibrant inside the smoke filled room. His non-threatening stance, handsome face, and friendly smile were the deceptive devices of a hunter, used to lower the defenses and make it easier to move in for the kill.

As if they needed another weapon against helpless, horny females—*fucking vampires.*

He winked at me like a practiced panty charmer, plopped a twenty onto the green felt, and leaned against the table. "Are you up for a game?"

"No can do, I'm already —"

"I'm done here," sourpuss loser interrupted, breaking down his stick. "Just don't let her break or play safety. You'll never get to the table."

I was left to gawk as the man I'd just hustled strode to the small round table with his belongings, collected his case and beer, and headed for the bar. Aside from my desire to chase the asshole down and force him back to the table, I cursed my decision to visit Shooter's Pool Hall versus Harry's Pub and Grill across town. It had been a hasty decision when I'd noticed Harry's was slammed to the gills and realized there wouldn't be a free table unless I won it and kept it.

The vampire grinned when I returned my attention to him, extending his hand. "Cash."

I didn't mirror the movement, keeping one hand in my pocket and the other on my stick, and sized him up. He wasn't carrying a cue or case, which didn't mean much. Most hustlers carried cues that resembled the cheap sticks the house kept lined along the walls, trying to pretend they didn't know what the fuck they were doing. It was easier to blend in as a newbie and scam those who didn't know better. His posture, however, told me he wanted to play for fun, and aside from the boots, he didn't appear to be someone who was in dire straits or feinding for drug money or the like.

To hell with it. If he wanted to play for money, I was game. There were enough people in the joint to keep things safe, and money from a vampire spent just as well as anyone else's. Shrugging, I turned toward the table holding my case and chalk.

"Cash works for me."

He laughed and the unexpected, humored sound caused me to glance in his direction. He was right on my ass but stopped before he got too close, as if he was aware I wasn't entirely comfortable with his company.

"That's my name. Not the score, sweetheart." His pronunciation of sweetheart left out the all important "h," making it sound more like *sweet-art.*

Terms of endearment, how I fucking hate them.

"That's nice." I blew him off and snagged my bottle of water. "I'm breaking. Go rack."

He hesitated and his smile slowly vanished, as if he found my disinterest unexpected. When he turned around and walked to the end of the table to rack the set, I noticed the set of his shoulders were now tense versus relaxed. They stayed that way even as he retrieved the balls from the pocket and pulled the wooden rack from the light fixture above the table.

Trying to find the mental headspace I went to when I needed to focus on a game, I took one final swig of my drink, screwed the lid on the top, and turned to place it on the table when I came face to face with another vampire seated on my barstool. Whereas the other vamp was friendly and offered an easygoing smile, this one studied me with a knowing expression, his eyes the color of pristine aquamarine. It was impossible to silence my alarmed gasp or mask the reaction that was second nature. I jerked back, moving away, and tripped over my cue case when it fell from the tabletop.

A large, cool hand wrapped around my forearm, keeping my ass from connecting with grimy carpet. He pulled me upright, his grip steady and firm, and released me when I regained my balance. As I stepped back, we faced off, although I was forced to look up to maintain eye contact.

His long, dark trench coat made it impossible to tell just how broad in the shoulders he was, but judging by the skin tight black turtleneck tucked into his tailored slacks, I was fairly certain the bulk was all him. His honey blond hair was neatly trimmed and brushed away from his face, bringing focus to defined cheekbones and the squared line of his jaw. Although he looked like he was nearing thirty or so, I knew he was a hell of a lot older. He didn't speak, sizing me up. To his credit, his gaze remained on my face versus taking a leisurely trip down my body as I was accustomed to.

Those eyes and the concentrated stare he was aiming in my direction caused my palms to go clammy and my breathing to stint. This was a vampire that could rip me wide open using his bare hands. I knew it, could feel it. He would eat my ass, leave my gnawed carcass in a dumpster in an abandoned alley, and continue on with the nightlife as usual. As much as I wanted to play off my nerves and act unaffected, I knew the vamp in black could see my fingers tremble as I bent at the waist and retrieved my case from the floor. Mr. Tall, Dark, and Terrifying was waiting for me when I righted myself and took the case before I dropped it again, confirming my suspicion.

Shit, shit, shit.

"All set," Cash called out from behind me and, for the first time in my life, I wanted to thank a goddamned creature of the night for saving my wretched ass.

Pivoting away from the vampire behind me, I faced the less-threatening but equally deadly fire crotch with the winning smile. Two vampires in one joint. What were the odds? Dismal. Which told me they were together.

Cash collected my stick from the table, brought it to me, and placed it into the hand I extended as my brain began functioning on automatic. "Take it easy on me," he said, keeping things light, as if he could tell just how rattled I was. "I'm fragile."

The moment he stepped past, walking toward the table to his friend, my brain kicked into gear. I felt the comforting weight of the cue in my hand and welcomed the smooth glide of the wood between my fingers, but I knew I was fucked. While it wasn't visible to those who weren't looking, I was trembling violently, like a lowly tree trapped in a category five hurricane. I'd left Miami to get away from this very thing; to keep a safe distance from what I knew would most certainly kill me. Past experience taught me that once you were on the blood sucking radar you'd better start working out an escape strategy, lay low until an opportunity to slip away presented itself, and get the hell out while you still could.

Placing the twenty onto the side of the table, I held my breath, hunkered down and got comfortable, and said a prayer to the pool gods that I made the nine on the break so I could call it a night. One stroke, then another, and I put all my strength into my hip as I stroked through the ball and shifted my weight into my shoulder. The tip connected with the cue, which then slammed into the first two balls on the right of the racked diamond. A loud crack resounded in my ears and the rounded spheres of resin scattered like pinballs. The cue ball rolled forward for a moment and, due to the draw I'd put on it, began creeping back toward the middle of the table as the two and eight ball dropped.

My heart felt as if it exploded in relief when the nine stopped in front of the corner pocket and the one ball slid into perfect alignment. I'd always loved slinging the money, and I found it rather damned poetic I was about to against a vampire. While it was apparent Cash wanted to play, I certainly didn't. Now, only a single combination stood between me and the door of the building.

Thank Christ for small favors.

As I lined up to take the shot and got comfortable, I noticed a lurker was standing just over the pocket. My focus quickly drifted from the pocket to the shadow he created, breaking my concentration. It was a diptwat thing to do, and I waited for the asshole to get out of the way. There was no way I was risking this combination and sticking around to shoot the breeze with vampires.

"Do you mind?" I grumbled loudly enough for him to hear while keeping my focus on the shiny yellow one ball. The alignment was just right. If I glanced up to glare at the person, I'd have to stand, take another look, and get back into position. Second guessing a shot caused you to take what was natural and apply additional pressure where none was necessary, which was something I didn't want to do.

"Need some help there?" Cash asked from just behind me, and I could hear the laughter in his voice.

"Hey, asshole," I yelled. Annoyed and out of patience, I unhinged the bridge my fingers created along the shaft, slapped my palm on the table, looked up at the shadow hovering over the nine ball and snarled, "Would you get the fuck out of the way?"

Horror swept through me the minute my furious gaze passed through the shadow, and I saw the people standing across the way who were looking at me as if I'd grown another head. A man wasn't standing over my pocket, a ghostly torso shrouded in black was. I gawked like a star-struck teenager who'd spied Robert Pattinson with K. Stew at the local 7-Eleven, eyes wide and mouth gaping, mortified that I'd not only slipped up, but had screamed at someone who, to the average person, wasn't even there.

"Who you talking to, chica?" Cash asked curiously, breaking the spell.

My face flushed, growing warm in embarrassment. It was damned hard to tear my eyes away from the ghost who stood at the end of the table staring directly at me, but somehow I did. Cash had come around the side of the table, and I didn't bother lining up my shot or taking my time. Relying purely on instinct, I crouched over the table, got into position, and let it rip. The cue popped the one into the nine and the striped ball sank with a deafening pop. I yanked my stick back, snagged the cash from the bumper rail, and rose in the same motion.

When I began breaking down my Sneaky Pete, Cash stepped in front of me. "Come on now. You can't leave yet. We were just getting started." His smile said he was at ease, but his jerky mannerisms and flickering glimpses behind me—which were uncharacteristic of his kind—gave him away. "You can't take my money and run."

"Watch me."

I turned, kept my attention on the ground, and hurried to retrieve my case. Unfortunately, the cheap leather holder was clutched inside the hands of the vampire with a black hard-on. When I looked him in the eye, silently dared him to fuck with me, and tried to take it from him, he hoisted his much longer arm up into the air, placing it out of my reach.

"What's your name?"

The expensive clothing and his immaculate appearance told me he was wealthy, but he carried himself like a street brawler; his observant, glittering eyes too disconcerting for comfort. I'd steeled myself for the cadence and dialect of a predator—braced to go head to head with another louse with a bad attitude and an ego to match—and was completely taken off guard when a sophisticated baritone caressed my ears.

I had no idea why he was staring at me so oddly, those glorious blue peepers far too inquisitive. However, it wasn't the fact that he was staring at me so directly that made my skin crawl and my stomach contort. It was the fact that the harshness in his face was gone, smoothed by what I perceived to be a dawning understanding and awareness—as well as something I didn't care to define.

Too proud to beg, I lowered my arm and narrowed my eyes. "Give me my case."

Apparently, my anger amused him. "Give me your name."

Anger—hot and welcome—pulsed through me. Right now, I wasn't alone in an alley or someplace he could play his hand. I was surrounded by people, meaning I was safe and he was shit out of luck.

Smiling sweetly, I lifted my arm, balled up my fist, and gave him a middle finger salute. "Wilma," I said. "Wilma Fingerdo."

"Don't antagonize her, Disco." Cash's voice at my ear caused me to jump to the right, and my elbow caught the side of the table. My water bottle fell from the surface, along with the wooden box that stored the fast food menu, salt and pepper, and mustard and ketchup.

"Shit," Cash muttered and moved to retrieve the mess, opening a window of opportunity for me to dart forward, grab the case that was now within my reach, and snag it from the hands of the asshole who flashed narrowed eyes of his own at me before I began a hasty retreat toward the bar.

I shoved the divided cue into the slots inside the hollowed leather without the normal care I usually gave them, forgoing the plastic joint protectors that were nestled inside the zippered compartment on the front. I'd only been at the table for an hour, which meant the twenty I'd swiped from the table would take care of things.

"BB," I yelled as I approached the counter, glancing past the shoulders in my way, and extended the bill to the graying bartender filling a mug full of Smithwick's on tap. He frowned when he saw me, stopped the tap, and immediately started walking to the end of the bar. I knew it was because he'd never seen me so demanding or edgy. Normally, I was cool as a cucumber. It was a necessary evil when hustling. Just like poker, you never revealed your hand. "Here's the money for the table."

"Everything okay, Rhiannon?"

"I just have somewhere I need to be. I lost track of time." I passed the money to him and smiled thinly, desperate to get the fuck out of the building.

He accepted the cash, but I knew he didn't buy my excuse. Not that it mattered. I didn't plan to return to Shooter's. Not for a long, long time. The truth was I'd gotten too comfortable, having forgotten cardinal rule number one—never let your guard down.

I felt eyes on me and glanced over my shoulder, wincing as I realized that BB had just given the vampire—Disco—my name. He stood just a few feet away, observing our conversation. His black trench coat was thrust back just enough for him to place his hands in the pockets of his slacks, his feet placed shoulder width apart. Gone was the curiosity and intrigue, replaced by the cool, aloof, and frankly terrifying demeanor that had created my first—and lasting—impression of him.

The ID checker at the door moved aside as I hustled for the exit. People were standing directly outside, smoking cigarettes. The grayish clouds parted when I rushed through them and began waving frantically at the lone cab that was steadily approaching. As it slowed to a stop, I stepped onto the street, yanked open the door, and lunged inside.

"Where to?" the cabbie asked as I slammed the door closed and he started the meter.

I was about to answer when I glanced out the window and I saw a dark form step through the misty vapor I'd just abandoned. His blond hair reflected the red neon light above the building, the red hues shadowing his shoulders making him appear far more sinister. He pulled a box of cigarettes from his pocket, plucked one out and placed it at his lips, and promptly lit it with a flick of the flashy Zippo that caused the neon to cast a mirrored shade of ruby across his face.

As he took a long, deliberate drag, he met my eyes, and didn't look away.

"Greenpoint," I replied hoarsely and moved away from the door.

The cab shifted and started to move down the street, putting distance between us, but my nerves didn't settle and heart continued to race. That horrible sense of intuition I'd always relied on warned me that while I might have gotten away tonight, this wasn't the last I'd see of him.

Rotating in the seat, I took a dangerous glance back. He remained in the same spot, toking on his cig.

As if he had all the time in the world.

Rhiannon's Law # 44: Don't believe the shit your parents pawned off on you to keep you in bed at night. The scariest monsters do not live in closets or come out from under your bed. They survive right along beside you, out in the open—right where you can see them.

BONUS MATERIAL:
MORE THAN WORDS

I wrote More than Words *before* Eyes on Me. *I knew many people wanted more Rhiannon and Disco and this was my way of giving them what they asked for. This scene takes place between the final chapter and epilogue of* Dead, Undead, or Somewhere in Between.

The sweet, earthy smell of burning wood and a delicious dash of smoke was the first thing that roused me from a deep, reviving sleep. Having grown accustomed to waking without an alarm, I was also aware the sun had risen. The past four weeks had been an extended break of sorts, time to mend, recoup, and recover. Unfortunately, that break would end in a week. It was time to figure out what I wanted to do, to make some big decisions, which brought me to the second reason I'd woken from a beautiful dream that included my own personal Adonis, a sandy beach, and a sunset to die for.

Disco's body was wrapped around me, bare skin against bare skin, our heartbeats in perfect harmony. His chest was flush against my back, wider hips snug against my ass, cradling mine. Although he didn't produce body heat, I was more than capable of warming him up. Right now, he was as balmy as a summer day, toasty warm and comforting.

For several minutes, I remained quiet and content in his arms, listening to the crackle of the wood as it split and withered. It was impossible not to feel the right-ness of the moment, of the two of us together. In the past few weeks, the feeling permeating my chest was becoming more and more apparent. This wasn't just a man I shared my bed with. He was a man that, whether I intended to or not, held my heart in his hands.

Even worse, he knew it. Living in his home except for the rare occasion when I ventured out to meet Goose, visit the doctor, or go to physical therapy, meant we were always with each other. For the most part, my appointments were later in the afternoon, when he could accompany me. However, when the rare occasion arose and I was forced to venture into the sun, he'd watch me go from the shadowed doorway, his displeasure notably apparent. It felt as if I was leaving a piece of myself behind as I crossed the threshold and entered the light he could never safely feel on his skin.

His cool breath caressed my nape, pulling me out of my thoughts, and his arm tightened around me as he whispered huskily, "Good morning, love."

My heart stuttered at the endearment, just as it had the first time he said it. Love was such a relative term, wasn't it? On one hand, hearing it could make someone the happiest person in the world. On the other, hearing it might scare the piss out of you. The people I loved always went away, even if they didn't want to. That made accepting and reciprocating the sentiment far more difficult. Wasn't it enough that I felt it? Or did I have to pony up, grow a pair, and find some way to force the one, tiny syllable from my mouth.

"Good morning," I wimped out and whispered, feeling like a goddamned pussy.

"Did you sleep well?" He nuzzled my neck and brushed his lips across my throat, intentionally lingering over my mark.

I groaned when his hand flattened over my belly, bringing me back against him. There was no need to answer the question; he was well aware of the response. The hard ridge that prodded between my thighs and ass told me he'd slept well too. Since he was a constant visitor in my dreams, we found all sorts of creative ways to pass the time. Last night, he'd given me glimpses of the things he wanted to do to me as soon as I opened my eyes and greeted a new day.

"I don't have the teddy on," I groaned when his teeth nipped at my shoulder.

"To hell with the teddy," he growled and rolled his hips, bathing my throat with his tongue.

His hand drifted down and I parted my thighs. His fingers slid over the mound below before they drifted to the folds beneath. I was already excited, my sex both wet and swollen. No matter how often I made love to Disco, I always wanted more—I always wanted *him*.

"I love it when you're like this, Rhiannon. It tells me what you're afraid to."

Before I could argue or protest, he had me flat on my back, settling between my legs. Dual, multicolored irises gazed down at me, the shimmering pools of blue so vast and breathtaking I could stare in them endlessly. His expression was one of desire and determination, something I witnessed more and more of late. I placed my hands on his chest, fingers lax on his skin.

Slowly, his face descended, until his lips brushed mine and the rest of the world faded away. His taste was a mixture of cinnamon and cloves, addictive and tantalizing. As his tongue slipped past my parted lips, I groaned into his mouth and mirrored the movements. He led the dance and I followed—rolling, dipping, sucking, and teasing.

Taking my right arm from his chest, I slid it down his body, along the defined muscles of his chest and abdomen. He shifted his pelvis upward as he got hip to where I was going, allowing me to caress the flaxen hair along the way until I took his erection in hand. He was hard yet velvety, a mixture of strength and vulnerability. He was fully engorged, the head of his cock larger and wider than the root below. I stroked him carefully, keeping my grip soft and my movements intentional, and was rewarded with a muffled curse and a throaty groan as he broke our kiss and pulled away.

"You have the softest touch," he said as he peered down into my face, allowing me to see the pleasure I gave him. The trust that involved—allowing me truly *see* him in all ways—was something I was only now becoming accustomed to. Sex was sex, until you added what we had into the mix. Disco left me no place to hide when I wanted to escape the world and forget. With him, I had to remain in the open, fighting my demons where he could watch and, in most circumstances, intervene.

Bowing his back, he dipped his head and took my right nipple into his mouth. I cried out, wrapped my free hand around his blond head, and continued to stroke him. He teased the skin, pebbling the flesh, before he went to work on the other side. Back and forth, he nipped, suckled, and licked, his attentions effectively coating the area between my legs in a scorching wetness.

"Gabriel," I moaned despite myself, falling into the habit I'd recently acquired. Disco didn't like his nickname, although he didn't argue when I used it. During moments like these, however, he had a definite preference.

"Not yet," he murmured against my skin. "I want to go down on you first."

He moved down my body, leaving wet kisses along the way, pausing as he nuzzled the area over my left breast that was marred by a lighter area of skin, the scar tissue almost gone but evident if you were looking. He bathed my navel, the scars along my abdomen, and finally stopped in front of the smooth skin below.

"I still can't believe you did this for me." His tenor changed, hoarse and deep as he stared at the now hairless valley of skin nestled between my parted legs. I was about to remind him that technically, I was the one gaining the reward after suffering the misery of a Brazilian, when he gave a firm lick from my sex to my clit that made it impossible to think.

He moved his tongue in perfect harmony with his fingers and lips, stroking, petting, and driving me out of my mind. He teased and tormented, knowing it was the trigger that never failed to send me soaring, only to pull away when I neared climax. Eager to experience heaven, I writhed beneath him, eliciting a chuckle as he pressed one hand against my belly to keep me still.

"Please," I begged, uncaring that I was giving him the power to control my responses and reactions.

The result was exactly what I knew it would be. He took that pearled bundle of nerves and sensation into his mouth and sucked gently, flicking his tongue back and forth as he did, and my body detonated like a Fourth of July bottle rocket. My cries echoed off the walls, carrying to the ceiling. Each wave of heat that spread from my stomach to my muscles was too much but not enough. I rode the feeling of bliss until my limbs quivered and I was limp on the mattress, my forehead sweaty and chest heaving.

Disco blanketed me until we were chest-to-chest, hip-to-hip, and entered my body in one expert thrust. I arched my back to take more of him, gloried in the way he felt inside me. Like this, we were not two people. We were whole, unified as one.

He studied me as he began moving, nice and slow. He feathered kisses along my jaw, my chin, my nose and mouth. I wrapped my arms around his waist and drove my nails into his skin. Although my right knee was still awkward to maneuver, the left continued to function just fine and I used it to meet each roll of his hips.

"Christ," he groaned and I knew he was close.

Doubling my efforts, I ground against him until I found the spot that would send me over for a second time. It didn't take much to reach the pinnacle, to know that one more solid touch would get the job done. As he slid home—once, twice—I quickened and tumbled over, quaking as my body gripped him tightly, tempting him to join me as I spasmed around him.

His thrusts became harder, the hands that were at my sides now used to hold my hips in place. He rose onto his knees, lifting me as he did, and plunged faster and faster. As he came, he threw his head back and shouted to the rafters. The muscles in his abdomen and chest corded, the twin lines running from his pelvis to his groin far more pronounced. Cool wetness jetted into me, tempering the heat where we were connected in the most profound way possible.

Disco released my hips and placed his arms on either side of my head, keeping his semi-hard length in my body. His expression was one that exhilarated and frightened me, so intense it was impossible to turn away. After a moment, he did what I thought he might and buried his face into my neck. He was aware of my hang-ups, but after witnessing my shock and consequent fear upon hearing his declaration the first time, I knew he wasn't up for a repeat.

"I love you," he said, words soft.

The same words surfaced on my lips, hanging on the tip of my tongue. Yet each time I opened my mouth, they refused to formulate. It was as if I was on mute, unable to express verbally what I felt physically and emotionally. Like a fish out of water, I opened my mouth and closed it several times. He must have felt it, because he lifted away and smiled down at me.

"It's all right." He kissed me tenderly before pulling away. "You'll tell me when you're ready."

This wasn't the first time he'd said or done something that made me feel absolutely worthless and undeserving of him, but it was the first time I felt guilty about it. Disco was everything a woman could possibly want. He was gorgeous, he was powerful, and he was the most generous soul I'd ever met. He never expected more than a person was willing to give, not even when he loved them. It said a lot about his character, why I was so torn, and why my feelings had changed so drastically regarding him in the past month.

So why couldn't I get over my mental shit and tell him? Why couldn't I bestow the three tiny little words he wanted to hear?

God help me, I had no fucking clue.

"Do you still want to go to your apartment?" he asked, breaching the quiet. "Or can I tempt you to stay and put it off for another day?"

"As much as I'd love to stay in bed, I have to go. There is no food in the apartment, I need more of my clothes, and I have to check my messages. I have to decide what I'm going to do about work."

"You wouldn't have to if you moved your things here," he reminded me, his eyes intent, deliberately forgoing the usual conversation about my ancient electronic devices that didn't allow someone to call and check for messages at another location. "And I thought you said you'd decided to stop working at the club."

"No, I said I was leaning toward that, not that I had decided." I started moving from the bed, uncomfortable with where the discussion was going. "One thing at a time, remember?"

"How could I forget?" he growled and moved so quickly I couldn't see, sweeping me off my feet.

Within seconds, I was in the bathroom and the nozzles inside the shower were turned at full blast. Waking up was a routine—we made love, we showered, and the rest was open to discussion. Most of the time, Disco could conduct business from his office. Since my near death experience, he sent Paine to take care of the things that required a formal meeting. The significance of that wasn't lost on me, which was another reason I was determined to put my life back in order. Disco was an important vampire in the area, and his lack of prominence was sure to be noticed. Considering how bloodthirsty their kind could be, he couldn't afford to look weak or disillusioned.

When the water was hot, he opened the door and led me inside. The crystalline beads adorning his skin were too much to resist and before I knew it, I was licking them away, until I went down on my knees before him. His heady groan told me that while it didn't go as far as the words he wanted to hear, it was more than enough to satisfy him until I was ready.

Rhiannon's Law #82: Fuck romantics who swear by the power of the "big three." Sometimes, if you want them to, actions *do* speak louder than words.

Read on for an excerpt from
The Renfield Syndrome by J.A. Saare,
coming August 2011 from Mundania Press.

CHAPTER ONE

Rhiannon's Law #22. You can't lie to yourself, so don't bother trying. Doing so only multiplies your douche bag level to the umpteenth power and confirms what others have been saying about you for years—that you are an idiot. Of course, I couldn't fault those guilty of breaking Law #22 from time to time, as I was prone to do so myself.

Like now, for instance.

From the moment I found myself on my ass, holding an issue of *The Blood Times*, I tried to convince myself it was all a bad dream. One minute I was in my apartment ready to get back to my vampire boyfriend. The next I was making a deal with a demon and getting my ass sent to the future as a part of the bargain.

It couldn't be real, but damn it, the concrete sure did feel cool and solid beneath my jeans, and my busted knee throbbed like a son of a bitch.

My gaze shifted back to the newspaper in hand. If it was meant as a joke, I wasn't laughing. The date on the paper indicated it was October 28, 2112. The feature article made my holy shit o-meter blare like a banshee. Humans were vanishing. Not as in going missing; as in they were ceasing to exist as a species. Something called the Renfield Syndrome was responsible. The side effect of the Renfield vaccine produced during the third world war between humans and vampires.

I flipped through the paper, desperate for more information.

The rest of the pages were full of ads, most of them chock-full of people offering themselves as blood slaves for immortality, money, and a decent place to live. Morbidly, the entries reminded me of the classifieds taken out when beloved pets spawned unwanted puppies and kittens and irresponsible owners were left to find them decent homes. Only these warm-blooded mammals weren't pets, they were people, and knowing that made my stomach roll and my hands tremble oh-so slightly.

I blew as steady stream of air through my pursed lips, attempted to slow the erratic beating of my heart, and tried to get a handle on things. The coolness of the shade against my face as the sun dipped further below the horizon got my attention, putting things in perspective.

It would be night soon, and I had to find Disco.

Disco. My heart spasmed at the thought and my chest felt as if a weight had been placed upon it. If not for my feelings for the man, I never would have made the deal to sever his debt, landing me one hundred and one years in the future. As fucked up as this shit was, I had to fulfill my part of the bargain with Zagan, the demon Disco was indebted to. Once I had the opportunity to speak with my vampire lover, his obligation to the sadistic creature from Hell would come to an end. One message was all it would take; a few short words to relay that the price to end their agreement had been paid. I didn't want to remain indebted to a demon—no matter what year it was—and there was no better time than now to get my shit together.

Groaning, I rose to my feet. The bastard right knee of mine was aching something fierce; a dull, throbbing ache that extended straight through the bone. Although the kneecap was mending, the process was agonizingly slow, and I resented how uncoordinated and helpless the injury made me.

The folded newspaper was oddly heavy in my hand as I headed south, in the direction of the Razor. Some things changed, but I hoped in this circumstance that some things remained the same. The Razor was a club that belonged to Paine—Disco's most trusted friend and the second in power to his family—which meant finding him wasn't a bad place to start. Not only would he be able to direct me to Disco, he could also offer me much needed protection in the surreal reality I now found myself.

I walked as fast as my leg would allow, wishing some of the vampire blood that saved my ass when I took on a deranged child vampire four weeks earlier stuck around for some physical healing. Not that I was complaining, mind you. A minor physical handicap was nothing when compared to crossing over to the other side. And I would know, since I'd almost stepped past the pearly gates into Heaven.

The streets were eerie, completely void of human elements. There were no cars, no traffic, no people, no pets and—something uncharacteristic of New York—no sounds. Each scrape of my sneakers on the pavement was the only distinguishable noise as I shuffled along the sidewalk, so loud in the misplaced silence that each step was almost deafening.

My attention flickered nervously from building to building, and I gazed disbelieving at what remained of the street. Several of the apartments were in shambles, doors and windows missing, the insides decimated and destroyed. A few of the residences I could see inside looked as though they'd been raided or burglarized. Garbage, clothing, and personal belongings were tossed next to stairs, spilling onto the street. It was as if the tenants had been permanently tossed out on their asses, with no time to gather their wardrobes or tend to their possessions.

I hobbled along each new street, hoping to escape the hellish nightmare only to be greeted with more of the same. A few of the doors that remained shut had huge crosses on them. Most were painted onto the surface of the entrance with white paint, but some had the real deal. Enormous pieces of wood interlocked to form a big fat, *Don't beware of dog, beware of fucking owner*, warning.

A couple of times I could have sworn heavy curtains shifted as I passed, but they immediately went still as I nervously strode by. It was a damned shame that I didn't have the time to play Nancy Drew, going door to door to unlock the mystery of the religious holy relics on display. If anything, it would have matched the surrealism of my situation.

For a moment, I paused and lifted my face toward the darkening sky. Vampires would be out soon, if they weren't already. The rays of the sun were only dangerous when they came from the direct source; the reflection of the light was as harmless as tap water to the creatures of the night, and it was well past sundown.

I breathed in through my mouth and released the air in a steady exhale through my nose, steeling myself to remain calm as I was forced to quicken my pace. I pushed my busted knee harder than I knew I should, ignoring the sharp, burning ache that started to pound deep in the joint with each step. I alternated the paper from my right hand to the left and shoved my fingers into my pocket.

My butterfly knife, rosary, and emplacement charm were still there.

Thank the Lord almighty.

At least I had something to protect myself with if necessary. Even though I was marked as Disco's familiar, I was still vulnerable without him around, and a lot can take place in a century. Where was he? What had happened to him in the time I had been missing? I wasn't entirely sure I wanted to know the answers to my own questions.

I cut down an alley, deciding on a short cut as each step I took became more painful, the fire in my knee now a blazing inferno. I was several blocks away from the Razor, and I wasn't sure I could go the distance. The sun was gone, the faintest grays and purples littering the sky as dusk lingered in those brief, final moments prior to the moon's takeover. The heaviness in my gut warned me it wasn't good to be caught outside at night, when the creepy crawlies came out to play.

My necromancer sixth sense alarm bells started shrilling, and I drew in a deep, ragged breath. A vampire was close, damned close. Since Disco had opened the mark between us, and fully introduced me to the source of my power, I was able to distinguish a hell of a lot more—including vampires anywhere in a twenty to thirty foot radius. From what I could gather—which, if I was being honest with myself, wasn't shit—there was only one. But one was more than enough cause for concern when you were a mere crippled mortal.

I didn't bother trying to hide, continuing on my path as I was already at the halfway mark. A vampire would know I was in the area regardless. Our uncanny senses homed in on each other, creating an undeniable pull. Sort of like a fly uncovering a steaming pile of shit, it was impossible to ignore.

The vampire I sensed made her appearance directly in front of me, approaching slowly from the other end of the alley. Her blonde hair was cut short, the inch long strands sticking on top of her head in a hairdo straight out of the eighties. I was pretty sure she bleached it since the strands were a blaring, platinum white. Her pale skin was bright and lovely, her full lips stained with bright, tomato red lipstick. The black heels that clicked over the pavement made her impossibly tall—well over six feet—and she was covered in leather. The black pants enclosing her lower half clutched and molded seamlessly to her hips, while the skimpy vest surrounding her torso stopped at her ribcage, displaying her smooth and lean stomach.

"Animator bait," she rasped in a throaty voice and stopped several feet away. She shifted her head, looking past my shoulder, as if she expected to find someone in my accompaniment.

"I'm not fishing, sister," I replied evenly and came to a stop.

"I smell them." She sneered, her nostrils flaring wide. "But the question is, how did they come across you?"

She crossed the distance using her vampire speed and was in front of me in the same instant she once stood across the alley. Her hand lashed out, and her cool fingers clamped around my throat. She shoved me into the wall, pressing into my chest, invading my personal space. She brushed her nose along my skin, breathing deeply. Suddenly, her head jerked back. She turned to glare into the darkness pervading the alley, and her deep navy blue eyes flared.

"What are *they* doing with you?" she whispered through clenched teeth, turning to study me.

"Who the hell are 'they' pray tell?" I questioned, trying to breathe easy versus pant as my oxygen supply was considerably limited by her hand around my throat.

She never had the opportunity to answer.

The rustling of multiple feet and rubber soles came from both sides of the alley. I rotated my head as best as I could in her unbreakable grip, first left, then right. The dusk was gone, and it was officially nighttime. My body hummed, a slight burning as more undead approached. However, the faces I could see with guns raised were not vampire, but human, and they were covered from head to toe with fun goodies like firearms, knives, and camouflage gear that made them resemble life-size G.I. Joes.

Barberella seemed to anticipate the company. Her lips curved into a Joker-like grin, and she relinquished her hold, stepping away from me in deliberate movements.

The camo posse moved in, guns pointed at both of us. My gaze flickered back and forth between the vampire and the men, and I lifted my hands into the air in a mock surrender. Having a gun pointed at you by someone who actually knows how to use it isn't funny or exciting—not at all. Even worse was being in the center of a soon to be shitstorm from which I might never be fully cleansed.

"Don't even think about it," one of the men in green snapped as the vampire moved, as if she was preparing to flee.

I rotated my head around, toward the sound of the voice. His black hair was unkempt on the top and short in the back, his resolute grey colored eyes intense and lethal. He kept his gun leveled on the vampire but turned his attention to me, his level stare traveling up and down my body, taking me in.

"Carter," Barberella purred. Stepping back, she shook her head and sniffed the air. "I should have known."

"Kate," he responded coolly. "Why am I not surprised to see you?"

"Must we do this night after night?" She sighed, rolling her eyes, and placed her hands on her hips. "Really, what's the point? We'll have you all eventually. It's only a matter of time."

My necromancy buzzer was raging full steam ahead, tingling under the surface of my skin like an itchy rash. I fought the urge to shift my feet and rub my arms. Movement in this circumstance wasn't good. Besides, the men with the guns were the least of my concerns.

Vampires were close, and they were plentiful.

I pushed my back against the wall, my right hand at the ready to grab my only two defenses from my pocket. I didn't know how long my leg would carry me, but

I was positive the adrenaline that was currently coursing through my veins would ensure I made it out of death pit alley.

"Get her," Carter ordered, his steely eyes sharp and intense.

A handful of people from each side of the alley approached, taking slow, cautious steps. They kept the guns trained on Kate, their movements intentional, calculated, and smooth. This shit wasn't good. One wrong move and it was game over. I cursed Zagan for sending me into the middle of a futuristic version of hell and damned myself for leaving the safety of Disco's home the morning when he'd all but begged me to stay.

Hindsight was such a cruel bitch.

Swiveling my head to the right, I peered down the alley. As I did, a solid and strong hand grasped my left arm, causing me to emit a loud yelp of panic. I jerked away from the touch and quite literally busted my ass, landing hard on my already sore posterior. I glared up at the owner of the appendage who touched without permission, angry and wary. It was one of the men who arrived on the scene armed to the gills, covered from shoulder to ankle with weapons, dressed in varying shades of green. He was in his forties, salt and pepper stubble spaced across his face, matching his shortly shorn hair.

"Come with me," he said quietly and extended his hand.

"Nuh-uh." I shook my head, scooting in the opposite direction. "I don't think so, All American Hero."

His frown was genuine; he didn't understand why I would refuse his help. I shoved my hand into my pocket, going for my trusty butterfly knife. My fingers wrapped around the outline of the warm metal, and I felt an insubstantial amount of comfort at its presence, which was better than none at all.

Vampires were here now. All around us.

"Incoming!" Carter yelled, eyes narrowed, mouth in a tight line. His chiseled arms flexed as he tightened his grip on the gun.

Vampires engulfed the alley, several dropping from the rooftops above. I pressed into the wall, attempting to remain miniscule. Whatever the hell was about to happen didn't involve me, and I didn't want to become a part of it. The alley erupted in gunfire, snarls, and the distinct symphony of fighting.

Someone snagged me by the shoulder, thrusting me upright, and yanked me forcefully to the left. I planted my feet and tried to lean my body in the opposite direction, stumbling as my weak knee caved. The hold didn't lessen, firm and unbreakable as the gargantuan soldier dragged me along behind him. I focused on the direction we were leaving, gaping at the sight. Vampires were attacking in bursts of speed, but they weren't killing their targets. Those suited in camouflage didn't offer the same courtesy, firing round after round into heads and torsos.

"Come on!" the man yanking on my arm snapped angrily. Too bad for him I was equally pissed.

"Let go of me!" I snarled, planting my feet again, and used my left leg to bear my weight. I pulled him up short, and his dark brown eyes flashed in warning.

"Get her out of there! We've got to move!" Carter bellowed.

A strange sensation brushed my skin, the slightest drizzle of beaded water tickling my face and hands. I stopped arguing with G.I. Joe and lifted my chin in the direction of the cooling sensation.

Then I heard the snarls.

Misty waves of condensation flittered down from the rooftops, floating in the air before dropping down. It started at the opposite end of the alley, carried down, and spread out. If the sun had been in the sky, it would have created a rainbow effect, much like a water hose with fork holes that created an instant, ghetto sprinkler.

The vampires hissed in outrage, and Kate pulled her lips back to reveal elongated fangs as steam erupted from their skin. It took a moment to compute, comprehension making my stomach knot as nausea made me want to toss my Cheerios. The water was blessed. It had to be.

"I don't have time for this," G.I. Joe grumbled, using my distraction as an opportunity to take control. He bent at the waist, shoved his shoulder into my midsection, and lifted me easily.

"Put me down, you dumb motherfucker!" I shouted, kicking, thrashing, and squirming.

He ignored my tirade, striding purposely to the camo army. My head flopped, and I tried to see through my hair as I continued squirming with each step he took. A few vampires were on their asses, bloody holes seeping their life's blood from their bodies. The bullets had to be blessed or silver as well. Their wounds would have started healing otherwise.

The walls of the alley disappeared from view, and my weight was shifted. Unexpectedly, the shoulder holding me was gone, and I was traveling backward. I attempted to brace myself for the fall that I knew was on the way, trying to relax instead of tense to ensure the connection with the ground didn't cause nearly as much harm. My back hit first and air exited my lungs in a painful exhale, causing me to gasp as I attempted to breathe in.

My knee cursed me as I scrambled to rise, but I stumbled over regardless, until I was safely on my stomach. I struggled to get my body in an upright position, using my hands as leverage. Several men in shades of green stared down at me from their seats, their expressions totally unreadable. A brand new spike of adrenaline overcame my fatigue.

Stay in a big ass van full of scary ass men from the future? Thanks for the offer, but I had to fucking pass.

After getting my feet under me properly, making sure my left leg would be the one I pushed off with, I lunged for the back door that was still wide open, my rubber soles squeaking loudly against the floor as I attempted to escape.

An arm lashed out, and I deflected it, pivoting in the opposite direction while using the flat portion of my palm to throw the blow off course. I stepped back in panic as two men stood to assist the one who had attempted to stop me. Watching them all, I pulled out my knife and flicked it open smoothly. As I peered down at the blade, and then gazed up at the men, I wanted to slap myself. It was laughable, really. All I had was a lame ass balisong to protect me from massive guys armed with Uzis.

Something hard and cold nudged the base of my skull, and I heard the very distinct double-click of a gun being cocked. My breath left my lungs, and I went stock-still.

"Drop the knife."

The voice was Carter's, and it wasn't friendly or open to discussion.

My horrified and anxious gaze darted around the bus, and I swallowed loudly. They all looked ready to roast me alive, and the rosary wouldn't to squat against any of them. I opened my right hand and shortly after a dull clack sounded at my feet.

"Good. Now, take a seat."

A firm hand gave me the initial get the move on shove. I staggered and bit back my diarrhea mouth. It wasn't easy. My temper always had a mind of its own. Carter put a hand on my shoulder and guided me to an empty seat on the right. I slid in and Carter walked past me, toward the front of the bus. He lowered the sidearm in an experienced grip and released the hammer. I cringed when my ears made out the violent sounds of guns being fired in rapid succession in the alley, followed by odd gurgles in the distance.

"Quinn has the second team," Carter spoke in hushed tones to the driver. "Take us back."

The bus started with a loud roar of engine and pistons, sputtering at the start until wheels rolled smoothly underneath. I jolted forward in the seat and quickly stared out the window, trying to figure what the hell was going on. Humans might be on the verge of extinction, but some of them obviously weren't down with being vampire Happy Meals.

Carter whipped around, and I felt his eyes burning a hole in my face. I returned his stare, thinning my lips and crossing my arms like a surly teen. He looked away as he strode back down the aisle. I returned my attention to the windows, gazing into the darkness. His footsteps stopped a short distance from my seat, scuffled, and started back in my direction. The all too familiar sound of metal sliding together chimed in my ears, and I turned in time to see Carter slide my knife into his pocket.

"These aren't so easy to come by. You can consider it a down payment for saving your ass," he said calmly and propped himself into the seat across from me. Leaning forward, he braced his elbows on his parted knees.

I drew in a breath and looked away, rolling my eyes as I muttered, "Don't be so quick. You didn't save shit."

"What were you doing out past curfew?"

I blew him off and kept staring out the window, wishing that I had the power to shut him out entirely. I had no idea there was a curfew to follow. It wasn't as if I'd experienced anything in the last century. Besides, I had my own set of problems to think about—namely finding Disco and delivering the message from Zagan. It was the only thing that would end the bargain between them and ensure the vampire I'd fallen in love with wouldn't pay the piper in spades. I had to take this one step at a time or run the risk of losing my goddamned mind.

Anger surfaced, a fire inside my chest. Maybe that was Zagan's intention all along; to have me freaking out and caught in something I couldn't control.

The rotten bastard.

"What were you doing out past curfew?" Carter asked again.

"You know what?" I titled my head back against the seat and peered in his direction, looking him in the eye. "You wouldn't believe me if I told you. So why don't you drop me off at the next stop and we'll call it a night."

"I'm afraid that's not possible. You should have stayed safe and sound where you belonged. Now we have to take you with us. It's protocol."

"Protocol, huh?" He didn't so much as nod, gazing at me in a manner that made my skin crawl, his expression unreadable. "Fuck me sideways," I muttered and leaned forward, until my head pressed against the brown leather seat in front of me. When I got home, I knew the first thing I was getting. A tattoo on my forehead that said, "Your ticket to insane shit stops here."

"I wouldn't say that any louder, if I were you." His grey eyes darkened, and his voice deepened as I glanced at him. "Someone might try to give you exactly what you're asking for."

"It wasn't an invitation."

He moved across the distance and rested his hands on the seat directly next to my leg. I felt my hair move as his face brushed the strands, and he whispered against my ear, "Then keep it to yourself."

I settled in and kept my big fat yap shut, fuming silently and safely, instead. The view from the window didn't lift my spirits. The landscape was as dead as the people I saw on a routine basis. In fact, I saw several of those along the way too. The ghosts we passed watched the bus as it drove by, sensing my presence. Their faces didn't tell me much, but their ravaged bodies did. Some had died horrifically, in ways I didn't want to think about. I could only guess as to what had transpired to make things so bad.

The entire city was a dead zone.

The driver turned right on Prospect Park West, and my eyes bulged in shock, the reality of my situation hitting me hard and fast. I was seeing the buildings that were only a conception during my century. Prospect Village, a mere idea in my time, had reached its completion in my absence. It was impressive, even on the darkened street, and I was fairly certain the contract on the leases had expired by now, leaving plenty of room for potential tenants.

The bus took a sharp turn around the corner and I ducked instinctively, thinking the top of the bus would rip off by way of the roof of the lower parking floor of the building. We barreled underneath without incident, into a dimly lit area. I latched onto the seat in front of me as the driver maneuvered the large vehicle, slammed the breaks, and tossed it in reverse. When he had the bus where he wanted it, he put the vehicle into park. The bus veered back and forth unsteadily before slowly going still. The sounds of shuffling bodies and feet echoed inside the enclosed space, and I glanced behind me to see the men filter out of the back door.

Carter stood, and his broad body encased the walkway. He stared down, studying me intently. He hadn't bothered speaking again, not since he'd imparted his earlier warning. It was cool, I didn't miss the conversation. I only wanted to get the hell off the bus—at some other location preferably.

He lifted his hand, pointing with his index finger down the aisle. "Let's go."

Pressing my lips together and biting my tongue, I rose from my seat as gracefully as possible. The men from the back of the bus were gone, but I could see them entering the building directly ahead. I reached the drop off, jumped, and landed awkwardly on my left foot. I wobbled unevenly, losing my balance as I tumbled forward. Hard and unyielding fingers gripped my arm, pulling me up and back. Carter waited until I regained my balance before he let go.

He motioned toward my bent knee. "What happened to your leg?"

"Oh, that?" I looked down at my lame leg and shrugged. "I was a professional river dancer until one of my jigs went terribly awry. It happens."

His brow crinkled in what I recognized as very real confusion—a look I was all too familiar with. He probably had no clue who in the hell Michael Flatly was, much less *The Lord of the Dance*.

He didn't press the issue, standing quietly behind me as I strode up the ramp and inside the building. The hallway was barren, the cream-colored walls spray-painted with multi-colored graffiti. He placed his hand under my left arm and guided me toward the elevator. The men from the bus moved aside, allowing us to pass. I felt the weight of their stares but tried to appear unfazed, looking directly ahead at the silver elevator doors.

When they slid open, I stepped inside and found there was one bonus to be had in the apocalyptic future—no whimsical flutes serenaded the inhabitants of the compartment with the sounds of music. Carter pushed the button to take us to the top floor, and the doors closed with a happy ding.

The horrible wretch of the elevator as it lifted caused my stomach to roll. I shifted my attention, glancing at Carter. He was as serious as ever. From what I could gather, he was probably in his thirties. But when his brow furrowed and creased, he looked damn near fifty.

When we reached the designated floor, the alarm chimed again and the doors opened. Directly ahead was a huge living room, complete with art deco furniture. Carter lifted his hands, indicating I should go first, and I nervously stepped inside of the room. Although he hadn't given the vibe that he would try to do something I wouldn't agree to, I was well aware of the masks people wore when they wanted to portray themselves as something they weren't.

"Take a seat," he instructed.

I took him up on the offer, not to be menial, but because my knee was betraying me like the two-faced bitch it was. The couch wasn't comfortable, but neither my bruised posterior nor my crippled leg complained.

I sat back, anxious and cautious, but physically relieved.

"Would you like something to drink?" Carter asked and stepped from the center of the room.

I remained silent as he walked around the bar and worked the holster off his broad, muscular shoulders before tossing it onto the counter. He unbuttoned the long sleeve camouflage shirt covering his body and revealed corded forearms with a scattering of dark hair. He shrugged out of it, folded the garment, and placed the shirt next to the holster. He walked to the fridge and I heard the pop of the door being opened as he called out, "Do you always make people repeat themselves?"

"Sure Martha, I'll take a drink. Why don't you whip me up some dinner while you're at it? I'm starving out here," I retorted tartly. My annoyance threshold was at its breaking point.

I heard glasses being dinged together, the slurping slosh of liquid being poured inside, and the refrigerator door slamming shut. He came around the bar with two drinks in hand.

"Here." He extended one of the glasses to me and I took it, keeping the beverage far, far away from my mouth. Silently, I balanced the glass on my knee, studying the amber colored liquid encased by thick crystal.

"Not thirsty?" he asked just before he downed his own drink.

Rhiannon's Law #5. Don't accept drinks from strangers. Not unless you want to be drugged, date raped, and given all sorts of STDs, and not necessarily in that order.

"I don't drink things unless they come from a sealed container." Anyone could drop something into an open glass. I was a bartender back in the normal world, and it was a known fact. I'd seen too many women fall victim to men who liked to add a little something extra to the concoctions they offered to them.

"Then you must be special to one of them. I haven't tasted soda since I was a boy." He plopped the glass down on the table in front of me. "I'm amazed your master let you stray so far. I'm sure he'll be upset to find you've been taken."

"Look." I sat up and placed my glass on the table. "This isn't what you think, and I don't really have the time or patience to explain. I have somewhere I needed to be yesterday."

"I bet you have somewhere you need to be, and lucky you, we've brought you here. Distance from that cesspit will allow you to see clearly." He smirked, lifting his glass in a mock salute, and returned to the kitchen.

"I am not staying here," I said quietly, refraining at screaming him like I wanted to. Acting like a raging bitch wouldn't help me now. I had to attempt to pacify him and, in the doing, bargain with the asshole.

"Oh yes you are. Your bedroom is right there." He pointed behind me, to the left. "I suggest you get comfortable." He shook his head. "All of you black swans are exactly the same, so don't think you're any different. You get swept up in the night side and forget all about your own kind. A few months here will open those eyes of yours. If it doesn't..." He cleared his throat, shaking his head again, and said, "Let's hope it won't come to that."

"You don't get it," I snapped, standing steadily without the betrayal of my knee, and walked toward the elevator. "I cannot stay here. I have something important I have to take care of. Fight your war with someone who gives a shit. Me? I'll take my chances with the creepy crawlies outside."

I pushed the button repeatedly, the round flickering yellow border indicating the device was working. My breathing increased, the few contents left in my stomach shifting past my abdomen and into my throat. I didn't want to vomit, not right now. However, once I was safely inside the confines of the neat and clean elevator, I could take care of that little problem. A ding sounded and the doors opened, revealing two men dressed in camo pants, wife beaters, and black Berettas.

"Is there a problem?" Their eyes trained on me as they asked the question, and their hands drifted to their sidearms. I loved men who felt superior simply because they had bulk and an automatic weapon on you.

Spineless pricks.

I lowered my head, exhaling in exasperation. This was the craziest fucking shit. Too bad I'd be repeating that same thing in the future. I couldn't seem to stop trumping myself.

"I think she understands the ramifications if she tries to leave," Carter answered from behind me, and I heard him settle into one of the seats and clunk his boots on the table. The big ass bastard on the right nodded his buzzed blond head, his biceps and chest flexing as he pushed the button and closed the doors with another cheery ding.

"So, this is what we've reverted to," I snapped angrily, turning to glare at Carter. "Kidnapping people and holding them hostage. It's good to see the human race has evolved during my sabbatical."

"Don't give me that bullshit," Carter said, his boots creating an earsplitting boom as they connected loudly with the floor as he sat up. "If you need someone to blame, take a look at those leeches you supply. They are the ones who have caused this, not us. We're doing what we can to survive. It is our responsibility to show those bred in captivity what it's like to be free."

"Bred in captivity." I grimaced in disgust. "You can't be serious."

"Where have you been the last forty years?" he asked in what I easily perceived as agitation. "Did you miss the aftereffects of the war? When we lost, they changed everything. You can't believe what they tell you, not even your parents can vouch for it. Blood slaves are tainted—all of them. You're nothing more than walking food."

I was curious by his statement, as well as completely confused. No better time than the present to get some answers. I wasn't very adept at playing a dumb ass—okay, I admit my douche bag level had increased recently—but with my lack of experience I hoped I pulled it off.

"So let me get this straight. They won the war and made us into walking meals on wheels? Even our children?"

"Have you learned nothing during your captivity? You're not a child, and you're far too old to have been allowed to remain with your family." His words conveyed his shock, surprise, and doubt.

"Let's just say," I answered cautiously, shaking off the skeevies at the notion of being taken from my parents like a newly minted, six-week old puppy. "The last time I was in the know, the world was slightly less messed up."

"How much do you know?" He was scrutinizing me, curiosity and disbelief overriding his annoyance. His eyes were a lighter color now. The steely grey softening to what reminded me of a calm sky. His expression was less skeptical, as if he no longer viewed me as a threat.

"I know something called the Renfield Syndrome wiped us out and that humans have resorted to whoring themselves out in the paper."

"Take a seat," he instructed quietly, raking his long fingers through his dark black hair, "and I'll tell you."

I nodded, rolling my eyes, and complied with the request. If I was stuck in this hellhole, at least I got cookies, milk, and story time. I took a seat and settled in.

"The first vampire came into the open in 2041. No one believed it at first, but after a few months when the world found out it wasn't a hoax, things started to change. The United States government, as well as the leaders across the globe banded together, calling for registration of all the vampires across the world. That was met with resistance. Some of the older vamps refused to participate, and a line was drawn. Those vampires who didn't submit to the request were deemed a danger to humanity. Within a few months, the fighting started. By 2044, the war was in full swing." He dry washed his hand across his shadowed face, hair falling across his forehead. "I need something stronger than tea."

He braced his hands on his knees and pushed his way to his feet. Swiveling around the couch, he quietly returned to the bar. He reached under the counter and produced a bottle. Some things might change, but liquor always stands the test of time. I recognized the label immediately. It was my old friend, Mr. Daniels. He reached for two short glasses, holding the rims between his fingers, and returned to his place to take a seat.

"Now." He put the glasses side by side, pouring the amber liquid carefully. "Vampires might have been weak during the day, but they slaughtered at night. The military dispatched soldiers to all largest neighborhoods, a worldwide curfew was established, and it became a game of cat and mouse."

He handed me a glass, and I took it. He threw his shot back, swallowing hard, and shook his head. He immediately poured another shot and sat the bottle on the table.

"Then the war on bloodsuckers got a new weapon. Something so accessible anyone could have it—the Renfield vaccine. It was engineered from vampire blood, and the way it worked was simple. You got the vaccination and if a vampire bit you, the vampire died. It seemed like an easy solution. All the leaders around the world showed a united front, televising the summit where they received the injection themselves. Before the end of the month, over three quarters of the world population had the shit floating around in their systems."

He downed the next shot and poured a third.

"It took almost thirty years for the side effects to occur. People started aging rapidly, their cellular levels going completely off the charts. They died within hours, all of them: men, woman, and children. The only populations that remained untainted were the third world nations that didn't have access to dependable health care, and we lost contact with them years ago. Since the first people to inject the tainted shit into their systems were the world's leaders, it was only a matter of time before the entire infrastructure combusted."

Eyes wide, I exhaled softly. "Jesus."

Carter smiled bitterly. "It was only weeks before what was known as the Renfield Syndrome wiped us out. When vampires started scouting for survivors, those who decided against receiving the vaccine got word there was a safe haven here in New York, which is where you currently find yourself. That was thirty years ago, and things still haven't changed. People are still fighting for the right to live, and vampires are still hunting them down and forcing them into slavery."

"So people are slaves?" I spoke slowly, thinking, *How does that work exactly?*

"They are nothing more than primped and preened cattle the vampires keep as pets. They try to fool you into believing you can live a normal life, that you can have a family and children. They clothe you, they feed you, but you're never free. You're always intended to provide what they need. Trust me, I know."

I twirled the glass between my palms, looking down at my hands. "Would it be too personal to ask how?"

"Someone here will tell you eventually. It's probably best you hear it from the direct source." He reclined back in the seat. "A few years after we arrived, my older brother started getting cabin fever. Each day Patrick ventured out, traveling further and further into the city, and one night he didn't come home. It was difficult, but we made our peace with the fact he was gone. When he showed up several years later, he was..." Carter paused, frowning. "He belonged to one of them. I won't go into detail, or explain why it was so reviled among us, as it's irrelevant. He claimed they only wanted to help rebuild society and that's when we learned they only demanded one thing in return—servitude. He was lucky to make it out the door alive. If he wasn't my brother, he wouldn't have."

"I'm sorry," I said, voice somber.

"Losing a sibling is painful, but I'd imagine losing a child would be worse, and that's what would happen. Once you agree to what they want, they own you. And that ownership extends down to your children. They aren't trying to rebuild the population because they care. They are doing what is necessary to ensure survival. Right now, children are a rarity, especially among us. Once we're gone they're fucked."

I crinkled my forehead, giving my brain time to filter through the new information. Things were worse than I could possibly imagine. Ending the debt to Zagan was going to be hell, but doing so in this reality was going to be almost impossible.

I put the glass to my lips, blocked off my nose and throat, and downed the shot in one gulp. I closed my eyes and drew in a nose full of fire-laced air, blinking several times to clear the tears from my eyes. I sniffed, clearing my throat, and plopped the glass down on the tabletop as I met his gaze.

"Now *that* is some fucked up shit."

"I'm glad you think so." He nodded his approval, leaned forward and downed his third shot, and then he lifted the bottle and refilled both of our glasses.

CHAPTER TWO

Despite having luxury accommodations, I slept like shit. Blessedly forgotten nightmares returned hard and fast, reminding me of why I sought refuge in the arms of my lover each night before I succumbed to sleep. Disco always took me to beautiful places when I slept, entering my mind to redirect my thoughts to more pleasurable things versus the hell that was my childhood after my parents were killed. No longer was I afraid to close my eyes to slumber. In fact, I had started to welcome the evenings spent in his embrace.

I tossed and turned on the queen-sized mattress each time I awoke in a cold sweat, terrified that the dreams were real. When I came to awareness, I told myself it would all be over when a new day greeted me. I had suffered this misery before and survived, before Disco was a part of my life. I could do it again without his assistance. When I finally drifted off to the land of dreams, it was out of sheer exhaustion. I woke the minute the sun's beams drifted through the glass wall, lighting my eyelids with shades of pale orange and yellow.

I stared at the ceiling as I came to awareness, trying to figure out what in the hell I was going to do. Carter wouldn't let me leave. He truly believed he was show-ing me the light. I pulled at the crunched cotton material at my throat, rubbing my fingers against the tiny tattoo created from Disco's bite hidden beneath. They didn't see my mark, and if I could help it, they wouldn't have the opportunity to. These people lived life to the extreme. Their very existence relied on it. If they discovered I was not only claimed by a vampire, but that I was also a necromancer beholden to one, my life expectancy was sure to take a nosedive.

I grinded my teeth together, wishing I could grind something else together in-stead. I bet Zagan was having a good old fashioned laugh at my expense, the rotten demon bastard. It had known exactly what it was doing when it made our deal, took the amulet I'd procured killing a child vampire, and sent my ass forward through time. Admittedly, I was never good at eating crow, but this went beyond any sort of good-humored joke.

Closing my eyes, I pictured Disco's face. His pale skin and distinct features were gorgeous, as all vampires were prone to be, but his eyes were his best attribute: deep multicolored pools of blue, green, aqua, yellow, and gold. I would give anything to feel his solid arms around me, his cool breath against my face. The night before had only shown me how much I'd started to depend on him, to force me to accept that I'd grown to need him.

I never would have agreed to Zagan's bargain if it weren't for him.

Pushing aside the duvet, I decided it was time to make it a new day. The bedroom was stark bone white, the linens, dresser, and nightstand matching perfectly. It was meant to look sophisticated, but it was merely plain and simple. I bet the decorator charged a bundle for his services, too.

The adjoining bathroom matched the bedroom except everything was elaborate. The sinks were deep and square, the faucets bright polished stainless steel that arched over like flower stems. I walked inside to rinse my putrid dragon's breath from my mouth; the result of the multiple shots of Jack I'd taken the night before. I cupped water in my hands and cleaned my face as I swished the liquid inside my mouth. I used the towel on the sink to pat my face dry when I was done, feeling slightly cleaner if not totally spring fresh.

I took a long look at myself in the mirror. The woman looking back at me hadn't changed. She still had long mahogany hair, chocolate brown eyes, a heart shaped face, delicate cheekbones and two eyebrows that arched like twin brush strokes. But the image didn't relay what resided inside the twenty-five-year-old who felt far older. That was more complex. No mirror in the world could accurately portray that woman.

When I walked out of the bedroom, the living room area was empty. I headed toward the glass door leading to a balcony outside. After I unlocked the handle and slid the glass partition aside, I silently stepped into the chilly morning air. I crossed to the railing across the way. Nothing but woodland greeted me, since the building was built near the accompanying park. There were no signs of life, no people going through daily morning rituals. It was as country as the city could possibly get.

The sun spread across the sky, distorting the horizon in variations of blue, red, purple, orange, and yellow. I took in breath and frowned, pausing as I took another shot, breathing deeply. There were no exhaust fumes or smells of food. There was just brisk air that burned my lungs, and the lingering moisture which accompanied morning dew.

Something touched my arm, and I tensed. Whipping around, I deflected the object forcefully away with the base of my palm. My right leg flew back automatically as I attempted to stand in a defensive position and wouldn't you know it, my bastard knee faltered. I cursed, using a flailing hand to brace myself and keep a precarious balance using the concrete barrier that kept me from toppling over the roof of the building.

"I bet you were quite the ass kicker before that knee of yours bummed out," Carter observed casually. He lifted a mug of coffee to his lips and leaned against the concrete barrier, staring into the sun. He had on his camouflage pants, boots, and a black wife beater. His dark hair was in disarray, messy around his shadowed face.

"I could hold my own," I growled, angry at myself and my injury.

"How did you hurt it?" He glanced over, lips curving around the mug. "Tell the truth this time."

"A vampire broke my knee cap," I answered before I could think, brute force honesty flowing easily from my lips. I cursed the lack of filters between my brain and my mouth the minute I heard myself say it aloud.

His curious smile vanished, and he lowered his mug, resting it on the barrier, and turned his upper torso around to face me. "No shit?"

"No shit," I responded, wishing I could kick myself in the ass.

"What happened?" His gaze was so intense that I had to look away. I took several long moments to formulate my answer, deciding honesty wouldn't hurt as long as I kept out essential details.

I returned my attention to him and shrugged. "I killed him."

"You killed him?" He threw back his head and laughed, thinking I was making a funny. When I didn't join in his laughter and smile faltered. His tone changed from teasing to sober. "You're serious."

"I don't joke about death," I told him quietly.

"How did you kill him?" He leaned closer, eyes curious. The muscles along his shoulders and biceps were clearly displayed, and they corded as he shifted the mug in his hands.

"Well..." I took my time responding, making sure I didn't give too much away. Kiwbe, the child vampire I'd killed, was an evil shit. He deserved to die for murdering and devouring his own kind. I didn't have any remorse for what I had done, and it was evident when I finally said, "First, I emptied a clip into his back. Then I cut off his head."

Carter's grey eyes darkened slightly, and his lips parted. Homeboy just got a shock. He didn't expect the damsel in distress to have a pair of balls. To his credit, he recovered quickly.

"Good for you." He gave a curt nod and took a heaping gulp of java.

"Since we had some fun share time, do you think it might be possible to let me walk out of here?" I asked with a hopeful expression, pretending that were friends now instead of total strangers.

He shook his head again, smiling. "Nope."

I sighed and pushed away from the railing. Stepping back and making sure I had decent balance, I walked away. A terrace circled the top of the building, and I took brief stops to take a look around.

The area between the two buildings had a garden, the soil tilled but empty, as the weather had turned too cool to plant. The vines intricately woven through the slats of wood and metal obscured a portion of the area from view. One thing was for certain—I couldn't leap from the building. If I did, there would be a nice red splatter for everyone below. I sat down in one of the metal chairs next to a matching rounded table. This shit was going to get old quick. Time that I didn't have to spare was slowly ticking away, and I didn't even have my tattered copy of *Jane Eyre* to distract me...

"Listen." Carter spoke from behind me, pulling an empty chair away from the table to take a seat. "We're going out to collect supplies in a few days. Normally, the newer residents remain behind. We don't have the time or resources to play babysitter. But I'm willing to extend you an olive branch. Promise to behave and you can tag along."

"What makes you so sure I won't haul ass the second you give me headway?" I narrowed my eyes and glared at him. "You are keeping me prisoner, after all."

"Because if you do, your privileges will be revoked for an undetermined period of time and you'll be kept in our hold in the basement. Besides, with that leg injury to slow you down, you won't make it far."

"Damn it," I snapped, leveling with him. "I can't stay here."

Carter chuckled, unperturbed. He finished his coffee off but remained seated, combing tanned fingers through his unruly hair. "You'll see the light. Give it time."

Give it time, my ass. If homeboy only knew just how much time I'd given up. Sighing, I asked cynically, "And just how many hostages have you taken in your effort to save humanity?"

Lifting his arms above his head, he stretched out, taking his time, muscles lengthening as he breathed in deeply. When he lowered his hands to the chair, he answered only, "Enough."

Struggling not to scream or toss my chair at him, I chose to make a hasty exit, rising as gracefully as I was able. Unfortunately, after a couple of steps, I was forced to hobble to the sliding glass door. The crisp air-conditioned condo was exactly as I left it, everything neat and in its proper place. I briefly wondered what Carter would think if I went on a demolition and ruined the entire decorative flow.

As I rounded the corner, I made solid contact with a body, and sent each of us off course and back. The blasted right knee of mine held out for a change, and I breathed a sigh of relief, thankful I wasn't gracing the floor with another ass mopping.

"You're the new one," the girl that crashed into me snarled, her sky blue eyes narrowed.

She was dressed in the fugly camouflage pants everyone seemed to love, a thin black wife beater, and combat boots. Guns protruded from holsters strapped under her arms and blades were situated in casings along her thick leather belt. Her features were soft—full lips, pert nose, dainty chin—but any illusion of femininity was ruined by her caramel brown hair cropped incredibly short. Not to mention the lean, rippling muscles along her tanned shoulders and arms that would do a man proud. I met her stare, crossing my arms defiantly over my chest. She-Ra was a good three or four inches taller than I was and could probably kick my ass considering I was lame and lacking her firepower, but I'd be damned if I backed down.

"I say," she said softly as she moved closer, leaning in so I heard her loud and clear, "that they let you go back. You deserve to rot."

"Well hello and greetings, fellow neighbor," I replied snarkily. "Top of the morning to you."

"Jax," Carter snapped, and I pivoted on my good leg to glance at him before I returned my focus to G.I. Jane. "What are you doing here?"

"She thinks you should let me go back." I turned my back to Carter and smiled at Jax, leaning close to whisper to her, "Personally, I think that's a fine idea. I've been trying to talk Mr. Serious over here" —I hiked my thumb in Carter's direction— "into giving it consideration. So far, he's not listening."

"I asked you a question, Jackson," Carter barked from just over my shoulder.

She didn't avert her focus from my face, reaching for the bag resting across her chest. She pulled it free, lifted it over her head, and threw it at my feet. "Quinn told me to bring her clothing to wear until she collected some of her own."

"That's great." I smiled and shifted my feet, gently prodding the bag on the floor. "You don't happen to have a spare pair of shit kickers? Do you?"

Jackson looked like she wanted to explode. Her lids slitted, her forehead creased, and her full, berry-tinted lips thinned. Chock it up to another person won over by my superb conversation skills and outstanding wit. I would have pumped my fist in the air, but I had a feeling it would have only made matters worse.

"Thank you, Jax." Carter intercepted what was sure to become a fistfight, stepping in directly beside me. "You can go. Tell everyone we'll be down after breakfast."

"Don't get too comfortable, vessel," Jax quipped before she lifted her chin at Carter. "You're not welcome here. Your time is short."

I smiled, goading her like a moron. "Talk about an understatement. You have no idea just how short my time is."

She started to step forward when a horrifying growl carried through the room. The sound was unlike anything I'd ever heard, so deep it felt as if the walls rattled and the floor shifted. Jackson glanced at Carter before she spun around and made her way to the elevator. I peered over at the man beside me, who was the source of the noise. He went quiet when our unexpected visitor stopped in front of the elevator.

"Vessel?" I asked him. "Am I about to tread water somewhere?"

He didn't look at me until the doors to the elevator dinged open, Jackson stepped inside, and they slid shut. "A vessel is a vampire blood donor."

Great. The more things changed, the more they stayed the same. Even with the world coming to an end, people were still determined to judge people with labels. I bent at the waist and retrieved the small black satchel. The contents were light, and when I flipped back the flap, I saw a pair of camouflage pants and a couple of black garments folded neatly inside.

"What is up with all the green and black?" I grumbled, placing the flap back over the satchel.

"Our clothing distinguishes us from average civilians."

"I hate to break it to you." I motioned at his face and then his very fit body. "But your entire look screams covert military asshole. Woodsy outdoor clothing is just the cherry on top."

Annoyed now, Carter muttered, "Are you always such a smartass?"

"No, not always. That character trait is generally reserved for the fucked up situations I find myself in. Like this one, for example."

Carter appeared legitimately uneasy and exhausted, gray eyes going dark as his shoulders drooped. He raked his fingers through his hair, shifting his feet.

"I'm going to be straight with you. A person that's just been taken off the grid would normally be quarantined and placed under observation. It's protocol and ensures no one falls into harm's way. The only reason you're not is because I've taken a personal interest in you. If not for that, you'd be hold up in a cell in the basement with the rats, a floor mat, and a water dish. No one here likes outsiders, especially human ones who've lived among vampires."

I was about to get snarky again when I internalized his last two words. Human ones? *Hello?*

Slowly, warily, I asked, "What do you mean human ones?"

"How old *are* you, Rhiannon?"

What a nice question to ask a girl you'd just gotten to quasi know after sharing a name exchange and a few shots of Jack Daniels with the night before. I pulled the satchel into my chest. "I'm certified antique at a quarter of a century, vintage twenty-five."

"How is it that you know so little? You couldn't have been kept so ignorant of everything taking place around you."

Nothing made me as warm and fuzzy inside as being referred to as an imbecile, but I couldn't tell Carter why I was ignorant of the world's happenings or why I had no idea what in the hell was going on. There was too much danger in honesty. I might find my throat cut or my body tossed over the side of the outdoor patio.

I stood there dumbly, unable to answer the question.

"Are you suddenly mute?" he snapped, staring at me as if he was fighting the compulsion to shake the hell out of me.

"What do you want me to say?" I blurted, grasping at straws. "I don't know what you're talking about. Does it really matter why? You refuse to let me leave, keeping me prisoner in this...this..." I waved my arm to the insanely odd and out of place apartment that was only an architect's wet dream before my ripple across the space time continuum. "*Better Home and Gardens* meets *The Jetsons* military fortress."

Carter moved quickly, taking my upper arms in his large hands. He squeezed harshly and growled, "You're lying."

"I don't know what you're talking about." I yelped, chest heaving, becoming furious and ready to give him more than he bargained for. I might be lame, but I knew how to defend myself, and there were plenty of objects in the vicinity to use as weapons.

His nostrils flared as he inhaled deeply, and my stomach sank as his irises became silver. He wasn't vampire, but he most definitely wasn't human. More than a virus had come along since the third world war.

"You're hiding something. I knew it the moment I scented the people, cars, and exhaust fumes all over you in the alley. No one smells like that anymore." He buried his face into the hair at my shoulder and breathed in deeply, murmuring on the exhale, "No one."

"What are you?" I whispered in a weak voice before meeting his unwavering eyes.

"I won't dignify that question with an answer. If you want to play dumb, so be it." Carter released me and took a step back. "Get a shower and get dressed. We'll eat, and I'll take you on a quick tour of the premises."

I watched quietly as he turned and stomped away; the muscles along his shoulders and arms flexed as he clenched his fists spastically, fingers squeezing before they relaxed. This entire situation was becoming worse and worse. And the most sickening part was that I had no idea of how to remedy it or what in the world I was dealing with.

Turning on my heel, I returned to the bedroom, stomping across the lush carpet that managed cushion my throbbing knee. I tossed the satchel onto the bed, ready to tear something apart, when something shiny caught my attention. As I neared the bed, my stomach knotted, sweat beaded across my forehead, and my heart increased tempo as fear swamped my senses.

It couldn't be.

No. Fucking. Way!

I lifted the amulet from atop the comforter with trembling fingers, causing the tiny bead of amber with the black teardrop in the center to quiver and shake midair.

I wasn't sure how it was here, considering I'd handed the damned thing over to Zagan myself, but the power it radiated was an all too familiar and eerie hum against my skin, an energy that crept past the barrier of my flesh and coursed through my blood.

Marigold Vesta's Amulet—spun by Lucifer's very own familiar—was once again in my possession.

ABOUT THE AUTHOR

J.A. Saare is a multi-published author in varying genres and has written stories featured in horror magazines, zombie romance anthologies, and flash fiction contests. Her work has a notable dark undertone, which she credits to her love of old eighties horror films, tastes in music, and choices in reading, and have been described as "full of sensual promise," "gritty and sexy," and "a breath of fresh air."

Currently she is penning numerous projects within the urban fantasy, erotic and contemporary, and of course, paranormal romance categories. Her website is www.jasaare.com. Those interested in her "naughtier" side can visit her alias, Aline Hunter, at www.alinehunter.com.

CPSIA information can be obtained at www.ICGtesting.com
Printed in the USA
LVOW051713130912

298648LV00003B/102/P